BEAST'S BETRAYAL

BOOK TWO OF THE GODS' LANDS TRILOGY

DEAN RICHARD KAYLER

Publishing Services provided by Paper Raven Books LLC

Printed in the United States of America

First Printing, 2024

Paperback ISBN: 979-8-9875138-3-5
Hardback ISBN: 979-8-9875138-2-8

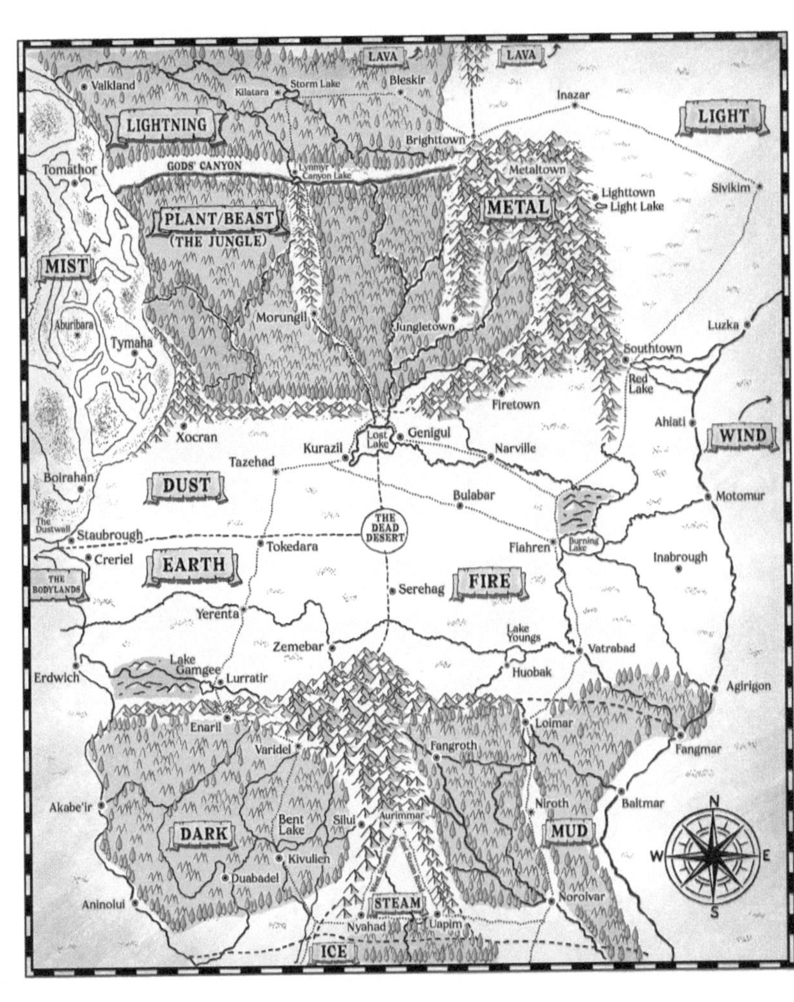

LAVA
LAVA
LIGHT
Valkland
Kilatara
Storm Lake
Bleskir
Inazar
LIGHTNING
Brighttown
Metaltown
Tomathor
GODS' CANYON
Lynmyr Canyon Lake
METAL
Lighttown
Light Lake
Sivikim
PLANT/BEAST
(THE JUNGLE)
MIST
Morungil
Jungletown
Luzka
Aburibara
Southtown
Tymaha
Red Lake
Firetown
Ahiati
WIND
Xocran
Lost Lake
Genigul
Narville
Tazehad
Kurazil
Boirahan
Bulabar
Motomur
DUST
THE DEAD DESERT
The Dustwall
Staubrough
Tokedara
Fiahren
Burning Lake
Inabrough
Creriel
EARTH
FIRE
THE BODYLANDS
Serehag
Yerenta
Lake Youngs
Zemebar
Vatrabad
Erdwich
Lake Gamgee
Lurratir
Huobak
Agirigon
Enaril
Loimar
Varidel
Fangroth
Fangmar
Akabe'ir
Niroth
Baltmar
Bent Lake
Silul
Aurimmar
DARK
MUD
N
Kivulien
W   E
Duabadel
Noroivar
S
Aninolui
STEAM
Nyahad
Uapim
ICE

To my parents: Carol and Dean
Your support allowed me to make my childhood dream
a reality, and share that dream with the world.

ACKNOWLEDGEMENTS

This book couldn't have been made without the work and support of many wonderful people: My parents, of course, who I dedicated this book to in thanks for their endless support, without which this entire series likely wouldn't even exist, much less this single entry. My friend Rey, to whom the first book, Fire's Folly, is dedicated. I still believe that without him these books would have taken twice as long to write and been only half as good. My many other friends who, while too numerous to individually name here, each supported me in their own ways as much they could. And the team from Paper Raven Books, who helped make this story shine in a way it never could have without them. The editors M.A., Colleen, and Ashley; the marketers Christine and Charlotte; the managers Brianna and Rachel; and the rest of the wonderful people at Paper Raven. Thank you all for everything you've done!

CONTENTS

PROLOGUE

It had been many hours since the two men left the small, insignificant village where they met, and not a word had been spoken by either of them since.

As they walked, Anderas found himself entranced by the slowly growing visage of the desert ahead of them as the dark silhouettes of the sand dunes began to form on the horizon. Forbidden as the desert was by every church, for it was nought but a place of sand and death, even for Blessed, he had never been so close to it before. Even if they weren't planning to enter the desert proper, being so close to such a forbidden place filled him with a mischievous, even heretical, thrill.

"Why now?" The sudden question broke through the silence, startling Anderas.

"Pardon?" he asked.

"Why now? It's been five years since my fight with that bastard. Why seek me out now?"

Anderas considered the question, shrugging to himself as he decided there was no reason to not share the answer. "I didn't feel ready."

"Ha!" Anderas couldn't tell if the single laugh was one of humor or mockery. "The 'Greatest Blessed Alive' didn't feel ready for a simple spar? For years?"

"That title is undeserved," Anderas pointed out. "Having been the greatest Descendant does not make me the greatest Blessed. Not yet, anyway."

"Mm. So what changed?"

"I've gotten more used to my new power. I always knew the Blessed had more raw power than Descendants did, but I didn't know just how vast a difference it was. I've spent the last few years practicing to make sure I'm in full control. The first time I tried to light a candle after my Blessing, I blew a hole in the wall."

"Ha! I've heard that before. Although mostly, I've heard how the whole wall was blown out. All that training as a Descendant came in handy, huh? It usually takes more than a few years for Blessed to gain the control to be confident enough for something like this."

"I was called the greatest Descendant for a reason."

"I've heard. Beat an Earth Blessed as a teenager, didn't you? Youngest Awakened in over a thousand years, right?"

"I was. Awakened at fourteen, fought Akamu three years later. The youngest daughter of the Lucerne family in Light has taken that title though. She's been Awakened at eleven."

"Damn. She must be quite something. Or the family is that desperate."

"Both, according to my sources. A talent that hasn't been seen since me, and a family that's lost too much power with too few allies. They're hoping that having such a young Awakened will raise them back up."

"Think it'll work?"

"I expect they'll be wiped out within the decade."

"Ha! And you people say I'm a savage."

"What did you ask me for as payment for this?"

"Fair," he snorted. "Anyway, think we're good? Unless you start burning up to the clouds, nobody's gonna see a thing all the way out here."

Anderas glanced around, noting the loose scattering of sand on the dry, hard ground beneath their feet. The last bits of sparse vegetation—stubborn dry shrubs and the ever-dwindling cacti—they had passed weren't even in sight anymore.

"Aye. We're good. Any further and we'll end up in the desert proper."

"What? Scared of a little sand? Or is the heat too much for ya?"

"There's simply no point. The desert defeated an entire great horde once. Why risk ourselves for nothing?" Anderas pointed out reasonably.

"Heh. Whatever. You ready then?" the Bone Merc asked, removing the leather cowl from his head and tucking it into a pocket, giving Anderas his first look at the man's hair. Or not-hair, he realized, as the Bone Merc shook his head and a clattering sound rang out. It was bone. All bone. In place of hair, the Bone Merc had hundreds of thin strands of segmented bones growing out of his scalp. Gods! It was no wonder the man kept his... *hair* tucked under a cowl all the time! It would be a dead giveaway to everybody who saw him who he was, since there was literally nobody else in the world who could get away with having bone hair!

"Aye, I'm ready." Anderas nodded, thinking it best not to comment on the strange feature, much as he had decided not to comment on how strange his white-irised eyes were.

Anderas had but a moment to see a mask of bone appear on the Bone Merc's face, growing instantly out of his very flesh, before he was suddenly flying through the air with an extraordinary pain burning in his side. He landed with a grunt, rolling a few feet before his mind caught up with him and he shifted into fire, reforming himself on his feet.

the Bone Merc hadn't moved. He was staring at Anderas, the bone mask covering his face hiding all expression, but Anderas could *feel* that he was being laughed at.

"Not as ready as you thought, eh?" the Bone Merc asked, humor clear in his voice.

"I admit, you surprised me. It's been a while since I was caught like that," Anderas replied, taking a moment to marvel at the fact his ribs actually hurt. He hadn't felt pain like that since he had been Blessed!

"A few years, yeah?"

"Aye." Anderas scowled, ignoring the flashes of fire, fear, and death that rushed through his mind at the reminder of his encounter with the Demon. Of all the things that his Blessing had brought him, freedom from the nightmares of that day was not one of them.

"Well, this is what you wanted, isn't it? To see just how strong I am, and how you compare?"

"Aye. It is."

"Well, let's go then!"

Anderas didn't bother responding, simply shooting two beams of fire out of his hands at the Bone Merc, the heat of them enough to start burning the sand on the ground. He wanted to experience for himself the power that had killed the Demon. It wouldn't do for him not to go all out. He threw himself backwards as a plume of sand exploded into the air in front of him, a jagged monument of bone erupting from the ground where his feet had been. He sent streams of fire into the obelisk, super-heating it until it exploded, launching shards of burning bone in all directions, feeling the strange sensation of thousands of small pieces flying through him. With his magic having burned out the Bone Merc's, the fragments couldn't harm him.

His eyes widened as a giant circle of pure white burst through the smoke and smashed into him. The force of the blow from an oversized shield knocked him off his feet. He twisted in midair, exploding fire out of the soles of his feet to launch himself over the Bone Merc's shield and behind him. Once again, he shot twin pillars of flame at the Bone Merc's back. The swarm of bone threads, which were the Bone Merc's hair, tunneled right through the streams and would have embedded themselves into Anderas' hands had he not cut off the fire and launched himself to the side.

the Bone Merc twisted around, throwing his oversized shield as though it weighed nothing directly at Anderas. It spun through the air; its whistling noise was the only warning Anderas had that it was razor sharp. He leaned to the side and let it cut past him, feeling the force of the air as it spun by his head. He locked eyes with the Bone Merc and couldn't help the grin that spread across his face, matched by the Bone Merc's own smirk. Feeling his magic singing in every fiber of his body, Anderas erupted into fire.

CHAPTER 1

Tala took a sip of wine, enjoying the sweet flavor as it washed over his tongue. It wasn't the best he had ever had, but he wasn't going to complain. Not with what his life had become. He sunk deeper into the water, trying to enjoy every last wisp of heat before it faded. A proper, hot bath paired with a nice, sweet wine. After everything that had happened, he hadn't known if he would ever get to enjoy such simple luxuries again. The moment he had killed Ignis Fatus back in Fiahren, accident or not, the likelihood of ever again enjoying simple pleasures had dropped to near zero. The moment that Anderas Anto had shown up in Southtown, right as they were on the cusp of fleeing the Fire country, the odds of doing anything ever again had dropped to completely zero. That he was now not only alive but basking in the pleasure of simple luxuries, was doing it in the manse of a noble family in the middle of Light country was, well… it was happening, and that was that.

His companions had mentioned on occasion that there were nobles who were sympathetic to the Dissident's cause.

Actual nobles, not vengeful former ones like Alina, whose entire family had been betrayed and slaughtered by their own church. But even after seeing it for himself with whatever game Anderas Anto was playing, hearing about sympathetic nobles was a very different matter to being welcomed into one's home with open arms! Yet here they were in a lord's manse at the edge of a small, forgettable, out-of-the-way farming town ruled over by one of the most minor noble families in the country—a family so unimportant that the Light Church barely even remembered either they or the town existed. A grievous oversight, seeing as said noble family and the entire town they ruled over was entirely populated by Dissidents and sympathizers!

Ex-Dissidents, really. People who, for one reason or another, had decided they didn't want to continue fighting in their countless millennia-old resistance against the Gods and the Churches, but still believed in the cause. An attitude that Tala could sympathize with: Gods know he wouldn't be fighting if he had a choice! He wouldn't even be with the Dissidents at all. He would be back in Fiahren, his beloved home city and capital of the Fire country. He would be staying up late working on projects at the Institute in peace and comfort, praying to the Gods for good fortune and inspiration. Not traversing the world as a wanted man, acutely aware of how little the Gods cared about the people and how tyrannical each of the Churches really were. Too bad he no longer had that choice. He wouldn't even be safe staying in a Dissident friendly town like Dritenik!

Which, apparently, was actually one of many small

settlements scattered throughout the world that Dissidents could "retire" to whenever they chose, living in peace right under the noses of the very people they were fighting against! The very idea of it all boggled Tala's mind. He had been learning over the past few months that the Churches weren't quite as "in control" of the world as they liked to claim, but for them to be so ignorant about entire towns of their most hated enemies was far beyond anything Tala had expected!

Although, how ignorant were they really? Or rather, how many of the people who made up the Churches' leadership were actually ignorant of such things? All of the Light Church's leadership, just like all the Churches, was comprised of families who descended from a man or woman who, at some point in the past, had been honored by their God and been made a Blessed, bestowed with overwhelming magical powers in their God's domain, and whose descendants still wielded a phenomenal, if much lesser, degree of said magic. While the Chand'ar family may currently be one of the most minor of the Descendant noble families in Light, they still were descended from at least one Blessed in the past, and thus were still officially a part of the Light Church's leadership, nonetheless. As would be the case for the lords of most of those other Dissident enclaves. Even Anderas Anto himself was clearly acting outside the interests of the Fire Church, if his actions of saving Tala's life in Southtown were any indication, and the man was not only a Blessed of the Fire God, but widely hailed as the greatest Blessed in the entire world! All the Churches portrayed themselves as being united in absolute totality under their respective God; just how false were their claims of unity?

Tala finished off his wine and rose from the now luke-warm water, feeling properly clean again. He would have to remember to ask Gazin about these things later. The old Flesh Descendant was an expert on politics, having been a member of the Dissidents for well over a century, and a slave to the nobles of Earth country before that. Or Alina. She had actually been a part of the Light Church once, the most promising Light Descendant of her generation, and might have some unique insights into it all. But that could wait for later.

For now, Tala was focused on finally feeling clean again! His light brown skin may not show dirt quite as clearly as the pale white of Gazin or Alina's, but it didn't hide it very well either. And his dark, curly hair seemed to trap every bit of filth he came across if he let it grow more than a half inch out. And nothing was better than having a clean pair of new clothes. He had spent almost two months wearing the same outfit he had worn the day he killed Ignis, sneaking through tunnels and trudging through hills in them, and he was looking forward to wearing clothes that weren't covered in blood and sweat stains, or riddled with patches to cover rips and tears. His shoes especially were falling apart, being even less suited to trekking through the wilds than his clothes, and even Dunlop was struggling to find ways to keep them on his feet. And there were few survival skills that the man lacked, as a former Wild Guard; one of the Mud country's most dangerous and respected non-Descendant soldiers, who traversed the wild forests and swamps of the Mud country by themselves, rooting out criminals of all kinds who sought to hide in the treacherous land. Even with Dunlop's aid, if the group hadn't kept the horses they had stolen from Southtown, Tala was positive he would have wound up completely barefoot long before they reached Dritenik.

Examining the clothes their hosts' servants had left for him in the room, Tala found himself satisfied with their choices: simple travel clothes, well suited for the life that was now his. Rough woolen tunic, pants, leather travel boots, and a treated cloak to help shelter him from wind and rain. All in dull shades of brown, unfortunately, but as decent of clothes he could ask for really. And probably of even better quality than he could normally get. As minor nobles or not, the Chand'ar family still had access to the Light Church's resources. Tala would forever mourn the soft cloth and bright colors he had worn as an apprentice Researcher. But not the shoes. Even if he could go back and undo everything that happened, he would never again wear shoes that weren't fit for traveling. No matter how much Gazin helped, Tala would never forget the feeling of his feet being so incredibly blistered after a long day of hiking. Give him a Blessed to fight any day before he had to endure that again!

Gods! What was he even thinking? No amount of sores and blisters in the world would be worse than facing any *more* Blessed! Tala reached out and gripped the handle of his ruined sword, the grip comforting him as he watched the strange way the light danced upon the Blessed metal of the chunky, misshapen blade. If he ever did face another Blessed again, this sword was his only chance at survival. A sword that Tala had dipped in the melted pools of metal that had poured off Elidor, the Metal Blessed lord of Southtown, in his fight with Anderas. A sword that Tala had then used to kill the Light Blessed Annelore—who had been trying to capture Tala—by sticking the metal hunk right into her head, where its own Blessed properties conflicted with hers and stopped her head from reforming after the blow, securing Tala's legacy as the world's first non-empowered person to kill a Blessed—bringing his count to two. And then Tala used that same idea to kill the weakened Elidor with a broken spear shaft shoved into his slowly reforming brain, bringing his count to three. If Anderas hadn't been the first and main reason that Tala had survived the arrivals of Elidor and Annelore in the first place, he might have even tried to use the blade to kill him, too. Even now, weeks after Southtown, he still felt both giddy and anxious at possessing such a weapon. A sword capable of killing Blessed! If only it didn't look quite so ridiculous, the Blessed metal having cooled in uneven lumps and chunks across the length of it.

He hoped Dunlop was right about being able to find a Metal Descendant in Lightning who would be able to reshape the blade into a proper sword and get him a proper sheath. It felt wrong to him for such a dangerous weapon to look so pathetic, and to be kept in such an ugly semi-sheath made of lashed-together bark and cloth. He knew it was his ego talking, but he felt proud and oddly protective of it, as its semi-unintentional creator, and wanted to give it the appearance it deserved.

Strapping it to his side as best he could without having

a proper sheath that fit, Tala took a moment to once again wonder what his life had become. With the rough clothes, daggers, and sword at his side, he felt he looked the part of a proper traveler, prepared for any trouble that might come his way. A far cry from the soft, naïve boy he had been before. Gods, he wished he could go back to being that person!

With a last squeeze of his sword's handle for comfort, Tala left the room he had been given with no particular goal in mind. It was their second day in the Chand'ar's home, and they were planning to leave first thing in the morning, it being far too dangerous for them to stay there for long. A proper day of rest and relaxation had done wonders for Tala's mood and, as much as he would have loved to stay longer, he was ready to move on. Maybe he would seek out Nuri, if the man wasn't otherwise engaged, and enjoy the smuggler's company for a last few hours. He was going to miss him moving forward.

It had been a surprise to Tala, if not the others, when Nuri had announced after their brief stop in Loastar (brief stop meaning Nuri and Caida had entered the town for supplies while the rest of them roamed widely around it) that he would be leaving their little group once they got to Dritenik. He had explained to Tala that his expertise as a smuggler was focused around Fire country, and the further they got from the Fire lands the less useful he would be to them. Better for him to return to where his services could be of use than stick with them when he had little more to offer.

It was going to be strange, traveling without Nuri. Tala had grown used to the man's constant litany of quips and mindless ramblings, always eager to help keep the group entertained and spirits high. He would miss the smuggler, as would they all, but he couldn't argue against Nuri's decision. The world was quickly spiraling into chaos, and Nuri would be needed where his skills were most useful.

That particular detail had been a shock to the rest of the group, but not for Tala, an irony he wished he could share with them. When they had arrived in Dritenik and been welcomed in by Gotam Chand'ar, he and his wife had shared with them all the news they could about how the wider world was reacting to the events of Southtown. War was coming. And coming fast.

There was a part of Tala that had found how shocked his companions had been at that amusing. Gazin, Alina, Serala, Caida, the people who usually seemed to know just about everything between them, and none had been expecting a great war to be brewing! For Metal to sequester itself, and declare both Fire and Light responsible for the disaster that had occurred in Southtown, formally removing itself from whatever conflict occurred between the two.

None of them had expected that outcome, not with Anderas Anto alive to spin the story to Metal. None except Tala. Anderas had saved his life, multiple times, and nearly at the cost of his own. The least he could do was keep the man's secret like he requested, and not tell anybody, including his companions, the truth about his actions in Southtown. He still didn't know what game Anderas was playing; why Fire's most beloved son had saved his life, or why the world's greatest Blessed would try to create another great war, but the man clearly had his own agenda, and Tala wouldn't betray his savior by revealing secrets he wanted kept hidden.

He was tempted though; he couldn't deny that. His companions, while confused as to how this situation had occurred, were ecstatic nonetheless that it was happening. Not just because of the destabilizing effect that a great war would have on the world, but because of how much easier it would make it to keep Tala himself safe: soldiers being sent off to fight a war were soldiers not hunting for Tala's head. Unfortunately, it also would make crossing borders that much harder, and as their next destination was Lightning country, they had a challenging road ahead of them. That border was normally quite easy to cross, as it had always been one of the more peaceful borders of the world. Both Light and Lightning had to focus so much on defending themselves from the endless incursions by Lava to the north, as well as protect themselves from Mist, the Jungle, Fire, and the Wind Raids respectively, that they were largely content to leave each other be instead of adding another challenge to deal with.

Despite their general passivity towards each other though, the two nations were far from friends, and from what Gotam had heard, tensions at the border were rapidly approaching breaking point. A situation that the Dissidents were actively working to worsen, of course. Tala sighed in annoyance: even his own allies were (unintentionally) making his life harder. He just hoped they managed to successfully sneak past the border this time and make it safely into Lightning. He did *not* need another Southtown to happen!

Nodding politely to some of the staff as he passed by them while they performed their various duties, Tala finally spotted Nuri through an open doorway that led onto one of the manse's many balconies, the back of his shaggy brown hair just visible over the chair he was lounging in. Sitting in her own chair beside him was Serala. Tala took a moment to stare at her. He was used to their group's strange, probably psychotic leader, being as dirty and road worn as the rest of them. Seeing her clean with her dark, silky hair hanging loosely down to her shoulders, her light olive skin practically shining after a thorough washing… He shook himself out of the impossible images that had started to stir within his head. Tala hesitated only a moment before stepping forward and interrupting. If it was an important or private conversation, they would have at least closed the door behind them.

"And how are you feeling, kid?" Nuri asked as Tala approached, bending his head back awkwardly, lazily, to peek at Tala. Even when he was trying to be quiet, Tala couldn't surprise them.

"Wonderful, really," he answered, sinking into an empty chair beside Nuri, smiling at Serala, who nodded at him in greeting. "First proper bath I've had in months. And new clothes, too!"

"Life on the road really makes you miss the little things, doesn't it?" Nuri chuckled, relaxing back into his chair as he took a sip of wine.

"Aye, that it does." Tala chuckled back. "So, what've you two been talking about?"

"Lil' Rala here has just been telling me how much she'll

miss me when I'm gone. How sad she'll be at night to not have me there, ready to help her warm up when it's cold out." Nuri winked at Tala. "How lonely she'll be—"

"We've been discussing his plans once he's back in Fiahren, now that it looks like a war is really happening," Serala cut in, shooting Nuri a bored glare. "There's going to be a lot of work for a smuggler like him."

Tala could well believe it. It had been Nuri who had helped them escape Fiahren by leading them through the labyrinthian tunnels of the Undercity, heavily aided by Alina's light magics. Tala still found it somewhat absurd how much his life had changed in that one day: he had never even left Fiahren before! Then he had seen a man abusing a girl in an alley and tried to stop it. For that man to have been Ignis Fatus, a Blessed, was absurd enough. But then Tala had killed him, accidentally, in self-defense, blowing his head all over the alley with a steam pipe (and thus discovering that he had been a Blessed). Then being rescued by Vail and Serala and taken to a Dissident safe house in the city, where the rest of their small group had joined them to help get Tala out of the city and save his life, bringing him all the way to Southtown on the border of Fire and Light, and beyond.

Tala looked out past the balcony they sat on toward the small town of Dritenik, which stretched out before them. The manse had been built on a hill on one edge of town, giving an amazing view of the place. Even knowing there was a war coming, it felt like such an abstract concept to him while he gazed at the lazy little town in the warm sunlight. He knew that, even if he couldn't see them, the town was preparing in its own way: stockpiling supplies, preparing homes for Dissident refugees, hiding the truth of the town's true loyalties for any other refugees that they wouldn't have the heart to turn away.

"What can I say? Talent like mine is always in high demand," Nuri said imperiously, nose hoisted in the air. "Of course, since you all will be bereft of some of my gentler talents, you'll need to fill in for me, kid. Caida can take of herself, of course, but if little Rala here starts getting a bit too testy, start her off with a bit of wine to relax, then take your hands and—" Nuri broke off with a gulp, one of Serala's many knives being held right under his chin. Tala only glanced over briefly to see Serala looking bored, despite the clear threat, before looking away again, face flushed. "Has anyone ever told you that you're far too quick to violence, Rala?" Nuri asked with an—in Tala's opinion—impressive calm.

"No, why?" she asked, sounding genuinely curious as she removed her blade. Tala shared a *look* with Nuri.

"No reason. Hey, here's an idea! Why don't y'all stay here for a bit longer? Nice, quiet little peaceful town like this. Could do you a bit of good, y'know? Relax for a week or two before moving on. What are the odds anybody finds you here?"

"No." Serala frowned. "Delaying will just make crossing into Lightning even harder. You should know that."

"Right, right." Nuri sighed, rolling his eyes at Tala, who chuckled. "Why would you ever want to risk it? It couldn't possibly be better than charging head first into a war. Anyway, Tala! This might be the last time we ever see each other. So, tell me, how much will *you* miss me?"

Tala shook his head even as he laughed.

CHAPTER 2

Two weeks. It had taken about that long for them to reach Dritenik from Southtown, and that long again to reach the southern edge of the Lightning border from there. Tala didn't even want to imagine how long the journey might have taken if they hadn't stolen the horses at Southtown. And now that he had finally gotten used to riding a horse, he was going to have to abandon it. There was no way they could cross the border into Lightning on horseback without being intercepted by either country attempting to commandeer their horses.

As of two weeks ago, it had become all but impossible, as horses were just too valuable for the coming war for either country to just let them pass unharassed. Even Serala's Dust merchant badge wouldn't do any good until the soldiers were close enough to see it, and by that point, the odds of them recognizing Tala would be too high to risk. Especially with them still being inside Light country, where another Descendant would easily notice if Alina used her magics to disguise him again. So, they were releasing their stolen horses into the wild. Better that than handing them to the Light Church, at least.

And he had proper boots for trekking through the wilderness this time, which was a huge improvement over the city shoes that he had been wearing during their escape from Fire. Small victories, but Tala had learned to take those wherever he could, no matter how small. Although from what he could see of the border from his crouched position hidden behind some rocks and shrubbery in the foothills of the Metal mountains, he was going to need more than a small victory to make it across that cleanly.

The two weeks it had taken them to reach the border from Dritenik had apparently been more than enough time for tensions to break into full violence, and Tala watched in morbid fascination as a mounted soldier charged forward and speared another through the torso. Whatever tenuous peace normally existed between the border forces of Light and Lightning had clearly broken down. Whether this was the first battle between the two or simply one of many, Tala had no way of knowing, but there were easily a couple hundred combatants on the field. Even from the distance, the sounds of battle were easy to hear: the screams of enraged or dying men and horses as various horn calls rang through the air.

Tala watched as a rider went down with his horse, then turned to his companions, all huddled nearby, some watching the battle, while others were busy trying to figure out what their plan would be from here.

"We should stay to the hills. Even if we go around this, who's to say we won't just be walking into another one? Or worse? I don't see any magic being used out there, and Lightning wielders aren't exactly known for their subtlety," Gazin suggested, stroking his red goatee in thought. Not for the first time, Tala wondered if the sheer red vibrance of Gazin's hair and beard were natural or the result of some sort of meddling the Flesh mage had done to himself. Hair wasn't exactly part of his domain as a Fleshy, but Tala could confess some level of ignorance to the intricacies of things such as hair color.

"These hills carry a risk of their own. Light and Lightning both have outposts to catch anybody doing exactly what we are. And there is a risk of running into a Metal patrol." Dunlop pointed out, sounding uncertain, flipping a dagger between his fingers in a common habit of his. Tala would never understand how Dunlop was comfortable carrying so many weapons on him: Tala was average height at best, and he had a good two inches on Dunlop, yet the former Wild Guard was easily carrying half his weight in various weapons. If he didn't know better, Tala would say that Dunlop was against going in the hills simply so he wouldn't have to hike with all that weight. Not that Dunlop ever showed the slightest sign of being tired or hurt, as evidenced by the practically glowing red burn that had started showing on his tanned face. Gazin would need to fix that at some point for him.

"There's risk either way. But what are the odds that any outposts haven't been wiped out by one or the other anyway? Even if we do run afoul of them, or a Metal patrol, we can just remove them and make it seem like the other side did it. And if Metal thinks that either of them slaughtered one of their patrols, that's only going to make things worse for all of them!" Gazin argued back, looking up at Dunlop. For all that, Tala had a solid couple inches on Dunlop, he had closer to a whole foot of height on Gazin.

"He makes a good point," Dunlop said, turning to Serala, who sat with the two as they worked out the plan. Mindlessly cleaning a knife in her hands as they talked, she was doing a poor job of pretending that she wasn't watching the battle in the distance. The girl wasn't as weapon obsessed as Dunlop, but she still carried far more than Tala thought was normal. Daggers, knives, short swords—she always had at least a dozen different blades on her, most of them hidden. Between her and Dunlop, Tala sometimes felt like he was under armed, what with only having the one sword, two daggers, and a hunting knife. He had learned that it was those two who were unusual, though, and that very few people normally carried so many weapons.

Ilan was standing near her, but like usual, the giant, dark-skinned man was silent and stoic, resting some of his weight on the massive great sword that he carried and had stabbed into the ground, watching their discussion with one eye as he kept the other on Vail. Vail sat watching the battle in the distance with his full attention. Or at least Tala thought it was his full attention; it was hard to tell with his ever-present hood up, obscuring his face in deep shadows like always, aside from the heavy stubble that was growing on his chin. After seeing how Vail—and Serala—had handled themselves during the events of Southtown, Tala didn't want to know what the man might be thinking as he watched the battle play out.

"So, we stick to the hills and kill anyone we come across, making it appear as though either Light or Lightning was responsible. Simple. Dunlop, you have the lead," Serala ordered absently, eyes transfixed on the battle with a hungry glint that did uncomfortable things to Tala's gut.

Dunlop nodded strictly, and without delay, began looking over the foothills ahead of them, already scouting out the best paths, completely uncaring about the battle that had so transfixed Serala and Vail. Gazin nodded far more calmly, and Tala saw the way his eyes danced between the two and the battle in the distance with a frown. Despite the nightmarish display the old Fleshy had made of himself in Southtown, Tala knew the man wasn't actually all that fond of violence. It was reassuring, if he was being honest, and knowing the man's true nature had helped abate some of the nightmares plaguing him since then.

At least the horrible nightmares about being flayed alive or being smothered or pierced by unholy masses of skin. Gazin's actions in Southtown, as helpful as they were, had lingered distressingly in Tala's mind. He was still struggling with the many nightmares about being stabbed, cut, or crushed, and the even worse nightmares of being burned alive, drowned in molten metal, having his eyes burned out of his skull, or having his head exploded by a misshapen sword. He was particularly upset he was having nightmares about his own actions on top of all the rest. Southtown, as a whole, had left scars on Tala's psyche.

He grabbed his sword's handle for comfort, not blaming

the blade despite its prominence in some of his many night-mares. Violence had never really been a part of his life, outside of the occasional trip to the arena, and he was struggling to come to terms with how much his life revolved around it now. There was supposed to be honor and glory in combat—Hells, Serala, and Vail clearly found it downright *fun*—but all he had found was fear and, later, nightmares.

He walked over to Caida and Alina, who were sitting on a large rock together, watching the battle in the distance. Caida was somehow looking as refined as ever, dark olive skin showing no sign of dirt or sweat, and her perfectly braided hair done up in some dizzying spiral that wrapped around itself to keep it out of her face. The two women had grown closer after Southtown, a development that gladdened Tala. Alina would greatly benefit from having more friends. While he liked the girl, and could openly admit he found her beautiful with her long, blonde hair and smooth, alabaster skin, she was always so withdrawn, as though she didn't know how to interact with people unless she had a purpose. It didn't surprise him that she struggled, not with her history. Still, he was happy she was starting to open up a bit more. And unlike with Nuri, Caida wasn't constantly trying to flirt with her, at least as far as Tala was aware, which probably helped her in getting more comfortable with the older woman. Caida was also surprisingly gentle with Alina, a softer side of her that Tala hadn't seen before. He shouldn't have been surprised, really. The woman was a professional courtesan (and spy/assassin) whose main clients (victims) were high-ranking members of the Church of Fire. She had to be able to play any persona to do what she did. Plus, the woman had a whole slew of "apprentices" that she had trained for the Dissidents back in Fire.

"I think we're heading out soon," Tala told the two women as he approached.

"Indeed. A nice, peaceful hike through the foothills," Caida said with only half-pretend exasperation. "I swear, we could have just kept the horses and ridden right on by that little scuffle. I doubt they'd even notice us with how focused they are on killing each other," she grumbled.

"We didn't know that was going to happen. It was too risky keeping the horses," Tala replied.

"Oh, I know. Doesn't mean I have to be happy about it. All this trouble to sneak around and for nothing!"

"Not entirely for nothing. We don't know what else is happening. This could be an isolated incident."

"Perhaps. But from what we heard from Lord Gotam, I doubt it. As does Alina."

Alina merely nodded her assent before standing and shouldering her pack. "Either way, it doesn't matter now. Besides, it's time to get moving."

Tala hadn't realized the others had already started grabbing their things, preparing to continue on, course decided. The group slowly shuffled into line behind Dunlop, most of them still keeping one eye on the battle in the distance as best they could before it was swallowed by the rocks and trees of the mountain's foothills.

Once again hiking through hills, Tala thought, not

particularly eager for the coming days. Hopefully it would be a much easier going than the Burning Hills had been, now that he was in far better shape and much more experienced with such travel. Even without Nuri there to help guide and entertain them.

CHAPTER 3

Well, at least I was right about the hiking being easier, Tala thought as he hastily dodged an axe a Metal soldier tried to cleave into his skull. A beam of light shot straight through the man's temple, dropping him instantly. Tala stared at the body, frowning as he slowly sheathed the dagger he had been hiding against his forearm like Dunlop had shown him. He didn't even need to look around to know there were no more soldiers—the silence said plenty.

Giving the corpse one last glare as he turned away, he wrestled with his conflicting feelings. Alina hadn't needed to dispatch the man for him—magic light powers be damned! She had killed plenty of the Metal soldiers already for it to be obvious that they had been slain by Light wielders. He could've beaten that soldier easily by himself! Another step, an easy parry with his unbreakable, albeit otherwise mostly useless sword, and his dagger would have slit his throat! Granted, he wasn't entirely sad he hadn't needed to do the deed himself, but this wasn't the first time this had happened.

In the last three days of hiking through the foothills, they had fought three Metal patrols, on top of the dozen others, who they had managed to hide from. And in all three fights, any soldier he faced off against ended up killed by one of the others: Serala, Dunlop, Ilan, Alina, and Gazin. Even Lito had stabbed one soldier in the back when he had challenged Tala, and Lito had nearly lost his head for it! The only ones who hadn't "saved" Tala yet were Caida and Vail. He was well aware he was by far the weakest fighter in the group, but being saved constantly by his friends, usually unnecessarily, and at risk to themselves, was starting to grate on him.

Of course, none of it would be a problem if they didn't keep encountering Metal patrols! They knew that trekking through the foothills would be dangerous, for this exact reason, but this was ridiculous! They had known patrols would be more common around Brightown, so they had spent two entire days just sneaking around that damned city. They spent one going as high into the mountains as they were comfortable to avoid the place, and then once again going back down into the foothills. They hadn't ever even gotten near the city and were practically tripping over soldiers! The patrols weren't even looking for Tala! They were just a show of force from Metal, telling their neighbors to keep their fighting in their own lands!

Although we may have royally cocked that up. Tala looked at the twenty dead Metal soldiers, all killed either from blades or Alina's magic. Since they wanted to increase the tensions between nations, they were being careful to make each patrol they were forced to fight appear as though it had been slaughtered by Light forces, with no magic from Gazin or Ilan. Tala wasn't sure how Metal would react to it, or if they would even believe it was Light forces that were responsible, but honestly, he didn't really care anymore.

He was tired. Tired of being hunted. Tired of people trying to kill him. Tired of caring. If people wanted to kill each other in the names of the Gods, then they were welcome to do it, as far as he was concerned.

He stared down at that last soldier, the one who he had nearly beaten before Alina blew a hole through his head. The man hadn't even recognized him as "the" Tala. He just saw an intruder on Metal's lands and that was enough reason to kill him. Tala hadn't even really been fighting when the man attacked him, having left it to the others who were so much better at it than he would ever be! *Is this really what people are under the Gods? Was I even a person to him? Or just a foreigner? An enemy? A body to be burned? Or buried? I think Metal buries the dead. If they'd even bother giving us the "honor" and didn't just leave us out for the birds.* Tala gripped his sword, feeling the smooth, leather wrap of the handle, which fit perfectly under his fingers. It didn't really matter in the end.

"Tala! What's the hold up?" Lito called. Tala's head shot up to see that the group had finished with their post-fight activities, their weapons cleaned and all the bodies looted, and were ready to continue on.

"Sorry! Sorry. I'm coming," he replied, releasing his sword's handle and scurrying over to them. His dark thoughts dispersing, they began moving westward again, picking their way over the rocks and brush that littered the foothills. With one last glance back at the bloody remains of the short battle, Tala vanished into the trees. They were almost deep enough past the border with Light that soon they could leave the foothills of the Metal Mountains and enter the lands of Lightning.

CHAPTER 4

"That is a lot of trees," Tala muttered as he gazed out over Lightning country.

"Right. Fiahren born. Not many trees there, are there?" Lito asked from beside him.

True, though Tala didn't bother answering beyond a simple nod to the slightly taller boy, who seemed more concerned with untangling something from his brown hair than on looking at the incredibly vast expanse of trees. He clearly didn't find it particularly exciting, unlike Tala. Lito had become something of Tala's best friend since fleeing from Fiahren—as much due to a lack of options as anything—but they had led very different lives and the things that Tala found new and exciting about traveling the world were common to Lito. The other boy had been an orphaned child raised in the Dissidents. He had spent the last few years traveling from place to place with Alina, helping the cause wherever their skills were needed. Seeing a massive forest wasn't new to him, and any sense of excitement about it had long worn away, no matter how many trees there were.

But in Tala's defense, there really were a *lot*. As they moved further west, and closer to the end of the mountain range, the group had climbed out of the foothills and into the mountains proper again to avoid a growing force of Lightning soldiers who had set up camp at the base of the hills, likely on their way to reinforce the border. From his new vantage point in the lower mountains, Tala could see for dozens of miles. And unlike the Fire and Light lands, Lightning was mostly made up of vast forests. Having grown up inside a city on the plains, he had often imagined what that might look like as a boy, but the actual sight of it was grander than he had ever imagined. He had never seen so many trees before! He hadn't even been able to *imagine* so many trees before! The immense forests of the Lightning Lands created a canopy of greens, browns, and reds that took his breath away. Getting to see sights such as this almost, *almost*, made everything that happened worth it. It wasn't a trade he would make again if he could go back and change things, but *still*!

"Are we really going to be walking through all *that*?" Tala asked, having a hard time picturing how anyone could travel through such a forest without getting lost for all eternity. While the Burning Hills and Metal Mountain foothills had had their fair share of trees, they hadn't passed through anywhere with enough of them to be called a forest. Add in Dunlop and the rest who had experience traveling through various wildernesses, and Tala had never really been worried about getting lost somehow before. Not in the hills and especially not in the Fire or Light Plains.

"Yes?" Lito answered, sounding confused. "Why wouldn't we?"

"I mean… is there light? Are there trails and stuff?"

"Gods, man, you really aren't used to trees, are you? It's really not that bad down there. I know it looks like the forest is super thick and stuff up here, but that's just 'cause the trees grow wide. It's not nearly like… whatever you're thinking it is."

"Really?"

"Yeah. Just wait till we get down there, you'll see what I mean. It'll be fine."

Tala grunted in acknowledgment, believing Lito, but kinda-sorta not at the same time.

"Although, I guess it's not all positive…" Lito trailed off, causing Tala to turn to him with suspicious eyes. "I mean, there are a lot of wild, dangerous animals like snakes and giant cats and poisonous frogs. And the air is pretty humid, so breathing can be kind of uncomfortable, and you'll always feel sort of damp, like you're constantly sweating. And it's noisy as all hells, with insects and birds and little critters and stuff constantly chirping or tweeting or whatever at all hours nonstop. And there's—"

"Enough! Stop! I get it! Just shut up, would you? Gods!" Tala exploded, not wanting to hear anything more about the miseries. The place sounded absolutely horrible! Why would anyone ever want to live there?

"It's not that bad," Alina sighed from beside Lito, although Tala would swear he could see her fighting a smirk. "And most of the really dangerous animals stay away from the roads. They keep to the deeper parts of the forests. They usually get killed by people when they venture too close to roads or villages."

"Well, that's better. Is it as humid as he said?"

"Oh, yes. But you'll get used to it. Mostly. Eventually. And you do still have to keep an eye out for bugs, snakes, bats, those sorts of creatures. Especially at night, they like to bite people in their sleep. And Gazin can only do so much to help if you get poisoned or catch a blood disease from some insect."

Despite the softness of her tone, Tala was certain that Alina was putting immense effort into not smiling. The way her cheeks were twitching was not a tick he had ever seen on her before.

"You both suck."

Lito laughed, while Alina finally broke and smiled, even giggling quietly. Tala sucked his teeth in annoyance, turning towards the others who were sitting on some large rocks, taking the short break as a chance to rest their legs.

Serala ran a dagger along a whetstone, five others laid out on the rock beside her. He sat on a small rock and took out his own daggers, examining them to see if they needed sharpening. They didn't. Dunlop and the rest had made a point of drilling into Tala's head the importance of keeping his weapons in pristine condition, even if they weren't really being used much. Even more so than in battle, a sharp blade could make the difference between life and death in the wilderness. A good dagger could be used to sharpen sticks, strike flint for a fire, skin animals, turn clothing or sinew into thread, and countless other little uses that could help him survive if he, somehow, ever got lost in the wilds by himself.

His friends' insistence on teaching him how to survive, coupled with all the—albeit theoretical—knowledge on wilderness survival he had from his time at the Institute, meant Tala actually felt quite confident he could survive if he ended up separated from the others. At least for a short while. He was still struggling with identifying plants correctly, even the ones he had learned about at the Institute, and more than once had nearly given Dunlop a conniption when he had mixed up medicinal plants with poisonous ones. Plants just really weren't his forte. Although, he was getting better at them. Especially after Dunlop forced him to ingest a concoction meant to help soothe digestion, but instead led to him spewing his guts out. At least he would never mistake *that* specific root again.

"We should get moving," he heard Serala say. She had finished with her daggers, which were once again all completely hidden from sight. "We should be able to reach the bottom before dark, and we can camp there before entering the forest."

Murmured assent sounded from the others, and Tala gave his daggers one last quick check over before sheathing them and following his companions down the mountain.

CHAPTER 5

Gazin pushed his hips forward as he arched his back, enjoying the popping feeling that ran up his spine. While the rigors of age didn't quite affect him like they did most people, he still wasn't immune to all the little aches and pains that came with such intense traveling. Well… most of them: aching muscles, sore tendons, cramps, spasms, and the like were all things he never had to worry about. Even the things outside of his domain, like joint pains and achy bones, rarely affected him. He may be not able to manipulate them like he could skin and muscle, but every part of his body was superior to normal humans, to Non-Body Descendants even. For all the downsides that came with being a Flesh wielder in the world—namely how they were either enslaved or killed simply for existing on this side of the Dustwall—there were some upsides too. And while stronger, healthier bodies were the norm for any Descendant, thanks to the Gods' powerful magics flowing through them, none were as naturally superior as Blood, Flesh, or Bone Descendants.

Still, he enjoyed that ever-so-slight feeling of relief brought about by some good bone popping, especially now that they finally had a chance to properly rest again. It was just a pity that he couldn't do much about the heat and humidity, although it didn't bother him nearly as much as his companions. He focused on his power, feeling all the little air streams that he had weaved throughout his skin, too small for a human eye to see, but numerous enough to help mitigate some of the overbearing heat.

He still vividly remembered his first trip to the humid hell that was Lightning Country, and how long he had suffered before finally figuring out a way to restructure his skin to help cool him down. It had taken him even longer to rework his trachea to filter out much of the moisture in the air, so that breathing came easier. Although rerouting that moisture into his stomach (while nice as it ensured he stayed well hydrated despite the heat) did cause him to have to pee quite often. Still, he would prefer having to empty his bladder over the unsatisfying, wet breaths that his companions were struggling with.

He glanced over at Tala. The poor boy was sprawled out on his bed, shirtless, trying to stay as still as he could in the hopes it would help him cool down a bit. It was a futile effort. Even though the air was a little cooler and drier at the inn where they were staying, it still wasn't exactly "cool" or "dry." The lad would just have to suffer until he adjusted, which he estimated shouldn't take more than a few days. Day or night there was no escape from heat or humidity in Lightning, and even normal humans were remarkably adaptable. Already Tala, along with the rest of their group, was faring better than he had when they first descended from the mountains. By the time they reached Kilatara, they should have adjusted enough that it wouldn't be immediately obvious they were foreigners, a small detail, but one that would help them avoid unwanted attention.

Thankfully, it wasn't much of an issue in this little town they had stopped in. It wasn't much more than an out-of-the-way trading post that had slowly grown over time and was pretty far removed from the main network of travel and information. Even if the residents here *had* heard about Tala yet, they were unlikely to ever suspect he would show up in their little sanctuary in the woods. He wouldn't be able to hide there for long, but at least for the next day or two they could all relax their guards somewhat as they rested.

And rest they were getting, Gazin chuckled as he picked up on Tala's steady, even breathing. The lad hadn't taken long to fall asleep, despite it not even being supper time yet. All the better though; he could use some rest. He had been quieter, more withdrawn than usual, ever since Southtown. Gazin recognized the heavy shadow he often saw in Tala's eyes, having seen it many times before. The lad was growing, maturing, maybe. Everything he had gone through over the last few months was tempering out the youthful naivety and reforging him into something new. Gazin just hoped that Tala could retain some of who he was through it all. He was an eager, optimistic, inquisitive, and all-around good kid, and Gazin was desperately hopeful he wouldn't lose all of that after all he had experienced. The lad had become close friends with Lito and Alina, surprisingly, so hopefully they would help keep him centered, being so close to him in age.

He had also befriended Serala, a frankly astounding accomplishment Gazin was both happy and worried about. He loved the lass as if she were his own family, but she wasn't exactly a shining beacon of health and sanity. Although for having been raised by Vail, she was far more stable and generally… kind than Gazin had expected. He suspected that had more to do with Ilan joining their strange little family than anything else. He only hoped that Tala's friendship (and obvious, if no less concerning, crush on her) might help show Serala that there was more to life than just fighting. The lad would be mortified if he learned that everyone—sans Vail and Serala herself, naturally—had easily recognized his crush on the girl, and they had all taken part in a running bet as to when (and if) Serala would realize his feelings for her. Or realize her own obvious fondness for him. Gazin wasn't honestly sure which of those was less likely to happen.

Regardless, Tala could be doing worse. Gazin would still keep an eye on him just to be safe. And for now, he could sleep, hopefully in peace. Exhaustion was a good way to prevent nightmares. Violent storms were common in Lightning, so Gazin checked that the wooden shutters over the window were closed and locked tight, then pushed open the door to their room. The lad would be safe without Gazin hovering over him, and Dunlop was in the room straight across the hall. He had his door open and a cloth out, inspecting all of his many weapons, ever-prepared for battle like any good Wild Guard. Just because the war would likely never touch this remote little town, didn't mean there would be no threats, such as military recruiters, deserters, or even just common bandits. In the off chance somebody came looking for Tala, they'd never get past Dunlop.

Happy with Tala's security, Gazin made his way downstairs, intending to enjoy a decent drink. It had been a while since he had been in Lightning, and the country had some pleasant meads. In the small common room of the inn, Gazin spotted Vail and Ilan sitting leisurely at a table and went over to join them after procuring himself a drink. Ilan appeared to be drinking a mead similar to Gazin's, but Vail had something different. Gazin didn't bother asking, he knew it was a tea of some kind. Even after all these years he'd never understood Vail's obsession with the drink. Not that he would complain: the last thing they needed was to discover what Vail would be like with alcohol in him.

"The others?" Gazin asked as he sat down.

"Caida's resting." Ilan responded languidly. Or Gazin thought it was languid, even to his ears Ilan didn't sound much different than usual, but his words were slightly slower than normal. "The kids are wandering the town."

Gazin nodded, taking a sip of his drink. He didn't recognize the flavor, some local variation probably, but it tasted good. He was happy to let the younger folk scout out the town for anything of note, they knew what was important to look for.

"Tala?" Ilan asked.

"Asleep. Dunlop's on watch." Ilan nodded, content with the answer.

The three of them sat quietly, each enjoying their drinks in the peaceful atmosphere of the quiet room, despite the ever-present heat and humidity. Even though Gazin cheated a bit with his magic, all three had long grown desensitized to such minor annoyances.

"How long has it been since you were in Lightning, Vail?"

"About five, six years," he answered absently, not bothering to even look at Gazin, who merely nodded again.

"Serala seems happy to be back."

"It's the air. Brings back fond memories for her."

"Good. They were good people. I'm glad she still has happy memories of them."

Vail hummed in his absent way. "They deserve that much, at least."

Gazin nodded solemnly. "Has she been back there? To the memorial? To Kurazil at all?"

Vail hummed again. "I brought her there after what happened in Mist. Thought it might help."

Gazin stared at him before closing his eyes with a huff. "Gods, Vail. And how'd that work out?"

Even with his eyes closed Gazin could feel the man's shrug. "Might not have been my best idea."

Gazin snorted in morbid amusement. The world would be a different place if Vail had ever had anything but bad ideas.

"How's the kid doing?" Vail asked, before Gazin could continue.

"Alright. Better than I feared, so far. He's adjusting."

"Good."

"He's very attached to that sword of his, though."

"Mm. It saved his life. And probably will again. Especially once we get it fixed up."

"You're sure an Unawakened can do the job?"

"Mm. It won't be easy, but they can do it."

"Metal is metal, Blessed or not. It will be slow, but it can be done," Ilan added, supporting Vail. "Even I can bring down a Blessed's earth wall if given enough time. A Metal Descendant should have little problem reshaping the sword."

Gazin just nodded. He already knew that all, of course, but the questions gave him an easy segue into the real question he wanted answered. "And then what?"

"Mm?"

"What's the plan, Vail? After the sword gets fixed up, what are we doing next?"

Vail finally deigned to look at him, raising his eyebrows in an attempt at an innocent expression. As if Gazin, of anyone, would ever believe that Vail even understood the concept.

"Is keeping the kid alive not enough for you?" the bastard had the audacity to ask.

"Don't bullshit me, Vail. Remember, I worked with you before. As much as anyone could back then. I know you're planning something. Something to do with the kid. And it's not about killing a few more Blessed."

"We keep moving, of course. Keep the kid alive. I was thinking of taking him into the Jungle next. That's all," Vail said nonchalantly.

"The Jungle?" Gazin's brows furrowed. "Why the Jungle?"

Vail shrugged in his nonchalant way. "Why not? It's safer on the move. Better the Jungle than Lava."

Gazin's eyes narrowed as he watched Vail languidly take a sip of tea. He had known the man for almost twenty years, knew him as well as anyone aside from Ilan and Serala could.

If that was all of Vail's reasoning, then Gazin would turn himself inside out and dance on the street. "And then what? Mist? Dust? What are you planning, Vail?"

Vail gave him that same innocent look. It reminded Gazin eerily of the way the man-eating shadow bear he had once had the misfortune of encountering in the eastern forests of Light had looked at him. Vail really couldn't pull off innocence. "What makes you think I'm planning anything? I'm just trying to keep the kid safe, same as you."

"Bullshit." It wasn't often Gazin would risk Vail's ire by calling him out, but Tala was too important for Gazin to just sit by and let him become a pawn in one of Vail's psychotic games. "We could keep the lad safe for years here. It was your idea to bring him to Lightning so he could get that sword fixed. A sword you're letting him keep. You wouldn't let a weapon like that go to waste. And now the Jungle? What are you plotting?"

"It was Serala's decision to come to Lightning, not mi—"

"Damnit, Vail!" Gazin bit out, catching himself at the last second from yelling at the man. Middle of nowhere or not, they didn't need to draw attention to themselves. "Don't give me that shit! You've been plotting something ever since Southtown!"

"I don't know what you're talking about—"

"Vail!" Gazin interrupted, frustration getting the better of him. He took a deep breath; anger wouldn't help him any when dealing with Vail. "Just tell me, what's the point of getting the lad lost in the damned Jungle?" Tala had been an excellent student in learning wilderness survival techniques, aside from his issue recognizing which plants were safe or not, but the Jungle was a different beast entirely to the rest of the known world. Even with the group, Tala wouldn't be truly safe, not when half the things they were teaching him didn't even apply there, or worse, would actually bring him more harm than good! Surviving in the Jungle meant following an entirely unique set of rules and common sense.

"Who said anything about getting him lost? He'll be with us the whole time. That's the opposite of getting lost. It'll take a while to get the sword fixed, and I think the Jungle is our best move after it's done. That's all. We're all just trying to keep the kid safe, I promise."

Gazin sighed, slumping down as he put his head in his hands. He had forgotten how often the bastard had made Gazin want to leap over a table and strangle him. He might have done it, too, if he believed for even a moment that Vail wouldn't kill him before he could even get close. But he was familiar with Vail's behavior, and he knew he would get no more details out of the bastard for now. He would just have to leave things be and resolve to keep an eye on him. And Tala. After all, Vail had promised that he was just trying to keep Tala safe. And that meant whatever Vail was planning would most certainly be putting Tala in grave danger.

CHAPTER 6

"So, what's Kilatara like?" Tala asked, curious about their destination. The group had just departed from the town after a pleasant, if simple, breakfast. While Tala had a vague idea of where Kilatara was on a map, he didn't know much about the capital city of Lightning beyond it being beside Storm Lake.

"Well, it's a city." Lito shrugged, walking next to Tala. "It's got a lot of buildings. And people."

"So, it's like Fiahren then?"

"Nowhere's like Fiahren." Lito snorted. Tala heard Alina hum in agreement from Lito's other side. "That city's a madhouse. No offense. Kilatara is… shiny? There's a lot of metal, like, every building has a metal roof, and there are lots of metal sidings and stuff. And they've all got these weird little pronged metal rods on the roofs too. Otherwise, it just kinda looks like a normal city. Although the docks are pretty cool; they're made out of this material called rubber that they get from trees that's bouncy, so it's really weird to walk on them. And they paint each dock a different color depending on what it's for, like docks for fishing boats are blue, military ships are red, and merchants are orange. It's really cool."

"Why do they make the docks out of rubber instead of wood? They live in a literal forest. They have plenty of wood to spare."

"It's something about the way rubber interacts with lightning, like it resists it. It's the same reason why all the buildings and boats are covered in metal, something about it making the lightning's power go into the ground so it doesn't damage the buildings or something. I don't really get a lot of it, but since lightning storms are so common there, they had to come up with ways to keep people safe. And wood catches fire real quick when hit by lightning."

"Oh, yeah, I remember hearing about that. We have—*they* have—some rubber back at the Institute, but apparently Lightning's really protective of the stuff so there isn't much. I think the Fire Church was really weird about it too, like they wouldn't let them research military applications for it. Which didn't make sense since if it's so good against lightning it would be a fantastic anti-Lightning weapon… although now that I think about it, maybe that's exactly why they didn't want us using it like that…" Tala trailed off as he thought about everything he had learned since "joining" the Dissidents.

He gripped his sword. He knew better than anybody just how badly the Churches reacted to people who found weaknesses to their powers. Although a rubber sword sounded ridiculous to him, against a Lightning Blessed it might actually be not so crazy of a weapon.

"It actually doesn't work as well as you'd think," Lito said.

"We've been trying for centuries to weaponize rubber and it's never gone well. Enough of it can protect you from weaker Unawakened, sure, if they're not really trying, but enough lightning melts it. I don't even want to think about how much would be needed just to survive a single attack from a Lightning Blessed. You'd probably have to drown them in a lake of the stuff."

"Oh. That's too bad." Too bad. Too bad! That was Tala's response to finding out he hadn't just discovered another way to kill Blessed, or at least Descendants! Gods! What had his life turned into? He shook his head, not sure if he was more disturbed by how casually he *wanted* another way to kill people or by how casually he wanted another way to *commit heresy*! Oh, how he missed the simpler times when his biggest concern was trying to figure out new ways of utilizing steam at his cozy little desk at the Institute!

"So, is that all then?" Tala asked, eager to get his mind away from those unwelcome thoughts. "Lots of metal and cool docks?"

Lito shrugged. "I guess? I mean, the Gods' palace is pretty cool, too, tallest building in the city by far, but that's not really unique for the capitals. And the lightning storms are pretty awesome to watch. They have viewing rooms throughout the city, mostly in the taller buildings or the ones higher in the hills, with special glass windows so people can watch the storms. Seriously, there's nothing like a Kilatara lightning storm. The lightning comes down like rain throughout the city and across the lake. It's amazing!"

"Aye, the lad speaks true," Gazin added, falling into step

next to Tala. "Nowhere else in the world will you see storms as magnificent as those at the heart of the Lightning God's domain. We'll see if we can't get ourselves a storm room while we're there. It's a sight you'll never forget, laddie, mark my words."

"I'll look forward to it." It did sound pretty amazing, Tala had to admit. Proper thunderstorms occurred on occasion around Fiahren, but the way the Fire Capital was built made it hard to really enjoy them. There weren't many places in the city with a clear enough view of the sky to be able to really see lightning, unless one got very lucky. The quick flash of light that accompanied the strike was often the closest any residents of Fiahren ever got to seeing a true lightning bolt. As a Researcher, he had been able to see plenty of storms from the Institute, it being one of the few places in the city that wasn't obstructed by all the other buildings.

"How long will we be there, anyway?" Tala asked. Their expected length of stay in Kilatara wasn't something he'd been told yet.

"Long as it takes to get that sword of yours fixed up," Gazin replied. "There are quite a few Metal Descendants in the city, and enough work with us that we'll have some options. It's just a matter of making sure we find one that's safe and willing to do a job like this, and then however long it takes them to do."

"What do you mean?"

"The Church keeps a close eye on the Metalborn, even if they're happy to welcome them. It'd be reckless of them to let foreign Descendants roam around unchecked, after all. So, we've got to find one who's discreet enough that they can do the job without the Church learning about it. And who'll be willing to do it without turning us in."

"I thought you said they were Dissidents? Would they really do that?"

"Hard to say, lad. They shouldn't. None of them should be that dumb, but these aren't exactly normal circumstances, are they? Turning this blade over to a Church could set them up for life, to say nothing of you. I don't even know what rewards Lightning would give to a Metal Descendant that turned you over to them. It'd be a Blessing for sure for anyone else."

"They wouldn't Bless a Metal Descendant? Even for me?"

"I don't know." Gazin shrugged. "Far as I'm aware no God has ever tried to Bless a foreign Descendant. I don't even know if it would work. Or if it did, if the Blessing would overwrite their Descendant powers, or if they would have control of two elements. And if that's the case, I can't see the other Churches being okay with it."

"Oh… no one has ever wielded two elements before? What about a kid with two different Descendant parents?"

"Well, that's a mighty rare thing to happen, two different types of Descendants getting together like that. I've known a few cases though, and heard about more, and it's never gone well."

"How so?"

"Babies rarely made it to birth. The few times those women even got pregnant they ended up miscarrying. No one's really sure why, but the general belief is that it's too much power for a fetus to handle. Similar to how Descendants usually aren't Awakened until they've reached their twenties. Awaken them younger than that and they usually end up losing control of their power and killing themselves, along with everybody around them."

"But not always," Tala pointed out.

"Aye, not always," Gazin agreed. "But it's common enough that it's rarely worth the risk. These days it's only done in the most dire of circumstances, or when whoever does the Awakening has the utmost faith in the kid's abilities. Anderas Anto was Awoken young, and despite his youth, and relative newness to his Blessing, he's already considered the greatest Blessed in the world. Even before it, he had a reputation as the greatest Descendant in the world, of any element. He beat an Earth Blessed in battle as an Awakened teenager! Barely more than a dozen years under him, and enough power it should have killed him, and he wielded it with more skill than some Blessed have! There was actually a string of early Awakenings after that happened; people thought that if their own kids were Awakened early, then they could be as great as Anderas. Most of 'em died, of course, and the few who survived were still nowhere near as gifted as him. A whole generation of dead Descendants later and early Awakenings became damn near taboo. Still are, and it's been damned near eighty years since."

"Really?" Tala was fascinated. He had never heard about any of this, except about how amazing young Anderas had been. "What about—" He stopped short, glancing at Alina, who was still walking beside Lito.

"Faith and dire circumstances," Alina answered his unfinished question, obviously knowing what he had been about to ask. Her voice was light, but there was a tenseness to her. Her shoulders were stiff as she stared straight ahead as they walked, not looking at him as she spoke. "My parents were confident in my skills, and my family needed something to give them more power in the Church. It wasn't enough, of course, and you know what happened then."

Tala just nodded with an ambiguous grunt, unsure how to properly respond to that. Her family had been betrayed and slaughtered by their former allies, the brutal politics of the Light Church showing no mercy to a family who had fallen out of favor, despite having a Blessed at its head.

CHAPTER 7

The journey to Kilatara through the forests of Lightning country was slow going and almost entirely uneventful, which left Tala with mixed feelings. On the one hand, uneventful was good, as it meant nobody was trying to kill him, but on the other hand, it was also boring. Their escape from Fiahren through Fire country had been similar, a lot of walking with little happening, but it had all been new and terrifying and exciting, so much so that Tala had never quite registered just how boring most of it had actually been. Their flight from Southtown had also been fraught with paranoia, as their escape into Light hadn't exactly been a subtle or quiet thing. They had also been on horses, which had taken a while for Tala to get used to, and had made that leg of their journey far quicker.

This time there had been no panicked escape, no real fear they were being followed by anyone, since no one should even know where they were. And so, while they never truly relaxed, their trek to Kilatara was bereft of the heightened levels of fear and tension that had been Tala's constant companion ever since that day he had killed Ignis. And so, Tala had discovered just how boring traveling could be, when his life wasn't in imminent danger. And Tala hated being bored. In his desperate quest to relieve some fraction of his boredom, Tala had taken to pestering the others to tell him about the things they had seen and done in the world. If he just happened to talk to Serala a bit more than the rest, well, he was sure nobody would think anything of it.

"The thing about Ice country is that it's not actually all ice and snow like people think," Serala continued. She still didn't speak casually overly much to the others, and Tala couldn't quite pretend that it didn't make him feel a little bit happy she was much more relaxed around him. Although being in Lightning had something to do with it. Ever since they had entered the overly humid forest, she had seemed just a bit happier, and a little more relaxed overall. Somehow, trying to ask about it had led into her telling him about what the Ice lands to the far south were like, not that he was complaining. "I mean, it is further south, but most of the population lives in the northern regions. It's still cold there, and there's a lot of snow in the winter, but it isn't a frozen wasteland or anything. I wouldn't want to live there myself. It's way too cold for me, but it's not that bad really."

Tala nodded along happily, enjoying listening to her talk so freely. For most of their time together, since leaving Fiahren, she would usually only talk for a little bit at a time before growing silent, when she wasn't acting as leader of the group. It was only recently she had started to engage with Tala and have long, drawn out conversations.

"You'd probably like it, I think." Serala hummed, looking at Tala, who turned his attention back to her. "Not the cold, obviously, but how different it is to Fiahren. You'd love the ice huts that they build further south. Igloos, I think they called them. They build these round buildings out of snow, with a little tunnel that you crawl through to get in, and light a fire inside. It's so cold the hut doesn't melt even with the fire keeping it warm."

Tala frowned, thinking about how that was even possible. The thermodynamics of such a structure would be fascinating to study! He wondered if Admani had written about these "igloos" in his travel journals. If he ever met up with his parents again, he'd have to ask them. Admani's journals had been restricted well beyond what an apprentice could access, but he knew his parents had read through the lot of them.

"Do you think we could go there?" Tala asked. "After we get my sword fixed up and whatever else you all have to do?"

"I don't see why not." Serala shrugged, smiling at him. He had a strange feeling she was pleased he had actually been listening to her. "We'll probably need to take you back down south eventually anyway. No reason we can't go all the way to Ice."

"Awesome!" Tala smiled back, feeling a fluttering in his gut as they smiled at each other. "What else is differ—" Tala broke off with a strangled sound as she turned to look ahead. A brilliant smile lit up her eyes, coinciding with sunlight spilling down onto her face as they broke through the tree line. Serala, bathed in sunlight with a smile happier than any Tala had ever seen on her before, stunned him so suddenly he gasped and breathed in a mouthful of saliva, making him choke and cough.

When he finally got his traitorous lungs to cooperate, Tala turned to see what had made Serala light up so drastically, and got his first look at Kilatara, the capital city of Lightning. His breath caught again as his eyes widened, and then hastily narrowed as they had yet to adjust to the bright sunlight from the darker depths of the forest.

In a word, Kilatara was spectacular! The entire city shone with the dancing and glimmering of countless lights, the entire place sparkling even brighter than the night sky on the clearest of nights when they were deep in the empty plains, as far from any cities as one could get. The sight was as mesmerizing as it was painful, and Tala had to pull his eyes away as they started watering from the overwhelming brilliance.

As Tala's eyes adjusted better to the sun and brightness of the city, he was able to make out more details he had missed. A city that was unlike any other he had ever seen. Although that wasn't saying much, as the only other proper city he had seen from a distance was Southtown. What stood out the most to Tala, aside from the shimmering, was the differing elevations of the city. While Southtown was built at the base of the Metal Mountains, nearly the entire city was built on flat ground, with only the lord's district being built slightly higher in the foothills. And Fiahren was entirely built upon the flat ground of the plains, despite pushing right up against the Burning Hills on its most northern side.

Kilatara, however, was entirely built on hills. While Tala had noticed during their journey that Lightning country wasn't nearly as flat as the Fire or Light lands were, he hadn't really thought about what a city built on such ground would be like. The highest point of the city seemed to be the west, although even there it started dropping back down before ending. From that highest point though, the city dropped chaotically east, getting lower, and sometimes higher, before hitting its lowest point right at the shores of Storm Lake, where he could faintly see the vague shapes of ships and what must have been the docks that Lito had told him about.

The lake itself was impressive, with its water shimmering in the afternoon sun, but Tala couldn't help comparing it to the Burning Lake, which bordered Fiahren, and thought the colossal lake of his home was a bit more impressive. It was certainly larger, even if Storm Lake looked properly massive from where they stood. So large, in fact, that even from their higher elevation he couldn't see the far shores of the lake. But from the maps he had seen back at the Institute, the Burning Lake was about three times bigger than Storm Lake, so it was easily the superior of the two.

"Quite the sight, isn't it?" Serala asked from beside him, the smile audible in her voice. "Have you ever seen anything more beautiful?"

"Only once." Tala breathed, glancing at her, to which she looked back at him questioningly. Realizing what he had said, Tala quickly turned his eyes back to the shining city and stumbled over his tongue. "I mean—Fiahren, I'm sure, looks better, from a distance, like this, from the hills. I mean—I didn't get a good look at it, after we left, or a look at all, really, I wish I had, though. But I've seen paintings, that people drew, other people, and I bet she's even prettier in person... it, I mean, it's prettier. In person. Fiahren." He stopped talking and bit his tongue.

He peeked at Serala from the corner of his eye and saw her staring at him, head slightly tilted with a bemused expression on her face. He felt his neck flushing and tried to fight down the blush before it reached his face. After what felt like an eternity of agony, she turned back towards Kilatara. "I guess it might be. Fiahren is certainly a... unique city. I'll have to look at it from the hills next time I get the chance."

Tala merely nodded in response, feeling both relieved and slightly... irritated? Disappointed? He mentally shook himself. This was neither the time, nor the place, nor the *person* for those sorts of thoughts.

"Well, let's keep moving," Serala called out to the group. "We want to get inside the city before nightfall. Clear skies can turn stormy in minutes around here." She led them off to the side, where the hill sloped less steeply. There were still trees on it, but not nearly as many as in the rest of the forest. Tala peered at the distance below them. The southern reaches of Kilatara didn't seem that far away from where they were, but he had learned that a short distance could still take a long time to cross when hills were involved.

As his companions passed by, Tala realized one was stopped right behind him and, judging from the shadow he had thought had been a tree, had been standing there the whole time. Tala turned his face, trying to keep his fear from showing, towards Ilan, the massive man had his arms crossed and a blank expression as he gazed out over the city of Lightning. Tala hesitated in the silence, nearly jumping when Ilan suddenly turned his head to him with a grin so small that Tala thought he might have imagined it. "Smooth, kid. Real smooth."

CHAPTER 8

Traveling through the forests of Lightning had been an utterly miserable, boring affair. Even Tala could only talk so much in a day. So far, the only thing breaking up the boredom had been the misery of the oppressive, humid heat. It had easily been the most boring time of his life. That record lasted only until entering Kilatara, where Tala was introduced to an entirely new level of boredom.

Upon entering the city, they beelined to an inn, which wasn't unusual for them, but in the week they had been in Kilatara, Tala had only been allowed to leave his room for meals downstairs or to use the privy. He understood their caution after Southtown but being stuck in the tiny room he shared with Gazin, always with at least one of his companions for "company," for an entire week, had been an utterly loathsome affair. The rest of them were all free to move about the city, as they had business to attend to. The most that Tala could see of the fascinating new city he was in was whatever he could glimpse out of the gaps in the window shutters, since it had been deemed too dangerous to have them open and risk his face being seen.

Had his companions not deemed the city safe enough to let him out after a week, Tala may have revolted. And Gods, how he was enjoying his new freedom! He had had a wonderful day seeing all the sights of Kilatara with Lito and Alina. Gazin and Dunlop had been with them as well, but the two older men had been hanging back all day. Tala appreciated that. It had been nice to just relax and see the city with his friends and pretend for a time that he wasn't the most wanted person in the world.

Even the specter of the great war that was rapidly escalating, and could be felt everywhere in the city, wasn't enough to ruin his day. He steadfastly ignored every little twinge of guilt he felt at every troop of soldiers that marched on by, knowing every one of those men and women may very well never return, all due to a war that he had unintentionally started. The biggest downside (that he was letting himself acknowledge, at least) to his new freedom was that his sword had been taken. Serala brought it to be fixed by whatever Metal Descendant they had found, and it would be weeks before he would get it back. He was uncomfortably aware of how much he missed the familiar weight of it at his side.

"So, what do you think?" Lito asked, legs dangling over the side of the low wall they were sitting on, admiring the multicolored docks and sparkling waters of Storm Lake. Tala was enjoying watching the various boats coming and going from the docks, even if the majority of them were military transports ferrying troops across the lake.

Tala took another small bite of the strange concoction in his hand, some sort of chilled, creamed fruit, and shuddered as another shock shot through his mouth and throughout his body.

"I don't know. It's delicious, yeah, but it's like static shock on my tongue, only stronger. It's not bad, really, but I'm not sure I like it."

"Yeah, I'm not a fan of the shocking stuff either," Lito said, taking a large bite of his own treat. He caught Tala's incredulous face and grinned. "You can get it without that. We just thought you should experience the whole thing first."

Tala's eye twitched, though whether it was because of Lito or the Lightning treat, he wasn't certain.

"Why do they make it if nobody likes it?"

"Oh, some people do. Most use it as a pick-me-up of sorts: a big bite of the stronger stuff can really get you going. There's all sorts of drinks and snacks and stuff you can get. It's supposed to be really popular among guards and soldiers, helps them stay awake during night shifts."

"I can believe that." Tala nodded, feeling another small jolt shoot through his body as he took another bite. "I'm surprised I've never heard of it. I wonder if this is what they've been trying to make back at the herbology labs."

"The what?" Lito questioned. Alina leaned forward next to him, appearing puzzled.

"The herbology labs. Back at the Institute?" They both stared back at him with blank faces. Tala sighed. "It's where they study plants and plant-related things. They've got these massive greenhouses they grow all kinds of different plants in, from all over the world. They've got some from Lightning, and they've been messing around with Lightning fruit for years, turning it into paste and freezing it and stuff. I wonder if this is what they're trying to make."

"Oh. That's cool."

Tala remembered well all the thousands of plants that were in the Institute's greenhouses, from enormous trees to the tiny little carnivorous snappers. As a youth, he had spent months tasked with caring for all the different plants, watering, and, when necessary, feeding them. It had been one of the most boring periods of his life, if he were honest. He knew that many Researchers loved working with plants, but they were decidedly *not* for him. Maybe that was why he was struggling with the plant-based survival lessons Dunlop had been giving him. Perhaps he had learned about so many plants (he had cared so little about) that he couldn't keep any of them straight anymore.

"You didn't know about the herbology labs?" Tala was surprised. Given the importance of the Institute, he'd have thought that Dissidents knew just about everything about the place.

"No? That's Institute stuff. That whole place is more trouble than it's worth to pay attention to. Most of us are happy to just let the people in Fire deal with it."

"Oh." Tala couldn't help feeling slightly offended. Even if he was no longer a Researcher, and had forsaken Fire (and the Gods, really) in general, he still held a deep love and pride for the Institute. "I guess I just thought it was more important than it is."

"What? No. That's not what I meant. It's just… I don't really know. It's just that it's kinda… off limits to us. Like *us*, us. All of us. It's not really an issue outside of Fire, or Fiahren, really, but when we're there? The Institute is forbidden. We aren't supposed to be involved with it *at all*. No sabotage, no spying, no killing or kidnapping or interrogating anybody that has anything to do with it."

"What? Why? I'd have thought it would be some sort of primary target for you all. The way the others talked made it sound like taking out the Institute would cripple Fire completely."

"It would. Or I think it would, anyway. Honestly, I don't know why, but it's a really strict rule we have. Any time someone gets sent to Fire, especially Fiahren, we're given this whole lecture about avoiding the Institute. Back when you first came to us, didn't you notice the way everyone reacted when you said your parents were Researchers?"

"I was a bit distracted," Tala said drily, trying not to think too hard about his parent's possible fates. He had heard nothing about them since the day he left Fiahren and could only hope that the Dissidents had gotten them out like they had promised.

"Right. Yeah. Well, that was kind of a big deal. I mean, we're supposed to have literally *nothing* to do with you lot, and then Vail and Serala of all people come dragging some random guy into one of our most secret hideouts, during a lockdown of all things, saying he killed a Blessed, and oh! He's a Researcher to boot! Honestly, I thought Hagan was going to have an aneurysm."

"Huh." Tala didn't really know what to say. "But Hagan knew who my parents are—he even knew who I was!"

Lito just shrugged, and Alina shook her head, having been silent so far, but paying close attention to the conversation. "He probably keeps track of everybody who works there, so he knows who to keep the rest of us away from. Somebody has to, or we'd never know who we can or can't touch."

"Could he have spies there? Inside, I mean? And that's why you're supposed to stay away, so you don't cause them problems?"

"Probably." Lito shrugged. "Honestly, that makes more sense than most of the theories I've heard. You're the one who's from there; do you think there could be spies?"

"I… guess? I mean, it's a big place. Biggest in Fiahren, even if the Fire God's palace is taller. And there are a lot of people who work there. So, it is possible, I suppose. Incredibly risky, though. The smartest people in the world work there; so spying right under their noses? And there's a lot of security. Nobody gets in unless they've been approved by the Church and Institute both. And the Church keeps a close eye on the place. We have to record and report everything we do, and they still send people to check in on things every couple of months."

"Wait, what do you mean 'send people to check in?' Don't they always have people there?" Lito asked, sharing a confused look with Alina.

"The Church mostly leaves us alone. I mean, they monitor everything we do, but they don't really get involved with us. They don't even send Empowered there, some sort of old agreement or something that only ordinary people are allowed on the grounds."

Lito and Alina were both giving him a strange look, like they thought he was going to start laughing and say he was joking. He wasn't really sure why.

"They never send Blessed? Or even Descendants? Ever?" Alina asked, her voice sounding even more confused than her baffled expression.

"No? Not that I know of. Even Ishaan never came back, and he was Blessed over eight hundred years ago. Like I said, it's some sort of ancient agreement or something. I don't know why it was made. I don't think anybody knows anymore. But no one I ever talked to had ever heard of an Empowered going there."

"That's weird. Like, that's really weird," Lito said, brow furrowed. "Churches always send Descendants for anything even remotely important. Why would they agree to let the Institute of all places have so much freedom?"

"I don't know." Tala shrugged. "It's just always been that way. The God of Fire himself gave the order, according to rumor, way back when Fiahren and the Institute were first founded. And in over seven thousand years, he's never changed his mind, at least not that I know of."

"The God gave that order? Not the High Priest, but the actual God himself!?" Lito sounded bewildered.

"That's the rumor. Why? Is it really that big of a deal?"

"I guess not…" Lito trailed off uncertainly. "If it was in the early days, He might just not care enough to bother changing it anymore, if He even remembers it. I mean, the Gods don't really do much these days. They haven't for a long time. But there aren't many places as old as the Institute around, so I guess it makes sense that a command the God gave back when they still did stuff is still being followed. We just don't hear about that sort of thing much anymore."

"Ah. Yeah. That makes sense," Tala agreed, unenthused. It was difficult to accept what he had learned of the Gods after a life of loyal service to them. Even though he now knew the truth, *believed* the truth, it still hurt somewhere, deep in his soul, every time he was reminded about what they were actually like.

The conversation died there, and the three of them sat quietly, each lost in their own thoughts. Above them, the sky quickly darkened as immense, menacing clouds began to coalesce overhead. Gazin and Dunlop walked up beside them, eyes pointed skyward.

"Well, lad, this is some fortunate timing. Want to go see what a true Lightning storm looks like?"

CHAPTER 9

Kilatara lightning storms, Tala could admit, might be one of the coolest things he had ever seen. Comparable only to the three-way fight between Blessed back in Southtown, a sight he was quite certain he was the only person, living or dead, to have ever witnessed from so close and survived.

They had a small viewing room all to themselves, tucked away in the corner near the top of one of the buildings on the hills, that gave them a fantastic view over the city and lake. It turned out that the Dissidents owned several private storm rooms throughout the city, which they often rented out to travelers for a tidy profit. Apparently, they doubled as highly valued meeting rooms between merchants when skies were clear; the thick, specialized glass, which kept the rooms safe from the lightning and thunder, also soundproofed them enough that there was little to no risk of eavesdroppers.

By the time that Tala and the others made it into the room, where the rest of their companions, sans Caida, were already waiting for them, it had begun raining extremely hard. So hard, in fact, that Tala hadn't been entirely convinced they would be able to see much of anything outside, even the brilliant brightness of lightning being little more than dull flashes in the absolute wall of rain pouring down.

The first clearly visible flash had surprised him while staring out at the black and rain beyond the window, to the point that he had missed actually seeing it beyond a sudden burst of light. The rumbling which came with it was mercifully muted by the design of the room, so it didn't burst his ears. He was more prepared for the second flash, although it came much sooner than he had expected. A towering, forked lance of brightest yellow tore its way through the blackness of the heavy clouds and the obfuscation of the rain. Tala's eyes hadn't quite adjusted to the dark again after the first flash, which helped quite a bit with properly seeing the second. As cool as it was to witness a lightning strike so close, and from such a vantage point, it wasn't quite as amazing as the others had made it sound. He wondered if, perhaps, they had oversold the experience slightly.

The third strike came shortly thereafter, huge and bright and thunderous, and Tala settled himself back in his chair to at least enjoy the uniqueness of the show. Then the fourth strike came, followed almost immediately by the fifth, then the sixth, then the seventh and eighth came simultaneously, creating a spectacular crash of jagged yellow lines that cut through the dark and sent a thrill up Tala's spine. Then the Lightning storm began!

With the preamble over, suddenly the twin strikes became a veritable shower of lightning, every second exploding the sky, the city, and the lake with immense bolts more numerous than Tala could even begin to count! They crashed and sang and roared through the blackness with a speed and ferocity grander than anything he could have ever imagined. The strikes grew bigger and stronger and faster until there was so much lightning crashing down from the heavens it was as if the sun had risen again, lighting up every inch of the shining city and the lake beyond with immense frequency. The darkness wasn't even given the smallest fraction of a second to return. Not just the room, but the entire building rumbled with the power of the storm. The overwhelming roar of the thunder so powerful that the very sound of it was making the earth shake beneath them!

And still the storm grew. The lightning came faster and stronger until Tala was pressed against the large glass wall, unaware he had stood as he watched mesmerized by the lightning falling like rain. Every building of the city lit up in whites, yellows, oranges, and reds. The lightning struck and followed the metal walls and rods and rails into the ground, turning the shining, shimmering city into a living monument to the glory and power of Lightning. The entire city shone with an endless, glistening light, sparking and screaming over the cacophony of thunder. The very air began to sing with an unearthly sound unlike anything Tala had ever heard before! The buildings themselves were so awash in the power of lightning, it looked as though they were creating their own. Tremendous fingers of energy, so white they almost looked purple, were shooting, stretching, *reaching* out of the buildings towards each other, towards the ground, and back towards the sky. Tala's world became nothing more than light and rumble and that haunting, buzzing singing hum of the purple lightning as it screamed its rage back out into the world!

He didn't know how long he stood there, watching the storm of the Lightning God rain its fury and glory onto the land below. Eventually, things began to calm. The lightning was coming less frequently. That beautiful, horrible song faded away as the purple lightning receded back into the dimming buildings, losing that effervescent glow that had brought the city to life in a way Tala could have never imagined! Almost as fast as it had begun, the storm died out. The clouds shrank and fled, revealing the moons and stars in the night sky behind them. It had stopped raining too, though when, Tala had no idea, so consumed he was with the show of nature's might.

Finally, when Tala despondently accepted that the storm was well and truly over, he turned away from the window and examined his companions. They all seemed to be in the same state, a sort of bittersweet melancholy—with three notable exceptions. Vail sat by himself in the back of the room, eyes far away with a strange sort of... *nostalgic* half-smile on his face. It might have been the most human expression Tala had ever seen him wear, and he couldn't help but feel a chill in his spine. The other two looking strange were Gazin and Serala. They sat closely together, with Gazin looking sad and Serala...

Serala looked almost like she was in agony but trying to hide it. Her stoic face had cracks that Tala was unused to. He would swear her eyes were wet, not that he would ever so much as even hint at having ever seen such a thing. The strangest part was that Serala, the girl who didn't seem to really understand the concept of vulnerability, grasped Gazin's hand in her own, with a grip so tight that her knuckles were bone white. Had it been anyone other than Gazin in her clutch, Tala would have expected their hand to have been crushed to a pulp.

Tala tore his eyes away before Serala could see him looking, for he had no wish to know what the girl would do to him if she knew he had witnessed such a vulnerable moment.

CHAPTER 10

I t was strange, to Alina, just… being in a city like they were. And a capital city, at that! No secret plans. No spying or assassinations. No *work*. Not really, anyway. Their only job in Kilatara was to protect Tala, and that wasn't exactly a challenge, not when no one knew he was there. He made their job easy by following their rules with little complaint, and she appreciated he had the good sense to do that. However, she could tell her friend (and that still felt strange to her, having someone other than Lito to call "friend") was struggling a bit, though Alina could empathize with that. Due to her powers, and her skill with them, she rarely got to enjoy any form of "downtime" ever since joining the Dissidents. Not that she ever had much before either, her mother having kept her on a busy schedule of training and education since she was young, but that was beside the point. Alina simply wasn't used to not having *something* to do, and she didn't find it a particularly pleasant experience.

She hoped the danger was past, though, at least as much as it could be. Southtown had been bad, really bad, even if it had resulted in an unprecedented victory for the Dissidents. But war was brewing—had already brewed, really—a massive war that somehow had the potential to be unlike any seen in millennia. She still didn't understand how that was possible, given that Anderas Anto had survived Southtown to be able to tell Metal whatever he wanted about what had happened. But events had spun in such a way that the world would be distracted from Tala, which meant that eventually he would be about as safe as any of them were. So long as they could keep him moving, and not let another Southtown occur to draw the world's attention back toward him.

Although, she was having some concerns about that, if she were being honest. As risky as Kilatara had been, it had worked out in their favor, and after having been safe for weeks there, she would have thought they would stay in Lightning for a while, moving between some of the smaller towns and settlements scattered throughout its many forests. However, she had managed to convince Serala to tell her of their next destination, and she was still confused by it.

"You're certain that the Jungle is the best place to go next?" Alina asked, tilting her head sideways in the tub to look at Serala, who was cleaning one of her many, many daggers, only to have Caida gently wrench her head straight again as she continued to work on Alina's hair.

The split-second of hesitation Serala showed before answering told volumes. Alina wasn't exactly sure *what* it was saying, but the fact she could see it at all meant there was something more about the plan than Serala was sharing. Serala was only present because Caida had insisted she join them for some "girl time," and had refused to accept Serala's refusal, practically dragging her into the bathing room with them. It had been rather amusing, in Alina's opinion, seeing Serala so clearly confused about what to do. She had ended up simply sitting in a chair off to the side cleaning one of her daggers (and how many of those things did the girl *have*?) while Alina entered the bath. While Alina did feel she had been growing closer with Serala over the last few months, having engaged in increasingly less stilted, awkward conversations with her as they traveled, it often felt like she had grown closer to Serala in the way that the group had grown closer to the Metal Mountains when they first appeared on the horizon earlier in their journey. Every day they knew they were getting closer to them, but Gods-be-damned did it not feel like they were ever making any progress, so large and distant were those peaks.

"Yes," Serala confirmed authoritatively. "Anywhere else is too risky with the war. The Canyon is barely guarded, and even then, only from people entering Lightning from the Jungle, not the other way around. The war shouldn't have any effect on that."

"I suppose that's Vail's reasoning, is it?" Caida asked mildly. Alina's eyes shot back to Serala even while her head was held firmly in place by Caida's hands.

"He agrees that the Jungle is the best plan," Serala said slowly.

"Hmm. I see." Caida hummed pleasantly, never stopping in her braiding of Alina's hair. "Well, I'm not sure I agree, but it's not my decision, is it?" She gave a husky, sensual laugh that sent chills up Alina's spine. Sometimes she forgot about what exactly Caida did for a living. "Regardless, I am looking forward to it. I've never been to the Jungle myself, and I hear that Morungil is quite the sight."

"Oh, it is!" Serala said, sounding far more enthusiastic than Alina was used to. "The Hale Kia'i are amazing, and they're all ancient. They've been around for so long nobody even knows when they were built, or how. Most people believe the Earth God, or some of his first Blessed, made them in the early days, before the nations were established. It would explain why they're still in such good condition even after thousands of years! And the Falms are fantastic! That's the Fal'marae, the big wooden platforms built around the Hale's. They're all shops and restaurants and stuff. There's something really cool about drinking tea on a platform hundreds of feet in the air, even if you can't really see the sky because the God Tree covers everything."

Alina stared at Serala, shocked. She had never heard the other girl… *gush*. Even Caida's hands were still in her hair.

"Sorry." Serala coughed, looking away with what Alina thought was an honest-to-Gods blush growing on her face. "I've… been talking to Tala too much. He likes hearing about all the different places in the world."

Alina turned her head in Caida's still motionless hands, sharing an intrigued look with her. Tala's feelings were obvious to all of them, as evidenced by the bet they all had paid into (even Ilan, to her enduring shock), but perhaps his little crush wasn't quite as unrequited as they expected. Alina wanted to say something, but what did you say to a girl like Serala about feelings that she probably didn't even realize she was having? Serala was many things, but emotionally intelligent she was not.

"He certainly does have a love of learning," Caida said. Alina noted the subtle hint of mischief in her voice. She had grown to recognize it from the many times Caida would tease her and the others. Caida restarted her ministrations of Alina's hair, and Alina relaxed back into the tub, attention subtly hooked on Serala. "And conversation. He does seem to enjoy talking to you in particular."

"Really?" Serala asked, making the single word sound both eager and doubtful simultaneously. "He talks to everybody though."

"Yes. But he talks to you the most. When he can."

"Oh." Serala blinked, clearly unsure what to do with that information. Alina felt a sudden pang of pity for the girl who was so obviously unused to dealing with such things as feelings.

"You enjoy talking to him too, don't you?" she asked. She took the quick, light squeeze of her shoulder as a sign of Caida's approval.

"I... do? I mean, yes, I do." Serala nodded, more to herself than them, frowning a little. Alina's pity for her grew.

"Then you should keep talking to him!" Caida said warmly. "You two are already friends, after all. Talking can only help you grow closer. And you want to get closer to him, don't you?"

"I... suppose?" Serala answered, sounding confused. "Close like Alina and Lito are?" Alina nearly choked on air. Where had that come from?

"Why, I suppose so." Caida said, and Alina felt a cold chill settle in her gut at her tone.

"Of course, Alina could be *closer* to Lito too, couldn't she?" Alina was not happy about the way Caida had leaned in and said that last bit right in her ear.

"I don't know what you're talking about," Alina said stiffly. She closed her eyes with a grimace, knowing she had said that far too quickly.

"She means marriage," Serala said bluntly, and Alina felt her face erupt in a blush.

"Well, I didn't quite mean that. Not yet, anyway," Caida said, losing her teasing tone in surprise. "I simply meant that they could be closer." She emphasized "closer" in a way that even Serala couldn't miss her meaning.

Serala, though, only tilted her head in confusion, frowning at Caida. Face aflame, Alina couldn't help but stare at Serala in astonishment. She had to understand, given how she always reacted to Nuri when he pushed her. "Aren't you two already fucking? What's between that and marriage?"

"What!?" Alina screeched, jaw dropping and eyes popping out at Serala, who only blinked confusedly back at her. Behind her, Caida laughed.

"Oh, no, dearest," Caida chuckled out, quickly suppressing her laughter. "They have yet to take that step. Gods only know why."

Alina couldn't believe this conversation was happening! "We aren't—we aren't like that! Lito's my friend! My best friend! We're not... together!"

"Why not?" Serala asked bluntly. Alina could only gape at her. "I thought you two were in love or something."

"I—That's—" Alina stumbled over her words, not even sure what she was trying to say. "What about Tala? Why aren't you sleeping with him?" She clasped her hands over her mouth, shocked at herself for asking Serala, of all people, such a question! She'd be lucky if she survived the bath with less than a dozen knives stuck in her now!

"Why would I sleep with Tala?" Serala instead asked, clearly bemused. Alina gaped at her again.

"Do you not want to?" Caida asked slowly, and Alina could hear the frown in her voice.

"I don't know. I haven't really thought about it." Serala shrugged. Alina felt like her head was buzzing at the strangeness of the entire conversation.

"Have you ever thought about having sex?" Caida asked.

"Sometimes." Serala shrugged. "But I'm not supposed to, so I try not to think about it too much."

"What do you mean, you're not supposed to?" Alina asked. She was well aware that she was far less open about such matters than was normal, but even she had fooled around with some of her closer handmaidens when she had been younger!

"Who told you that?" Caida asked.

"Vail."

Alina and Caida shared another look. "And why did Vail tell you that?" Caida asked slowly. Dangerously. Alina didn't know much about Serala's relationship with Vail, but Serala had been with him since she was a child. She was terrified of Vail, but if Serala was saying what Alina thought she might be, what she knew Caida was thinking, she might have to face her fear sooner rather than later.

"I don't know. When I was a kid, Vail told me I shouldn't have sex, and if anyone kept trying after I said no, I should stab them. He never actually told me why, although I've had to stab a lot of people over it. Especially men. They don't always respond well to being turned down." She shrugged, as if stabbing people was an ordinary, everyday occurrence. Which, given that it was Serala, might actually be the case. Still, she was relieved Vail hadn't been abusing Serala like she had first feared.

At least he wasn't abusing her in that way.

"That man, I swear." Caida huffed. "And Ilan never explained it? That it is okay to have sex sometimes?"

"No." Serala shook her head, looking confused again. "I know that you all have sex a lot. I just thought that there was something wrong with me."

"Oh, by the Gods." Caida swore, a sentiment Alina shared. She didn't know how Vail had ended up caring for Serala, if she was his daughter or niece or what, but that man had no business raising a child!

"Serala, dear, you and I need to have a chat sometime. Privately. After I've talked to Vail… after I've talked to Ilan. Alright?"

"Yeah, alright." Serala shrugged, giving Caida a puzzled look. Alina contemplated if Caida would allow her into that little chat. Serala clearly needed the support.

CHAPTER 11

Tala eyed Serala eagerly as she entered the room, trying to contain his excitement. When Gazin had told him to meet her in one of the Dissidents' storm rooms, his heart started racing. There was only one reason she would want to meet him in such a place. Well, two reasons, but he tried not to think about that. Not when Gazin, Dunlop, Lito, and Alina were all joining him, and Dunlop was acting like an excited little boy—to their collective amusement—practically bouncing on the balls of his feet as they waited for Serala to arrive.

He could almost feel Dunlop restraining himself as Serala arrived. She smiled at Tala strangely as she closed the door behind her. Ever since she had started having private "girl time" with Caida and Alina, her smile kept changing. It was like she was trying out different smiles on him for some reason. He had noticed Alina doing the same thing to Lito sometimes but had no idea why. It definitely all went back to Caida, and whatever little game she was playing with them, but he'd probably have a better time prying info from Vail than her.

All thoughts of weird smiles were driven from his mind when Serala pulled a sword out from under her cloak and all his attention was pulled instantly to the—rather normal—sheath and handle. They were nice, certainly, but not exactly attention-grabbing. Still, Tala's heart skipped a beat as he focused on them while Dunlop drew a reverent breath beside him. Smiling more normally now, Serala handed Tala the sword, and he took a moment to relish how perfectly the new handle fit in his palm before drawing the blade.

It was a thing of beauty.

It was still shaped like the classic longsword it had been born from, straight and sharp on both sides, but even Tala could tell that it was no ordinary weapon. The smith, whatever Metal Descendant they had found to work on it, had forgone all pretense of normality with the naked blade and had embraced the Blessed metal fully. The tiniest twitch of his hand had Tala mesmerized, the blade shining and rippling with a dancing rainbow hue at even the slightest shift. He gave it a slow, careful swing and marveled at how smoothly it cut through the air. *This is a weapon.*

Holding it sideways, the blade carefully nestled on its side in his palm, he studied every inch. Simple though it may be, the hilt had been entirely redone. Where before the handle had just been a normal grip covered in leather, it was now a work of true craftsmanship. The top half of the handle was still a leather grip, one sized perfectly for Tala's hand. The bottom however was pure metal, ending with a rounded, slightly studded pommel whose weight balanced out the sword perfectly.

"There was more Blessed Metal than the blade needed,

so the smith used it in the handle," Serala explained, gleefully. "And in the tang and pommel. Said that it would make both nearly unbreakable and would also prevent too much backlash from reaching your hands if you hit something hard with it. The cross guard too. It and the pommel are a mixture so they don't have the same sheen of the blade. That way, it won't catch people's attention at your side. And since it's Blessed Metal, it won't break if you hit something with it. That's why she gave them that teardrop shape at the ends. They're too small to hurt a Blessed, from how you explained the sword worked, but they'll hurt like the hells if you hit anybody else with them. Basically, if you ever need to fight without people realizing what that sword is, you can just keep it sheathed, turn it around, and beat them to death with the handle. The sheath is reinforced with some of the extra metal too, so you don't have to worry about it."

"It's wonderful," Tala breathed, examining the sheathe to see if he could spot any difference to it from a normal one. He thought he might be able to see glints of color when peeking inside it, but that was all. "That Metalsmith did an amazing job."

"Oh, she knows. And she was paid more than well for it. She was sad she couldn't put her mark anywhere, but if any of the Churches ever found out she made it, she'd be executed immediately."

Tala nodded somberly, feeling sympathy for the unknown smith. He would have hated making an important invention back at the Institute and not be able to put his name anywhere on it. Dunlop was practically salivating as he gazed lustfully at the sword. As relieved as Tala was at having the sword back in his hands—he hadn't realized how tense he had been without it—he was worried Dunlop might maul him if he didn't let him examine it himself. Wordlessly, he offered the hilt to Dunlop. For a moment, Tala thought Dunlop might kiss him before he reverently took the blade, turning his back to them as he brought it right up to his eye.

Leaving Dunlop to do his thing (was that crooning he was hearing?) Tala turned to the others. "So. Thoughts?" he asked.

"That's a damned nice sword," Lito replied succinctly, shooting a worried look of his own at Dunlop. "He's not going to lick it, is he?" he hissed in a concerned whisper.

"Nay, he wouldn't do something like…" Gazin trailed off awkwardly. Dunlop was definitely crooning. They shared looks, shifting around in awkward silence as they tried to ignore whatever was happening behind Tala.

"We're headed to Lynmyr, right?" Tala asked, desperate for something, anything, to distract them.

"Aye, that we are, lad!" Gazin exclaimed, just as eager as Tala. "Great city. Lynmyr. Great city! That's even its nickname, y'know? 'The Great City of Lynmyr'. Or 'Lynmyr, the Great City.' The Bazaar is excellent! You'll love it, I'm sure! You can buy things there you can't find just about anywhere else."

"And the Canyon is cool, too!" Lito quickly added before the not-quite silence could return. "Or so I've heard. Never actually seen it myself. But I've heard it's gorgeous. The Bridge too. It's supposed to be unique, made with some old, lost technique."

"It's certainly different," Serala added slowly, seeming

confused. Tala had a bad feeling that she thought Dunlop's crooning to a sword was perfectly normal behavior. "Definitely something you'll want to see." She nodded at Tala. "Even Vail said he's never seen anything like the bridge before."

"Cool, cool. Can't wait," Tala said. And it was true, too, mostly. He knew Researchers had been trying to study the Canyon and Bridge both for a long time, but Fire wouldn't risk letting them go in person, so it was a slow, tedious process to learn anything new.

"This is quite the sword, kid."

Tala jumped. He hadn't been expecting Dunlop to be right behind him like that! He hadn't even noticed the weird crooning stop.

"Ah, yeah, it is. Thanks," Tala replied, smiling shakily at Dunlop as he took back his sword.

Dunlop, to his credit, seemed entirely unbothered by the awkward atmosphere. "If there's no other business, we should get moving," he said. "We shouldn't linger any longer now that we have the sword. We've been in this city too long already."

Tala winced and nodded. Army recruiters were being seen more and more frequently on the streets, and it was getting harder to avoid them. They would end up getting conscripted into Lightning's forces if they stayed much longer. And that was the best-case scenario.

CHAPTER 12

"I'm gonna be honest, I'm not really seeing why it's called the 'great city,'" Tala commented idly. The journey from Kilatara had gone as smoothly as could be, and they had made it inside Lynmyr with little problem, Alina's magic having been more than sufficient to hide him from the rather more attentive guards at the city's gates. "I mean, it's nice and all, but it's nowhere near Fiahren. Or Kilatara even. It's more like Southtown, just… taller." The buildings of Lynmyr mostly seemed to stretch up a good few stories, higher than most of those in Southtown had, but the city lacked any of the chaos or beauty that had been present in either of the capitals Tala had been to.

"Don't think on it too much, lad," Gazin responded from beside him, a place he had taken to occupying quite often since leaving Kilatara. Tala wasn't annoyed by his constant presence, per se, but he was growing increasingly curious as to why Gazin was hovering so much, like he was expecting something bad was going to happen to Tala and wanted to be there to stop it. None of the others seemed to have developed that same worry, though, and Gazin had acted oblivious when Tala had tried to ask some subtle questions about it. "It's a large city, and a central trade hub at that, being the only real place to cross the Canyon, but it only started becoming known as 'the great city' after they stopped the Demon from destroying the bridge and he fell off into the Canyon. But after Lady Asifah claimed to have killed him, the name just kinda stuck."

"Fell?" Lito questioned from Tala's other side. "I thought Asifah blasted him off?"

"Aye, that's what she claims," Gazin said with an amused snort. "I have it on… good authority, you might say, that the Demon wasn't entirely paying attention and slipped off. Took a step without looking and tumbled right down."

Tala gave Gazin a look, feeling both Lito and Alina peering around him at the man too. Of the many, many tales told about the Demon from Wind, slipping off of the world's most famous bridge due to carelessness didn't exactly fit in with his usual image. Apparently, from what Tala had heard, the Demon had been silent for a few months after that event, and Lady Asifah had taken to claiming she had killed the Demon, before he showed up again and destroyed half of Lostrego.

"And who exactly is this 'good source' of yours?" Tala asked skeptically.

"Hm? Oh, don't you worry about that, lad. Just somebody who happened to be there for it all. No one important," Gazin said dismissively, flicking his hand in the air. Tala narrowed his eyes at the Fleshy, who was studiously ignoring him, before sharing a look with Lito and Alina. There was definitely something more to that than Gazin was saying. Unfortunately, they were unlikely to ever discover what it was. Even though Gazin was possibly the worst gossip Tala had ever met, if the man wanted to keep something a secret, he could be unbelievably stubborn about it.

Probably comes with being a ranking member of the Dissidents. The Dissidents didn't actually have ranks, but Tala had learned in his time with the group that certain people in the cause were listened to and followed as though they were in charge, even if they didn't hold a formal position like Hagan's, where their leadership was obvious. Gazin could order others about, although apparently, he rarely ever acted in such a way, preferring to follow along with the plans of others than be in charge himself.

To be honest, the whole leadership and general organizational system of the Dissidents quite confused Tala. He thought it might make more sense if he ever actually encountered other members, but the group was careful to hide him away from friend and foe alike. He doubted any Dissidents in Kilatara had ever even known he was there, despite the weeks he had spent in the city. Not that he was complaining about it. After Southtown, he was heartily on board with the concept of "operational security."

"So, it's known as 'the great city' because the Demon was an idiot?" Tala couldn't help but ask, amused at the astonished faces Lito and Alina gave him.

Gazin coughed like he was choking on something, an action Tala thought he would never see from a man who could literally open up his own throat on a whim. Gazin had demonstrated that particular ability one night when discussing with Tala about the peculiarities of the human larynx and how it affected a person's voice. Tala had been morbidly fascinated to be able to watch the way the larynx and other parts of the throat moved as Gazin spoke in different volumes and pitches. Greatly disturbed, yes, but fascinated.

Gazin cleared his throat. "That's not—well..." Gazin didn't seem to quite know how to respond, much to Tala's own personal amusement. "Maybe just don't say something like that again, aye, lad? It's just, uh, probably wiser not to," Gazin finished strongly, with a firm nod of his head as though the entire thing was resolved.

Tala snickered, although he caught the strange look that Gazin had sent to Those Three: the trio of Vail, Ilan, and Serala, who were leading their little party through the streets. For a second Gazin had looked extremely uncomfortable. Nervous, almost. There weren't many things that could scare Gazin.

He was about to ask when Gazin, clearly intent on preventing exactly that sort of thing from happening, spoke. "Looks like we're just about to the Inn, methinks. Let's pick it up, eh? I could use a hearty meal and some ale myself." And with that said, the short man sped up, pacing ahead of Tala and the other two.

Tala, for his part, shared a bemused look with Alina and Lito. The Demon was a topic that made many people uncomfortable—even amongst the Dissidents, oddly enough, according to Lito—but Gazin always had the strangest reactions whenever the Demon was brought up as anything more than a passing reference. Not for the first time, Tala wondered if Gazin had, somehow, *known* the Demon. Unfortunately, it was one of the few topics they could never get Gazin to speak much about. The annoyingly restrained gossip.

Tala glanced back at Dunlop, who was bringing up the rear of the party, just a few steps behind them. The man just gave him a blank stare in return, along with the slightest motion of the shoulders, the tiniest shrug that Tala had ever seen. Tala shrugged back, exaggerating the motion and receiving a raised brow from Dunlop in return. Suppressing a chuckle, Tala turned forward again, following the others as they continued up the street before turning into the inn.

CHAPTER 13

They weren't planning to stay in Lynmyr for very long. A couple days, three at most, to get a bit of rest and stock up on whatever supplies they needed. The trip from Kilatara had gone quickly, the benefits of traveling on the Lightning Road. The global network of trade roads that connected the capitals and most major cities of each nation (except for Lava and the Bodylands, naturally) were almost always the quickest way to get anywhere.

Unlike most of the lesser roads throughout the world that were usually just packed and hardened dirt after millennia of use, the interconnected series of roads that made up the main trade network were made of stone, cut and connected in such a way that rain would neither flood nor wash them away, high winds wouldn't move them an inch, and even extensive use would barely wear away at them. There was little to no risk of a hole appearing for a foot to get caught in, be it human or animal, nor of mud or overgrowth to hinder travel. As such, after having had weeks in Kilatara to stock up, there was very little that Tala or his companions needed to replenish in Lynmyr.

Which was a bit of a shame, in Tala's opinion. Even if Lynmyr wasn't quite as great as its reputation made it out to be, it was still a major foreign city, unique in its own ways, and Tala would have loved the chance to explore it properly, much like he had Kilatara. Despite being a border city, Lynmyr was one of the last places anybody would expect Tala to show up. The only reason he would have for being there was if he intended to head back south by going through the Jungle, which no sane person would ever expect an internationally wanted criminal to do, given that they couldn't safely use the Jungle Road and stepping off it might as well be suicide.

With how smoothly their time in Kilatara had gone, and how low the risk was of Tala being recognized in Lynmyr, it had been agreed he could take the next day to explore the city before they left the following morning, crossing the Canyon Bridge along with the morning mass of southbound traders.

Gazin and Dunlop, as usual, were to accompany Tala for the day, just to mitigate whatever small risk there still was. Tala didn't mind. Not really. He was growing used to always having shadows. There was something comforting in knowing that whatever happened—even if nothing happened—he had some of the most dangerous people in the world protecting him. Even if there was nothing in particular they needed to protect him from in Lynmyr. Even if the biggest threat to him was to show up—a Blessed—he would be more capable of defending himself than either Gazin or Dunlop.

Maybe months of being constantly babysat was starting to get to him. Hopefully, he'd feel better about it in the morning.

Thankfully, Tala's mood indeed improved after a good night's sleep, and after having an enjoyable breakfast, Tala eagerly rushed out the door, Gazin and Dunlop following close behind.

"Slow down there, lad!" Gazin chuckled, gently grabbing Tala's elbow. "We've got all day. There isn't enough in this city to warrant that kind of haste. What are you so eager to see, anyway?"

"I wanted to see the lake!" Tala said after taking a breath to calm himself. "It may not be half as big as the Burning Lake, but it's in a basin one-hundred feet below the city, and you can walk right up to the edge and look straight down at the water! I've never done anything like that!"

"Aye, it's worth seeing." Gazin chuckled fondly. "But it won't take but an hour to get there, so slow yourself down a little."

"Yeah, sorry." Tala grinned sheepishly. He knew that it wasn't because either of his minders would have trouble keeping up—even on his best day, both men could leave him in the dust if they wanted—but moving with any sort of speed would only draw attention to them. Despite their many months together, Tala still sometimes forgot such small concerns. "I also want to see the markets! The bazaar. It's supposed to be huge, with all sorts of goods from all over the world! I've heard you can even buy live animals from the Jungle!"

"Aye, lad, the markets of Lynmyr are famous for a reason.

Although I'd suggest staying away from any Jungle animals. They can be vicious beasts, with all sorts of nasty surprises."

"I'm not gonna buy any! I just want to see them! I've heard weird things about Jungle animals."

"That's 'cause they are weird. Remember what we told you on the road here? Be wary while we're in the Jungle. You never know what anything really is. What you think is a plant might actually be an animal, and what you think is an animal might really be a plant. And both might want to eat you regardless. And even if you do know it, it might behave differently than its cousins elsewhere do. That's no less true just 'cause some poachers have smuggled them 'cross the Canyon."

"Which makes the markets a safe place to see them in person before having to face them for real in the Jungle," Tala pointed out, perhaps a bit more smugly than he had meant to.

"He's got you there," came Dunlop's quiet voice, a slight smirk on his lips. Tala felt his own quirk up in response; it was always vindicating to have Dunlop agree with him. Especially for something that had nothing to do with weapons.

Gazin just sighed, although Tala could tell it was done more in jest than anything. "Alright, lad. Just don't go getting too close. It wouldn't do for you to get strangled by creep vines or poisoned by some cat spraying on you."

"I—what? Jungle cats are poisonous? Or venomous? Or… what?"

Gazin sighed again, this time less humorlessly. "Some, lad, some are. There's no rhyme or reason to animals in the Jungle. Or plants, for that matter. There are cats with poisonous piss, snakes that can sing, plants that can think, all sorts of crazy things. I myself almost got eaten by a tree once. Fell asleep one night, woke up covered in roots with my left foot being chewed on by a trunk with teeth. One of the less pleasant experiences I've had, truth be told."

Tala gaped at him in horror, trying to imagine what it would be like to wake up to such a thing. "And uh… why are we going there again?" he asked with a shaky voice.

"Because that mad bastard thinks it's a good idea," Gazin grumbled, clearly unhappy about it. Tala was confused. He thought it had been Serala's idea to go to the Jungle. It must have been Vail's. He was the only person Tala knew of who Gazin would speak of like that.

But why did Vail care where they went? Despite their strange conversation the morning after escaping Southtown, where Vail actually spoke and acted like a mostly normal human being, the man had acted just as absently aloof as ever afterwards, rarely indicating he was even aware of their plans.

"And why does he think it's a good idea?" Tala tried to ask as casually as possible. If he tried to confirm who they were talking about, Gazin would notice his slip and immediately refuse to say anything more. It was slightly manipulative of him, Tala knew, but he could live with it. The raised eyebrow Dunlop sent him showed that he, at least, knew what Tala was doing.

If Gazin wasn't clearly caught up in his—likely less than flattering—thoughts about Vail, he most definitely would've caught on too. "Gods know what that man's ever thinking. Hells, even they've no idea I'd wager." Gazin continued to grumble. *He must be really aggravated about this. He'd never say so much otherwise.*

Gazin peered at Tala with narrowed eyes, and Tala knew he wouldn't get any more about their enigmatic maybe-leader at the moment. Instead of chastising him though, Gazin gave him a strange warning that seemed rather out of place, given the topic was one of their companions. "Just stick close to us while we're in there, you hear me, lad?" Tala just nodded. It wasn't the first time he had been told such, especially from Gazin. "Even off the road you'll be safer with us, but no matter what, do not get yourself lost. The Jungle will eat you alive. Literally."

"Yes, Gazin, I know. I've no intention of getting separated from you lot," Tala said, rolling his eyes as he turned away. He appreciated their concern, mostly, but Gazin had been overbearingly obsessive about making sure Tala knew to Never. Get. Separated. whilst in the Jungle. "And if, Gods forbid, something does happen, follow the Split south until I reach Morungil, where we'll all meet up again."

The Split was the small mountain range that ran in a straight line from the Jungle capital of Morungil almost all the way to the southern edge of the Gods' Canyon, directly across from Lynmyr. From the southern side of the city, without the buildings getting in the way, the northernmost reaches of the Split were visible on a clear day.

"Good." Gazin nodded, appearing—at least slightly—mollified. They left that conversation behind as they continued walking, occasionally getting some input from Dunlop, until they reached the eastern edge of the city.

Tala finally got his view of Canyon Lake, and it was spectacular!

Canyon Lake was, as its name implied, a lake connected to the Gods' Canyon that ran all the way from the northern reaches of the Metal Mountains in the east to the waters of the Misty Sea in the west. The Canyon was over a mile deep at its most extreme and ranged anywhere from a few hundred feet to many miles in width. The Canyon was the barrier that separated the lands of Lightning from the Jungle, and the primary defense that prevented Lightning from getting devoured by the wildness of the Jungle. Not even the raging, rampant growth of flora Plant wielders could generate could cross the Canyon before a Lightning patrol, watch tower, or guard post discovered the attempt. Despite Plant's best efforts, as the long stalemate between the two countries could attest to.

Lightning itself had long since given up on trying to cross the Canyon themselves to secure land on the other side, for they had learned long ago that once the Jungle had claimed an area, it was all but impossible to retake. Even Fire, who naturally held an extreme advantage against plant life, had long since given up on trying to push the Jungle back at their small, shared border, and for centuries had contented themselves with merely preventing the Jungle from encroaching any further south.

That didn't mean there was no way to cross the Canyon, however. Along its sprawling expanse, there were a few small ways across, although all of them were heavily monitored by Lightning. The other crossings had no proper locations on their southern side, the paths merely leading into the wilds of the Jungle. That was why Tala and his companions had left Kilatara following the Lightning Road due south to Lynmyr. The great city sat less than half a mile from the edge of the Canyon, at its lowest point, and was built right up to the side of the giant basin which housed Canyon Lake a hundred feet below, where the canyon walls on the northern side broke and the river spilled out to fill the lake before rerouting back into the grand river that had carved its place across the land.

Due to the way the city had been built on the edges of the lake's cliffs, it was easy for a person to gaze across the vast lake and see all the way to the cliffs on the other side—an amazing sight. There was something very strange about seeing a whole lake spread out below him like that. Like it was being kept in a giant bowl carved into the earth. Looking straight down from the barrier fence, the sheer cliff ran all the way down to the water. Off to his left a ways, a bit further up the curve that was the lake bowl, there were a series of stairs and ramps carved into the cliff face, leading down to a series of jetties and docks. There were some fishing boats moored there, although most were spread out across the lake.

Looking back down, he felt an urge to jump in the back of his mind, but easily ignored it. He had felt the same urge when looking out from some of the higher windows or balconies at the Institute. A natural feeling, he had been assured, an urge that many people felt when gazing down from any noteworthy height. He wondered if anybody had ever actually followed that urge here, where there was water to fall into. One-hundred feet would certainly hurt, but it was a survivable distance.

They spent some more time gawking out over the lake

and wandering up the street that ran alongside it. There wasn't a whole lot to see, truth be told, after the initial awe of the lake faded. The steep sides of the lake made using it for transporting goods far too inconvenient, and taking boats out into the canyon was just asking for them to be destroyed in the various rapids or shallows of the river. So, the only vessels on the lake were fishing boats, and those weren't exactly the most exciting things to watch. Feeling satisfied he had seen everything worth seeing about the lake, Tala and his minders turned back towards the city. Gazin led the way as they maneuvered to the famous markets.

Tala could tell they were getting close to the markets far before he could see them, for the noise of the city changed. The sounds of life with a heavy populace didn't seem to change much really, although he had noted there were significantly fewer merchants and streetside stalls in Lynmyr than had been in the capitals or Southtown. Now Tala knew why. All the merchants were set up at the bazaar! As he got closer, turning corners and going down streets, he started hearing the calls of merchants and peddlers hawking their wares, along with the loud bustle of many, many people all packed together, much like Market Street in Fiahren on Market Day. Over the din of people, Tala could hear animals: cheeps and chirps, screeches and growls, and other, much stranger sounds he couldn't identify. Even before the markets were in sight, Tala felt a thrill run through him at the sheer vibrancy of life he could feel in the air.

Finally, they turned one last corner, and Tala froze, eyes widening in amazement as his breath left him. The markets.

Were. Amazing! His eyes darted around as he took in every-thing he could see. Even at the very edge, Tala could tell they were like nothing he had ever seen before! Right before him was a small plaza, empty of anything but people milling about, with stalls ringing it on the very edges, mostly selling various foodstuffs: meats, fruits, and vegetables. Directly across the plaza from him, the entrance to the markets opened up like a magical doorway, welcoming him to enter.

Just from what little he could see inside, the wide city street turned into little more than an alley, one so narrow a horse cart would barely be able to squeeze through, even if it was entirely empty of people or things—which it wasn't. The alley was filled with people, even more than the plaza. The market stalls seemed to be built inside the buildings, along both sides of the alley. People constantly shuffled in and out of the buildings as they perused the racks or crates or piles of goods lining the street itself.

Tala drifted through the plaza, barely aware of Gazin and Dunlop with him, as his head turned every which way and he squeezed through the crowd into the alley. The market stalls indeed were part of the buildings lining the alley, and most of them even had small spaces inside the buildings where even more things were kept! There were stores for all manner of clothing, and stores that specialized: some selling exclusively footwear, others hats, others trousers, or tunics, or belts, or gloves! As Tala drifted through the crowd, he saw one store that seemed to be only selling nightwear! And there was so much more than just clothing. There were stores selling fab-rics of all kinds, wooden sculptures, tools, instruments even!

Barely even conscious of what he was doing, Tala's feet took him over to a rack of scrolls that most people were passing by with nary a glance, and he stooped over to peruse them more closely. Written on the scrolls in careful ink were titles. Most meant nothing to him, but a few Tala recognized as bedtime stories his parents had told him as a child. They were selling bedtime tales written down!

The shop behind the scrolls was barely more than a hole in the wall, but in it were easily hundreds of scrolls, all arranged in piles. And carefully placed on shelves along the wall were books! Properly bound books! Feeling his heart soar, Tala rushed into the nearly empty shop, easily dodging the only other patron that was inside it: a bland figure covered in a dull cloak and plain cowl on their head. Aside from thinking that the cloak reminded him a fair bit of Vail, Tala ignored the person to focus on the treasure before him.

On one wall, the books seemed to be instruction manuals: written teachings of how to fish, or carve wood, or make different types of food. There were manuals for all sorts of things! Another wall was full of history, legends, and tales from the past. Most of those Tala recognized, having read them in his youth as part of the required studying to become a Researcher. He was surprised to find them in a random shop in a city, even if it was the famous markets of Lynmyr. It took a lot of time and effort to make even a single book, so they weren't very common outside of the walls of rich and powerful families, or the Institute and its Researchers. The markets of Lynmyr really *did* have everything!

Although Tala noticed on closer inspection, none of the

books were on more… sensitive histories. They all covered topics that were fairly well known to the wider world already, such as the Vanishing of Water, the Great Bodylands Hordes, the Wind Raids, and other similar topics. Tala couldn't help but be slightly disappointed that even on the other side of the Jungle, the Churches still clearly kept a tight hold over what information the common people were allowed to access. Assuming they even knew how to read, which most didn't.

Tala was just reaching for *The Origin And Evolutions Of The Dustwall Through The Ages* (a favorite book he had read many times back home) when a hand grabbed his arm, stopping him. He started for a moment and turned to see Gazin, giving him a look of fond exasperation.

"C'mon, lad. No point torturing yourself in here. We won't be buying any."

Tala felt a whine rise unbidden in his throat but stopped it before he actually made such a pathetic sound. It had been *months* since he had been able to sit back (or hunch over, which was much more common) and feel like a Researcher again! Gazin was right, though. Books—or even scrolls—were an unnecessary burden to carry with them. Even worse, no matter how careful they were, any that they did bring with them were bound to end up dirty and damaged eventually. The mere thought of which made Tala cringe. Reluctantly, he nodded his agreement. With a last forlorn gaze at the array of books and scrolls, he followed Gazin out of the shop, noticing the other patron of the small store giving him a strange—possibly amused—look. The person was lacking eyebrows, making it hard to tell what their actual expression was.

Spirits rising as he fell back into the abundant energy of the markets, Tala continued perusing every stall he passed, often giving little more than a glance before moving on. With Gazin and Dunlop hot on his heels, Tala passed through a maze of streets, not paying the slightest attention to where he was going. Most of the market's alleys were covered with wooden beams and cloth, providing shelter from rain and sun alike. Although on a sunny day like that one, the many different colors of cloth (and in some places colored glass, which Tala found beautiful) meant the light that shone through into the markets was a mottled array of shifting shades, which only made the whole experience that much more magical to him.

After passing an entire section dedicated to weapons and armor (where Tala had to slow down immensely so Dunlop could take his time ogling over some of the best pieces), they finally emerged into another wide-open plaza, one full of cages and fences behind which were all manner of creatures. Here, Tala really slowed down, so he could take his time examining all the unique and utterly bizarre beasts. In one corner, coiled in a dip in the ground that was itself situated behind waist-high walls, were a dozen snakes, each of which had scales shining in a variety of colors. One was a vibrant blue with bright pink streaks shooting through it, and another was an emerald green wrapped in bands of gold and silver. One was striped all in red and white, giving it an oddly disorienting appearance.

As Tala stared at the snakes, and they stared back at him in turn, one opened its mouth and—instead of the hiss that Tala expected—a clear, ringing note sounded. The other snakes all joined in, creating a beautiful, wordless chorus.

"Singing snakes. Must be young. The older ones can do more than one note apiece," Gazin said.

Waving off the snake merchant who tried to sell them the collection, the three moved on, looking at the whole variety of animals. Birds that could change size, some sort of monkey that seemed to have flexible bones judging by the knots it kept getting itself to, a head-sized ball of fur with no discernible features rolling around in its cage. Tala was mesmerized by all of it!

There was a pool set up behind another low wall with a couple of fish in it. Tala watched as the merchant held out some sort of giant insect over the pool, hand covered in a very thick glove. After a few seconds of nothing, one fish poked its head out of the water. Without warning, a burst of fire shot out of the fish's mouth, incinerating the insect, which was then immediately gobbled up by the fish as it leapt out of the water, eating the flambéed bug right out of the singed glove on the merchant's hand. Tala clapped along with the rest of the crowd who had seen the display, while internally trying to figure out what sort of benefits a fish might find from being able to spit fire. It seemed kind of like a pointless ability to him, if he were being honest. How did the Jungle have fire-breathing fish when the actual country of Fire, and its vast array of fire-wielding animals, didn't?

Questions for another time, he decided, eagerly moving on to see what else there was. Tala passed through the plaza and into another set of alleys, ones quite a bit wider than before, making them ideal for keeping the cages and habitats for the various animals while still allowing traffic. There were also plants, many of which were just as amazing as the animals: some sort of flower with spinning petals had drawn him right up to its cage when Gazin pulled him back, just shaking his head and gesturing for Tala to continue on. He gave the flower one last glance—and thought it seemed disappointed, for as much sense as that made for a flower—and kept moving. (He only thought to wonder later why a flower might be in a cage.)

As Tala was looking at some sort of strange golden flower, whose petals were gently dripping a golden liquid into an array of open flasks beneath it, he heard a choked scream and some sort of commotion behind him. He quickly turned around to see a person whose entire upper body seemed to be encased in wriggling tentacles. *Vines!* he realized. The person was being attacked by a giant mass of moving *vines!* The person's legs rose from the ground as their body was pulled further into the wildly thrashing, pulsating vines. Gazin had positioned himself in front of Tala, one hand held back toward him, protecting him from whatever was happening. Dunlop, meanwhile, was hacking at the vines with his axe alongside a few guardsmen, all trying to rescue the poor soul who was being… eaten? Maybe?

Tala just barely had enough time to wonder what exactly had happened when two hands grabbed the sides of his head, and everything went black.

CHAPTER 14

Gazin continued to furtively scan the crowd, making sure no one was approaching them, prepared to act in whatever way was necessary to protect Tala. Dunlop was still hacking away at the carnivorous vines, trying to save their prey from a most foul death. Gazin had seen the hanging cage that the vines were in, and the way they were bound, and they should have been unable to break free on their own. Someone had intentionally let the vines loose, likely knowing they would grab the closest person they could. The odds of that happening when Tala was there were slim, and that made Gazin nervous. But the lad was safe, pressed up against the wall behind him, where Gazin had shoved him the moment he heard the first scream. No one could get to Tala without going through Gazin first (and there were few people in the world who could accomplish such a feat).

But nothing was happening, aside from Dunlop, the guards, and a few other good Samaritans fighting against the vines. There were no soldiers rushing towards them, no furtive figures ducking through the crowd—nothing. Could it just be somebody causing chaos at an unfortunate time, unaware that Tala was present? Or an assassination attempt entirely unrelated to them? Not the most reliable method for that, but still possible, though looking increasingly unlikely.

One guard had grabbed onto the victim's feet and, thanks to the many blades cutting away at the vines, managed to pull a terrified man out of their grasp. The man was no noble, rich merchant, or anything like that. His clothes were too simple, brown, drab, and worn. Not somebody worth such a public and unreliable method of assassination. Gazin tensed even further. Something was wrong. He could feel it.

He reached back again, almost subconsciously, to make sure Tala was still there. There wasn't anywhere the lad *could* go, but it would make Gazin feel better to be sure as he kept his eyes scanning the crowd. His arm reached back further than it should, until it hit the stone wall behind him. He groped the wall for a second, uncomprehending of what he was feeling, before spinning around in a panic. Tala was gone! That was impossible! There was a table covered in pelts to his left, and a protruding doorway to his right! There was nothing on the wall or ground either, no window, grate, or sewer access. Nothing!

He craned his neck up, looking at the coverings above them. Gazin almost snarled in frustration. There was a hole in the fabric covering the wooden beams that crisscrossed the alley, right above him. Somebody had to have grabbed Tala and carried him up. Or a few somebodies; one person alone couldn't have done it from that height unless they had grabbed him with their feet. Or hung upside down from their feet, but that was even less likely. But how had they avoided his notice? Even in the noise of the markets and commotion of the vines, Gazin had excellent hearing! And Tala hadn't made a sound!

All of these thoughts flashed through his mind in a second before Gazin jumped, his enhanced legs giving him enough force to clear the hole easily, landing perfectly atop one of the wooden beams. He eyed the top of the markets, the empty roads of cloth stretching out, seeing nothing. He jumped again, latching onto the wall of the building beside him and hoisting himself up onto the roof. The buildings that encompassed the markets weren't hugely tall, usually only two or three floors, but he would still have a much better vantage point from the roof of one. He peered out across the spread of the markets, looking for any sign that a person, or persons, had been there.

He saw nothing. No Tala, no soldiers, no anybody. It was empty. He had lost Tala.

Gazin stepped off the roof, falling through the same hole in the fabrics (seeing that it had been made simply by someone pulling the cloth sheet off to the side from above) and landed with a heavy thud back where he had been standing in the alley. Everybody was still distracted by the rampaging (although no longer threatening) vines and the man they had almost eaten, so no one saw Gazin's superhuman feat of landing a few dozen foot fall without shattering his legs.

No one but Dunlop, who had just finished shoving his way through the lingering crowd to reach Gazin. "Where is he?" he demanded.

"Gone. Grabbed through the roof. No sign of whoever took him," Gazin reported shortly, trying to work out just who had taken Tala, and how. It was the type of method he might have used, not the usual way that the Lightning Church would have gone about it. Or even been able to. Not while escaping Gazin's notice. This was bad.

"C'mon." He grabbed Dunlop, who looked like he was about to start scrambling up the wall himself. "We need to tell the others. Even you can't track over stone and cloth."

CHAPTER 15

"How is this possible?" Serala demanded, her voice barely contained below a shriek. They had gotten lucky, and everyone was back at the inn when they had arrived, except Caida. They were surrounding a table in the common room, the bedrooms too small for all seven of them, and Gazin knew that was the only reason Serala was even trying to stay quiet. Her face was alternately turning darker and paler, her fear and fury about losing Tala warring within her. Not that any of them were faring particularly well.

Lito and Alina were both pale (paler than usual in Alina's case), terrified for their friend and charge. Dunlop was glaring down at the table, teeth gritted so hard it looked as though he was ready to begin chewing it in his anger. Gazin himself felt similarly, and he had struggled to maintain his temperament when explaining what had happened. Even Ilan appeared angry and frustrated, rare as that was. Only Vail wasn't obviously affected by the news that they had lost Tala, but Gazin knew the man well enough he could see the slight tension in his face, the slimmest of frowns on his brow. After finding Tala, keeping Vail calm was the most important thing. If he got angry, and acted out, things would get even worse.

"I don't know," Gazin answered Serala. "It shouldn't have been possible. Not without me noticing. He was inches away from me. I should have *felt* him moving, I don't know how I didn't!"

"Could it have been a Dark wielder?" Lito piped up, looking nauseous. "Could they have just… disappeared him?"

"No. Believe me, lad, those powers are not exactly subtle. Even an expert who can manage to use them like that without killing everyone around wouldn't be able to do it undetected. There are no magics that would have been able to grab him without me knowing."

"Then what do we do?"

"Get the local cells involved," Vail said, still sounding as disinterested as ever. That was good, at least. If Vail was still acting like Vail, then Gazin didn't have to worry too much about him doing something stupid. "Have them all mobilize and scout the city, cover every access point and place of interest. Jails, manors, anywhere he might have been taken."

Gazin nodded, along with Serala and the rest. Except Dunlop, who was still glaring furiously at the table, as though it was personally responsible for everything wrong with the world.

"Won't that cause us problems?" Lito asked, his tone making it clear what he meant by "us." Every Dissident in Lynmyr would be compromised.

"Aye, lad, but it's worth it. We can afford to lose this city for a few years more than we can afford to lose him."

They all nodded again. Serala looked strangely relieved by Gazin's words. But also worried, as well as furious, which made him arch an eyebrow. That was interesting.

"We'll spread out, hit every safe house, master, and everyone else in the city. The faster we get them all moving the better."

They all nodded again and rose, prepared to begin their campaign through the city, when Caida came hustling through the door of the inn. That was odd. Caida wasn't one to hustle, *ever*. Wherever she had been, something must have gone very, very wrong for her to come in like that. Gazin wasn't sure if he wanted it to be something involving Tala or not. She rushed over to their table, seemingly oblivious to their own agitation, a lack of attention that was also terrifyingly out of character for her. The whole thing reminded Gazin far too much of Southtown, and how she had acted right before that disaster struck.

"We have a problem. We have to leave the city. Now!" she spat out. *Just like Southtown, indeed.* Gazin closed his eyes in exasperation. She was acting even worse than she had then, which was worrying. He wasn't sure what could be worse than *"Blessed in the city,"* but this journey had already broken his expectations of the world. "Wait, what's happening? Where's Tala?"

"Gone. He vanished in the markets. We think somebody grabbed him," Lito told her, voice pitching.

"Shit!"

Gazin raised his brows. It wasn't often that he got to hear Caida swear.

"Shit, shit, shit! We need to—no! Shit!"

Oh, things were very bad indeed for Caida to be this flustered. Gazin closed his eyes again, dreading to hear the answer to what he was about to ask.

"Caida. What happened? What did you learn?" he asked, as calmly as possible.

"He—*He* is here. In Lynmyr. If He took Tala, we've lost him, it's over!" She moaned, falling into Lito's vacated chair, head slumped in her hands.

"Who is 'he?'"

"the Bone Merc. the Bone Merc is here."

Oh.

Oh.

Well, that would explain how Tala vanished. the Bone Merc could have easily taken him right under even Gazin's nose. But things may not be as bad as Caida believed. the Bone Merc wasn't their enemy; he could be negotiated with. As long as he hadn't already accepted a contract for Tala, they could probably get him back without much fuss. If they could find them, that is. If the Bone Merc *had* accepted a contract, then they would have a problem. He rarely broke contracts. Or failed them. But it still wasn't impossible. He had refused their many efforts to recruit him to their cause in the past, but that didn't mean they couldn't talk him into letting Tala go. After all, they had...

Oh. Yeah. Gazin glanced at Serala, and winced. The poor girl was frozen, her face a rictus of conflicting emotions. She definitely shouldn't take charge of this one. Gazin would have to make sure Ilan kept her in check. If the man could. He would have asked Vail, who might be the only person who could actually keep Serala in check, but, well…

Gazin peeked at Vail and felt his heart shudder in fear. Vail's eyes were practically sparkling. And he was smiling. Gazin sighed, lamenting that he had ever agreed to join this accursed venture. At least they might be able to negotiate for Tala's release, if the Bone Merc did indeed have him. After all, they had possibly the only person in the world who the Bone Merc might actually consider a friend.

"Vail," Gazin warned lowly.

Vail calmed down. Barely. His smile vanished, but his eyes retained that same manic look.

"Relax, Gazin," Vail said flippantly. "We have a lost little lamb to go find, don't we? Come on then, don't want to lose him!"

Gazin glared at Vail, barely suppressing a snarl. "What about the plan? Getting the others looking for him? Even if *he* did take him, we have no idea where they went, or what he'll do to him!"

"Forget the plan." Vail waved absently. "Even if they find them, what will any of them do? Os could tear this whole city down if they get in his way. Besides, I'm pretty sure I can find him myself just fine. So, let's go before he does something we'll all regret." Without waiting for a response, Vail all but strutted out the door, leaving the rest of them to follow or be left behind.

CHAPTER 16

Tala groaned and shifted, bringing his hand up to rub the sleep out of his eyes. Except he didn't feel his hand on his face. Actually, he couldn't feel his *hand!* What in the Hells? He blinked his eyes open, confusion swirling before slowly warping into panic. What was happening? Where was he? He was sitting on a chair in some dingy room with little more than an old table in front of him with another chair at its side and some light pouring through the gaps of a couple of wood-covered windows. His attention was captured by the cloaked person leaning over the table, rolling up some sort of scroll, and completely ignoring him. Tala stayed quiet, trying not to alert his presumed captor that he was awake.

He couldn't move. He was completely paralyzed. Everything below the neck, at least. His arms, his legs, his torso, he couldn't control any of it. Panic began to mix with terror in an unholy combination of emotion inside of him. He was certain he would have been sick were he able to feel his stomach. He wasn't even bound or anything: there were no ropes or chains on his legs, and his hands were resting limply, one in his lap and the other dangling down by his side. Whatever this person had done to him had left him able to move only his head and neck.

Tala's mind rapidly shifted through his memories, trying to reconstruct everything. There had been singing snakes, and fire breathing fish, and carnivorous vines, and… nothing. The last thing he remembered was Gazin shielding him against a wall as Dunlop battled a mass of vines trying to consume a person. What had happened after that? It was hard to imagine something bad happening to Gazin and Dunlop, of all people, but then where were they? What had happened that Tala was now alone with a stranger?

With a start, Tala realized the person at the table was watching him. With his face pointed at him, Tala recognized the man! It was the other person who had been in the bookshop! The one with no eyebrows! And he was still wearing the same brown cowl over his head! Tala groaned internally. *Of course* he had been recognized in the one place where he wasn't just another face in the crowd! And by someone who was, apparently, capable of abducting him away from the likes of Gazin and Dunlop. What absolutely terrible, terrible luck he had.

Tala took a deep breath to steady himself. He was getting far too used to feeling panicked and terrified if he could still think clearly despite his situation. "Hi!" he chirped, as cheerily as he could. "Can I help you with something?"

The man stared at him. The skin over his eye shifted weirdly, like he would be raising a single eyebrow if he had one. Tala stared back, refusing to back down or lose his pleasant smile. There was something wrong with the man's eyes, he noticed, beyond the lack of brow or even eyelashes. He couldn't tell what, but a shiver started at the base of his neck. He was unable to tell if it had progressed lower than that.

"Most people tend to scream or cry when they wake up like that," the man said blandly. There was something off about his voice too; it changed slightly in pitch when he spoke, each word coming out just a little bit differently than the one before. Who in the Hells was this?

"Kidnap people often, do you?" Tala queried, trying to hide his anxiety behind genuine curiosity.

"You could say that." The man smirked. Silence descended once again.

"I see." Tala nodded. It probably wasn't the best idea to antagonize this person, but frankly, Tala didn't care. "So, what's the plan then? Or did you just want to have a friendly chat with me? I'm certainly amenable to that, you know. Although, I think it would be a bit more friendly if I could move, you know?" Tala's sword was still hanging at his side, as were his smaller blades. Whoever this man was, he was clearly overconfident if he hadn't thought to disarm Tala—and he obviously didn't realize just how special his sword was. If Tala could just wait out whatever poison had been used to paralyze him, he might get a chance to strike. Even if his kidnapper was a Lightning Blessed, the sword should work. The same element of surprise that had killed Ignis, that had killed Annelore, and technically Elidor, would work here too. He just needed to buy time.

But the man didn't respond. He just continued to eye

Tala with an amused grin. The skin of his brow moved again, like it was being raised. It was strange seeing the skin move without any hair on it.

"Right," Tala said after a few more seconds of silence, enough that it was quite clear the man wouldn't be answering. "Well, I'm assuming you know who I am, seeing as you kidnapped me and all. But, to be blunt, I have no idea whatsoever who you are. So, would you mind sharing your name with me? It's quite off-putting, being all… stuck, like this without even having a name for my oh so gracious host!" Now that he had gotten started, Tala was finding it hard not to keep escalating this overly friendly persona of his. He really hoped that, since he was still alive, the man wouldn't simply kill him for being annoying. The man was beginning to look a bit less amused at Tala's antics.

"My name?" he asked, sounding genuinely surprised. Tala was growing increasingly unnerved. Who was this person? "You can call me Osson, I guess."

"Okay then! Nice to meet you, Osson!" Osson frowned. "So, not to be a bother, but I am going to keep asking, so you might as well just tell me! What are we doing here? What's your plan, exactly? Because, you know, my friends are going to be coming to save me, and you really don't want to get on their bad side. Like, you really, *really* don't," Tala said, trying to mix threatening with his otherwise overly cheery tone.

Osson snorted, clearly amused. Tala tried not to let his real grin slip through. Whoever Osson was, he had no idea just who Tala's friends were!

"Friends like Gazin the Flesh wielder?" Osson replied drily.

A chill shot through what little of his body he could feel. If the man knew, actually knew, who Gazin was? That was bad. That was really, really terrible. He tried not to let his sudden fear show but had a feeling that Osson had seen it clearly, regardless.

"Yeah, I'm not too worried. But we've wasted enough time. Here's the deal: we're going to go on a little journey, and if you behave, I'll let you—mostly—be in control of yourself. If you don't, I won't. And if you scream, or try to get anybody to help you, I'll seal your mouth shut. And believe me, that is *miserable*, especially when you're walking. You'll constantly feel like you're suffocating, and the more you panic, the worse it'll be, but you'll still be breathing just enough through your nose that you won't pass out. So don't make me have to do that, okay?"

Tala's smile died a quick death. Who in the Hells was this person? He must be a Body Descendant like Gazin to be able to do the things he was talking about. That must be how he had paralyzed Tala too. Some sort of body manipulation. That meant there would be no waiting him out. *Crap.* Tala didn't know enough about what exactly Body wielders could do with their respective powers to guess which one Osson was. But things might not be all bad. The only Body wielders east of the Dustwall were either slaves, fugitives, or Dissidents. And none of them were friends of the Churches. If he could figure out what Osson's plan was, why he had kidnapped him, maybe he could still talk his way out of this?

"Well? Are you going to cooperate?" Osson asked, leaning down to stare Tala dead in the eye. Tala nodded shakily, feeling another chill in his neck as he got a closer look at Osson's eyes. Everything about them was wrong! The whites were too white, with no hint of the red or pink of blood vessels. They were the color of bleached bone. They looked about as solid as bone too, as there was no moisture or shine to them at all. There were also no irises, the white of his sclera ending suddenly at the yawning black of his pupils. The pupils slightly grew in size though, so whatever was wrong with his eyes, they clearly still worked. Gazin's eyes appeared perfectly normal. So was this a conscious choice Osson had made for some reason?

"Good, then let's go. And remember, don't scream, don't cry, don't even talk." Tala nodded again as Osson poked him in the forehead. His body suddenly sagged, feeling returning to Tala in a rush of sensory bliss. Never before had Tala felt so happy to be able to feel; even the burning of muscles that had been in one position for too long felt amazing!

Osson grabbed him and hauled him to his feet, holding onto Tala as he regained his sense of balance. A surprisingly kind and thoughtful gesture from the man, an act which gave Tala hope he might be able to talk him out of whatever Osson was planning. An idea that quickly vanished when Osson removed his hand. A sudden, sharp pain shot through Tala's neck, and he found himself unable to breathe. It was like a hedgehog had been suddenly shoved down his throat (although thankfully not a Fire hedgehog, whose quills often burst into flame when they stabbed something).

Osson put his hand on Tala again, and the pain and

choking vanished as quickly as they came. Tala gawked at him in fear and confusion, the question clear on his face as his throat was busy sucking down lungfuls of sweet, sweet air. Gazin might be able to fix it, but Osson had made it clear he knew about Gazin, so Gazin likely couldn't easily undo whatever he had done. Given Gazin's age and skill, that meant Osson was likely a Blood or Bone wielder. And he had made some sort of permanent change to Tala's throat, if his power was letting Tala breathe and he suffocated without it. Oh, this was a bad, terrible, miserable situation. He really hoped he would be able to talk Osson out of his plan, if he could even figure out what that plan was in the first place!

"A little insurance that you won't try to escape. We stop touching, that happens. So, if you don't want to die a miserable, painful death, you won't try anything, okay?"

Tala nodded again, breaths coming more evenly. This was a disaster! Even if his friends saved him, how would they keep him alive?

CHAPTER 17

"You never actually said where we're going." Tala commented idly as he carefully stepped through the crowd, acutely aware of Osson's grip on his arm. They had been walking quietly for only a few minutes, staying so close to each other that people were probably mistaking them for lovers, and the stress was starting to wear on Tala.

Osson didn't answer. The kidnapper didn't act like he had heard Tala at all.

"So, where are we going?" The hand on Tala's arm tightened, making him smirk. "It's not like I can get away from you after all. And really, don't you think this whole thing will be a bit more pleasant if we're at least—"

"By The Three!" Osson hissed in annoyance, grabbing Tala's arm even harder. "Didn't I say I would seal your mouth shut if you talked?"

"Yeah, but where's the fun in that? I'm already being kidnapped. Does it really need to be more miserable? Besides, people would notice if my mouth was sealed shut. And since you're trying to avoid attention, I figure that you won't risk it."

Tala's throat immediately closed up as hundreds of agonizing pinpricks shot through it, although the feeling lasted for only a moment before abating. He coughed at the sensation of air suddenly stopping and starting in his throat.

"I can do worse than seal your mouth."

Tala coughed again and cleared his throat. "True," he rasped. "But you can't do much. People will notice if I start choking or seizing or something. Or if you start having to drag me."

"Gods!" Osson spat. "You have been awake for ten minutes! How are you already so annoying?"

"It's a gift," Tala said smugly, smile quickly vanishing at the murderous glare Osson sent him. Maybe he shouldn't keep pushing the man.

Less than a minute later, Tala spoke again. "So, where are we going?"

Osson breathed in sharply, and Tala heard a muted snap before his arm erupted in agonizing pain right under Osson's hand. It lasted for barely a second before the pain vanished completely. Had Osson just broken his arm and then healed it just as quickly? A Bone wielder then. That was one question answered. Too bad it didn't really help Tala any.

"We are going to Mist. Okay? We are going to Mist, because I want to go to Mist, and I want to take you to Mist. Now will you shut the Hells up? Please?" *Huh.* Tala must have been really getting to him for Osson to even say please!

Tala flexed his fingers, trying to feel if his arm was okay. It seemed perfectly fine. He was pretty sure Osson had broken it by accident, so it probably wouldn't happen again, lest Tala attract attention. At least, Tala really hoped that was the case. It had hurt!

"Mist, huh? What's so important in Mist? Did they hire you to capture me?" He felt Osson's hand tighten on his arm again. No pain, yet. Good. Osson was too busy trying to temper his obvious frustration while keeping an eye on the crowds to notice that Tala was speaking just a bit louder than necessary. His friends would be looking for him. Anything that might help them was worth trying.

"No. I just thought it would make for a romantic get-away for us. Somewhere nice and quiet where I can strip the flesh from your bones as you scream in agony. Doesn't that sound lovely?"

"Not really, no. I'm quite attached to my flesh. And my bones. Both of them together, really. I'd rather they not separate, personally." Tala noticed a few curious glances their way by passersby at his words. Unsurprising given the way his voice had pitched in fear. It wasn't even on purpose, but it served to help attract some small attention without Osson realizing what he was doing.

"You might be one of the most aggravating people I have ever met."

"Just one of? Clearly, I need to try harder. Who's more aggravating than I am?"

"By The Three! Would you just shut up?"

"Nope! If I'm really that annoying, you could just let me go, y'know?"

"Or I could just kill you."

"But then Mist would be mad at you for not bringing me to them."

"Mist doesn't even know! They didn't hire me!" Osson jerked Tala forward, not letting him lag behind as he picked up their pace. Osson had spoken far louder than he had clearly meant to, drawing even more looks their way.

"Then why are you bringing me to them?"

"Because they'll agree to whatever terms I want in exchange for you!"

"Ah! So, you're trying to trade me for something! Well, whatever it is, I'm sure we can work out a deal ourselves! The Dissidents, I mean. They're rather protective of me. I'm sure they'll make whatever deal you want with Mist." At the last second, Tala remembered to lower his voice. He had been steadily, if slowly, talking louder and louder, but mentioning the Dissidents, especially his affiliation with them, would bring the sort of attention that even he didn't want. There was risk, and then there was foolish risk.

"Nice try, but they don't have what I want. Mist does. So, we go to Mist. Are you happy now? Will you stop asking inane questions and just stay quiet?"

"Maybe. What does Mist have that Lightning doesn't?"

"Mist. It has mist. It's misty. Lots of mist there."

"Lightning has mist. Especially in the mornings. It's pretty humid up here. And it's a forest, so there's a lot of trees. Makes for a lot of mist."

"By the Gods, kid, you may actually be the second most annoying person I've ever met."

"Really? Second? Already? It's only been a few minutes."

"I usually kill them before they can be more annoying."

"Oh. Does that mean you didn't kill the first most annoying person? Why not? Did you try? Did you fail? Were they a Blessed so you just couldn't? 'Cause I don't know if you've heard, but I'm pretty good at doing that. We could make a deal about it even! Let me go and I'll kill your Blessed!" Tala left out that he had absolutely no intention of ever facing another Blessed again, much less hunt one down to try and kill them.

Osson sighed again, a weary sound. "Yes. Because. Yes. Yes. No. And no. And no again. Killing Blessed isn't as hard as they like to believe, as you've discovered yourself. If I wanted to kill one, I'd just do it myself."

Tala blinked in surprise. Osson sounded more tired and annoyed than anything, not at all like he was bragging. But Tala had discovered a rather specific weakness when it came to Blessed. That was a far cry from having Osson's calm certainty that he could just… *murder* a Blessed on a whim. Who the Hells was he? Also, he had tried and failed to kill the most annoying person he had ever met.

"Who was it?"

"Hmm?"

"Your most annoying person? Who you tried and failed to kill? Who was it?"

"No."

"Oh, c'mon, we're buddies! Pals! You can tell—heurgk!" Tala choked off as his throat closed with the agony of an angry wasp's nest. The pain and suffocation lasted longer this time, only a few seconds more, but more than enough for him to understand that Osson was not willing to entertain the topic any longer. *Fine, message received,* Tala grumbled mentally, massaging his poor throat with his free hand. Osson seemed far happier now that Tala was being quiet again. Well, he couldn't let his torturous kidnapper off quite so easily! If he was going to be kidnapped, he could at least make it as painful an experience for his kidnapper as he could!

"So, who—or what—are 'The Three?'" Tala asked once his throat was a bit less sore.

"What?" Osson sighed, sounding simultaneously resigned and confused.

"The Three? You've sworn by 'The Three' a couple of times now. I've heard the two Jungle Gods called 'The Pair' before. Or 'The Two' or 'The Duo,' things like that. But I've never heard anyone mention 'The Three' before. Aside from Those Three, but I doubt that's who you're talking about. Are they the Body Gods? I've never heard anyone swear by them before. Is it because you're a Boney?"

"Oh, by the—!" Osson exclaimed, ending in an unintelligible, angry snarl. "Will you just shut up? Please? For the love of their unholy mass, will you just stop talking?"

"Their unholy mass? What in the Hells is that?"

"Fuck it! I'm done!" Osson spat, turning on his heel and grabbing Tala by the throat.

His eyes shot open, thinking that he had finally pushed too far and Osson was going to kill him. Instead, after only a few seconds, Osson relaxed, dropping his hand and continuing on like nothing had happened, Tala's arm still caught firmly in his grip.

Tala was confused. What just happened? He opened his mouth to ask, but…

He couldn't speak! He kept opening his mouth, but no sound was coming out! He could breathe, but that was it! He tapped Osson on the arm, but the man ignored him. He tapped him again. And again. Until he was just beating a rhythm of taps on Osson's shoulder, who refused to acknowledge him at all. After a minute of Tala's incessant tapping, his arm suddenly dropped lifelessly to his side. It was exactly like back in the room when he had awoken, but this time only his arm was paralyzed!

Annoyed, Tala tried to figure out something else he could do to get Osson's attention. He couldn't talk, couldn't move his arm, and his other arm was locked in Osson's grip (a grip that was keeping him alive, so he wasn't too keen to risk that anyway). What else could he do that wouldn't risk Osson letting go? He breathed a loud sigh, the air whistling through his lips, when his eyes lit up with an idea.

Tala began whistling softly, their closeness putting Tala's mouth very close to Osson's ear. He whistled a jaunty, half-forgotten tune from his youth, stumbling constantly in pitch and volume as he tried to remember.

With a snarl, Osson tightened his grip painfully and yanked Tala into a side alley, away from the bustle of the busy street.

"What? What do you want? Why are you being so Gods-damned annoying? Can't you just *not* be an insufferable little prick?"

Tala responded the only way he physically could by

giving Osson his most blank, Vail-like stare. To his credit, Osson huffed and rolled his eyes. A strange rushing feeling shot through Tala's throat and arm, and he was able to feel and use both properly again.

"Do you really not know why I might have a problem with being kidnapped and turned over to a Church who will torture me to death?"

"Get over yourself, kid," Osson said bluntly. "It's going to happen sooner or later, Dissident friends or no. Tell you what, I'll make you a deal. You don't make this trip as annoying as humanly possible, and I'll make sure that Mist agrees to kill you quickly, okay? No torture, no prolonged suffering, or humiliation. Deal?"

"No! No deal! A quick death is still death! I'm trying not to die! That's why I stuck with the Dissidents in the first place! And by the way, they've done a good job of keeping me alive so far, so yeah, I'm going to trust them! And if you were smart, you'd let me go before they find us, because however big and bad and dangerous you are, my friends are worse! I've seen them fight! They slaughtered trained soldiers by the hundreds in Southtown, and at least half a dozen Descendants! And *I* killed Blessed! I killed Elidor of Southtown! One of the strongest Blessed alive! I killed Annelore! I survived Anderas Anto! I'm actually pretty confident that with the Dissidents' help I can keep staying alive! And when they come to rescue me—and they *will* come—you'll find out just how weak you are compared to them!"

Osson gave him a strange look, like he was confused.

What was there to be confused about? Tala was world famous by now, and wasn't that the reason Osson had kidnapped him to trade to Mist in the first place?

"You really don't know who I am, do you?" Osson asked slowly.

The question caught Tala off guard. Why would he? Free Bone wielders weren't exactly well known! The Churches would hunt them relentlessly, same as Blood and Flesh wielders! The only two free body wielders Tala even knew were Gazin, a Dissident, and… oh no. Oh no, no, no.

"Figured it out then?" Osson smirked.

Tala's mind froze. His entire being was in shock, just as he had been when Anderas Anto had walked out of the fire back in Southtown. If any person alive *might* be worse of an opponent than Anderas Anto, it was the Bone Merc.

the Bone Merc, whose actual name was Osson, apparently. He never would have guessed that.

"You understand why I'm not exactly worried about your friends now, don't you?"

Tala could only nod, acutely aware of the iron grip still crushing his arm. He had been intentionally annoying one of the most dangerous people in the world! The person who killed the Demon! How stupid was he?!

"Good. Now, enough with your mindless chatter. Come along, nice and quietly, and I'll still make sure Mist gives you a swift, peaceful death, okay?"

Tala nodded again, his mouth dry. Osson—the Bone Merc!—was probably the only person alive who *could* force a

Church into giving Tala a quick death instead of whatever else they might want to do. Dear Gods, what had his life become?

"Don't kill them," Tala managed to force out, barely more than a whisper.

"What? Who?"

"My friends. If they come to rescue me. Don't kill them. Please."

Osson gave him a considering stare. "Agreed. I need you, but I have no fight with them. If they do happen to find us, I'll let them go. Alive and as unhurt as I can manage."

"Well, that's mighty kind of ya, isn't it, Merc?" A voice rang out down the alley, a voice that Tala recognized instantly. "But I think you'll agree to letting the lad go without it coming down to a fight."

"Huh. So, they did find us. I guess I underestimated them," Osson muttered. "And why, Gazin, would I do that? You know better than most just how little of a threat to me you all are." He said much louder to the short, redheaded man striding toward them.

"Not all of us, Merc. How do you think I found you so quick? Now you better undo whatever you've done to the lad and get right on out of here before it's too late!"

Osson smirked bemusedly at Gazin, disbelief clear. "Is that so? And just who has you so certain… oh no…" Osson trailed off, sounding absolutely terrified. His grip on Tala's arm went slack as he stared at Gazin in mounting horror, forcing Tala to quickly use his empty hand to keep Osson's locked around his.

"Yep." Gazin nodded, sounding more annoyed than

anything. "And he'll be here any minute. So how 'bout we just end things here and go our separate ways? We're heading south, so you might want to go any other way."

Tala was stupefied. Who in the Hells could scare the Bone Merc of all people?

"Godsdamnit!" Osson suddenly cursed, enraged. "Always! That Godsdamned bastard! Fine! Fine! Take your stupid kid and his stupid talking mouth, and for the love of every God, just keep *him* away from me!"

Osson threw his hands up in the air, throwing off Tala's own grip like it wasn't even there. Tala panicked for a moment before realizing that nothing was wrong. He could breathe just fine, and there was no pain in his throat. What the Hells? Just the threat of somebody nearby was enough to make the Bone Merc give up just like that? What in the Hells was happening?

"Gazin? What—" Tala started to say but was cut off by the man.

"Later, lad, later. For now, let's get out of here before—"

"Os!" a voice cried out, loud and happy and carrying through the alley. Osson's body shot completely rigid, the cowl on his head suddenly stretching as though something was trying to rip it apart from the inside. Gazin sighed, a lost and defeated sound, chock full of suffering and regret.

"Oh no. No, please dear Gods, no," Osson, the legendary, dreaded Bone Merc, whimpered.

Tala turned, both curious and scared to see who this person was. To his utter shock, it was none other than Vail! It took him a moment to recognize the man. Despite still wearing his normal cloak and hood, there was a wide, happy smile on Vail's face, an expression Tala never thought he would see. *What? Vail? But... what?*

"Os! How long's it been? What? Seven, eight years? How've you been!?" Vail cried cheerily. He walked right up to the stiff Osson, the feared and dreaded Bone Merc, and swept the man up into a full-bodied hug.

Tala could only stare, his mind refusing to accept that what it was seeing was actually happening. Beside him, Gazin put his face in his hands, and Tala could swear he heard him muttering curses. Or prayers. Both, maybe? Looking at Osson's blank, pale face and Vail's wide, sunny smile and happy eyes, Tala had a feeling it was both.

CHAPTER 18

"Hello, Vail," Osson groaned, sounding as weary as anyone Tala had ever heard.

"Oh, don't be like that! You should act happier to see your old friend after all this time!" Vail chirped, wearing a bright smile that lived somewhere between genuinely happy and unbearably smug. He had released Osson from his crushing-hug but still had one arm slung around the aggrieved man. "And you've met our new baby hero! What do you think of our little Blessed Killer, eh?"

"He's almost as annoying as you are," Osson bit out through a tightly clenched jaw.

"Really? Well done, kid!" Vail said cheerily to Tala, who could do nothing more than blink in response.

"What have you been up to the last few years? You should come back with us, get a drink, meet the crew! I think you'll be impressed! You haven't met any of them except Gazin. And Ilan and Rala, of course."

"Serala is still with you?"

Vail nodded.

"The last time I saw her, she tried to kill me."

"She was still just a kid! And that was ages ago. I'm sure she's over it now."

"Over it? Are you serious?"

Vail gave him a confused look.

"Right. Never mind. I forgot who I'm talking to," Osson muttered, somehow sounding even more annoyed. "Look, Vail. I'm not going anywhere with you. At all. We are going to part ways here and now, before you ruin everything. Forget we ever saw each other, okay?"

"When have I ruined anything?" Vail asked, sounding offended. The sharp glare Osson shot him sent shivers down Tala's spine, made even worse by the man's strange eyes. "That was just a bit of fun! You enjoyed yourself too!"

"I don't enjoy pissing off the Churches, Vail! You have the little mouthy asshole back, so just leave me be! I'm going!" Osson stormed past Vail, striding out of the alley with an angry gait.

"Oh, thank the Gods!" Gazin whispered, looking incredibly relieved. "Come along, lad. Let's get back to the others. They should be nearby." Tala was still too stunned to say anything, feet following Gazin more out of habit than conscious choice. Vail fell into step beside him, still grinning softly, like he was eternally amused at some joke only he understood.

Tala walked out of the alley with his companions in a daze, paying no attention to his surroundings until he felt a tight grip on his arm. Gazin had reached back to grab Tala and was standing protectively in front of him. Confused, again, Tala brought his eyes up to see what the fuss was and felt one lid start to twitch. Half a dozen city guards were arrayed in a half circle in the street in front of them, surrounding Osson and, behind him, Tala, Vail, and Gazin.

Osson had been saying something to the guard's leader—what exactly Tala didn't know—but cut himself off with a long, aggrieved sigh as the guard captain's eyes scanned the three of them before darting back to Tala. Confusion flitted over his face before morphing into looks of recognition, surprise, and then horror.

"That's—that's—" the captain stuttered, choking on his own breath, sweat beading on his forehead as his eyes bulged, locked dead onto Tala.

"That's nobody you want to have seen. Nor am I. All you saw was a couple of unimportant nobodies having an argument in an alley. No big deal, and nobody has to die. Understand?" Osson asked the captain, calmly, yet forcefully.

The guard captain turned back to Osson, and it was clear, even to Tala, that he had no idea who Osson was. His eyes flitted between Tala and Osson a few times before his back straightened. He drew his sword, shouting so loud and shrill that it was little more than a terrified scream. "Tala'Keahi! The Blessed Killer! In the city! Alert the Church! Alert Lady—hurgk!"

His screeching was cut off as a white shape lodged itself in his throat. The street was silent. Nobody moved as all eyes went to the long, white, strangely segmented length of bone. With a sick squelching sound, it slid out of the guard's neck and quickly retracted back into Osson's hand.

For just a moment, there was no movement in the street,

aside from the bleeding corpse of the guard captain as it thumped limply to the ground. All eyes followed Osson's other hand as he palmed his face with it, and the whispered words of "Godsdamnit, Vail!" were clearly heard in the silence.

Tala had but an instant to wonder why Osson was blaming Vail before the man suddenly moved, faster than Tala's eyes could follow. The other five guards collapsed, each with a large shard of bone sticking out of their throats or faces.

Screams erupted all around them. The people in the street, who had before been giving their group and the guards a large berth, panicked, running away from the Bone Merc and his newest victims as fast as they could. In front of Tala, Gazin spat out curses as beside him Vail laughed in unrestrained glee.

Still laughing and wearing a sadistic grin, Vail strolled up next to Osson. "Well then. Still think we should go our separate ways?"

Osson growled, a deep, animalistic sound.

"Great!" Vail exclaimed cheerfully. "Gazin? Tala? We might want to run. Things are about to get fun!"

CHAPTER 19

Well, this feels familiar. Tala ran down the street, closely following Vail and Osson. Of the four major cities that he had been to in his life, three of them he had now run for his life through. Part of him—a small part, admittedly—was actually glad it had been the Bone Merc who had kidnapped him, for he was likely the only person alive who wouldn't have bothered taking Tala's sword from him. And when running for one's life through a city, a sword was a very comforting thing to have.

Although I might not actually need it this time. Tala watched as a small squad of guards stepped out onto the street, swords and clubs in hand. In an instant, all of their necks were sliced open by that strange bone… Whip? Yeah, a whip that came out of Osson's hand. Having the Bone Merc on their side meant there wasn't much that could truly threaten them. Although the way that Osson was cursing Vail's name, face, existence, and parents as they ran was making Tala second-guess just how much he was actually on their side.

And there are the bells. That brings back memories. Of

course, the last time that Tala had heard a city's bells was after killing Ignis back in Fiahren, the event that had started the whole mess his life had become. Back then, he had been terrified beyond belief at hearing the city bells ring out, knowing they were for him. Now, he just rolled his eyes at the sound. His companions, his *friends*, were some of the most dangerous people in the world, barring the Blessed, and Tala himself had gained worldwide notoriety as the *killer* of Blessed. Multiple, even! And at his side was the sword that could do, *had done*, it! And now he was being protected, however temporarily, by the Bone Merc!

His companions came barreling out of a side street right in front of them, almost seamlessly joining Tala and Gazin in following Vail and Osson through the city. The only hiccup was Serala, oddly, who had stumbled and almost fallen when she caught sight of Osson. She was kept up and moving by Ilan's massive hand gripping her shoulder. Tala couldn't blame her. She had met Osson before, apparently, so of course she would recognize him, and anyone could be forgiven for a momentary stumble at realizing that they were in the presence of the Bone Merc.

A pack was shoved into Tala's hands as they ran. Dunlop must have grabbed it from his room back at the inn before they had set out to rescue him. *How considerate!* He gave his friend and trainer a nod of thanks as he maneuvered the pack onto his back, tightening the straps so it didn't jostle too much. It was comforting to know he wouldn't have to sleep on the bare ground without even a bed roll once they reached the Jungle, and he wouldn't have to share the other's water skins.

With a rather nice sense of calm—and a thoroughly pleasant lack of any real fear or anxiety—Tala ran through the city. He even managed to feel some sympathy for the poor guards who got in their way, only to be mercilessly slaughtered by the Bone Merc. It was nice to be fleeing a city and not be scared out of his wits for once… Dear Gods, his life had gotten strange these last few months!

And it was nice to be fleeing a city that *hadn't* been prepared for them, unlike Southtown. The standing force of Lynmyr was only a fraction of the size of the combined forces that had suffused Southtown in preparation to ambush Tala, and none of them had been prepared to deal with a group of Dissidents charging through the city, to say nothing of the Bone Merc who led them. As the southern gates of Lynmyr came into view, only a small force of guards had arrayed themselves in front of the large double doors, securely closed. The guards clearly had no idea just who they were defending the gates from, as they were grouped together in a tight cluster *right in front* of the gates.

Tala sighed in pity for the poor bastards as the sounds of his companions' footsteps suddenly got much louder. Or rather, the footsteps of *one* of his companions got much louder and faster. Ilan picked up his pace and charged out in front of the group, entirely encased in that stone armor of his.

The guards—to their credit—saw the stone giant heading right for them and tightened their formation instead of fleeing. The few with shields buckled down front and center. *Brave, but worst possible move.* Ilan only increased his speed even further before smashing through the shields and the guards behind them, sending splintered wood and screaming people flying without slowing down. Ilan's charge didn't stop there, though. He continued forward, head down and shoulders hunched, until he reached the gate's double doors, almost twice as tall as the giant man was.

With a deafening smash, the bottom half of the steel-reinforced, thick wooden doors exploded outward. Their strong design was meant to stop people from breaking through them to get *into* the city and fell short at preventing somebody from breaking through them from the *inside*. Tala was curious if the doors would have been able to stop Ilan had he been coming at them from the outside. They weren't exactly weak on the inside, and Ilan had blasted through them quite easily.

Questions for another time! Tala barely ducked to avoid a hastily thrown wooden club from one of the few remaining guards. Dunlop grabbed it out of midair without looking and tossed it back at the guard, not even breaking his stride to do so. The club whirled through the air with unnerving accuracy before smashing the guard who threw it right in the face. The guard collapsed limply to the ground. Tala grinned, amused at just how... impudent Dunlop had made such an impressive move seem.

With the gates wide open—more or less—before them, their escape from Lynmyr was all but certain, but Tala spared a quick check behind them just to be safe. A few scattered guards chased them at a distance, although they seemed to be having second thoughts about actually catching them after Ilan's little destructive episode. But that was it: no priests that Tala could see. Finally: a simple, easy escape. As he passed through the broken gates, Tala peered ahead and saw nothing but a stretch of empty plain between them and the Gods' Canyon. Just a bit more running and they would reach the Canyon Bridge, cross it, and then be safe in the Jungle.

Well, safe from Lightning, at least; nobody from Lightning, be it soldier or Blessed, would dare follow them across the bridge.

CHAPTER 20

"Arrows! Fall tight! Alina!" Dunlop yelled, and Tala rushed over. The others converged on Alina, all of them still running but matching pace with the girl. She spun around, running backward. Behind their backs, a soft light began to glow, coming from the shield that Alina had conjured.

"Hard light," she had told him it was called. Light with an actual *physical* presence that could be touched and maintain its shape. She had demonstrated it to him a few times before, and Tala still struggled to understand the physics behind it. A challenge that wasn't helped by Alina's inability to properly explain just *how* it worked. For her, there was little more involved than, "I tell it to do, and it does." Apparently, even most Light Blessed struggled with creating hard light, and despite her prodigious talents, Alina admitted she was limited in what she could do with it.

One of the things she *could* do was create a solid sheet of hard light in midair, one more than strong enough to withstand a rain of arrows. As they jogged (having to follow

Alina's much slower pace as she ran backwards while holding up their shield), many strange plinking sounds echoed as the arrows impacted Alina's shield.

Tala grinned; it was almost funny just how stupidly powerful their group was together. All ten of them were protected by a lethal rain of arrows thanks to just one. Well… nine of them were protected. Osson ran off to their side, seeming entirely unbothered by all the arrows falling around him. And on him, only to plink off like he was a solid wall. Tala smirked; it would take a lot more than arrows to hurt the Bone Merc.

"Oh shi—!" Tala heard Alina curse before the light of her shield suddenly intensified, followed by a powerful flash as an incredible rumbling sound tore through the air. Alina stumbled, held up by Lito, shield gone. She was able to recover in seconds. Running backwards, she shot off two intense beams of light out of her hands, forming another hard light shield afterwards without wasting a moment. Just in time, too, as another volley of arrows bounced off the shield as others rained around the group.

The shield suddenly grew much brighter again. Tala squinted in reflex as another bright flash erupted, and a bolt of lightning smashed into the shield, shattering it into pieces that quickly vanished. Another rumble tore through the air. Alina was better prepared this time and didn't falter. She launched four more light beams, two from each hand, before forming another shield. Whatever Lightning Descendant was chasing them, they were no match for the Light prodigy. A part of Tala—a small part—was slightly sad that they were stuck running instead of fighting. He would have loved to see a battle between Alina and a Lightning Descendant. Alina would win, of course, but it would still be a fascinating sight.

They were making good progress even at their slightly slower pace. They were out of range of the archers, and he could see the Canyon clearly, a massive gash in the land that ran off far past the horizons. And directly ahead of them, spanning the canyon at its narrowest point, was the legendary Canyon Bridge. Even though it was still distant enough to not be quite clear, Tala could tell the bridge was different from what he had expected. First, it was *large*! The bridge had to be at least fifty feet wide, or close to it! Who would have ever made a bridge that wide? And why? A dozen carriages could cross that thing side by side!

The second thing Tala noticed was that the bridge looked *weird*, aside from its sheer size. It was practically shining in the afternoon sun, as though the entire thing was made from clean steel! The bridge was supposed to be old, so old in fact that nobody even knew who had built it, or when. So why was such an old, large bridge so… shiny? Did Lightning take that good care of it?

His thoughts on the bridge were disrupted when he noticed the large guard buildings on either side, both looking distinctly different—more normal. Soldiers were streaming out of them. At a quick count, there must have been over a hundred soldiers pouring out of the two buildings and creating a defensive formation in front of the bridge. The large spear wall brought back memories of Southtown. Unlike Southtown, though, Tala didn't really feel any great sense of fear this time, not when he had a better idea of just what his companions were capable of. While Alina was busy fending off the Lightning Descendant behind them, she wasn't the only one capable of dealing with a group of soldiers.

Right on cue, Ilan moved ahead. More and more stone flowed up the man's body with each step. But Tala frowned when Ilan's pace slowed. The man fell back again as the stone armor stopped forming, although it stayed around his lower half. In his place, Osson was charging ahead, covered in—as far as Tala could tell—a complete armor set made entirely of stark white bone. As the Bone Merc bore down on the soldiers, a lightning bolt shot through the empty space between them, hitting Osson dead on. The man didn't even flinch as another lightning bolt struck him, followed by another and another. Two Descendants, one from each building, Tala guessed, were striking Osson in tandem, loosing an impressive onslaught of Lightning.

Two Descendants were nothing for the infamous Bone Merc. As Osson got closer, two bone whips shot out of his hands. Both moved almost as fast as the lightning did, striking the Descendants right in their throats. *He certainly has a penchant for aiming for the throat,* Tala thought idly. Instead of retracting the whips like he had before, Osson instead wrenched his hands in opposite directions across his body. Whips following the motion, they flew through the formation of soldiers, slicing through every single one with barely any resistance.

That… was a bit more brutal than Tala would have preferred, if he was being honest. He had seen his companions slaughter more soldiers than that back in Southtown; Hells,

Alina herself had incinerated more than that with a single attack back then. There was something different about seeing (and not even really seeing, as his eyes had been covered at the time) hundreds of people vaporized in an instant and seeing a hundred people cut into two or three, bodies falling to pieces right in front of him. Tala had heard the stories of how brutal the Bone Merc could be but seeing it firsthand was… just disturbing. Every time Tala started to think he was getting used to the violence of his new life, something would come along and remind him how uncomfortable he really was with it all.

Still, it certainly made life easier for them, as the group quickly reached the line of death. Not a single one of the soldiers had survived the Bone Merc's attack, not that Tala was surprised given the stories. He made a point of not looking down as he passed through the bodies. He still had the occasional nightmare about Southtown and didn't really need to add to the images that haunted him.

Thoughts of death and horror quickly fled Tala's mind as he got his first proper look at the Great Canyon Bridge. Eyes opening wide, his brain jumped into action. Who in the Hells had made the thing!? The bridge was made of metal, but it wasn't a metal like any he had ever seen before! It wasn't even like his Blessed metal sword, although between the two he might have said his sword still looked better. No, the bridge was just so… clean! It was like every inch had been polished to perfection, but Tala couldn't see any signs of wear at all! For something that was so old, and was used so often, it looked like it had never been touched! Lightning must keep it tidy, as there wasn't even any dirt or detritus laying on the bridge, but nothing could make the entire bridge look so fresh. He had heard that the bridge was a marvel of design and engineering, but now he understood what that meant. No wonder Lightning had never managed to replicate it. Even the Institute didn't have the knowledge, much less the means, to create something like this!

And the design of the bridge itself only reinforced the idea that the bridge was special. It definitely wasn't like any bridge he had ever seen, or even seen theorized back at the Institute. Strange metal and cleanliness aside, the bridge was straight, flat, and had no upper support. However the bridge was held up, it was only supported from underneath. Pillars at most, Tala reasoned, or it would block the flow of the river that ran through the canyon. But for such a long, wide bridge to be supported only by a few pillars? Gods, how he wished he could stay and study the thing!

And what was the deal with the… railings? He wasn't sure what else to call them. The sides of the bridge, preventing people from falling off, were two unbroken lines of the strange metal, a solid barrier on both sides that extended from the floor to just above Tala's waist. Whoever had built the bridge must have had an excess of the strange metal to use so much just to make such a fancy and excessive guard rail. It also curved as it went up, so the top of the railing (that couldn't really even be called a "rail" in Tala's opinion) was rounded at the top, instead of flat. There were no solid corners on the bridge *at all.*

"Keep moving, laddie! We aren't safe yet!" Gazin called from the back of the group. Tala glanced back and nodded, picking his pace back up. There were a lot of soldiers streaming behind them, charging down the road from Lynmyr. Only a few had caught up to them, and they were swiftly dispatched by the others who were playing rearguard. There must have been more left in the guard buildings after Osson had wiped them out. The ones coming from Lynmyr were far enough away that they should be safely across the bridge before the enemy reached them.

"You're doing well, kid," came a soft voice from beside him, and Tala almost stumbled. Vail was keeping pace right next to him. When had he gotten there? And why wasn't he in the back fighting with the others? Although the rest were quickly closing in on them, so maybe Vail had just moved first? Either way, it was weird. Why was the man wasting time encouraging Tala?

"Remember what we've taught you about the Jungle. You know how to survive in it." What in the Hells was Vail talking about? It really wasn't the time for this! The probably insane man was reaching into his pocket while he ran.

"No matter what, remember to keep these wi—" Vail cut himself off suddenly, spinning and throwing his free hand up towards the sky. Not a moment later, a thunderous boom roared out. A massive flash erupted on the bridge, not even a dozen feet away from Tala.

Whatever had exploded launched Tala away, close as he was to it. He smashed into the barrier railing at such an angle that he skidded quite smoothly on it down the bridge a ways. Groaning, he lay on the ground. Blinking the spots out of his eyes, Tala saw Vail next to him, acting similarly groggy. Vail shakily rose to his feet, seeming more annoyed than anything. Looking back, Tala saw that the rest of the group had been blasted off their feet, too, on the other side of the explosion.

Standing between them, directly where the lightning blast had landed, was an old man in strange garb: loose, flowing pants cinched at the waist and connected to an open top, leaving his heavily muscled torso exposed to the world. His outfit was a deep blue, covered in stylized white lines reminiscent of lightning strikes. A Lightning Blessed had come. Tala dropped his head and groaned. He was getting sick of this shit.

CHAPTER 21

As Tala slowly climbed to his feet, he gripped the hilt of his sword, prepared to draw it at any moment. He wasn't sure how useful it would be against a Lightning Blessed, but it would be an unexpected surprise nonetheless. Even if it only bought him a few seconds, those seconds could well mean the difference between life and death, as he knew only too well. He observed the new arrival intently, trying to discern everything he could about the man, anything that he could use to his advantage.

He was drawing some rather bleak conclusions. The first thing he noticed about the man, besides for his rather unique clothes, was that he was old. Old enough to *look* old, which for a Blessed meant that he was likely well over five hundred. Probably closer to seven hundred, at Tala's estimate. It was notoriously difficult to tell a Blessed's age by their appearance, but this new arrival was almost entirely bald with only two large tufts of almost entirely gray and white hair sticking up from the sides of his head, only a few scant, dull streaks of black left behind to show what color it had once been. Even the man's angry mustache was entirely gray.

To make matters worse, he was clearly not one of the many Blessed who grew lazy and complacent with their powers. His entire body, much of which was visible due to the way he wore his strange robe open, practically rippled with muscle, and was littered with small scars, with even a few larger ones visible on his arms and torso. There were few things that could leave a scar on a Blessed, and those were mostly other Blessed.

"I am Denhei! Master of techniques passed down through my family for ten thousand years! Who dares to bring chaos to this city and disturb my rest?"

Tala blinked, mind stalling at the Blessed's… boasting? He wasn't really sure what to call it. It was late afternoon. What rest were they disturbing? And techniques passed down over ten thousand years? The Gods had only descended some time a little over seven thousand years ago! His claims were nonsense! Surely a Blessed of all people would know that! And was he wearing sandals?

Tala wasn't the only one who didn't seem to know quite how to react to the Blessed's announcement. The rest of his friends were all standing in different battle-ready positions on Denhei's other side, staring blankly at him. Even the soldiers still alive behind them were unmoving, blinking in bemusement.

"Oh, for the love of—! It's not even his city!" Tala heard Vail groan, pulling his attention away from the Blessed's… posing?

Yeah, posing. Denhei was standing in place, shoulders

back, head tilted high, eyes closed, and hands planted on his hips. He must have heard Vail, though, for his eyes snapped open and zeroed in on the man standing beside Tala. "Indeed! It is not my city, but is it not my prerogative to go where I wish? To visit where I wish? Me? The inheritor of techniques perfected over ten thousand years?"

Tala watched as Vail said nothing and just stared back at the Blessed with his classic blankness, the silence stretching awkwardly on.

"You clearly recognize who I am, to be aware that I, the great Denhei, am not the lord of Lynmyr! But I do not know who you are! Tell me your name so that we may conclude our business here as proper warriors!" Denhei commanded, still posing dramatically. Tala wasn't sure if he wanted to laugh or cry at the fact that such a ridiculous man was actually a threat.

Vail, of course, didn't answer, and continued to stare at the man, unimpressed, without so much as a twitch. He was so still that Tala wasn't even sure he was breathing. In fact, Tala suspected Vail may not be breathing just to make his blank, derisive stare even more dramatic. It seemed like something Vail would do.

"Lor—Lord Denhei!" one of the soldiers called out, pointing past the Blessed, hand shaking even worse than his voice. "That's him! Tala'Keahi! The Blessed Killer!"

"Oh?" Denhei lifted one of his bushy gray eyebrows as his eyes slid off Vail and onto Tala, who felt every hair on his body raise as the Blessed scrutinized him. "Hmm, he does match the description! Tell me, boy, are you indeed *the*

Tala'Keahi? Killer of Elidor? Slayer of Annelore? Murderer of Ignis? Defeater of the great Anderas Anto?"

"Tala. I just go by Tala, actually." Tala had to fight the urge to close his eyes, keeping them trained on Denhei. Out of all the thousands of possible responses that he could have given, why was *that* the one that came out of his mouth?

Denhei's other eyebrow rose to join the first. "Tala, then! And just what is Tala, the Blessed Killer, doing here, hmm? Have you come to add me to your list of victims? You will find, boy, that I am not so easy to kill! Not me, the great Denhei Mishima, heir to techniques passed down through my family for ten thousand years! Lord of combat! Master of foot, fist, and lightning!"

Denhei posed again, his chest thrust out, looking as though he expected everyone present to begin cheering. Tala just stared blankly, entirely unsure of how to respond to the ridiculous man.

"Lord Denhei! the Bone Merc! the Bone Merc is with them!" a soldier called out, this one sounding far less nervous than the first.

Denhei whipped around, turning his back on Tala and Vail entirely. Tala cursed his bad luck. If he were only a little bit closer, he could have stabbed Denhei from behind with his Blessed sword.

"Where? What? Who? Which one of you is the Bone Merc? Where is he?" Denhei roared, and Tala was certain he heard a hint of fear in his voice.

"...Over there, milord," another guard hesitantly said, finger pointing past all of them. Collectively, every eye on the bridge turned to follow the finger. Osson leaned against the railing on the far end of the bridge, arms crossed as he watched them all.

"Really? Os? Really?" Vail called out to the man, sounding annoyed.

"Screw you, Vail! I'm not part of any of this!"

"Oh, you cowardly shit," Vail muttered in clear irritation, turning his back to Osson and looking again at a nonplussed Denhei.

"Right. Well… it seems even the infamous Bone Merc knows better than to face off against me, Denhei Mishima, master of techniques passed down through my family for—"

"Ten thousand years! Yes! We get it! Would you please shut up about it now!" a voice cried. After a few moments of pure silence (broken only by the distant laughing of Osson), Tala realized that *he* had been the one to interrupt Denhei! Again, he resisted the urge to close his eyes, wondering what in the Hells was wrong with him?

"You dare?" Denhei growled, and Tala became acutely aware of the smell of ozone. "You dare disrespect my family's techniques? That have been passed down for over ten thousand years? I will sear the flesh—"

Denhei's furious threats were interrupted as his head burst into a spray of lightning, a dagger flying straight through the center. Head reforming in an instant, Denhei again whirled around to see who had committed such a blasphemous act. Instead, he received another dagger through the face. Tala's friends once again begun fighting against the soldiers encroaching on them.

Seizing the opportunity of Denhei's distraction made by Serala's daggers, Tala drew his sword and charged at the Blessed, hoping that his sword would work on him the same as it had on Annelore. Unfortunately, as ridiculous of a person as Denhei seemed to be, his boastfulness was not entirely without warrant. Seeming able to sense Tala's approach, he spun around, striking out straight with an open palm infused with crackling lightning right at Tala's chest.

Through instinct more than anything—thanks to the many nights spent training with Dunlop and Lito—Tala managed to block the strike with his sword, catching the hand on the flat of his blade. He was launched backward, flying off his feet, sliding along the smooth metal floor of the bridge until his back hit the railing again. To his immense relief, he felt none of the burning or shocking that he had been told came with being hit by a lightning attack. He checked the sword. It was completely unmarred, not even a scorch mark on it. His sword was lightning resistant. Neat.

In a moment Vail was beside him, hauling him up to his feet and checking for injuries. Tala assured him he was okay, briefly explaining his sword's newfound resistance. He would have sworn Vail smirked at that. Meanwhile, Denhei marched straight at Tala's friends, clearly intent on killing them all as lightning crackled around his hands and feet. It was curious, Tala thought, how a Blessed was using his magic to empower his martial abilities instead of just overwhelming his opponents from where he stood with sheer magical might.

Regardless, Tala wasn't going to complain. It gave him

the time to hopefully save his friends. They didn't have a lightning-resistant sword to save them if Denhei struck.

"Hey! Bastard! I'm still here! Your little attack didn't work!" Tala shouted, having no real plan beyond "stop his friends from getting murdered by an enraged Blessed." From beside him, he thought he heard Vail sigh.

His not-really-a-plan worked, as Denhei stopped where he was and slowly turned around, giving Tala a considering look. It must be quite a surprise to the Blessed that he was still alive, and perfectly fine, since Denhei didn't know about his sword. It was too bad that trick probably wouldn't work again.

"So you are. Maybe there is something to you after all. No matter. You shall die a warrior's death then! Come at me, Blessed Killer! Let me show you the might of ten thousand years!" Denhei got into another pose—no, not a pose. It was strange to see a Blessed in a proper fighting stance, one very similar to some of the unarmed combat stances that Dunlop had shown him.

Tala, however, had no intention of going *to* the Blessed. Fighting a Blessed was suicide, despite his previous successes at it. He was not eager to fight one who had actually been trained in martial arts with his sub-par sword skills, magic sword or no. Unsurprisingly, it seemed Denhei wasn't going to give him a choice. After a few seconds of staring at each other without moving, the Blessed began striding back toward Tala, whole body crackling with lightning.

Before Denhei could get within reach of Tala, his head erupted into another storm of lightning, courtesy of another of Serala's daggers. Tala's companions had, predictably, had little difficulty with the remaining soldiers. Slowly, they fell back onto the bridge, keeping the swarm of soldiers that had followed them out of Lynmyr at bay.

Denhei, it seemed, had finally lost patience with Serala's antics. Spinning around even as his head was reforming, Denhei locked his gaze onto Serala, casually dodging another dagger that she sent his way.

"Fine, girl, you first!" Denhei roared. With a crackling burst, the man charged towards Serala faster than Tala had seen him move yet. Serala dodged the first, second, and third strikes from the Blessed's hands and feet, but his incredible speed finally caught her. To Tala's horror, Denhei slammed a fist, covered in so much lightning it could barely even be seen, straight into Serala's gut. Lightning erupted around her. She was blown off her feet and sent flying through the air, sailing clear over the side of the bridge before falling out of view.

Tala stared at the place Serala fell. Completely frozen, he struggled to process what had just happened. Serala couldn't… she *couldn't* be dead. It—she *couldn't*. Tala kept staring at the railing, at the spot where she vanished, waiting for her to come climbing over the strange metal, ready to continue the fight.

An aborted choking noise from beside him drew Tala's attention. Vail, eyes wide and face slack, stared at the same place Tala had. The man was completely still, as still as Tala had ever seen him. Tala was pretty sure he wasn't breathing and, this time, Tala was positive the man wasn't doing it on purpose. Oh Gods! Tala didn't know what to do! Serala had just… oh Gods! Tala looked at Vail, then at Denhei, who had turned back and was walking toward them again, looking smug.

A hand gripped Tala's arm. Vail stared at him with an intensity he had never seen before. Unspeaking, Vail grabbed Tala's sword hand and turned it over, pushing the sword back into its sheath. Tala wanted to ask just what he was doing when a Blessed was quickly bearing down on them, but the cold fury visible on Vail's face prevented him from being able to even open his mouth.

Once Tala's sword was secure at his side again, Vail reached into his pocket, and Tala was reminded of Vail's strange behavior right before Denhei had arrived. Mute and in shock, Tala watched numbly as Vail withdrew a small cloth bundle from his pocket. He grabbed Tala and pulled him close. Tala thought for a moment that Vail might be hugging him before he recognized the feelings on his back. Vail was shoving that cloth bundle deep into Tala's pack and pulling it tightly shut with the water guard well secured over the opening.

Pulling back, Vail stared deeply into Tala's eyes with the same intensity as before. "When you surface, keep those on you at all times. In a pocket or tied to your pack. Make sure they can be smelled. And remember, find the split, follow it south. We'll meet you at Morungil." Vail hesitated for a moment, uncharacteristically uncertain. "And if—if Serala's alive… save her. Whatever it takes, save her."

Tala goggled back at Vail uncomprehendingly. What was the man talking about? What had he put in his pack? Why did it smell? How was *he* supposed to save Serala? She—she had been—

Without waiting for an answer, Vail grabbed Tala roughly and spun. Tala, unprepared for such an act, stumbled along and hit the railing. He was lifted up, sliding over the bridge's strangely round rail guard. Panicking, grasping for a handhold that didn't exist, the last thing Tala saw was Vail's face morphing into unimaginable rage as he turned around.

Then Tala slid down the rail guard and fell towards the water a hundred feet below.

CHAPTER 22

After everything they had survived, everything that had happened after Tala, after surviving Southtown and *Anderas Anto*, Alina had almost started to think their little group was invincible. Seeing Serala, their strange, psychotic, fearless leader, killed so suddenly, so… *easily*, all Alina could do was stare in horror at the man who murdered her… not friend, exactly, but a girl she at least respected.

The Blessed, obviously feeling satisfied at having dealt with her, turned around, ready to kill Tala, who was most definitely one of Alina's few friends, before stopping, clearly confused about something. Forcing her eyes to drag off of Serala's killer, Alina followed his gaze to Tala, hoping beyond hope the boy had, once again, done something world changing.

Tala was nowhere. Confused, Alina looked back to Denhei, and then at her companions, and even the soldiers behind them. They were all looking at where Tala should have been with different levels of confusion clear on their faces. The bridge was silent as they all turned to Vail, the man standing with his back to them all, looking over the side. The man slowly turned around, and Alina was struck by the look on his face: pure, unadulterated rage—an emotion Alina hadn't even known the man could feel, much less express. If anything could get such a reaction out of the man though, she supposed it would be the murder of his… daughter? Maybe? Alina still didn't know what his relationship with Serala was—had been.

"Where is he? The Blessed Killer, where did he go?" Denhei asked into the silence, sounding just as confused as he looked.

"He fell." Vail shrugged carelessly, and Alina felt her heart plummet: Tala had fallen!? Off the bridge? How? When? What about the guard rail? It was perfectly fine! Such a fall could kill him! Why was Vail acting so nonchalant about the possible death of their most important member!? Her mind spun in dizzying circles, refusing to accept just how badly things were going. Serala and Tala gone, with a Blessed just standing there, more than capable of killing them all.

After everything, was this really the end? All of them dying together on a bridge at the hands of this one Blessed?

"Fell! Ha! I bet he jumped rather than fight me, Denhei, master of techniques passed down for over ten thousand years!"

"The kid was right. You do say that way too much," Vail commented casually, stretching his arms across his body. His voice contrasted sharply with the angry glare on his face.

"You can die next," Denhei said shortly. Without further warning, the Blessed charged at Vail, who seemed entirely unbothered by his imminent death, still stretching.

Alina couldn't move as Denhei bore down on Vail. She wanted to close her eyes, to turn away at least, so she didn't have to see another one of her companions die, as strange and distant as this one was. Tears streamed down her cheeks as Denhei, arms and legs crackling with lightning, swung a fist at Vail.

The bridge, once again, descended into silence. Alina was so shocked, even her tears had stopped.

"Godsdamnit, Vail," Gazin muttered, sounding thoroughly frustrated. Although Alina barely processed the words as she gawked at the scene in front of her.

Vail stood there, stance barely changed, holding Denhei's fist in one hand. All the lightning that had been on the man was completely gone. Vail's mouth slowly morphed into a grin: an evil, sadistic, bloodthirsty sneer that sent chills down her spine.

Vail struck out with his own fist. To her further surprise, the blow landed solidly on Denhei's cheek, snapping the unprepared Blessed's head to the side. A small spray of blood flew out of his mouth. What the Hells!? That was—that wasn't even possible! Only a Wielder—a Blessed or Descendant or *at least* a Marked—could hurt a Blessed! Tala was so special because he had found ways around that rule! But even then, he had used clever tactics and weapons, utilizing his own knowledge and the inherent weaknesses of the different magics to kill the Blessed that he had! How in the Hells had Vail accomplished the same thing with simply his fist? There was no fire surrounding his fist! No ice or light or metal or steam or water or blood or—or *anything*! Even Blessed had to *actually use magic* to hurt another Blessed!

Vail punched Denhei again. The Blessed stumbled with

the blow, Vail still holding solidly onto his fist. But that second blow knocked sense back into Denhei, and the man flowed with the motion of his stumble. Doing a half-spin, he struck out at Vail with his elbow, still a competent fighter despite the like of lightning. As smooth as anything Alina had ever seen, Vail ducked under the strike. Tucking himself in close to Denhei, he used his own elbow to smash the Blessed in the chest while still holding his fist, pulling Denhei into the hit so that it struck even harder. Denhei coughed and wheezed as the air was forced out of his lungs.

Unrelenting, Vail swung his arm up and smacked Denhei dead in the face with the back of his hand. The blow was weak, coming at such an angle, but it still had enough force behind it that Denhei's nose crunched and began bleeding.

Denhei roared, a choking sound full of pain. Weak lightning sparked across his body, and Vail dropped his fist, jumping backwards and shaking his hand lightly. Alina could barely believe—scratch that, she *couldn't believe*—her eyes. A Blessed's magic could kill a person with barely any effort. How was Vail alive at all?

She wasn't the only one who was struggling to understand what was happening. "What—what are you?" Denhei choked out, still struggling to catch his breath even as lightning raged to life across his body.

Vail didn't answer, but beneath the shadows of his hood (*the hood he never took off,* Alina's mind whispered), that same angry, evil grin hadn't shifted. Moving swiftly, Vail charged at Denhei. Denhei, clearly also caught by surprise, reacted on instinct, and tried to deflect Vail's strike with his arm.

The moment Vail's hand connected with Denhei's forearm, all the lightning on Denhei's body weakened; the lightning on his arm vanished entirely. Vail grabbed Denhei's arm and jumped, swinging himself around the larger man's body in an acrobatic maneuver the likes of which Alina had only ever seen Serala perform. Vail smashed an elbow into Denhei's face as he swung behind him. Spinning his whole body in the air, he ended up firmly on Denhei's shoulders, legs locked around his throat as he began raining punches down on his face and head. As Vail unleashed his wrath, all lightning on Denhei died out once again.

Blood flew and at least one tooth as Vail proceeded to vent his rage upon the man who had killed Serala. Showing amazing endurance, especially for a Blessed who were rarely ever injured or experienced pain, Denhei ducked his head, protecting his face as best he could. He grabbed Vail's legs, spinning around as he tried to wrench the much smaller man off him.

Alina wasn't sure if it was intentional or an accident, but Denhei suddenly dropped backwards, nearly crushing Vail under him between the ground and his back. Vail had apparently been prepared for such a move. With uncanny expediency, as though he had done it a hundred times before, he spun around Denhei's head. His legs stayed in his grip, leaving himself awkwardly caught in Denhei's hands, a position that would have likely resulted in his death if Denhei hadn't landed hard on the ground, groaning in pain as his back and head smashed into the hard metal of the bridge. Vail quickly freed himself.

Instead of recommencing the assault, Vail jumped backwards, moments before an explosion of lightning erupted out of Denhei's body. With another groan, Denhei lifted his legs up and kicked out, jumping from flat on his back to a standing position. He was clearly ready for a fight despite the beaten and bloodied state of his face.

"How!? How are you doing this?" Denhei roared, staring at Vail with a mixture of fear and hatred. Vail, again, remained silent. His back was to Alina so she couldn't see his face, but judging by the growing fear on Denhei's, she could imagine just how deranged his smile must have grown.

Screaming his rage to the world, Denhei threw out a massive bolt of lightning at Vail, one that would have easily vaporized Alina and all the rest of them in an instant. Instead of striking Vail, it spun, twisting around and around the man in a crackling cyclone, growing weaker by the moment. After a few seconds—where everyone, including Denhei, stared at Vail in horror—the lightning died completely, leaving Vail completely unharmed.

The stillness encompassing the bridge was broken by the motion of Vail's shoulders, quickly followed by the man's still hooded head as he threw it back and laughed. It was a deep belly laugh, a sound of unfiltered mirth. In all her life, Alina had never heard such a pure laugh sound so unnervingly *evil*.

Denhei, however, seemed to recognize it. The old, battle-scarred Blessed's eyes grew wide as his face paled, an expression of abject fear taking over his face.

"It-it can't be! You-you-you…"

"Me," Vail said.

Alina had never heard anyone, much less *Vail*, sound so smug.

Alina thought there were only two people alive who could make Blessed feel fear who weren't themselves Blessed. the Bone Merc, that legendary (and apparently asshole-ish) figure with powers that nobody knew the true extent of, and Tala, the boy who broke the world. Never in her wildest dreams did she think she would ever see a third, or for that third to be *Vail*.

Nevertheless, when Vail took a simple, casual step forward, Denhei, as though on instinct, took a step back. That one step was apparently all that Vail needed. Without wasting another moment, he lunged forward again, engaging Denhei in a hand-to-hand fight that the "master of ten-thousand-year techniques" was barely managing to keep up with. Alina could barely tell what was happening, but Denhei was being beaten bloody, his lightning sparking weakly between Vail's relentless blows. Every strike Denhei attempted in return was either dodged or parried by Vail; the smaller man treating the attacks as minor nuisances at worst. Eventually, Denhei fell to his knees, and then onto the ground, curled up in a fetal position, arms covering his face and stomach.

Vail stopped, looking down at the beaten, moaning Blessed before him. Vail knelt by Denhei's head, and said something to the man, too quiet for Alina to hear. After a few seconds of nothing, perhaps waiting for Denhei to respond, or perhaps waiting for something else, Vail slowly stood. Taking a deep breath, Vail took a small step forward, twisted sideways, and stomped his foot down on Denhei's temple, smashing the Blessed's head against the bridge.

Alina stared at the casual murder of one of the most powerful people in the world, unable to believe what she had just witnessed.

CHAPTER 23

"You called for me, High Priest?" Anderas bowed, softly shutting the door behind him. The room was warm, heated both by the vast amounts of sunlight streaming in through the large glass window, which stretched across the wall and part of the ceiling on his right, and the merrily flickering flames in the hearth set in the wall on his left. Soleil sat hunched over his desk, scribbling furiously with a quill. As Blessed of the Fire God, they were both unbothered by all temperatures, hot or cold, save for the most extreme of either. Why Soleil insisted on keeping his personal quarters hot enough that the slower servants often collapsed during the course of their work was a mystery even to him. Although rumors said it was somehow related to his time serving at the Dustwall.

"Anderas. Good. Sit. I'll be just a moment," Soleil ordered absently, barely glancing at Anderas as his quill scratched across the page. Anderas arched an eyebrow but stayed silent as he strode towards the desk and settled himself in one of the two rather spartan seats before it. For all that Soleil loved his comforts and luxuries, his personal solar was as utilitarian as could be. It was a place for business, not pleasure, in Soleil's mind, and the High Priest had taken to spending more and more time in it over the last few weeks.

Anderas had only been waiting for a minute before Soleil finished, quickly running his hand over the parchment to dry the ink with a steady stream of heat. He still refused to adopt the newer, and arguably much higher quality, tools the Institute had created, clinging stubbornly to older materials like quills and parchment. Without wasting a moment, Soleil rolled up the parchment, sealed it with wax, and rang a small bell on his desk. He passed the scroll to the servant, who came through the hidden doorway behind him, bowed, and left as quickly as he came. Anderas waited quietly as Soleil took a long drink of water (he never imbibed wine or other alcohol while in his solar) before turning to him, and regarded Anderas with a heavy, weary gaze.

"Trouble, my lord?" Anderas asked sarcastically. Soleil snorted as he stood and made his way over to a large table covered with a map of the world. Anderas rose silently to join him. All across the map were markings and small figures, showing the state of the ramping war. Anderas eyed it, noting how thin Fire's forces were spread compared to the other countries.

"There's always trouble these days, it seems," Soleil said, not bothering to try and hide his exhaustion. "Ever since that bloody disaster at Southtown. You really burnt the sheets on that one, Anto."

Anderas didn't deign to respond. They had gone over the details of Southtown a dozen times already, and Soleil had accepted that none of what had happened was truly Anderas' fault. That didn't stop him from griping about it to Anderas every chance he got, however. Not that Anderas blamed him, really. They had lost all access to Southtown in the aftermath, and Firetown had closed itself shortly after—a devastating blow to the Fire Church who relied heavily on the trade with Metal that occurred in those two cities. The large mass of Light troops shown on the map, clustered in the Three Rivers east of Southtown, wasn't helping. They overwhelmingly outnumbered the Fire forces that were arrayed at Ahiati. An invasion was imminent, if it hadn't started already.

"You haven't had any luck with the people protecting that boy, have you?" Soleil asked, as he frowned down at the map.

"Very little, I'm afraid," Anderas replied, hiding his annoyance at how true that statement was. He had been heavily invested the last few months in trying to learn about Tala's companions but still had little more than theories and conjecture. Even less than that, for some of them.

The only two that Anderas' network had been able to piece any real information together about had been the two… not non-combatants, but *lesser* combatants, the man and woman who had stayed on the fringes of the battle. The man was Nuri (the most likely to be his real name, as he was known by many), a smuggler of remarkable skill and renown in certain circles. That had been fairly easy for Anderas to discover, as his own network had worked with the man many times before. (Not that "Nuri" ever learned just *who* he was actually dealing with on those jobs.) Nuri had, in fact, been recently spotted in the city again after a conspicuously timed absence. For whatever reason, he had left Tala's little group. Anderas would be careful to keep an eye on him going forward.

While Nuri the smuggler was an interesting, if not overly important, discovery, the woman was another matter entirely. Caida: Fiahren's most prestigious prostitute. He was still working out all the implications of that discovery. She was a frequent guest to various noble estates and even the Gods' palace itself. In the last few months, she had been "traveling." Anderas had heard everyone from petty nobles to Blessed alike whine about her absence. Just as he did whenever she had left the city in the past, as though her many apprentices weren't more than making up for it.

At first, Anderas had simply been impressed when he learned who she was: a Dissident with personal access to (almost) every man and woman of note in the city. One who had hidden her true allegiance so well that even he had never suspected her of being a traitor. The ultimate spy in many ways. And possibly an assassin, as Anderas had started connecting many unfortunate deaths that had occurred over the years to the woman. Although, the more Anderas investigated her, the more disturbing the picture he was forming became. Most of the best brothels in the city belonged to her—that was common knowledge—but she controlled far more than just a few high-end establishments. A large portion of Fiahren's industry—not just carnal pleasure, but services of all sorts, from food to military production—could be tied back to the woman in one way or another.

For years, Anderas had suspected there was a shadow figure who held immense power in the city. He had always thought it to be Sulien, the Blessed who secretly served as the Church's spymaster. He was now beginning to believe it was, in fact, Caida. A woman who he had personally spoken with many times as she glided between the city's nobility during parties or as he passed her in the halls! He couldn't begin to guess why she had risked herself and everything she had built to join Tala's group. He would have to speak to her again if he ever got the chance. If she was indeed the shadow power in Fiahren, he would need her cooperation—or her successors—to achieve his goals. The fact she was apparently a Dissident (something he still found hard to believe despite seeing it himself) should only make it easier. If he took the risk of explaining to her what he intended. He would have to be *certain* before he took that chance.

It was the final figure that bothered Anderas the most. The cloaked man. If it wouldn't have risked everything Anderas had been working towards for the last two decades, he would have had his servants' agents' Dissident contacts captured and brought to him to personally interrogate. They had refused to acknowledge the cloaked man even existed, but they knew something! That *man's* laughter while he slaughtered countless soldiers in Southtown had revived nightmares Anderas hadn't had in *years*! He knew who he *couldn't* be, but he still needed to learn who he *was*!

For now, he had to keep playing nice with Soleil while keeping what little he did know to himself. "We know they escaped into Light, and didn't circle back to the south, but I haven't heard anything solid about them since."

"Neither have I," Soleil grumbled. "Damned Dissidents!

They're a cancer on this world. Anyway, that's not what I called you here for. I'm sending you to Huobak. Mud is pushing towards that city aggressively, and I want you there to remind them just who it is they're dealing with!"

"Huobak?" Anderas questioned, looking over the region on the map. There was a large concentration of Mud units on the border near the city. "I suppose that would be easier to take than Vatrabad. And more valuable than Agirigon. I would have thought you would send me to Serehag, though. Earth is mustering their forces, and from what I've heard, they're intent on taking back that city." Anderas didn't even have to look to see the overwhelming number of Earth troops arranged near Serehag. It was easily the largest single force on the table, by a fair amount.

"They are. But I'm sending others to reinforce your uncle. There's no other city Earth can reach without taking Serehag, so we need numbers there more than raw power. Mud is the bigger threat at the moment. If they take Huobak, they can make a deal with Earth, and the entire southern half of the country would be in danger. The other two will be reinforced as well, but Huobak is the most vulnerable, and the most important. That city won't fall as long as you're there, so that's where you're going."

"Understood, High Priest." Anderas nodded, hiding his annoyance. Soleil was right about the importance of Huobak in the current climate, but Anderas had other interests he cared far more about, and being sent to Huobak wouldn't benefit any of them! But he couldn't refuse a direct order from the

High Priest, not if he didn't want to give up everything he'd been working toward. "Is there anything else?"

"No." Soleil slumped over the table, eyes slowly roaming over it. "A war on three sides, when we'd be hard pressed to win on one. However this ends, Anderas, we're going to come away bloody. I—*we*—need you to be The Great Anderas Anto if we're going to win this thing, in any sense of the word."

"Are things truly so dire?" Anderas couldn't help but ask, managing to make himself sound concerned. *Of course,* he knew how dire things were. He was the one who had conspired to make them that way! None of it would be happening if he hadn't played the Metal priests like he had. Tala's actions, as surprising and miraculous as they had been, had provided a once in a lifetime opportunity Anderas would not squander, even if it meant moving up his plans by centuries. Prepared or not, change was coming, and Anderas would ride that chaos as far as he could.

"Aye." Soleil nodded tiredly. "We were stretched too thin already, I know you know that. Light has already started crossing the Three Rivers, and we can't afford to stop them. I'm only sending our weakest and most worthless assets to contest them. Necessary sacrifices. We can't do nothing as Light invades, but Earth and Mud are more important. Light doesn't have the resources to hold whatever they take anyway. They'll pillage the region, probably sack Ahiati, but in the end they'll fall back to their own lands regardless. Ahiati is the poorest city in the country anyway. Everything of value was taken in the Wind Raids."

"I understand," Anderas said empathetically. "If we have to lose somewhere, let it be where it doesn't really matter."

"Aye." Soleil chuckled weakly. "But if we lose Serehag, or one of the three southern, it may be centuries before we get them back, if ever."

Anderas nodded solemnly. "Forever burning," he said, the ancient words falling easily from his lips.

"Forever burning," Soleil replied resolvedly.

CHAPTER 24

Gazin sighed, growing tired of the constant whispering buzzing through the air from the two remaining kids. Lito and Alina had been furiously discussing what had happened on the bridge, how it had happened, ever since they had crossed the damned thing. The two had fallen well behind the rest of the group, so they could talk without being overheard, but Gazin's enhanced ears could hear them clear as day. Normally, he would have reduced his hearing to save himself the irritation, but he didn't dare do such a thing in the Jungle. Even if they should be safe on the Jungle Road, only a fool let their guard down in such a place. Hearing the slightest change in the animal chatter deep in the trees, or the rustle of a leaf being brushed, could very well mean the difference between life and death, road or no.

Although, the kids did have a point. With Tala lost, what was the plan? They all were just following Vail as the man stormed down the road. None of them were willing to ask him and risk turning his wrath on themselves. Even Osson was quiet, having rejoined the group after they left the bridge.

He had been waiting for them at the far end, unwilling to involve himself in the fighting. When he had made to say something to Vail, Vail had given him such a glare that even the infamous Bone Merc had balked.

Gazin huffed. If they were going to get anything, he would have to do it. And they had been walking long enough; the bridge was far behind them. It was time for answers.

"Vail. Stop," Gazin called out. He could tell that his companions were feeling both anxious and relieved.

Thankfully, Vail didn't make an issue of it, like Gazin had half-expected he would, and stopped where he was, although he didn't turn around or change his body language at all.

"What is it, Gazin?"

"We need to talk. Tala's gone. What are we going to do?"

Vail spun around, face almost as blank as usual, but Gazin could see the tension hiding beneath the surface. In fact, he had a feeling they all could see it. "The plan hasn't changed. We're going to Morungil. The kid knows to meet us there."

"He fell off the bridge, Vail! We don't even know if he's alive! And even if he is, that's hundreds of miles of Jungle that he'll have to get through! Alone! He isn't prepared for that!"

"So?"

"So? What do you mean 'so?' Are we just supposed to wait in that damned city for the rest of our lives, waiting for him to *maybe* show up one day?"

"If that's what it takes." Vail shrugged, beginning to turn around, clearly expecting that to be the end of the conversation.

"No, Vail! Damnit! We need more than that!"

"Like what?"

Gazin spluttered, anger overtaking him—anger towards Vail for acting so nonchalant and anger towards himself for being unable to answer the simple question.

"Shouldn't we-shouldn't we try to find him? Them? Him?" Lito spoke up, voice betraying his nerves.

"How? Search through thousands of miles of dense jungle?" Vail sounded unamused.

"Couldn't we follow the canyon? The river? If he's alive, he'll wash up somewhere."

"That's hundreds of miles of winding canyon. Despite what maps show, the canyon isn't just some straight line cut through the world. Even if we had tried to follow the moment he fell, we'd never catch up. And the kid isn't dumb enough to wait around at the river for us. He knew that if we got separated to meet us at Morungil. So that's what we're going to do."

Gazin's eyes narrowed, mind mulling over Vail's words. "Why not? Why wouldn't the kid wait for us by the river? We never made a plan for if he fell in. We never thought it was even a risk."

"We didn't think there would be a Blessed to get in our way either."

"Vail!" Gazin took a breath. "He was fine. Denhei was-was distracted. How did the kid fall over the barrier when nobody was even looking at him?"

"I don't know. I wasn't looking at the kid either. Maybe he slipped."

Gazin *knew* Tala didn't just slip and happen to fall over a solid railing that was higher than his waist. It had to have been Vail, but why? Gazin had never agreed, nor even understood, why Vail had been so set on going to the Jungle. On bring-ing Tala through Lynmyr, as small of a risk as it might have been. Gazin knew Vail hadn't been aware that Osson was in the city, so that wasn't it. Vail had been planning something. Something he had been unnaturally cagey about, even for him. But what could Vail possibly be planning that required throwing Tala off the bridge? Assuming the kid survived the fall, assuming he climbed out on the south side, what good could possibly come from Tala being alone in the untamed depths of the Jungle?

Gazin opened his mouth, prepared to ask those questions. Whatever was worth risking Tala like that, they had a right to know. Serala had more than likely died for whatever this insane plan was, even if that had *definitely* not been part of it. He stopped short of speaking as a motion caught his eye. By his side, Vail's hand was making a sign, hidden from the rest of the group, so that only Gazin could see it. *Stop,* it said, a special hand sign, long used by the Dissidents as part of an entire secret language used in only the most dire of circum-stances, when silence and secrecy were paramount.

Gazin glared back at Vail, giving no indication that he had seen his sign. He didn't need to. Vail knew. Gazin hated trusting Vail. He was never, *could never,* be certain when the man was being honest, or when he was simply fostering chaos for his own twisted amusement. But he had, much to Gazin's surprise, given it all—most of it all—up when he had taken in Serala. He had actually tried to be a decent father to the girl, as incompetent as he was at such a thing. Even Vail wouldn't be so cold as to continue on with business like normal after what had happened to her if it wasn't for a good reason. Hells, he had murdered a Blessed in vengeance for her, something Gazin hadn't even known he could do, although he had long suspected.

So as much as it rankled him, as unnatural as it felt, Gazin backed down. It was too bad that that didn't solve all their problems. "Are we really just going to wait around and hope he manages? We have people who know the Jungle. We can hurry to the city and send them out to search for him, at least!"

"No," Vail refused. "We don't want to risk drawing attention to him like that."

Gazin's eye twitched. It had been less than a minute, and Vail was already stretching the limits of his trust.

"Osson." Vail turned to the Bone Merc, who blinked back in surprise, clearly not expecting to be drawn into the conversation. "Go find the Carnival. Wait around for a while. I wouldn't be surprised if the kid ends up there. He may even have Serala with him."

"What? No! I'm not one of your people, Vail. You can't just order me around!"

In a flash, Osson was pushed up against a tree, Vail's hand gripped tight around his throat. "You owe me. I'm calling in your debt. Go to the Carnival. Wait for the kid. If he doesn't show after a while, go find him. Both of them. Bring them back to us, or news of their fate. Afterwards, you can go back to doing whatever you want. Clear?"

Osson nodded, looking both angry and resigned in equal measure. "Fine. But the debt's clean after."

Vail stepped back, releasing his grip. Osson shifted

awkwardly, his entire body shivering in a deeply unnatural way. After one last silent glare at Vail, Osson stalked off, disappearing between the brush without so much as a word to the rest of them.

CHAPTER 25

Tala groaned, keeping his eyes shut as he enjoyed the feeling of the warm sun on his skin. He just wanted to keep lying there, calm and peaceful, but knew he couldn't for much longer. He didn't know where he was, and, frankly, he didn't really care. The last thing he remembered was Vail throwing him off the bridge and into the waters of the Canyon River. After that, his memories were a jumbled mess of water, pain, and panic.

No, he would much prefer to just keep basking in the sunlight, dry, calm, and pain-free, aside from the growing ache in his spine. He grumbled and shifted his shoulders, trying to readjust his pack with minimal effort, to no avail.

Sighing, Tala gave up and opened his eyes, staring straight up at the blue sky above. Only a few scattered clouds slowly drifted along. What time was it? He tilted his head back and forth a tiny bit, scanning the sky. The sun was on his left, lower than he had first thought, given the heat. Far down past his feet, the mottled hues of the first night moon appeared. Late afternoon, then. It would probably start getting dark soon.

Squeezing his eyes shut for a futile moment of protest against everything, Tala reluctantly pushed himself up into a sitting position, looking around properly to see where he was. Right on the edge of a river, apparently. Not surprising, given his last memories. Strangely, he was entirely clear of the river itself. A few feet of soft grass stretched out from his feet before becoming mud and sloping gently into the water. Looking up the river, presumably where he came from, the land rose sharply on both sides, blocking his view of what was probably the Gods' Canyon. He must have floated down some small tributary that ran out of the canyon.

"Ah, you're up. I was wondering how long you'd doze for." The voice was calm, cultured, with subtle hints of a strange accent. Tala's head whipped to the left, feeling his heart spike into a frenzied beat. Not very far away, on a large, gray rock, sat the speaker: a man, completely naked, with skin a similar shade to Tala's own, only a slight bit paler. The man sat casually, entirely unbothered by his nudity, and stared at Tala with a gentle frown, his face full of curiosity, but showing no signs of malice. Tala stared back, not sure how to react to this naked, unarmed man. His eyes flicked down for a moment, scanning the man's body, only to lock onto a still figure lying in the grass near the man's feet.

"Serala!" Tala gasped, scrambling to his feet and rushing over to the girl, forgetting to be wary of the stranger in his rush to check on his friend. She was unconscious but alive, with a weak pulse and steady breaths. Even so, Tala could tell that she wasn't simply sleeping. If she didn't get medical attention soon, she wouldn't stay alive for long. He gazed up at the naked stranger, who was now leaning over them, sympathy clear on his face. "Help! She needs help! Can you—? Is there anybody nearby?"

"I've already done all that I can for her, I'm afraid." The man shook his head, sounding genuinely sorry. "The body is outside my domain. She should be stable, I think, long enough for you to get her to aid, if you so desire."

Domain? Tala wanted to ask but shook the thought off. Serala was more important.

"Are you certain? How do you know? What did you do?"

The stranger leaned back, analyzing Tala with an amused look. "As much as I could. Her heartbeat was erratic, failing. That was my most immediate concern, but I'm not very familiar with healing or the human body, so I don't know if that was the only thing. Otherwise, she seems alright, as far as I can tell. No severe damage to her brain, I think, and I was able to soothe some of the damage to her organs. What exactly happened to her? From the fist mark at the center of the scarring, I'd guess punched by a Lightning wielder, maybe?"

Tala blinked repeatedly, trying to process everything the man had just said. He was coming to some very unpleasant conclusions about this strange person, but they were being offset by how caring he seemed to be. "Yes. A Blessed. He punched her."

"Really? What were you two doing that led to her getting punched by a Lightning Blessed? And ending up in my river? Did you jump off that bridge or something?"

"Yes. And-well… that's not really important."

The stranger was looking vaguely amused, although he

also had that curious look again, frowning lightly at Tala like he was trying to figure something out, eyes dancing over Tala's features. Tala could see the moment the man figured out whatever he was trying to. His face was incredibly expressive.

"You're Tala'Keahi! The infamous Blessed Killer! Well! That would certainly explain how you got into a fight with a Lightning Blessed and survived! Tell me, did you kill him? That would bring you up to four, right?"

The stranger seemed entirely unbothered by the fact that Tala had grasped his sword's handle the moment he heard his name. In fact, the stranger seemed almost *excited* to be meeting Tala and was staring at him with an expression of pure fascination. The sheer openness of the man's face and his emotions felt jarring to Tala, who had gotten used to the stoicism and self-control of his companions.

"What? No, I didn't. I, uh… I fell off the bridge before I could fight him."

"Oh? Pity, that. Still, I never thought I'd be meeting The Tala'Keahi! You've really been making some waves since you killed Ignis Fatus!"

"…Thank you?" Tala half questioned, not entirely sure how he was supposed to respond. Tala had thought the man was an Empowered of some sort, based on his comments earlier, but now he wasn't so sure, given that the man seemed happy in a not-an-enemy-and-not-going-to-try-and-kill-him kind of way. "Are you a Dissident?" That was the only real explanation he could come up with for… everything about him.

"Hmm? Oh no, no. Unfortunately, no. I'm more of an…

observer, I guess you could say. Just supposed to watch what happens around here and record anything that seems like it might be important. Not supposed to interfere, either, but I can't really help myself sometimes. Thousands of years and we're still not supposed to get involved? At some point, it just starts seeming pointless, you know?"

Tala didn't know. He stared bemused at the stranger, who was beginning to speak faster and faster, as though he hadn't said anything in a long time and was desperate to get the words out while he had the chance.

"And Gods, does it get boring! Do you know what happens in and around this river? A few times a year, maybe, a person or two will fall in, and that's it! Because what else are people going to be doing in a river that runs through a giant canyon? Nothing! You wanna fish? There's better, easier places to go to do that! Wanna ride a boat? Same thing! Wanna go for a swim? Guess what? Elsewhere is better! And yes, I know, people use the lake! But they don't *do* anything there! They fish! That's it! People don't even swim there! And I can't even get into that city by the lake because they barely understand how the plumbing system works, so they use slaves for half of it and there's nowhere for me to access! Gods, I swear I'd go up there and teach them how to use the damn thing properly myself if it wouldn't get me landlocked for the next hundred years!"

The stranger was glaring back at the canyon in the direction of Lynmyr. Tala didn't move, trying to understand just what he was talking about. The stranger wasn't making a lot of sense.

"So, no, I just float around up and down the world's

most boring river all day with the occasional peek into the world's most boring lake waiting for people like you to fall in so I can at least do *something*! Which, by the way, you have to keep to yourself! I'm not even supposed to save anybody who falls in, just let them get themselves out or die, because I'm just supposed to observe, from a distance, and never get involved! So, you owe me, for saving your life, and you must never tell anybody about me, 'cause if my people hear about it—and believe me, my people *will* hear about it—then I'll get sent back home and landlocked, and you have *no idea* how much it sucks to be landlocked. Well, you do, I guess, but that's only 'cause you don't have a choice, and you've never not been landlocked, so you don't actually know how much it sucks when you have an alternative."

Tala nodded along absently, caught up in the stranger's frenetic pace. He wasn't really sure, at all, what being 'land-locked' meant, or why it was such a big deal. Maybe the stranger was from the Mist islands? The theory fit. Sort of. Ish.

"So, just, please, keep this to yourself? If you feel any gratitude whatsoever to me for saving your life, and your friend's, don't ever tell anybody about me. Ever. Normally, I wouldn't have even shown myself to you so it wouldn't be an issue, but with the shape your friend was in, I thought I should take the risk 'cause I didn't think she'd make it if I didn't help you out a bit. A bit more, I guess, but still. But, anyway, you won't tell anybody about me, right?"

Tala stared at the strange, naked man as his rant finished, taking more than a few seconds to realize he had been asked a question. There was so, *so* much to unpack from that little…

speech, that Tala didn't even know where to start. "Sure. I can-I won't tell anyone."

The man slumped back, entire body relaxing like a huge weight had been lifted off him. "Great! Thanks! I really appreciate it!" He beamed at Tala, looking so genuinely happy that Tala thought he would keep the promise not to tell anyone if only so he wouldn't feel guilty when looking back on that strange moment.

"Are you a Water wielder?" The words were out of his mouth before he could stop them. The idea was ridiculous, completely so. No one had seen any sign of the Water God or his followers for thousands of years.

The man shot rigid, looking back at Tala in a panic, eyes wide and fearful. After a few moments, he slumped again, looking defeated as he closed his eyes, as an embarrassed blush spread rapidly across his face, neck, and upper body. "Damnit." He groaned, opened his eyes, and peered pleadingly into Tala's own. "Please, please never tell anybody about me. Most of you don't even believe we exist anymore, and we really want to keep it that way."

"…Is that a yes then?"

The man heaved a great sigh. "Yes, yes, it is. My name's Wade, I'm a Water Blessed, it's nice to meet you."

"… A Water Blessed?"

He nodded morosely. "Yep. Please don't tell anyone about me. And please don't kill me either, eh, Tala'Keahi? Oh, great Blessed Killer?" Wade peeked at him through downcast eyes, but with a teasing smirk dancing on his face.

"You're a Water Blessed named Wade?"

Wade slumped even further. "Yes. I know. Believe me, I've heard all the jokes. Blame my parents. But it could be worse. They named my eldest sister Aqua." Tala blinked, deciding to just move past that little tidbit.

"If you're a Water Blessed, why are you here? Where are your people? The Water God? You all vanished thousands of years ago!"

"Yeahhh. About that… I can't say much, but basically, most of our ancestors, and the Water God himself, didn't want to be part of this whole endless war thing going on between the nations, so we left. Made a home elsewhere. And us Blessed are sent back over here to keep an eye on how things are going, see if anybody has figured out how to get rid of the Gods yet. There was that guy a few years ago, the Demon, I think you call him? We'd never seen someone like that before, but then he was killed by that Bone Merc guy, so that fell apart. Shame, really. The Water God got really excited when he heard about what the Demon could do, said he thought it sounded like something he thought he remembered from before, whatever that means, but that was it. It's been a long time since the Gods came and he doesn't remember much about the early days anymore. You know, I don't think I was really supposed to tell you any of that either, so maybe don't mention any of that to anybody, yeah? 'Course, I'm not supposed to be talking to you in the first place, so I guess it's kind of a moot point, but still." Wade shrugged.

"Okayyy, then. Sure, why not? That all makes total sense." Tala shook his head. "So, what? You guys just hang out in rivers and lakes and stuff spying on the world, waiting for something to happen?"

"Yeah, basically. It gets really boring, but, I mean, we have orders, y'know? They're actually pretty strict about making sure you people don't realize we still exist. Not really sure why it matters, myself, since it's not like any of you could ever actually get to us to try anything, but still. Of course, we aren't always perfect about it, but nobody's ever figured out the truth. We—us scouts, I mean—have become something of a myth to your people. 'River Ghosts,' I think you call us."

"What? I've seen one before! One of you, I mean! In a river back in Fire! I thought someone was watching me through some bushes that hung over the water, but nobody was there! My friends said it was a water ghost, or a frog, and laughed it off!"

"Oh, really? Well, yeah, it was probably one of us. Fair warning, if you ever see one again like that? Don't acknowledge them. Definitely do not let them know that you know what they are. I may be friendly enough, but it really is a big secret, and if any of the others find out you know, they'll probably kill you to protect our secret. It's nothing personal, just, you know, it's the rules."

"Right. Fair enough. I'll just keep this all a secret. If anyone ever asks how I survived after the bridge, I'll just tell them a River Ghost saved me!" Tala grinned at Wade, who grinned back.

"I'd appreciate that. Anyway, you should probably get moving. There's a few hours of sunlight left, and you don't want to be anywhere near the river when it gets dark. There are some nasty creatures that come out of the Jungle to drink at night, and you really don't want to have to deal with them, especially not if you're going to try to take care of her." He nodded towards Serala. "Oh! That reminds me! I made this while I was waiting for you to wake up!"

Wade spun around on the rock and pulled something around the other side. Tala analyzed it and blinked before a smile worked its way onto his face. Wade was pulling around a crude sled, one that had been cobbled together from sticks, leaves, and vines. It wasn't very impressive, not that Tala was going to say that, but it would fit a person and seemed stable enough that he should be able to pull Serala around on it.

"Oh, my Gods! Thank you! But, uh…where-where are we supposed to go?"

Wade shrugged sheepishly. "Sorry, but I can't really help you with that. I could take you near Lynmyr, but it sounds like that's probably the last place you want to go right now."

Tala nodded. Wade wasn't exactly wrong. "The Jungle it is then, I guess. Have any advice, by chance?"

"Not really, sorry. Follow the Split? I've heard people say that."

"Yeah, that's my plan too." Tala couldn't even see the mountains that made up the Split. He guessed they were east, based on the direction the river flowed. So at least he could find them to follow eventually. Although it sounded like he should head south first, to get away from the river. Gods, he wasn't looking forward to dragging an unconscious Serala through the wilds of the Jungle!

Wade helped Tala get Serala situated on the sled as best

they could and stepped back, giving Tala a grimacing sort of smile. "Well, best of luck, Tala'Keahi! I hope you succeed at whatever it is you're doing!"

"All I'm trying to do is survive!" Tala laughed. "So, thanks!" He turned around and grabbed the handles of the sled before stopping and turning back to Wade. "Actually, before we go, I have a favor to ask."

"What?"

"Well, she's in a coma, right?" Tala hesitated.

"As far as I can tell." Wade nodded.

"Even if she's stable, she can't eat or drink. She won't make it a week. Is there anything you can do to help? Like, fill her stomach with slow digesting water or something?"

"Is it really that much of a problem?" Wade asked. "I thought it took a month for someone to starve to death?"

"Starve, yeah. Dehydration kills in a few days."

"Really? Huh. I never would have guessed. My people don't really have that problem." Wade frowned. "I... maybe could do something, but it won't last very long. Only a day or two. And it would only be water, no food. Would that be enough?"

"It'll help, at least. But I don't think it'll be enough." Tala sighed. He only knew of a few ways to hydrate someone who couldn't drink, and he didn't have the equipment for the better options. A Water wielder though, he could maybe work with. "Could you make balls out of water? Small ones that won't break? That I could carry in a bag?"

"Sure." Wade shrugged. "Sounds easy enough. What

for? I don't think you'll be able to push water balls down her throat. Unless they're for you?"

"No, no. They're not for that. Or me." Tala sighed and began explaining his idea. Wade was both baffled and amused, but in the end, Tala had a sack full of small, slimy water balls that he carefully tucked into his pack.

Tala returned to Serala's sled, grabbed the handles, and began walking towards the Jungle. "Good luck. I'll be rooting for you," Wade called. Tala turned back to see nothing but an empty riverbank. No sign of Wade anywhere he looked.

With a deep breath, Tala started forward again, determined to somehow, impossibly, find somebody in the depths of the Jungle, the most dangerous place in the world, who could help Serala.

CHAPTER 26

Tala thought he had been prepared. His friends had told him how to survive in the Jungle, what to eat and what to avoid, how to spot signs of danger, and how to find water. All sorts of things. He hadn't planned to ever be alone in the Jungle, but he had eagerly learned what he could anyway, just in case.

Well, he was still alive, so that was something, but he had made a mistake. He had been in the stifling darkness of the Jungle for days and had been hungry. And so, he'd begun foraging food to add to his dwindling supplies. But he had foraged something he shouldn't have. He wasn't sure what (though his money was on some plant he had misidentified), but ever since then, the world had been *wrong*. He was seeing things that weren't there, hearing and smelling things that didn't exist. Vines would reach for him and vanish when he tried to fight them off. He couldn't keep track of his own body—how many arms he had, how many legs. Sometimes, he spoke to himself and no sound came out, other times he would speak and hear a dozen voices all speaking back.

Tala glared at the vine reaching for him, growing out of the trunk of a tree. He swung a hand (which hand? He wasn't sure. He had lost count of how many hands he had a while ago) at the vine, his hand (was it a hand? He couldn't remember) passing straight through the vine, which then instantly vanished. A fake vine then. Or a snake? It could have been a snake. A fake snake? Or a fake vine? It could have been either. Or both. It wasn't real, though; he was confident about that. Real things didn't vanish when he touched them. Or did they? No, no, they stayed there, he was sure of it. His hands (five hands? Since when did he have five? He must have lost one somewhere) went to the snakes wrapped around his waist. Snakes? No, they were ropes. No, they were vines. Green vines, although sometimes they were brown, and sometimes purple. Once they had been blue, and he thought he was going to drown, but then they changed to yellow and he felt warm in the sun.

What was he doing? Oh yeah, he was checking the snake-ropes he had tied to his waist. They were still there, still solid and there even after he touched them. Why did he have braids of sparkly hair tied around his waist again? He took a step and almost fell, held up by the same ropes of hair that had stopped him from walking forward. Oh yeah, he was pulling something: a cart. It was on square wheels behind him. He was a horse, pulling a sled over the purple water, between the yellow buildings with their pipes all reaching up and blocking the sun with green feathers. Green? They were green. They were leaves. They were on trees!

He was in the Jungle! He was a human! He was pulling a sled with his friend on it! She was hurt! She needed help! He had to get help! He stepped forward, straining as he pulled the weight of the girl on the sled behind him. He had tied the sled to himself after he almost left her behind the first time everything went strange.

Or was it saving him? He couldn't really tell anymore. There was no pain, except for when there was *only* pain. He had tripped once and thought he had fallen into the sky, only to realize he had fallen on his hands and knees, scraping his palms badly on the roots and rocks of the forest floor. His hands had bled, but there was no pain. Later, there was no blood, but his hands burned like they were on fire. He couldn't tell if he was hurt or not.

An animal had attacked him once. Or maybe a few had. Or maybe the same animal many times? That sounded wrong. He was sure they had been different. But then again, he had been sure that he had lost a hand somewhere, but he checked and he still had six, so maybe he was wrong. Either way, at least one animal had attacked him. His sleeve was ripped, and his second left arm was hung limply at his side and had glimmering streaks running down it. His first left arm also had a shredded sleeve, but it was made of wood, so he didn't think it was injured.

Could wood be injured? He had tried to ask one of the trees, but it blew smoke in his face and turned away. Trees were rude. Except for when they were nice. A tree had sung to him once, and then others had joined in, until the air was alive with the melody of the forest. That had been before the animal attack. Unless it had been after. It had been one of those. Before or after. Unless there had been more, then it could have been before and after. He laughed at the joke. What joke? Animal attacks weren't a joke. They were bad. Dangerous. He had been attacked by an animal. Or many, he wasn't sure. It had eaten him. Then it hadn't. It had run away after. He wasn't sure why; he didn't want it to run away! He was alone. He could've used the company! Except he had company, but it didn't talk, it just laid on the ground and stared at him, following him no matter how he tried to get away from it.

Was he supposed to get away from it? That felt wrong. Something in him was saying he was wrong. But then why was it following him? Was it going to attack? It hadn't yet. But it had long, sinewy arms that were wrapped around his waist; it wouldn't let him go. But it wasn't hurting him. Nothing hurt him: he didn't feel pain! He laughed, spraying the air with shiny sparkles, like the kind that flowed down his left arm, the one that wasn't made of wood. His arm was pretty, even if it unsettled him to look at it. He stared at his right arm, the one that ended in a sharp point. It shouldn't be sharp. The sharp belonged on his hip, by its brother. He put the sharp in the hole at his hip, where its brother waited for him. The sharp was sparkly like his breath; like his left arm (the one that wasn't made of wood). He didn't want to look at the sharp; it was better in its hole. Why was he looking at the sharp? He couldn't remember.

He stumbled forward, stepping left, then left, then right, then center, then right. He had a lot of feet. He had to move them all to go forward. It didn't help that the monster on the ground kept pulling him back, trying to pull him down. He didn't know why it didn't try harder, it just held on to him, and followed behind, floating through the air. The air must be heavy, and hard, because it always slowed him down, made every step so much harder to take.

Why was he walking? Why couldn't he just sit down like the monster? He was tired. He didn't want to walk anymore. He could sit down, sit with the monster. It wouldn't hurt him; he couldn't be hurt. But he was tired. He wanted to rest. Why couldn't he rest? He stepped forward. He lost track of which leg was moving. He had so many! Why was he still walking? He couldn't stop. He couldn't stop. He had to keep moving. The monster needed him to keep moving. He didn't know why it didn't help him then, why it only made moving harder, and not easier. But it didn't matter. He had to keep moving. He couldn't stop. It was important to keep moving. He took a step forward. And another step forward. He tripped on something: a rock, a root, a beast, a bug. They all tripped him. They all tried to stop him. He couldn't stop. He stood up, his second left arm didn't do anything, it just dripped shiny on the ground. His first left arm couldn't help him stand; it was made of wood. Wood couldn't help him stand! He stood up, his right arms helped him.

He took a step forward. He couldn't stop. He stepped forward. Another step forward. Another step...

CHAPTER 27

There were strange noises in the trees. Or, rather, the noises in the trees were acting strangely. He thought. Tala was still having trouble telling what was real and what wasn't. Hallucinations of all sorts still assaulted him at random intervals. They weren't constant anymore, which was good, but that almost made it harder for him to tell the difference between real and fake. Truth be told, he would happily take another bite of whatever it was that had affected him so, if only because he hadn't been able to feel the immense pain his body was in when he was under its effects.

With the substance wearing off, he could feel the ache in his… everywhere, really. His left arm (of which he was now reasonably certain—usually—he only had one) was by far the worst: the entire arm, from hand to shoulder, was completely shredded. His sleeve was little more than a collection of resilient string, and his arm itself was, well… he was making a concerted effort to not look at it anymore, after using some loose vines (that only occasionally turned into snakes) to create a makeshift tourniquet. Glimpsing his own bones through the ravished skin and muscles was not a pleasant sight. He really hoped he'd be able to reach Gazin while his arm was at least still attached.

He was attempting to not think about just how unlikely that actually was, though. He was lost in the Jungle, exhausted, and heavily wounded. His only real idea of what to do was "go south." But that was difficult to accomplish in the darkness. Daylight was obscured to the point of non-existence by the thick canopy of the trees above. Normally he would try to climb a tree (not that he really knew how, but still) to get a peek above, maybe get a glimpse of the Split to judge how far he had come, and how far he still had to go. But with one arm completely (and agonizingly) unusable, it wasn't worth the attempt. Part of him was relieved, he would admit, that he had an excuse to not try climbing the trees. He *really* didn't want to find out what types of horrifying bugs, plants, or other critters he might encounter trying to climb a Jungle tree.

So instead, he was making do with what little light trickled down to the ground, trying to use the angle and intensity to judge what time of day it was and, from there, which way was south. He thought he was managing it alright. Given the random lights he would sometimes see that may-or-may-not actually exist and the world's annoying tendency to shift colors, including occasionally turning entirely black and white, he was less confident than he would like. But he didn't really have any better options, so he kept on, dragging Serala on the makeshift sled behind him. He felt grateful he had thought to tie her to his waist when the hallucinations first started, for there was no way he'd be able to pull her by hand with his left arm in such a state.

Speaking of, it was probably about time to give her some more water. Or close enough to it, at any rate. He couldn't really keep track of time much better than *it may be day* and *it may be night*, what with the dim lighting of the forest and his general problem perceiving the world. But he was pretty sure it had been a while since he had last given her water, and he had just arrived at a clearing that would make the process a bit easier on him. (It wasn't much of a clearing, really, but it was a big enough gap in all the trees and bushes for them to both easily fit inside, along with relatively smooth ground.) So, Tala pulled the sled all the way in and gingerly dropped to his knees beside it. He desperately wished he could lean against a tree but knew better than to risk it after the last time he had done that. Some sort of bite-happy fanged-beetle-like thing had tried to eat his eyeballs. He refused to so much as stop moving after that unless he wasn't touching anything higher than his ankles to avoid any more such surprises.

Tala pulled his bag around his side as best he could with one arm and untied the water skin hanging off it. He had quite a few of them filled up when he had entered the Jungle, but they were nearly all empty now. Even though it had rained a few times, the sheer amount of foliage the water had to pass through to reach Tala meant he was not going to trust drinking it, not after picking up all sorts of *extras* as it slid along the leaves and branches. He and Serala both already had some burns on their bodies from acidic rainwater.

Tala took a small drink from the skin before re-tying it

to his bag. He had a few more days at best before he ran out and would have to take desperate measures. He had passed some pools and small streams, but he didn't want to risk drinking whatever might be living in those. Even in normal circumstances, he would be very hesitant to do that. In the Jungle? Absolute last resort.

Much like how he was giving Serala water. He had no other choice, unless he was willing to let her die. Praying desperately that she wouldn't kill him after she woke up and found out just how he kept her alive, Tala pulled out the sack nestled safety in his bag, the one full of slippery, semi-solid globules of water he had had Wade create. Rectal rehydration had been an interesting, if short, segment in his education about the human body at the Institute, but he had never expected to actually be utilizing said knowledge! Of course, over the last few months, he had made use of a lot of the things he had learned back then that he had never expected to. At least he could do it all quickly now, some small mercy: untie Serala from the sled, remove her protective coverings, turn her on her side, pants down, water-pill in (thank you, Wade!), pants up, done. It had gotten slightly less mortifying with repetition, but still, it was not a process Tala enjoyed. It worked, at least. They had been in the Jungle for at least a week, and Serala hadn't died from dehydration.

Returning the water-globule holding skin to the safe confines of his bag, Tala started on the other mortifying task of caring for Serala in the Jungle: checking her body for any unwanted passengers. Bugs and other critters were an issue for Tala, who was awake and moving. They were even worse for the unconscious Serala. He had done what he could to protect her, covering all her skin with the spare clothing in her bag, and then wrapping what he could of her up in all the extra cloth they both had. For the most part, it worked pretty well. Whenever he stopped to give her water and check for bugs, most got caught in the cloth wrappings, sparing her from their predations. But a few managed to worm their way down to her skin, so Tala kept his mind focused on his task. He methodically stripped her, removed every little creature on her, and redressed her, careful to make sure no new bugs had hitched a ride in the process.

Finally, after making sure she was clear, re-covered, and tied to the sled again, Tala allowed himself to fall back on his butt, (after carefully checking there were no critters nearby who would try to hitch a ride onto him) and allowed himself a brief rest. He wouldn't lie down, for that would risk falling asleep and thus both their lives would probably end, but a few minutes off his feet to recover as best he could was acceptable.

He stared up at the vast canopy above him, the dark leaves and branches covering up even the tiniest glimpse of the sky he so desperately missed, enjoying the peaceful silence. Then he huffed in annoyance. His hearing had gone out again. Having his sight go all weird was annoying, but not particularly dangerous, since he could still *see*. Having his hearing go out was horrible. In the Jungle, sounds were often the first indicator that there was something nearby. Aside from the immense pain he was already in, sure to get even worse once his system finally finished flushing out whatever he had ingested, he was looking forward to the hallucinations and general mind-altering effects ending.

Dropping his head to scan his surroundings, which had become a deeply ingrained habit over the past few days, Tala didn't see anything particularly concerning. The only unusual things were the glowing eyes of a creature peering out at him from the darkness of the Jungle a few feet away, just outside the other end of the clearing. Thankfully, he determined it was nothing more than another hallucination. No real creature—even in the mad hell that was the Jungle—could ever be quite like *that*. Every part of the creature was constantly moving, changing, shifting into the features of different animals all at once. Even in the few seconds he was looking, the thing's paws became feet, then hooves, then paws, then claws, then they became feet again. Its eyes became slitted and square and bigger and narrow; two became four, then became eight; and grew smaller, then wider; became two, then became segmented, and then became round. Its muzzle became a beak, which became a mouth, then a beak which grew lips, then teeth, but then lost teeth with a big tongue, then a small tongue became a forked tongue with sharp teeth, big teeth, lots of teeth, and then no teeth.

Even the wildest of Tala's hallucinations so far hadn't been quite so… *unstable*. Even when he couldn't keep track of how many arms or legs or tails he was supposed to have (being none for the latter), his body hadn't been shifting quite that much. Maybe it was the final hallucination? One last wild burst of random reality before his system finally cleared? He hoped so.

Stretching his shoulders as much as he could (meaning

he barely stretched one shoulder, as the other was attached to an agonizing lump of brutalized meat that was formerly his arm), Tala closed his eyes. Groaning, he prepared to pop back to his feet so he could continue his wretched trek south (or what he really hoped was south).

"It has been a very long time since anything ignored me like that," a screeching-braying-hissing-rumbling-growling-purring voice said in a vast array of tones.

Tala stopped his stretching and looked at the hundred-in-one creature. Was his hearing working again, or was it just because it was coming from his own head? He dug a small rock from the ground, relieved it wasn't some sort of acid-spitting spider disguised as a rock, and loosely tossed it at a tree, watching as it bounced off with a dull thud.

"Well, at least that's working again," he said to himself, happy that he wouldn't be trudging through the Jungle without one of his major senses. Not being able to hear in that place sucked. With a groan, Tala prepared to tie the sled around his waist again. A difficult task to do, one-handed, but he had gotten pretty good at it over the last few days.

"Are you an idiot? Or has your brain become as damaged as your body?" the voices asked, shifting through a thousand throats all at once.

"I'd say the latter, probably," Tala answered flippantly. Talking to his own hallucination probably wasn't the sanest thing he could do but, at this point, he didn't really care. At least this hallucination was making sense. That was better than the flying frog he had seen singing in wordless rhymes. He still hadn't quite figured out how rhymes could be wordless but was both disturbed and impressed by his brain's ability to conjure up such a thing, regardless.

"Is that so?"

"Well, I'm talking to you, aren't I? I think I am, at least. Although, I suppose it doesn't really matter if I am or not, since I think I am, and that's probably the same thing as far as we're concerned. Or I'm concerned. Either way, doesn't really paint me as the picture of sanity now, does it? And, frankly, given the shit I've been through since I entered this damned place, I wouldn't be surprised at all if my brain isn't entirely working properly anymore. It certainly wouldn't be the only part of me, would it?" He gestured vaguely towards his limp and mangled arm, beginning the arduous process of tying the vines around his waist one handed.

"Indeed. I should have expected some level of insanity with that smell on you."

Tala squinted back at the creature. Was he not noticing a bad smell, and this was his brain's way of trying to draw his attention to it? But what could be smelling bad? With a grimace, he tilted his head as best he could and sniffed what he could of his ruined arm. It wasn't a pleasant scent by any means, mostly blood, but he detected none of the putrescence that would indicate it had started to rot.

"Okay. I'll bite. What smell?" Because asking his own imagination questions he didn't already know the answer to made *perfect* sense.

"His smell. The Null wielder. It is on you both, but much stronger on you."

"Uh-huh. And who is this—" He stopped. He was

carrying a foreign smell with him: the bundle that Vail had shoved in his bag before throwing him off the bridge. When Tala had remembered about the bundle, he had been tempted to just throw it away, out of spite towards the man who threw him off the damned bridge. The only reason he hadn't was because Vail clearly had some sort of greater plan—one that involved *throwing Tala off of the Godsdamned bridge!*—and had something to do with the bundle.

As infuriating as Vail could be sometimes—most of the time—Tala owed him for saving his life many times over, so he had decided to give him the benefit of the doubt (for now) and do as the man had asked. Although when he did find the group again, he was most definitely going to be having a serious talk with Vail—and probably punching him in the face too, for good measure. Especially once Tala had pulled the bundle out of his bag and found it to be nothing more than a balled-up pair of dirty socks. He still had tied them to the outside of his pack like Vail had said.

"Are you talking about Vail? Is he the smell you're smelling?"

"Perhaps. I do not know his name. If I ever learned it, I have forgotten. But he wielded Null magics, the first I had seen since the old days."

"Oookay. I've never heard of 'Null' magic before, but I'm pretty sure Vail doesn't have magic of any sort anyway, so I think you're mistaken. Or I'm mistaken, I guess. We're mistaken? Gods, this is hard to keep straight!"

The illusion walked-slithered-stepped-crawled-hopped closer, sniffing Tala with its nose-snout-trunk-beak-mouth.

"No. I have forgotten much, but I remember that scent. I had hoped he would bring an end to this cursed existence. Did he send you here?"

"No one sent me anywhere. Except for Vail, when he pushed me off the damned bridge! So, I guess he did? He didn't say a thing about you, though, just something about making sure his dirty-ass socks could be smelled. Which hasn't really done me any good so far, considering." He gestured again to his mangled arm.

"So, he did send you."

Tala's eye twitched. Why was he arguing with his own hallucination anyway?

"Do you also share his magic? Are you stronger than him? Can you free me?" The creature's curled-bushy-long-straight-scaly-short-sharp tail was swaying, giving Tala the impression the thing was excited, or nervous.

"No. Sorry. I don't have any magic either. And if I could just choose to get rid of you, you'd already be gone anyway. But my brain doesn't like to cooperate with me, apparently. Unless you want me to try this sword out. It can kill Blessed, after all. Maybe it'll work on you too?" He drew his sword, the fantastical metal reflecting what little light there was in a beautiful display. The creature inspected the sword, sniffing it and even poking it with its amorphous barbed-smooth-toothed-slimy-dry tongue.

"No. This blade is merely a product of-of-" the creature trailed off, confusion ringing in the discordant voice. "I no longer remember his name. Any of their names. How long has it been since I last remembered?" The creature sounded morose. The cacophony of sounds that made up its voice were quiet, almost mournful. "It doesn't matter. That blade is only a minor product of my…compatriots' magics. It cannot harm me."

"Mhmm. Well, that's too bad," Tala said, feeling confused as he re-sheathed the sword. Addled or not, his brain was going through a lot of trouble to make this hallucination seem real. If it was trying to tell him something, he was at a complete loss as to what. At least it was more entertaining than the endless trees and general suckage that the Jungle had been so far. Maybe that's really all his brain was trying to do?

"Indeed. But it has been some time since I saw the Null wielder, and you are the first he has sent to me. I did not know if he was even still alive. He gave you no clues as to why he sent you?"

"I don't even know if he actually had a plan when he threw me off the bridge. He's annoying like that. Maybe he wants me to prove myself? Survive the Jungle all alone? 'Course, I don't think Serala was part of whatever he was thinking, really. But whatever. Honestly, I don't know. And I kind of don't really care. I'm just trying to survive this Godsdamned place, and I'm wasting my time standing here talking to a Godsdamned hallucination. I need to keep moving."

Finally, shaking himself out of the insane conversation he was having with his own mind, Tala returned to tying the vines of the sled around his waist, trying to ignore the illusory creature as it watched him silently.

"You should turn west," it eventually said.

Tala huffed. "Follow the Split to Morungil. That's what I'm supposed to do. Go south. Why in all the Hells would I go west instead?"

"Because you will not survive to reach the city. It is too far for you in your condition. If you go west, you will find those who can help you and your friend. That is your only chance of survival."

Tala gave the hallucination a suspicious look. Although, maybe this was the point of this whole little… experience. He knew he wouldn't make it to Morungil as he was. He wasn't sure what was to the west, but maybe he was subconsciously remembering something? A town or village he had forgotten hearing about and his fevered, intoxicated brain was using this hallucination to try and get him there? One last desperate act of survival?

"You know what? Sure. Why not?"

"Good. I shall summon a creature to guide you. Follow it, and it will lead you to help. And I will leave you with a small imprint of my power, so that you will be safe from any creature that would wish to do you any more harm."

"Er, right. Okay. Thanks, I guess?" The conversation was getting weird again. Had his brain finally exhausted its ability to be somewhat functional and was returning to the madness of before?

A small monkey-like creature, with red fur and a long tail, came bounding into the small clearing, coming to a stop next to the hallucination. Tala blinked. This new creature seemed rather normal, especially compared to the walking chaos he had been conversing with. He felt a bad headache coming on.

"Follow the little one. He will not lead you wrong." Tala just nodded dumbly. "And remember this, for I do not believe he would send you to me for nothing. Perhaps you can do what he could not with it: Find the legacy of Tora, the once greatest city in the world. It was destroyed in our birth, and I long believed that nothing remained. The existence of a Null wielder in this world again makes me think I was mistaken. If there is any hope of fixing what they did, it would come from Tora's remains."

Tala stared blankly at the creature, who was looking him deep in the eyes, as much as it could while constantly changing in shape and size and number. "Okay. I'll remember that. Sure. Why not? 'Cause that made *all* the sense. I've never heard of Tora, though." Actually, the name was ringing a faint bell in Tala's mind. He had no idea where from, but he wasn't surprised. This was all a hallucination, after all; it must be a name he had heard *somewhere*. Although it wasn't a city. He had studied maps of the world and knew every city that existed outside of Wind and the Bodylands (and Water, he supposed, now that he knew they still existed somewhere). He had never heard of any place belonging to those lands though, of that he was completely positive, so this "message" was probably just some more nonsense that his brain had conjured up.

"I doubt you would have. My brethren would have endeavored to destroy all traces of it, determined as they are to erase the existence of Before from the memory of the world. I would tell you more if I could, but it has been so long. I remember almost nothing of Before. I will leave you now, to find aid in the west. I hope you discover the reason the Null wielder sent you to me, and that you can use what little I have told you. Good luck."

The creature turned away and vanished back into the darkness of the Jungle. Tala watched it go, bemused. "Well," he said to himself. "That was a thing." The little red monkey creature was still there, though, staring at him with big eyes. "Either you're a hallucination too, or I'm completely insane. Although, I guess one would kind of mean the other, so whatever. Lead the way, little guy!"

The monkey-thing bounded off into the trees, pausing on a branch to look back at Tala. With a sigh, Tala started moving, following an imaginary monkey in the completely wrong direction. He missed his old life.

After a few hours of following the monkey through the dense jungle, Tala had been really questioning the wisdom of his decision. Or he would have been, if he had been capable of such thoughts by that point. He was so tired by then that his entire world had collapsed down to one single concept: follow the monkey. If the monkey didn't have such vibrantly red fur, which starkly stood out against the greens and browns of the rest of their surroundings, he wouldn't have even been able to do that much, not with how dim his vision had grown. So, when the monkey stopped moving, and began to alternate staring at Tala and the way forward, before rushing back into the depths of the jungle faster than he ever could have hoped to follow, Tala thought it was the end for him.

He had been only vaguely aware of the sounds drifting

around him, most definitely not the normal noises he had grown used to since venturing into the Jungle. Simply more falsehoods conjured up by his poisoned mind, he had believed. Without even trying to look at what the monkey had been showing him, Tala took a step forward, tripped, and fell to the ground. Lacking the strength to do anything, Tala simply lay there, finally letting go of his grip on consciousness. He had given all he had, more than he knew he could, and he was spent.

CHAPTER 28

Tala was quite surprised when he woke up and felt… perfectly fine. Better, in fact, than he had felt since being thrown off the bridge. His eyes snapped open, and he blinked in the darkness, trying to understand what he was seeing and, more importantly, what he was *feeling*. He knew he shouldn't be feeling anything remotely near okay. The last few… days? Weeks? He wasn't sure, but they had been hell. His memories were fuzzy, and strange, entirely nonsensical for the most part, but full of misery. So how, exactly, did he go from that to lying on his back in what could only be a bed (there was something soft beneath his head and his whole body was tucked under some sort of warm covering), staring up at what appeared to be the top of a large tent?

Looking around, he could make out the shapes of a few other small beds also in the tent, sitting very low to the ground. There didn't seem to be much else. There was a small bit of light coming from what must be the entrance flap, though it was closed. And he could faintly hear various other sounds coming from outside, including people's voices. He wasn't restrained or anything. Had he been rescued, somehow? Was Serala okay? She wasn't in the tent with him!

Pushing the blankets off himself, Tala carefully sat up, sliding his feet until they were firmly on the ground. He seemed to be moving perfectly fine, no aches or sudden pains flaring up. He checked his left arm over, feeling oddly disoriented at it seeming perfectly normal. Hadn't it been all but destroyed? He had (when he was capable of thinking clearly enough) been concerned about even being able to *keep* it, given the state it was in. Was that a hallucination too? Because it seemed like his arm was perfectly fine, without even any scars! He could make a fist and clench it tight with no trouble whatsoever!

Oh! He had missed it when lying down, but on the ground next to the bed was his pack, along with a small pile of what were probably clothes beside it. Slowly standing up, on alert for any negative responses from his body, Tala briefly stretched his muscles before donning the clothes that had been left for him: a simple tunic and breeches, in decent condition. His weapons were gone, though, and Tala felt a bout of anxiety shoot through him. He probably wasn't in any danger, given that wherever he was, someone had cared for him and left him unsecured and unattended. But his weapons, the sword especially, had become a source of comfort for him.

He eyed the tent's exit, taking a deep breath to steel himself. Physically, he seemed fine, so waiting around in the tent wouldn't help him any. But there was no point being reckless about things, so Tala crept over to the heavy flap covering the opening and, slowly, moved it aside as little as he could, peeking with one eye through the tiny slit he opened.

Well, he was definitely in a camp of some sort! There were lots of other tents, in a surprising variety of colors, arranged in two halves all around an open stretch of ground. He couldn't see very much, as his tent seemed to be tucked away in a row further back from the open stretch, but he still had a direct line of sight to it, between a few other tents in front of his. The noises were a lot louder now that the flap was opened, even if barely, the sounds of talking and children's laughter. That was a good sign. There wouldn't be laughing children if he was somewhere dangerous. Not seeing anybody nearby, Tala cautiously stepped out of the tent, taking in everything he could.

To his mild surprise, it seemed like he was still in the Jungle, as in all directions he could see the giant, dense trees stretching out into the distance. Yet there didn't seem to be any trees within the area of tents. The ground under him, in fact, was nothing more than simple grass and mud, the type created by lots of people walking around on it. A large clearing, then, in the depths of the Jungle. Perhaps he had stumbled, in his delirious state, into some small town or village? While the Jungle only had one proper city inside of it—the capital of Morungil—there were plenty of smaller settlements scattered throughout it. Nobody knew how many there were, or even where most of them were, as few dared to step off the Jungle Road and fewer still survived.

He remembered something about a monkey? With red fur? Leading him to... safety? Had that been real? He had been told to follow the monkey by... something. Something he had thought was a hallucination even while in the depths of delirium. He shook his head. He could deal with whatever *that* all was later, when he had time to think on it all instead of figuring out just where he was.

Moving slowly forward, walking between tents towards the main thoroughfare, Tala continued looking around. Whatever settlement he was in was surrounded by a tall wooden barrier, a palisade of sharpened tree trunks. Some form of barrier to protect people from the dangers of the Jungle only made sense, even if he questioned how effective such a wall would be against any of the more dangerous elements of the Jungle.

Tala kept creeping closer to the center, trying to not draw attention to himself as he stopped by the last row of tents, staying right behind the corner of one as he peered out at the village. It was nothing like any settlement he had ever seen before! Not only because it was made up entirely of tents of various designs and materials (and colors! It was easily as colorful as Fiahren!) but because—even on what he assumed was their equivalent to a main road—he couldn't tell what any of the tents were for! None were obviously a shop, or apothecary, or tavern, or anything! Although there must be a blacksmith somewhere, because Tala could hear the distinct ringing of metal.

"So, what do you think of our little home?" a voice questioned from behind, making Tala jump and spin around, fumbling for a sword that wasn't there. The woman gave Tala a kind smile, a hint of laughter in her eyes. Tala surveyed her quickly, checking for weapons or any other signs of danger, as he had been trained to do. She was unarmed, as far as he could tell, and he felt himself relax. She was wearing light clothing, mostly soft greens and browns, a long skirt and simple top that covered her skin but was so thin he almost felt like he could see through it. Probably could if they were of different colors. He couldn't tell her age; her skin was tan and smooth and soft, but she might be a few years older than him. A decade at most, maybe. And she had vibrantly red hair that was braided in a strange design behind her neck. She was absolutely gorgeous, in Tala's opinion, but having spent so much time around Serala and Alina (and Caida especially) had rather desensitized him to the nerves he would likely otherwise be feeling in her presence.

"I-I don't know. Yet. I just woke up. It's… different."

"It is that." She hummed, and her voice flowed like soothing honey, making Tala feel oddly calm. "Even more so for one such as yourself, I imagine."

Tala blinked at her, unsure of what she meant. The woman merely smiled serenely back at him, waiting for him to respond.

"I guess…?" He faltered, but the woman didn't move, continuing to softly smile. "I'm-Lito. By the way." He hadn't meant to use his friend's name, but it was the first one that had popped into his head. Using his own name was danger-ous when the whole world wanted his head. Lito's name was entirely unknown, at least to his knowledge, and was fairly common at that, at least in Light country. Even in Fire, Tala itself was rather unique, to say nothing of his full name.

The woman rose an eyebrow. "If that is what you wish to be called."

Tala blinked again. *What?*

"Tell me, Lito," he swore he could hear a note of amusement in how she said the name, "how did you find yourself arriving at our doorstep? Especially in such a horrible condition?"

"I, uh, I don't really know, to be honest. It's all kind of a…blur. But S-my friend? What about my friend? I had someone with me, a girl. She was unconscious! Where is she?"

The woman gave him a calculating look. "Your friend will be okay. She is still recovering. Her condition was unusual, though. Even some of our most skilled weren't certain what had happened to her. Perhaps you could enlighten us?"

"Well, I'm not sure how much I can tell you, really. Like I said, a lot of the past few-well, a lot of it's kind of a blur. I'm not sure about a lot of it, really."

The woman gave him an amused look. "I'm not surprised. Your condition was atrocious when we found you. We were surprised you were still alive."

"Yeah, so am I. Do you… know what all was wrong with me, by chance? I thought, well, I'm not sure what was real and what wasn't, to be honest."

"That would be because of the Somiocanic venom. You had quite a lot of it in your system."

"Oh! I've heard of that! Gods! I had no idea! No wonder I was so messed up!"

"Oh? I was under the impression that Somic was practically unknown outside of the Jungle."

Crap. He had heard of Somiocanic venom at the Institute. He had to be more careful about letting his disguise slip. Even if they didn't know exactly *who* he was, a lost Researcher was worth a lot.

"I just heard about it in passing, when I was at the border. I was told to avoid it. Guess I kind of… didn't."

The woman merely hummed in response, sounding amused.

"So where am I, exactly? And who are you?"

She smiled; a grin chock-full of mischief. "My name is Gwyar. And this is the Carnival of Blood."

CHAPTER 29

Tala huffed a laugh, but faltered as her face didn't change. She was serious, albeit amused. "You're joking, right? That's a myth. It can't be real."

"Is it? Why can it not be real?" she asked.

"Well, none of the Churches would allow it to exist, would they? A bunch of Body mages running around, all together like that? How would that even work?"

"By being thought of as a myth, of course." She chuckled. "Who would hear of such a place and not think it must be but a story? But why couldn't it exist? What else would become of Body mages who were free of slavery?"

"Die? Or join the Dissidents?"

"Many do. But why could there not be a third option? Few ever wish to die, but not all want to fight, either. Especially for a cause that is so widely misunderstood, or believed futile. Is it so hard to believe that those who wished for neither option would find an alternative for themselves? A way to live, free, without having to fight?"

"I suppose so." It made sense that, over millennia, escaped

Body slaves would have come together and found a way to live. And he could understand not wanting to join the Dissidents in their eternal struggle. He wouldn't have chosen to do so himself if he had had any real alternative.

"So, this is really it then? The Carnival of Blood?" he asked skeptically. The town of tents he was in was nothing like the stories of the Carnival he had heard: a place of unholy monsters and depraved acts, the epitome of the unfettered skills of Body mages left to run rampant, free to explore the limits of their abilities without care for law or morality. Aside from the town being made entirely out of large tents, it seemed like a rather normal, peaceful place.

"Aye, 'tis indeed. 'Tis not what you were expecting?"

"It doesn't really fit any of the stories," he said bluntly.

"Nay, it does not. 'Tis why we encourage those stories to spread. Our greatest protection is that few believe we exist. Even if they should happen to find themselves in our midst, why would they ever believe our little troupe are the same monsters they have heard about? There is no reason to ever think it, so long as they don't witness our magics."

"Then why did you tell me who you are? I haven't seen you do anything. Hells, you're the only person I've even spoken to so far." Gwyar gave him another mischievous smile as she stepped out onto the wide, open path that made up the main road of the town, forcing Tala to hurry to stay beside her. They barely garnered a glance from the people who could now see them.

"That is because I already know you are no enemy to us, Tala'Keahi."

Tala stumbled, surprised at the unexpected use of his real name. How did she know? The Carnival's existence, its people's very lives as free folk, were crimes as far as the Churches were concerned. It made sense that they didn't consider him a threat, given his relationship to the Churches. That didn't answer how she knew who he was.

He rushed to catch up to her again, Gwyar having not slowed her pace when he fell behind. "How?" he asked, resignedly, not needing to say more for her to know what he was asking.

"Even we have heard of you, oh great Blessed Killer. But regardless, a friend of yours has been waiting for your arrival, expecting you would end up here. Although how he knew, he has refused to say."

"A friend? Who?" Was Vail there? Did he know about the Carnival? It wouldn't have surprised him. But how could he have known Tala would end up there? It wasn't even in the same direction he had been going until he had decided to follow what he had (increasingly less now) believed to be a hallucination. But who else could it be?

"You'll see. He's just in here." Gwyar led him into a large, open tent, with rows of tables and benches arranged inside it, where many groups of people sat eating and talking. Tala scanned the tables, looking for a familiar face, and stiffened in surprise when he caught one. Sitting by himself off in a corner, as far from the rest of the occupants as he could be, Osson bent over a bowl, taking a bite of a hunk of bread that he had dipped into it.

Tala turned to Gwyar, incredulously. Why would Osson,

of all people, be waiting for him? How was the Bone Merc even there? Tala mentally revoked that last question. Of course, the *Bone Merc* would know about the Carnival of *Blood*. It was a safe haven for people like him! Tala was starting to think that Gazin had been lying when he said it was a myth, instead of simply not knowing about it.

"He arrived a few days ago. He said that you might show up, so he would wait. He seemed annoyed that you actually did, but relieved that the girl was alive, which is unusual for him."

There was a *lot* to unpack in that statement. Not least of which was that Gwyar apparently knew Osson well enough to know what unusual behavior for him was. Once again, a headache formed at the absurdity that was his life.

"The first time I met him was because he kidnapped me," he said bluntly, earning a raised eyebrow from Gwyar. "He isn't going to try that again, right?"

She chuckled. "I do not believe that is his intent, no."

"If he does, is there any chance of you lot stopping him?"

"Nay. Even were we willing to risk it, I doubt we would succeed."

"Really? Don't you outnumber him by, like, a lot?"

"Numbers mean little against someone like him. Even for our kind."

Right. Okay. Apparently, a whole town (or whatever the Carnival was considered) of Body mages didn't like their chances against the Bone Merc. How could one lone Bone wielder be so much more dangerous than a whole group of other Bone wielders, along with Blood and Flesh wielders besides? The man was considered the most dangerous person in the world, but *still!* Tala missed the days when life made sense.

He took a deep breath, trying to erase the irritation he felt percolating in his whole body. He was only mildly successful. With an annoyed huff, he strode towards Osson, deciding to just get it—whatever exactly *it* was—out of the way. He walked up to the table, standing across from Osson, who didn't look up or show any other awareness of him.

"Well, hi, Osson! Fancy seeing you-"

Osson's hand whipped up, pointing straight at his face, unnervingly still. The man didn't even bother to raise his head as he spoke. "No. I've heard you talk enough for a lifetime. Be silent or leave."

Tala huffed. *How rude!*

CHAPTER 30

Tala sat down at the table, fully conscious of how Osson tensed at the action. He didn't really feel any sympathy for the man who had kidnapped him. Plus, he wanted answers, and Osson was the most likely person to have any until he reunited with Vail.

"You've heard me talk for, like, an hour. And if you hadn't kidnapped me, we never even would have met. So, really, it's your own fault. Deal with it."

Finally, Osson raised his head, just enough to glare at him. "My way of dealing with annoyances is to kill them."

"Eh, maybe. But you won't kill me. You wouldn't have waited around here for days if you were going to do that. So why are you here?"

"Maybe I decided to take you to Mist. That was my original plan."

"Yeah, but I doubt it. Gwyar said you were waiting for me but seemed annoyed I showed up. So, you're here for me, but not for your own reasons. So, what are you doing here? Did Vail send you to meet us?" Tala had a feeling few people could get away with making the Bone Merc's eye twitch like that. At least not with all their limbs still attached.

"If you can figure all that out on your own, you don't need me to answer. So just do that quietly in your own head."

"Nuh-uh. There's plenty I don't know and can't figure out. So, if you want me to stop annoying you, it'd be easiest for us both if you just answered my questions. Like, did you know that Vail *threw me off of the Godsdamned bridge?*"

Osson closed his eyes, and Tala could practically feel the irritation pouring out of the man.

"Yes. I saw that," he growled.

"Okay. Do you know why?"

"Kid, what makes you think I know why that mad bastard does anything? I don't believe anybody understands what he's thinking. Hells, I'm pretty sure he doesn't know half the time!"

"Mmm. Fair," Tala conceded. "Well, what about this place? How did you know to come here? Is everybody out searching the Jungle for us and you came here? Or did he send you specifically to meet us?"

"He sent me here specifically," Osson bit out, sounding like the words physically pained him. "Don't ask me how he knew. My turn for a question. This place is a secret and never stays in one place for long. How did you happen to just stumble across it while half dead and out of your mind?"

Tala faltered at that. His memories since entering the Jungle were a jumbled mess of what was real and what were hallucinations. "I'm not entirely sure. I-I saw… something, which told me to come here. Well, it told me to follow this monkey-thing, and that led me here. Honestly, I'm pretty sure they were hallucinations, but the… *thing* said I would find help, and the monkey did lead me here, where there was help, so… I don't know."

Osson was giving him a blank look. Somehow still portraying irritated despite the complete lack of expression. Tala was actually kind of impressed.

"A *thing*," he stressed the word sardonically, "that you imagined, told you to follow a monkey—that you also imagined—to what is possibly the only place in the Jungle that could have saved you?"

"Well… yes?" Tala knew how it sounded, but it had *worked*! Somehow! "I was out of my mind, to be fair."

"Mhmm." Osson seemed thoroughly unimpressed. "And what, pray tell, exactly was this… *thing* that told you to come here?"

"I don't know. Like I said, I was out of my mind! It was a hallucination! A really weird one. It was an animal, but, like… *every* animal, you know? It was changing constantly. It would have wings, then no wings, and four feet, then two feet, then no feet, then eight feet, or like two eyes, then one eye, then compound eyes, then eight eyes. Definitely the weirdest thing I saw, including when I thought my body was made of pudding."

Osson was staring at him with a weird expression, one Tala wasn't sure how to read. It was… shock? Maybe? Mixed with the usual irritation and aggravation that Osson always seemed to be feeling? Eventually Osson sighed, a slow, defeated sound, and slumped down, closing his eyes again.

"Of course you did," he said, in little more than a whisper.

Tala wasn't sure Osson was even still talking to him anymore. "Why wouldn't you? Alright, okay, fine! Did this… *thing*," he said the word oddly, no longer sounding sardonic, "say anything else to you? Give you the deep secrets of life, perhaps?"

"No? I mean, it said some other things, but they didn't make much sense. An ancient city, I think? It wasn't one I've ever heard of, though, so I think it was just my brain being confused. It also said something about how I smelled like 'him,' whoever 'he' is. I thought it might have meant Vail, since he gave me those socks and told me to make sure they could be smelled, but it didn't know his name, so I don't know. Honestly, the whole thing was just weird. I mean, my whole time out there was—my brain was practically melting—but yeah, that was probably the weirdest. Probably because I actually felt coherent, more or less, at the time, so it seemed… realer than a lot of the other stuff. I guess."

Osson was back to staring at him blankly. "Socks?" he questioned, after far too long of utter silence.

"Huh? Oh, yeah, Vail gave me a pair of his dirty socks before he pushed me off the bridge, told me to keep them out so they could be smelled. Not really sure what that was about. Thought it might deter predators and the like from attacking me, but that sure as shit didn't happen. Do you know?"

Osson was rubbing his temples. "Before I met that bastard, I thought I couldn't get headaches. It shouldn't be physically possible, but somehow, he does it anyway. I shouldn't be surprised, I really shouldn't, because when did he ever care about things like 'possible' and 'reason' and 'not being the most

Godsdamned annoying moron in the entire Godsdamned world?' He doesn't!"

Tala eyed Osson in concern. He wouldn't claim to know the man all that well—or at all, really—but the way he was muttering to himself didn't sound very healthy. Although, if anyone could give a person like the Bone Merc a headache, he supposed it would be Vail.

"Okay, kid? Save your questions for Vail. When you get back to him, you can ask him about-about everything. He may even answer you. Who knows! But I don't want anything to do with any of this, okay?"

"You know something?" Tala frowned. What was there for him to know and not want to say? Tala had still been—mostly—convinced that what he had seen had been nothing more than a mixture of hallucinations and luck, but that didn't make sense with how Osson was acting.

"I don't. Now shut up and leave me alone."

"Yes, you do. Why else would you tell me to tell Vail about something I hallucinated? Why would he have answers? Osson, what's going on? What was that thing I saw? How could it be real?"

"By The Three! How are you still so Godsdamned annoying? I don't have any answers for you! I've already been dragged into Vail's bullshit far more than I ever wanted to be! Now shut up and leave me alone!"

Tala huffed but stayed silent, annoyed by Osson's refusal to cooperate. He just wanted some answers! What was so difficult about that? Osson didn't have to do anything but talk! Tala sat there in silence, frowning at Osson as the man finished his stew. Eventually, he spoke again, taking a sadistic pleasure in the pained groan Osson made when he did so.

"Why are you here then? If you don't want anything to do with us, why'd you come here to get me?"

"Gods! It's none of your business! I'm here, and when Serala awakens, I'm going to take you both to Vail in Morungil, and then I'm leaving! Okay? Hopefully to never see you again! So, until she's up, just stay the Hells away from me, okay?" Osson stood and stormed out of the pavilion, leaving Tala sitting alone.

Eventually, he too rose and left, rejoining Gwyar, who had been speaking to a couple of people outside. He waited while she finished her conversation, turning to him after.

"Well. 'Tis not often I see that man get so worked up. Nice talk?" she asked with a chuckle.

"Yeah, I guess you could say that. He's not really a nice person, is he?"

Gwyar's brows rose. "Nay, he isn't. I doubt there are many who would say otherwise. Did you at least find out why he came here for you?"

"Yeah. He's going to take us to Morungil, once Serala awakens, to meet back up with our friends."

"Truly?" she asked, sounding surprised. "And what was offered that got *him*, of all people, to agree to escort you?"

"I have no idea." Tala shook his head. "He wouldn't tell me either."

"Well, there are few you would be safer with when passing through the wilds of the Jungle. 'Tis a dangerous place. You must have good friends indeed for them to have hired him."

"Yeah, something like that," Tala replied, trying—and failing—to not think about being thrown off the bridge. "How is Serala doing? Do you have any idea when she might wake?"

"Nay. Her injuries were severe. Such… *intense* damage from a Blessed is difficult even for our kind to heal. In addition to the other… oddities we found with her condition. Are you certain you don't know what happened to her?"

"No, I really don't." He tried to sound sincere, feeling a twinge of guilt in his gut at lying to her. "What oddities are you talking about?"

"For taking such a direct blow from a Blessed, a Lightning one at that, her injuries are inconsistent. 'Tis as though someone tried to heal her already, using magic. But 'twas not Body magics that were used. In fact, we don't recognize the type of magic lingering in her system at all, nor how it worked. It has made the task of healing her properly even more difficult than it already was, although she would certainly have been long dead without it. There were also traces of such magic within you, though much fainter."

"Oh. Well, that's a… that's a thing. Then. I guess." As kind as Gwyar had been so far, and as grateful as he was to her and the Carnival for everything they had done for him and Serala, Tala wasn't going to betray Wade's trust in him. Or reveal anything about Water's continued existence. He still hadn't quite finished processing that fact himself. Not with how the man had saved both their lives, violating strict and ancient orders to do so.

"Indeed," Gwyar said, giving him a strange look. He had a feeling she didn't entirely believe his professed ignorance.

"And how did you keep her alive? She was heavily malnourished and dehydrated, but the latter should have killed her many days ago."

"Oh." Tala blushed and turned away from her, wishing he could keep that to himself. Unlike Wade's existence, he didn't really have a good enough reason to justify keeping it a secret from Gwyar. Delaying as best he could by looking at the Carnival, Tala couldn't help but admire how incredibly peaceful it seemed, despite its location. He could hear the sounds of people working and laughing, and a group of children ran gleefully by without giving him a second thought. He wondered what it would have been like to grow up in such a place, so removed from the Churches.

Resolutely watching the Carnival to avoid looking at Gwyar, Tala explained that he "just happened to have, just in case" some dissolvable water capsules, and the method with which he had used them.

"Ingenious!" Gwyar breathed, truly sounding impressed. "I wasn't aware that there were many outside of our kind who knew the body well enough to know such a method would work!"

"I don't think there are, really. I'm a-I was a Researcher at the Fire Institute. I learned a lot about the human body and how it works in my training. Didn't really think I'd ever need to know a lot of it back then. Glad I paid attention now."

"Ah, that explains much. Even here we've heard about your Institute of Fire. In fact, you aren't the first Researcher who has graced our little Carnival."

"Really?" Tala asked, shocked. "Who else has been here? When?"

"Some years ago, I do not know precisely how long. His name was Admani. We quite enjoyed having him. I'm glad to see he kept his promise to keep our existence a secret."

"Admani? Really? That makes sense. He's one of the few who ever actually got permission to leave Fiahren. I've heard people talk about his journals, and weird references he made when talking about his time in the Jungle. Making friends and such. Nobody was ever quite sure what he had been talking about."

"You speak of him as though he is dead. 'Twasn't that long ago he was here, unless I've truly lost track of time. What happened to him?"

"Nobody knows. He just vanished one day. The investigations into it never got anywhere as far as I know."

"How odd. But somehow, that doesn't surprise me. He was a strange man, and I can certainly see him vanishing into the night in search of some grand secret without telling anyone."

"Yeah, a lot of my teachers said the same thing. The Church was angry as all hells about it."

"Mm. I can imagine. I've heard the Church of Fire can be quite jealous over their Researchers."

"They are. Hey, can I get some food somewhere? I've got money for it."

Gwyar laughed. "Indeed, you can satiate your hunger at the next tent over. And don't worry about money. We don't bother with it much when we're on our own. We are perfectly happy to feed you for free."

"Oh, great! Thanks!" Tala said happily as he started walking to the next tent, Gwyar beside him. "But what do you mean when you're on your own?"

"Well, we are a carnival! We don't live here year-round! There are numerous towns and villages scattered throughout the Jungle, and we visit many of them! They pay for entertainment, and we return the money in exchange for goods or the occasional service that we cannot perform ourselves. 'Tis quite lucky for you we happened to be at this campground, in fact!" She sounded merry about it, but Tala noticed the strange look she gave him as she spoke of luck. As they entered a tent smelling deliciously of hot foods, Tala thought it might be worth something to ask her about the strange creature that he may *not* have hallucinated.

CHAPTER 31

For all he had believed—like most of the world—the Carnival of Blood was a myth, Tala still found himself slightly off-kilter at how different the Carnival was now that he knew it was real. He had seen no evidence of grotesque monsters or evil deeds. In fact, the people who made up the Carnival, in his experience so far, were almost disappointingly normal. Despite the majority of them being Body Descendants, generally feared and reviled throughout the world, they were just people. Even if Tala still felt an instinctive shock whenever he saw someone casually perform Body magic: a hand suddenly growing a thick layer of bone or hardened flesh as someone went to grab something hot, or a small squirt of blood that quickly receded as a splinter was pushed out of a body. They were mostly small, subtle, casual uses of their wielder's magics, in a way that Tala could well believe no outsider had ever realized the true nature of the Carnival.

Although, there weren't only Body Descendants living there. It was a safe haven for any person who wished to live a life of peace, away from the tyranny of the Churches. Along with many regular, unpowered people, the Carnival consisted of Descendants of all different types. There were wielders of almost every other God, in fact, even Lava wielders (who Tala had never seen before) from the far north of the world, to a pair of twin Ice wielders from the far south. The only elemental wielders missing from the Carnival, in fact, were Wind and Water, neither of which surprised Tala in the least. The Wind Raids had only ever affected the eastern coast. None ever delved far enough to even see the Jungle. And even the mythical Carnival of Blood didn't know what had happened to Water, or that they still existed in the world. Seeing wielders of so many different magics all in one place, and so casually using them for everyday tasks from fun to work, was a surreal experience for Tala. There were even some Awakened of a few different Gods!

Even if the Carnival were ever discovered, Tala wasn't sure just how the Churches would deal with it! With Descendants of seventeen different elements all living and working together, to say nothing of the large number of Body Descendants who were the most feared of them all, the Carnival could boast a military power unlike anything Tala had ever imagined! If it weren't for the existence of the Blessed, the Carnival could probably conquer the world (though Tala had no idea how the Gods might react if such a unified force of diverse magics ever actually tried to do so).

Oh, how Gwyar had laughed at that thought when Tala had relayed it to her! The Blood wielder was apparently the leader of the Carnival—although she rarely had to do much in that role—and had taken it upon herself to act as Tala's personal guide and host during his time there. Although Tala had a niggling feeling she was simply keeping an eye on him as much as being a gracious host. She had explained to him in no uncertain terms that the Carnival was a place for peaceful living, and that was it. Anybody who wished to leave was free to do so, but few did. Those who did choose to leave were most often children who had grown up in the Carnival, and upon becoming adults, wanted to experience the wider world. Some simply left to adventure and see the world, while many joined the Dissidents to fight against the injustice and tyranny of the Churches. Regardless of their reasoning, all left with the understanding that they were to never speak to an outsider about the Carnival's existence.

It turned out that there were a few outsiders who did know about them, mostly Dissident leaders. Osson was also counted as an outsider in the know, but Gwyar had refused to elaborate on why. Osson himself, when Tala managed to find the man, had been quite unwilling to explain either.

The Dissidents would accept anyone from the Carnival who wished to join the fight, and in turn the Dissidents would sometimes bring them people who wished for the life of the Carnival, free from the fighting and danger of the world. Not all the Dissidents who knew about the Carnival were happy with the agreement, however. Gazin, who apparently not only knew of the Carnival, but knew it well, was a long-time detractor of their agreement. He strongly believed the Carnival should be fighting alongside the Dissidents instead of hiding away, adding their immense power to the cause. Tala quickly learned that Gazin and the Carnival held a mutual contempt for each other, an alleged fact that surprised Tala about the affable man who had treated him so well.

In truth, if Tala wasn't *the* Tala, Blessed Killer and world's most wanted man, he wouldn't have minded staying at the Carnival himself. He had never really thought about what a life free of the Gods would be like, having never even considered such a thing as possible before. For all that he had been a loyal servant of the Gods, the idea of being free from them had become incredibly appealing. Neither the Plant nor Beast Churches bothered the Carnival. Gwyar was certain neither had any idea about the Carnival's true nature, and the Carnival wasn't wealthy enough to bother taxing (as far as the Churches were aware). They were as free from the Gods as anyone could get.

Even criminals who lived outside of society—bandits and the like—spent their short lives in fear of being caught by the Churches. And even the Dissident towns like Dritenik still had to present themselves as loyal: paying tithes and taxes, supplying troops and goods, and whatever else the relevant church demanded of them. Had Tala been anyone else, he probably would have decided to stay with the Carnival—Vail, Osson, and the rest of the Dissidents be damned!

But even the Carnival couldn't truly protect him forever. Eventually the Plant and Beast Churches would learn, if they didn't already know, that he was in the Jungle, and would send people to find him or his body. No, he would have to leave sooner or later.

And so, Tala spent his days waiting for Serala to recover, enjoying what time he had with the Carnival. He was able to relax in a way that had eluded him, even in Dritenik. If it wasn't for his concern over the still-comatose Serala, he might have considered it heaven. And while the Carnival had few books—or highly learned people like at the Institute—he still learned quite a bit about the world simply from talking to everybody he could. The Jungle, for all its danger, wasn't that difficult a place to live for those who knew how.

When Gwyar had first told him the Carnival traveled to different settlements in the Jungle, he had assumed she meant there were a couple large ones that had managed to eke out survival long enough to become, while maybe not cities, large enough to be safe havens. It turned out that there were well over a hundred little towns and villages scattered throughout, and very few were anywhere close to being large enough to be considered a city. Most ranged from a few dozen to a few hundred people living in them and—as long as they were careful—they usually managed fine. Although Gwyar had known a few which had been destroyed by the Jungle after growing complacent or arrogant in their assumed safety. The Carnival itself had been around for a few thousand years, and in that time, they had learned how to survive, not only *in* the Jungle, but constantly moving around in it, a much more difficult feat, according to Gwyar. But with a healthy amount of both respect and fear towards the place, it was doable.

Although there were some places, deep in the Jungle, that even the Carnival didn't dare tread. Places that, according to Gwyar and some of the others that Tala spoke to, were entirely uninhabitable to humans, even Descendants. While most of the things Tala heard about the Jungle meshed with stories he had heard outside of it, these "forbidden" places were unlike any of the stories he had heard before. The people of the Carnival spoke of giant monsters, both regular animals of immense size and other large creatures that had no comparison to anything else they knew. They told him of giant spider nests, whose webs could ensnare even the largest person and whose venom could kill in seconds, working so fast that not even Blood wielders could save themselves. At least, not Unawakened Descendants, which was all there were of Body wielders at the Carnival. They told tales of trees that moved and *hunted*, similar to but far worse than the tales he had already heard.

Tala already thought that it was a miracle he had survived alone so far, especially with Serala in tow, but hearing the stories of horrors in the deep places of the Jungle gave him a whole new degree of nightmares when he went to sleep. If Tala had his say, he would never return to the Jungle again once he finally left the cursed place. Even the allure of the Carnival might not be enough to ever bring him back. Although, he could admit, it was tempting: a place free of the Gods and the Churches was *extraordinarily* appealing.

CHAPTER 32

Four days after Tala awoke at the Carnival, he was allowed to see Serala. Between the severity of her injuries and the difficulties in healing wounds caused by a Blessed (along with the complications of the unknown Water magic in her and anything else that had infected her while in the Jungle) the Carnival's healers had taken that long to bring her to what they considered a "healthy" state. She was still unconscious, but they assured Tala it was more akin to a deep sleep for her to recover than the coma she had been in before. By their estimates, she should awaken within a few hours, so Tala had elected to sit in her tent and wait.

A pained groan sounded in the small tent, making Tala's head whip up to the bed. His mind was yanked out of its musings and into the present, focused solely on Serala. The girl's face was scrunched, eyes tightly shut, as she made another pained moan and began stirring. She stretched her arms out to the sides, but her left hand caught in the thin blankets that draped her. Her eyes shot open, and she attempted to sit up, falling back with another pained sound before making it even halfway. Her eyes barely skimmed the tent before locking firmly onto Tala's, and she relaxed even as he saw a multitude of questions form in her eyes.

"What… happened?" she forced out before he could speak, her voice harsh and rough.

"It's okay! You're okay. Everyone's okay," he rushed to reassure her. He had never spent much time in the medical wing at the Institute, beyond what was necessitated by his apprentice training, and couldn't recall how he was supposed to handle a person waking up after a traumatic injury. Although he had a feeling that acting gentle and calming wouldn't help much with Serala.

"What. Happened?" Speaking must have been agony, but Tala wasn't surprised that wasn't stopping her.

"First, have some water. Then I'll tell you everything." He grabbed the skin full of boiled water that had been left beside her bed and opened it, offering to help her drink. She glared at him for a moment before her thirst took over. Instead of accepting his help, she reached for the skin, despite how much effort it was clearly taking her to do so. He let her take it, prepared to catch it if her strength failed her. Stubbornly, she brought it to her mouth. Tala drew her ire when he grabbed the skin, stopping her from gulping it down.

"Small sips, slowly. You're still recovering. Take it slow." She glared at him but acquiesced, sipping the water. Tala felt his eye twitch as she continued to slowly, slowly drink the water until the entire skin was empty, staring him straight in the eyes the entire time. She gave the empty skin a quick shake before dropping it, and raised an eyebrow at Tala, clearly expecting him to finally answer her now. He sighed in both relief and exhaustion. It was nice, in a way, to see that she was still the same, despite her injuries.

"Okay. Well… we were in Lynmyr. Do you remember that?" She nodded, face blank. "And we fled the city with O—the Bone Merc after he kidnapped me, right?" A flash of rage, strong but brief, crossed her face, although Tala noticed the new tenseness in her jaw and eyes. Osson had refused to explain any of his history to Tala over the last few days, including whatever was between him, Vail, and Serala. "We got to the bridge, over the Canyon, when we were ambushed by a Lightning Blessed."

Her eyes narrowed, and her brow furrowed. "Denhei," she said, her voice still rough, but not quite as bad as before. Suddenly, her eyes widened, and she scrambled into a half-sitting position, leaning back on the pillows as she threw the blankets off her upper body. Tala threw his head up, staring intently at the ceiling, trying to give the topless girl some privacy. He couldn't resist a few quick peeks down, though. Her hands slowly traced the myriad of scars now emanating across her torso. They were centered just a few inches below her breasts, in a patch of strange, pinkish scarred skin a bit bigger than a large fist, right where Denhei had hit her. Branching out from that patch were jagged lines of similarly pinkish skin, in a pattern that vaguely resembled some fern plants crawling their way across her body. Only a few small lines made their way onto her arms and neck before tapering off. He knew it was the same for her legs, hidden beneath the blankets.

"I should be dead," she stated. Tala wasn't surprised at how matter-of-factly she said that.

"It—it was a close thing. You got lucky. *Really* lucky." His eyes flickered down to her again, to her face this time, and caught her eye as she frowned back at him. Her frown turned into a smirk as she glanced down at her bare torso. To Tala's mix of relief and displeasure, she settled herself back onto the pillows a bit more and pulled the blankets back up, covering herself again.

"Was it Gazin?" she asked, and it took Tala a second to realize what she was talking about.

"No. I-mmm… when-when Denhei hit you, he kind of punched you off the bridge," Tala said awkwardly, looking away from Serala. Her smirk had vanished, and she was frowning again, looking properly confused. "You fell. Into the river. We all thought you were dead."

Her frown persisted. "Where are the others?" Even with her broken voice, Tala could tell she wasn't giving him a choice on answering.

"Ah. Not… here. I was, umm, I kind of fell after you? Into the river?" He hadn't meant for it to sound like a question, but he really didn't want to get into the whole "Vail threw me off the bridge" thing so soon after she had awoken. Especially not when she was still clearly recovering.

"You… fell? Did you… jump? After me?"

"No! No. I just… fell? It wasn't on-I didn't mean to!" Best to just continue on, he thought, distract her before she gets too focused on what he wasn't telling her. "Just… I fell, too, and we both washed up on a bank downriver. You were unconscious and in bad shape. I made a small sled with some wood and vines I found and pulled you into the Jungle on it. We couldn't cross the river, so that was the only option. I carried you through the Jungle until we found help." He really hoped that she would focus on the big picture. He was not looking forward to when she started prying for more details about everything.

"Help? In the Jungle? Where are we?" Well, at least she was willing to gloss over the details for now. He was grateful for that. But how was he going to explain who exactly had saved them and was now caring for them?

"Funny thing, that," he started, having no idea where his mouth was going. "We're at the Carnival of Blood. Turns out it's real. And not evil." Well, he would have liked to break the news a bit more gently, but whatever.

"Oh. Good." Even for Serala, that reaction was very underwhelming. "How'd you find them? Even I don't know how." Tala sighed internally. *Of course* she already knew that the Carnival was real!

"I kind of… didn't? It was an accident. I think. Honestly, I'm still figuring out a lot of it. I ended up getting a lot of Somic—Somiocanic venom—in my system somehow, so my memories are a bit fuzzy after entering the Jungle."

Her eyebrows raised in surprise. "Oh. So, they healed me? Us?"

"Yeah. They've been really nice, too! They just ask that we keep their existence a secret. Which I guess you were already doing."

She nodded absently, confirming for him she had indeed already known about them. "Is there a plan?"

"Yes, actually! The others should be all safe and sound in Morungil, so once you're ready, we'll head there!"

"How do you know?" Tala flinched. He had a feeling this wouldn't go over well.

"Well, apparently, Vail thought we might end up here, so he sent someone to meet us and help us."

"Who?" she asked suspiciously, eyes narrowed.

"Osson. You know, the-the Bone Merc?" He hadn't needed to include the epithet, apparently. Serala's entire body went rigid at the name, hands clenched so hard he was worried she would hurt herself.

"He's here?" she hissed.

"Look, I don't know what happened between you two, but he's here on Vail's order. To help us. I promise!"

She didn't relax. In fact, Tala thought she might be even angrier than before. She slid down into the bed, breaking eye contact with him. "I'm tired. I need to sleep."

Tala hesitated, uncertain. After a minute of silence, in which Serala didn't move nor make noise, he slowly got up and walked to the entrance of the tent. With a last glance at her, lying in the bed and resolutely not looking at him, he slipped out of the tent and back into the Carnival. He had known there was some sort of history between Osson and her but had been (mostly) content to let things stay there, as both were rather secretive people. But he wasn't willing to stay out of it any longer. Not when he would soon be stuck in the depths of the Jungle with the two of them.

CHAPTER 33

"What's your history with Serala?" Tala demanded. He had hunted down Osson determined to get the truth from the man, who once again was eating alone in the large mess tent.

Osson clearly hadn't been expecting the question, for he stumbled as he started his usual dismissal. "What?" he ended up asking, actually looking at Tala properly for the first time since they had been reunited.

"Serala and you. She woke up. She's fine, by the way. But she completely shut down when she found out you were here. If I'm going to be stuck with you two, I want to know whatever it is that's between you." Somewhere in the back of his mind, Tala was marveling at himself. But if the Bone Merc hadn't turned on him yet (and Tala took a sadistic pleasure in irritating him as much as he could) then he figured he could get away with this much. Especially when he actually had a reason to know.

Osson stared at Tala, who stared back expectantly. He watched the subtle signs that Osson was going to give in: the twitch of his brow skin, the slight slump of his shoulders. Osson made a vague gesture towards the seat across from him. Tala took it, subtly enjoying the sense of victory.

"She blames me for killing her parents," Osson said bluntly, before taking another bite of meat, looking at Tala with a bored face.

"Oh." That was not what he had been expecting. Granted, he hadn't really had many expectations. With the people he now found populating his life, he had learned better than to think he could anticipate them, but still. "Did you? Kill her parents?"

"Yep." He nodded, unconcerned, as he took another bite. "Why?"

"Accident. Collateral damage."

"What?"

"I was in a fight. Lots of people got hurt. They were two of them. Shit happens."

Tala wasn't surprised, per se, at how callously Osson could discuss innocent people dying accidentally at his hands, but he still felt fairly disgusted with the man. "That's awful! Don't you feel bad about it? At all?"

"Not really." He shrugged. "I don't care. Like I said, shit happens. People die. Sometimes it's my fault. Sometimes not. I'm not going to get worked up over every random idiot I kill. Accident or not."

"If you didn't care at all, you wouldn't remember two people who were collateral damage!"

"I don't. I wouldn't even know they existed if it weren't for Vail."

"What?"

Osson sighed, clearly getting annoyed. "Vail was friends with them. Or something. Honestly, I don't know, and I don't really care. He took her in after they died. I don't know why. Hells, I doubt he knows why, mad bastard that he is. Maybe he actually felt a twinge of sympathy for the first time in his life when he saw their daughter crying over their bloody corpses. Either way, he raised her himself, and she's never forgiven me for killing them. Which, if you haven't noticed, isn't something that bastard seems to understand. Last time I saw them, she tried to kill me, and he laughed it off, said it was good training for her. I don't think it even occurred to him that she had reason to hate me. That was about a decade ago. Six, maybe seven years or so after he pulled her off her parents, covered in their blood."

Tala was speechless. What in all the Hells was wrong with him? Wrong with Vail? So many things about Serala were being explained. Gods! He didn't even know what to do about everything he had just heard!

"There. Now you know what's 'between us.' Our history together. Happy?"

Tala's mind was rushing, trying to sort things out, put pieces of the story into place. As horrific as it was, everything Osson was saying rang true to him. Although, if it was true, he had been seriously misunderstanding Vail's character. Hells, being thrown off the Canyon Bridge for some insane scheme nobody knew about suddenly sounded a lot less surprising! Just what kind of monster had Tala been traveling with? Admired even, when he wasn't questioning his sanity.

"How… What happened? Who were you fighting?"

Osson snorted a laugh, a sound of dark amusement. "What? Can't figure it out? You've probably heard about all my battles. Least in the last few decades. You tell me. What fight was I in just under twenty years ago that killed a whole lot of people?"

Tala didn't even need to think. There probably wasn't a person alive who didn't know the answer to that question. It was the most famous fight in history, eclipsing even the stories of Anderas Anto.

"The Demon," Tala half-whispered. "The fight that killed a city."

"Aye," Osson said blithely. "Although we didn't really kill a city. Not all of one, at least. A few thousand people, maybe? Most of the buildings were still standing after too. Like I said, collateral damage. Her parents weren't special. Besides, even the Lightning Church was happy with that trade. What's a few thousand people, or even a whole city for that matter, compared to the Demon? A lot more than that had already died to him, and a lot more would have died if he'd kept going."

"So, what? You don't care if you kill people, but don't like it when somebody else does?"

Osson gave him a funny look. "I don't give a shit either way. I was paid, a lot, to take out the Demon. Didn't matter to me what he was doing. Lightning paid me a king's bounty afterwards. Almost all the countries gave me gifts in thanks for ending him. It was nice. Although, I do miss the fights sometimes. Blessed stop hunting me down after that. They were the only ones who ever gave me a decent challenge before. Least on this side. None were half as annoying as he was to fight, though. But that Anderas? Anderas Anto? He was an excellent fight. I enjoyed that one. I'd love to go all out against him sometime."

"Wait. Wait, wait, wait! You fought Anderas Anto? When? He only even became a Blessed like, a year before you killed the Demon!"

"Yeah, I've heard. No idea how he survived that fight, to be honest. He was good, damned good, but I'm not sure how much that would've helped him. Especially as a Descendant. Anyway, when he was still a new Blessed, a few years in, he contacted me privately, asking to meet in secret. He wanted to fight the person who killed the Demon. So, we had ourselves a friendly spar out near the desert, where nobody would know about it. One of the hardest fights I've ever been in. I'd love to do it again. Properly. Where only one of us walks away. I'd probably win, of course, but I might not. Especially now that he's had time to grow into being a Blessed. You don't know just how big of a power difference there is between a Descendant and a Blessed. Even Awakened. I could tell in our fight he was still learning his new powers. Honestly, he might be the second most terrifying person I've ever met. On this side, at least. Hells, maybe that's what I'll do next, while I wait for things to cool down with the Lightning Church. See how strong he is now."

Tala was done. Osson had spoken more in this one conversation than Tala had heard him say in total all the rest of the time they had spent together (however unwillingly), and he couldn't decide if he was regretting it. Serala's tragic history.

Osson's utter disregard for people's lives. Vail's complete inhumanity. And now, Anderas Anto, Fire's most beloved son (and loyal, allegedly, although Tala had been questioning that part ever since Southtown), had secretly sought out the Bone Merc to have a 'friendly spar' 'near the *desert*,' a place forbidden to everyone by all the Churches. Tala had the same thirst for learning that was shared and cultivated by all Researchers at the Institute, but this conversation was beginning to be just a bit too much for him.

"What could he do, exactly? The Demon, I mean." Tala might have been done, but apparently his mouth—and curiosity—wasn't. "Even Blessed fear him, but no one has ever actually said what made him so strong. Most people think he was a Wind Blessed, but the Churches have never said anything about it, which is weird for them. Even the Institute was forbidden from studying him."

"Honestly? I've got no Godsdamned idea. That's one of the things that made him so annoying to fight. I have no idea what he did or how he did it."

"What? But you fought him! You broke *some* of a city fighting him! You killed him! How do you not know what he could do?"

"Because he's an annoying little prick, that's why! He did *something*, yes, but I've no bloody idea what! I don't even know if it was magic! Maybe he's a Wind user! I've never even seen one, so who knows? All I can tell you is that he could screw with *my* magic, and even on the other side of the Wall, not many people can do that shit. And he wasn't using Body magic, so damned if I know! Biggest fight of my life and I couldn't enjoy myself! But who in the Hells cares? You wanted to know about me and Serala, now you know. Get the Hells out of here, kid!"

Tala stood woodenly, feeling neither the need nor desire to respond to Osson's rude dismissal. He had already been so done with that conversation, and Osson's last answer had only made things worse. Just what in every last Hell could the Demon do that even the Bone Merc didn't understand it?

CHAPTER 34

After talking to Osson, Tala spent most of the rest of the day by himself, thinking over everything Osson had told him. Serala's history was tragic but explained so much about her. The Demon was, unbelievably, still a complete mystery. How did the man who killed him—in one of the biggest fights in living memory—not even know what he could do? The Researcher in Tala—the part of him who lived for unearthing the secrets of the world—was being driven mad by it all. So much so, Tala had almost missed the references Osson made to the "other side" of the "wall." Tala only knew about one "wall," and that idea brought on a headache all its own. There were descendants of Great Horde survivors at the Carnival—few, but they were there—but none living who had actually seen the Bodylands. All they knew about them were the scant few horror stories their parents had been willing to share, passed down from their own parents, and so on.

If Osson had actually crossed the Dustwall somehow (which should be impossible, by land or ship, no one crossed the Dustwall outside of Great Hordes) then he knew about an entire region of the world Researchers had only theorized about for millennia! Asking Osson about it would have to wait. For now, Tala had to focus on Serala and dealing with her… complicated past with Osson. Which is why, the next morning, Tala slipped into her tent after making sure she was awake.

"How are you feeling?" he asked, approaching her bed carefully.

"Alright." Serala shrugged. Tala was glad to see she seemed to be a lot better—and in a better mood—than when he had left her the day before. "I've been better, but I've been a lot worse too." As if to prove her point, Serala threw off her blankets and shifted her legs sideways and out of the bed. Far too recklessly in Tala's opinion, she stood, swaying unevenly. Without thinking, Tala rushed forward to help steady her, placing one hand on her back with the other hovering in front, prepared to catch her if she fell forward. After everything he had had to do while caring for her in the Jungle, he barely even registered how the sleeping garments the healers had dressed her in hardly covered anything. She simply smirked amusedly at his actions.

"You really shouldn't get up yet," he told her. "I'll get the healers back in. They can check you over and tell you if it's okay for you to be up."

"They're Body mages, Tala. They've already done everything I could need. Now I'm hungry, and I want to see the Carnival."

Tala made a point of looking her up and down.

"Right. Let me get dressed. Then take me to the food."

Tala sighed. "I'll wait outside."

Serala nodded absently, already examining the pants and tunic that had been laid out for her.

It took only a matter of minutes for Serala to dress and for them to get a variety of meats, fruits, and vegetables all laid out on the large plank-like leaves the Carnival was fond of using. When Tala led her to the dining pavilion to eat, he was glad to see that Osson was absent. He would need to talk to Serala about him soon, but his presence would only complicate things.

"Gods, this is good!" Serala mumbled through a mouthful of food.

Tala lightly whacked her on the head. "Don't talk with your mouth full." He grumbled as he took another bite of… giant lizard? Even in the Jungle he had to correct his friends' manners… Tala's head shot up, realizing all too suddenly, and too late, just who he was eating with, and that no, this wasn't one of his Institute friends being gross.

He stared at Serala wide-eyed, waiting for one of her ever-present daggers to make an appearance. Instead, Serala was just staring back at him, dumbfounded.

"Sorry! I'm sorry!" Tala squeaked out. "It's just-habit! It's habit! Back at the Institute, my friends would do that sometimes, talk with their mouths full, and it's a bad habit, and we'd get in trouble when we were kids for it. And I stopped. But they'd still do it sometimes and get in trouble with the Researchers, so whenever one of them did, we'd all whack them because it's a bad habit!"

He watched nervously as Serala swallowed her mouthful of food. "It's okay. Just… there's not a lot of people who would've dared. Not to me, at least. You're right, though. I shouldn't do that."

Tala nodded, relieved. He couldn't believe he had just done that!

"So, what've you been doing the last few days here?" Serala asked after taking another bite, gesturing to the Carnival around them. "Do they have some big secret library you've been devouring? Or is there some nice Jungle girl or boy who's been entertaining you?"

Tala faltered; that was a strange thing for Serala to ask. Clearly, she had been spending too much time with Caida.

"No." He chuckled. "No library. Or anybody specific. I've mostly just been talking to all the people, learning about the Carnival, and the Jungle."

It was Serala's turn to chuckle. "Of course you have. You're kind of predictable, you know?" Tala wasn't sure if he should be offended or not. Predictable people didn't end up hunted throughout the known world, thank you very much! "Did you learn anything interesting?"

Tala smiled and immediately jumped into telling her the stories about the deep Jungle. He'd learned details about the different nations the Carnival residents came from, and various things he had learned about the different magics. Their wielders had happily humored him as he engaged in the ultimate forbidden sin for a Researcher: Arcane Research. She laughed when he told her about how he may have accidentally set the Ice twins on a path to learning Ice enchanting (or creating it, he wasn't really sure how it worked), based on what he could remember of Alina's enchanting of rocks to hide their campsites at night.

As much as Tala enjoyed talking to all of his companions, none could engage with him quite like Serala. While she wasn't as broadly educated as he was, her experiences in the world allowed her deeper insight into things than Tala's purely theoretical knowledge did. In a different life, he had a feeling she would have made an exceptional Researcher.

Hours passed like that, food long since consumed and forgotten as they talked. Carnival members came and went from the pavilion without notice as the two were wrapped up in their own little world. He didn't even know when, or how, the conversation had circled back to the Carnival. "It still seems unbelievable to me that a place like this can exist."

"It's different for sure." Serala shrugged. "It's not really all that special though, is it? Aside from all the different Descendants living together. I mean, people who don't want to actually fight can always live in Dissident towns too. That way, they're still helping the cause at least."

"That's my point!" Tala exclaimed. "The Carnival is separate from all of that! The Gods, the Dissidents, all of it. They're free. Freer than anybody. They helped us because they're good people, not because they had to. Those that want to leave can go. Those that want to fight join the Dissidents. But it's all their own choice. No Gods, no Dissidents. Just people living their lives free."

Serala had her head tilted as she watched Tala, bemused. "I guess so," she said slowly when he had finally stopped. "You think it's okay, then? Them refusing to fight with us? Even knowing all they could do?"

"I… it's not ideal, I guess," Tala answered, uncomfortable. "They could completely change the-the balance of power, if they wanted to. I understand why Gazin has issues with them for refusing. But at the same time, I don't really blame them. I mean, I was loyal. Before you told me the truth about the Gods and the Churches. But if I could go back to my life? Go back in time to before I killed Ignis, even knowing everything I do now? I don't know what I would do."

"You wouldn't join us again?" Serala asked quietly. Tala thought she sounded hurt, but he couldn't bring himself to lie.

"I don't know. I just… I didn't choose any of this, you know? I'm not a fighter. Not like you or Dunlop or Alina or even Caida. I'm glad I met you all. I am. And I'm glad I know the truth about the Churches and everything now. But this fight? I don't really want to be a part of it. I do support the cause, I do, but it's not really who I am. I wanted to study the world, learn about it, create things to make life better for people. Be remembered for the good I did. Instead, I'm running around the world fearing for my life, known only for the people I've killed and the chaos I've caused. Even if it's all been for a greater good, it feels like I'm living somebody else's life sometimes."

Serala was quiet, frowning at the table. Tala took a deep breath, resting his chin on his hands. He was just now noticing how late it had gotten; the sun was well on its way down. It wasn't quite dinner time yet, but there were plenty of other people relaxing in the pavilion with them. Well, they had been relaxing. While none were looking their way, Tala could tell that they were all listening to him and Serala. Some looked ashamed, while others relieved, and many were shooting him quick, furtive glances of sympathy and pity. Tala knew that if anyone could understand his feelings, it was the people of the Carnival. Once again, he wished he could just stay there.

"You are a fighter," Serala eventually said somberly. "Even before everything, you were a fighter. I saw what happened with Ignis, remember? In that alley. You chose to confront him. You had no idea who he was, or why he was hurting that girl, but you chose to stop him. You could have walked away. Most people would have. Even without knowing who he was, nobody would have blamed you for walking away. Even calling for guards would have been more than most would have done. And even after you saw who he was"—Tala tried to interrupt her, but she barreled over him—"you didn't know he was a Blessed, but you knew he was Empowered. You still chose to fight instead of give in. And then you kept fighting. You didn't have to come with us. We wanted you to, but we couldn't have forced you, not in the middle of the city. And you chose to leave Fiahren with us, even after learning who we were. And again, in Southtown. You could have surrendered, you could have tried to run, you didn't. I would be dead right now if you hadn't fought the entire Jungle just to keep me alive. Every time things went bad, you had a choice. And every time you've chosen to fight. You may not be a fighter like me or Dunlop or even Caida, but you are a fighter. It's just in your own way."

Tala didn't know what to say. From a certain perspective,

everything she had said was true. But he hadn't been trying to fight! He had been trying to survive! But that was her point. He didn't have to make the choices he had. He had other options, slim as they may have been. But he kept seeing the easy path and refusing to take it. Because he knew it was the wrong way, even when he wanted it to be the right one. Even before he learned the truth, when he had believed it to be the right way, he still—somewhere, deep in his heart or his mind or somewhere—had chosen not to take it. Had chosen to fight.

He still didn't want to, though. It had always been out of necessity, desperation, and simple conscience.

"You're right." Tala was glad to see Serala smile at him. "I have chosen to fight, and I will continue to do so. I've fought because I've had to, not because I've wanted to. I just wish I had another option—like the Carnival. Where I could live my own life, and be free of being 'The' Tala'Keahi, killer of Blessed."

"You'd really leave?" Serala asked, looking confused again. "Even knowing how evil the Churches are? How unworthy the Gods are?"

Tala sighed, conflicted. "I don't know. In truth, I'm not sure if I could. You're right; I could have ignored Ignis, should have, but I didn't. Even if I would be safe here, I don't know how long I could stay, knowing what's happening out there."

"So maybe you fit into your new life better than you thought."

"I don't know." Tala shook his head. "I'm not even sure that's what would bother me the most about staying here in the Carnival. It's nice, but it's barely involved in the wider world.

There would be no more learning beyond what the people here can tell me. I could become an expert on the Jungle, and Arcane Research, but that would be it. And more than I'm a fighter, I'm a Researcher. As much as I hate what my life has become, there are some good things in it. You. And the others. Getting to see the world, meet new people, learn things I never would have in a lifetime at the Institute. I just wish I could experience it without a dagger to my throat the entire time. If I could be like the people in Dritenik, but mobile, I think I'd be happy. Exploring the world, helping the cause where and when I can, but without being actively involved. I could meet new people without having to hide my identity for fear they'll turn me in. I could enter a city openly, marvel at its construction and design, without having to sneak around like a criminal. Don't you think that sounds nice?"

"It does," Serala said wistfully, a faraway look in her eyes. "I've never thought about leaving the Dissidents. But I think, if it were possible, I would enjoy a life like that."

"Really?" Tala couldn't help but ask, skeptical. "It seems like you love your life. Traveling around, fighting and killing your enemies wherever they may be."

"I do." Serala smiled impishly. "I know you don't feel it, but something about fighting makes my blood sing. Life and death, sitting in the palm of my hand. Every move a life taken, every move my life saved. I do love it. But ever since... ever since Vail took me in, fighting is the only thing I've really known. It's the only thing he cares about. I know that. I'm not blind.

"When I was a kid, I would pretend he cared about me.

Loved me. And I think he does, in his own way. But he's never cared about me like other people care about those they love. I don't think he can. And he's never really understood my interests outside of fighting. Like you, I loved seeing new places. Whenever we got to a new city, I wanted to go everywhere, see everything. He indulged me, but the first time he took me to Fiahren, and I saw the pipe network, he made me think of how best to sabotage it. Where I could do the most damage. When we saw the dam at Fangroth, he taught me where its weaknesses were, so that I could bring it down if I ever wanted to flood the city. The first time I saw the markets of Lynmyr, he questioned me for a week about where the best place would be to start a fire; where it would do the most damage, where it would kill the most people, where it would be hardest to put out. I think I would like to see the world without having to plan how to destroy it. Without having to plan how to kill everyone I meet."

Tala stared at her, horrified. Every time he thought Vail couldn't get any worse, he learned something new about the man. He didn't need to see her face to know that would be wrong to say at the moment, though. "How about it, then?" he ended up asking.

"How about what?" she asked, bemused.

"If we ever get the chance to... to leave. To be rid of the Gods and the Dissidents and the war and all of it. If we ever get the chance to be free, would you come with me?"

Serala offered him a half-smile. "And where would that be? The Bodylands? The Wind lands? Hop in a boat and sail off the edge of the world looking for the mythical lands of

Water far off to the west? I think we're both stuck here, in this life, whether we like it or not."

Tala was silent. He wanted so, so badly to tell her what he had learned. That the people of Water still lived somewhere off to the west, where no boats ever returned from. Somewhere near, or even past, the Bodylands. He couldn't. Not when so many people were around. Not when he had promised the man who had saved both their lives he would never speak of it. But now that the idea was in his head, he couldn't shake it.

No matter how small the chance, how impossible the dream, he still wanted to have hope that someday, somehow, he could be free of the life he had so unwittingly entered.

"You know, most of the Researchers believe the world is round," Tala said instead. "That there is no edge. The Gods have never actually said either way. Not that the Institute has recorded, and they have records going as far back as the early days. Some of them believe that there are more lands out there, past Wind and Body, and maybe Water. The Churches deny it. Hells, even the Gods have said there's nothing else out there. But we already know they aren't perfect, don't we? That's what the Dissidents' fight is all about. What if they are wrong? Or, more likely, are lying? What if there are lands outside of the Gods' control?"

"Like the Far Shore?" Serala asked doubtfully. "The mythical land on the other side of Wind? Even if it does exist, who's to say there aren't just more Gods? If they lied about its existence, they could be lying about there only being nineteen Gods in the first place."

Tala frowned internally, thinking. The Far Shore was a

myth. But so were the Water lands, and he now knew that they existed—and River Ghosts. The Carnival of Blood was a myth, and he had been living peacefully, pleasantly, there for days. He couldn't tell Serala why he was starting to believe, perhaps, there was more to the ancient myths and legends than most people thought. At least, he couldn't tell her most of his reasoning. But that wasn't important, was it? All that was important, at the moment, was hope.

"Maybe it doesn't. Or maybe it is ruled by other Gods. Even so, I'd-we'd-be unknown there. If it is possible, would you at least consider leaving with me?"

"Sure, Tala." Serala smiled at him, half happy and half sad. "If you manage another impossible miracle and find us a place free of the Gods—our Gods, at least—I'll go there with you."

Tala gave her the brightest smile he could, and Serala responded with a laugh. But behind his silliness, Tala was furiously thinking. If he ever got the chance, if he ever found himself near the Gods' Canyon again, he might just have to see if Wade was around. He had some questions for the Water Blessed.

CHAPTER 35

"'Tis been a pleasure having you here," Gwyar said, smiling warmly, holding Tala's hand softly between her own. "You are always welcome to return, if you ever find yourself in these parts again."

"Thank you." Tala chuckled. "But I can't say I'll ever be eager to return, much as I've enjoyed my time with you all."

"Aye." She laughed. "These lands are not for everybody. Or even most, I wager. But should life ever unfold for you thus, know you have friends here. I wish you great fortune, wherever your path should take you."

Tala nodded, smiling gently as Gwyar gave him one last affectionate pat before turning around and walking back through the large wooden gates of the Carnival's encampment. Tala watched her leave with mixed emotions. He had enjoyed his time at the Carnival of Blood, ridiculous as the notion would seem to any who did not know the truth about the place. It had been fascinating speaking to all the different people who lived there. Tala had learned a lot about the different places in the world that he had never known. More importantly, he had learned a lot about the different magics he had not yet encountered, leaving him feeling far better prepared for any future Descendants—or, Gods forbid, Blessed—that he might face. Having access to so many different Descendants, most of whom were more than happy to share everything they knew about their magics with him, had been a dream come true for the heretical-Researcher side of him.

He almost wished he could stay longer, as even a full week had not been nearly enough to learn everything he could have there. But with Serala all healed up and perfectly capable of traveling again, it was time to continue on.

If he were being honest, he was not particularly excited about the upcoming journey to Morungil. Even though it should be perfectly safe with both Serala and Osson at his side, the idea of once again having to trudge his way through the oppressive darkness and ceaseless noise of the Jungle made his heart race anxiously. According to Osson, the journey shouldn't take much more than about twelve days or so to reach the city, but even that was far too long for Tala's comfort. He'd had enough of the Jungle to last a lifetime already.

As he turned around, checking the straps of his bag one last time, he looked at the small strip of cleared land that stood between the Carnival's walls and the trees. Every encampment the Carnival had throughout the Jungle was encircled by such a strip, no more than ten feet wide. Most encampments had a couple dozen people or so who lived there year-round and kept the strip clear. A necessary task as the Jungle would easily overwhelm the entire place within a matter of months if not constantly held in check. Even the path through the trees that the Carnival had carved out when it had arrived a few weeks prior was almost indistinguishable from the rest of the Jungle already, a testament to the lingering power of the Plant God infusing the whole country, flowing through every root and stem, spurring on the growth of all flora to a frankly ridiculous degree.

"Well, let's get going," Tala said aloud, trying—and failing—to sound nonchalant about reentering the cursed wilds. He only got a single grunt in response from Osson, who without ceremony turned and followed the slightly less overgrown remnants of a trail left by the Carnival. Serala didn't respond at all. She followed silently, face blank but eyes swimming with compressed rage. This was the other reason Tala wasn't looking forward to the journey. After learning about Serala's history from Osson, he had been at a complete loss as to how to help his friend deal with Osson's presence. He couldn't imagine what it must be like for her! As such, he was stuck with the ever-surly Osson and the brooding, rage-filled Serala. It was not going to be a fun experience.

Over the next few days, Tala's patience with both his companions wore thinner and thinner. Osson was perfectly content to travel in complete silence, all but ignoring the presence of the other two. Tala wouldn't have minded if he had been able to talk to Serala, but she was even worse! He didn't understand how she managed to so ceaselessly maintain her silent, seething anger for days on end! Anger was exhausting! Tala was usually exhausted after a few minutes! And yet Serala showed no signs of calming down! Her every action was taken with a violent mien! While Osson walked so quietly it was like the man wasn't even there, and Tala tried to not make too much noise, her every step might as well have been a stomp! And Tala was almost certain she was intentionally stepping on every twig and leaf and brittle rock they passed just to feel it crunch under her foot! At least Tala never had to take watch at night, as Osson had decided to just do it himself every night since he didn't trust Serala wouldn't try to kill him in his sleep (and Tala wasn't going to question Osson's claim that he could go weeks without sleep with no ill effects)!

But by the fourth day, Tala couldn't deal with it all anymore! Despite not having come across a single aggressive animal, the aggressive and often violent plant life was still a hassle to deal with. Just being in the Jungle was wearing at Tala's nerves, and the behavior of his companions was only making things worse. After what must have been his dozenth attempt at trying to engage Serala in some sort of conversation, only to be completely rebuffed by the girl as she glared either at Osson's back or the ground, he finally lost his patience.

"Enough!" he suddenly yelled, voice sounding incredibly loud even to his own ears. The sounds of the Jungle instantly fell silent. Osson and Serala both turned to him, one with what (he assumed was) a raised brow, and the other with a glare, although one that held confusion as much as anger.

"Serala, I'm sorry, but for the love of the Gods you have to stop… moping! And glaring! And just-just everything!" Serala's face went from confused, to angry again, to angry at *him*, and he hurried to continue speaking before she could. "No! Look, I know why you're upset! I get it! He," he gestured at Osson, "told me about what happened. To your parents.

What he did, and everything! And yes, you have the right to hate him! To be pissed and want to kill him and whatnot! But we're stuck in the middle of the Godsdamned Jungle, just the three of us, and will be for at least another week! So please, for my sake, if nothing else, figure out *something*! Talk! Fight! Fuck! I don't care! Just *deal with it*! Please!"

Tala panted as he finished his impromptu tirade, wishing he had at least taken the time to think of something a bit more eloquent and persuasive. He glared at Serala, unwilling to relent despite his sloppy words. To his surprise, the girl's glare had lessened. While still there, the anger was now mixed with signs of guilt, confusion, and awkwardness. He glanced at Osson. The man stared at him with his non-existent eyebrows definitely raised.

The three stood there in silence, none of them moving. Tala's eyes darting back and forth between Osson and Serala, hoping one of them would do *something*. He had absolutely no idea what to do next, besides pray to every God that neither of them would kill him for his outburst (willfully ignoring the fact that most of the Gods likely wanted him dead).

"By The Three," Osson sighed out, so quietly that Tala wouldn't have been able to hear it had the Jungle still not been so quiet from his shouting. "I don't like the kid, but he has a point. You haven't slept since we started. If you slip up, things in here can kill you before even I can save you."

Serala whirled on Osson, face a rictus of fury. "Save me?" she spat out. Tala had never heard her speak with such venom. "Save me? You? Are you joking?"

Osson sighed and sent an angry glare at Tala, who frankly

couldn't care less. "What do you want? An apology? I'm sorry your parents died because of me. It was an accident. I feel terrible about it. Happy?" Tala stared blankly at Osson. The man hadn't even tried to sound sincere! Why was he cursed to be stuck with such awful people?

A sudden motion caught Tala's eye. A dagger appeared in the middle of Osson's forehead, quivering slightly. The man went cross-eyed as he looked up at it.

"Really?" Osson asked, sounding vaguely annoyed. A blur of silver and another dagger buried itself in his chest, just left of center. Osson didn't even bother acknowledging it. "Feel better?" More flashes in the air and three more daggers appeared: one in the right side of his chest, one sticking out of his groin, and one held in Osson's hand, not two inches away from his eye. "Okay. You? Leave," he said, pointing at Tala. "We need to work some things out."

"Wait, what?" Tala chirped. "What do you mean, leave? Where? We're in the middle of the Jungle!"

"Just keep going south. We'll catch up."

"We're in the middle of the Jungle!" Tala shouted.

"Yes. And you survived by yourself for weeks in here already. While caring for her, while out of your mind from poison and injured so badly even I'm impressed you're alive. You'll be fine on your own for however long this takes."

"He's right. Go," Serala growled. Tala gawked at her. This was not what he had in mind! He *did not* want to be alone in the Jungle, no matter how short of a time! He made to protest again but was stopped when Serala turned to him with a glower that he didn't even want to try and interpret.

Choking on his aborted words, Tala coughed and closed his mouth. He took a step toward Osson, feeling Serala's glare on him. He continued walking, passing Osson, who ignored him as he picked the daggers out of his body. He stopped and glanced back at the two, both ignoring him entirely. With an aggrieved sigh, Tala continued, swearing under his breath with every step that took him deeper into the Jungle, and away from his psychotic companions. In less than a minute, an almighty boom rumbled through the woods, as though one of the giant trees had come crashing down. Tala just shook his head and stormed by a bush, confident that those two would be able to follow his trail when they were finished. He almost wanted some Jungle beast to attack him, just so he would have an excuse to stab something!

CHAPTER 36

Tala had lost track of how long it had been since he had left Serala and Osson behind. Not that he had ever really started keeping track of time in the first place, as the deep gloom of the Jungle made it all but impossible anyway. Still, it had been at least an hour since the two had sent him on ahead. He wondered how long it would be before they caught up to him, and what condition they would be in. He was pretty sure that Osson wasn't going to kill or maim Serala, and—as dangerous as the girl was—he didn't think she was actually *capable* of truly hurting the Bone Merc, not that she wouldn't try. But Osson was an existence more on par with the likes of Blessed than regular humans like him or Serala. Tala happily ignored the twinge of doubt that thought raised, what with him being 'The Blessed Killer' and all. The point stood, the absurdity that was his life notwithstanding. He was sure the two would be fine.

Although, after another hour, perhaps two, passed, he was growing worried. Maybe he should turn around and head back towards them. The thought grew stronger by the minute, when he started hearing the sounds of movement behind him, like something human-sized was coming. Relief washed through him even as he drew his sword, prepared just in case. His solo walk had been strangely calm, much like their last few days, but it wouldn't do to grow complacent in the Jungle. So he waited, sword poised to strike as the noises grew louder.

He smiled as Serala came crashing through a particularly dense set of bushes, followed by Osson. His smile morphed into a frown as he saw their conditions. Osson appeared fine as ever, although his clothes were a bit more ragged, but Serala was covered in dirt and small cuts and bruises, along with a few bigger scratches, including some that were strangely uniform, as though made by claws. Splotches of blood were smeared all over, and her clothing was a mess.

"Are you okay?" Tala scurried forward, sheathing his blade as he tried to get a closer look at Serala in the gloom.

"Fine. I'm fine," she said tiredly, waving him off.

"Was this really necessary?" Tala asked hotly, turning on Osson. He figured they would fight, but the legendary Bone Merc should have been able to win easily without hurting her!

"Wasn't me," Osson said shortly, shooting Tala an annoyed glare. "Bunch of damned animals attacked us. She'd be dead if I hadn't saved her. You're welcome."

"Oh." Tala blinked. "Thanks, then. Did the noise bring them? We haven't seen any beasts since we left the Carnival."

"Maybe. None attacked you?"

"No."

"Hmm." Osson gave Tala a searching look. "I'm not paid enough for this shit." He grumbled to himself after a few moments before sitting and leaning against a tree. Tala almost warned him to check that the tree wouldn't try to eat him but caught himself at the last second. Even if it was a carnivorous tree, it wasn't exactly a danger to Osson. Instead, he turned to Serala, who was checking over her wounds in a blasé manner.

"Are you okay?" Tala asked. Some of her injuries looked pretty nasty.

"I'll be fine. I have some ointment that will heal them."

"Why not have—" He stopped at the glare she sent him.

"I'll be fine," she repeated testily. She sighed and closed her eyes, taking a deep breath before opening them and giving Tala a piercing look. "I'm sorry. Alright? About making you deal with... all of this. You were right. I was letting it get in the way, and I was putting us in danger."

"It's alright." He went for a grin, but it turned out more of a grimace. "I get it. Well, not really, but you know what I mean. Your... history, together. I can understand why you'd have some issues with... this."

She gave him a tired smile. "Still. Things will be better going forward. I promise."

Tala raised an eyebrow. "Oh? Did you two work everything out?"

She snorted in amusement. "Not even close. But it was enough. We fought, we talked, we fought off a bunch of damned Jungle monstrosities together. Stabbing somebody multiple times can be incredibly cathartic anyways. Even if it doesn't really hurt them." She shot a glare at Osson, looking for all the world like he was asleep against the tree. Tala knew the man was awake and likely could hear every word they said despite his trying to talk quietly. Serala didn't seem to care either way.

"I can imagine." Tala chuckled, having grown too used to her twisted sense of... well, everything to feel properly disturbed by it anymore. "Maybe I should try stabbing Vail a time or two when we get to them."

She gave him a bemused look. "Most people usually want to stab him at one point or another, but why do you?"

Oh. Right. He hadn't told her yet. "Ah. Well... he's kind of the reason I'm here right now. In the Jungle. With you. He threw me off the bridge into the canyon after you fell."

"He what!?" Serala yelped, a higher-pitched sound than Tala had ever heard her make before. "Why? What? That doesn't make any sense! Was he... was it the Blessed? Denhei, right? Was he really that strong? I know he's famous, but..." She trailed off, eyes wide in confusion as she tried to work out Vail's motive.

"I don't know. I don't think so. He was planning it from the start, even before Denhei showed up."

"What? Why in the Hells would he do that? Are you sure?"

"Pretty sure, yeah. Osson saw it too." Her head whipped to the man, who didn't open his eyes or even move, other than his mouth to speak. Barely.

"Aye. He threw him off when no one was looking. Pretty sure he'd been planning to do it all along. Tell her the rest."

"The rest of what?" Serala demanded, looking furious.

"Well, he said to save you, if I could. So, there's that!" Tala tried another smile, although this one was definitely a grimace. "He also... gave me a pair of dirty socks." Her face went slack as she processed what he just said. "Told me to keep them out after I surfaced. Said to make sure they could be smelled. I don't suppose you know what that's about?"

Judging by the confounded frown on Serala's face, he could tell she didn't know any better than he or Osson had. It was actually kind of funny; he had never seen her quite so flustered before.

"Smell? What-why? His socks? Dirty socks? Something was supposed to smell him? Why throw *you* over, though? Literally anyone would be a better choice! He could've jumped over himself!"

"I have no idea."

"Tell her about your talking weird thing," Osson said.

"Your what thing?"

Tala closed his eyes and sighed. "I don't know. You know how I was high on Somic? Completely out of my mind and hallucinating heavily? Well, a bit before... finding... the Carnival, I hallucinated—or *thought* I hallucinated—some sort of creature." He explained the whole story, with plenty of caveats, since he still wasn't sure what was real.

Serala was frowning at him, confused, but not quite as disbelieving as Tala had expected. She looked down, and he could tell she was thinking hard about something, although he had no idea what. It wasn't like there was a lot to go off of from what little he could remember. Eventually, she raised her head, staring him square in the eye.

"Have you heard the rumors of the Feral God?" she asked, and it was Tala's turn to frown in confusion.

"Of course. They say the Beast God went wild and abandoned his followers one day, running off into the Jungle to never be seen again. But that's a myth. There's still Beast Blessed around. And how could a God just run off like that without anybody knowing anyway?"

"Don't you remember the stories? About how Beast Descendants will vanish into the Jungle, and the ones who return, sometimes, will be Blessed? And how often did you, or anybody, see the Fire God? If he left and the Fire Church kept it quiet, how long would it take before anybody learned he was missing?"

The Fire God was only ever seen once a year, on Gods' Day, making a short appearance on the balcony of his tower, and rarely for more than a minute. A balcony so high up and far away that the Church could dress anybody up in the God's robes and nobody would ever know it wasn't him. As a child, Tala had loved getting to catch a glimpse of the Fire God every year, fleeting as it was.

"So, what? You think that... *thing* I saw was the Beast God? That's crazy! I'm literally the most wanted person in the world! They should want me dead! On sight!"

"Would they even know about you? Rumors of the Feral God have been around for centuries, at least. They may have no idea you exist. Did they say anything that made it seem like they knew you?"

"No. They didn't even know Vail's name. They said that they forgot it, if they had ever even learned it. It sounded like they'd forgotten a lot of stuff. And a God wouldn't just forget things, would they?"

"How do you know? The Gods are the most reclusive beings in the world. They've been alive forever, after all. Maybe being in the world, having a physical body, means that they can have physical side effects, like forgetfulness. They've been around for millennia, after all. And they can be hurt and feel fear and stuff. Be affected by drugs, with each other's blood, yes, but still."

"But I'm pretty sure it talked about getting killed! By 'him,' or Vail, or whoever! And by me! Like it was sad, *disappointed*, that he couldn't kill it, and that I couldn't either! If they wanted to die, they could just... end themselves, couldn't they?"

"Maybe. Maybe not. We know practically nothing about the Gods themselves. Maybe they want to return to the heavens, are tired of being in the world, but can't. Maybe they're stuck here. What if that's what happened to Water? Their God wanted to go home and found a way to do it? Maybe the Beast God wants to go home but can't figure out how, so they tried to lose themselves as an animal! Went feral! But a God can't completely lose themselves like that! Like Beast Blessed can!"

"But Water—" Tala faltered. He couldn't say anything about Water.

"Oy! You two!" Osson growled, standing up, ripping off a few tree roots that had started to wrap around him. "Let's keep moving. The trees here are hungry. Boy, you're losing your pack."

"What?" Tala whipped around to see some sort of vine had wrapped around a loop of his pack and was slowly pulling it away from him. With an irritated growl, Tala drew a dagger and cut the vine, which gave off a high-pitched whine as the rest of it quickly slithered back into the brush. "I hate this place," Tala grumbled, standing to follow Osson as he led the way.

"Okay," Tala continued the conversation with Serala. "So, let's say that this is all true, and the Beast God wants to die, to go home. Now what? We can't do anything about it!"

"Maybe not. But what if this is what Vail had planned? It was his idea to leave Lightning and go to the Jungle! He wanted something to smell you! Maybe he wanted you to meet the Beast God for some reason! Also, there's a flower growing on you."

Eye twitching, Tala let Serala pull the parasitic bud off his neck, shivering at the creepy feeling of bloodthirsty roots sliding out of his skin. "But why? I couldn't do anything! I can kill Blessed, *kind of*! The Gods are completely different! And shouldn't you know? If it *was* the Beast God, wouldn't Vail have mentioned to you sometime that he *knew one of the Godsdamned Gods*?"

Serala let out a sigh, a noise of long-suffering exhaustion. "You would think. Vail keeps a lot to himself, even from me. Honestly, I wouldn't be surprised."

"Seriously? I-I don't... What the hells?"

Osson snorted again. "Welcome to Vail, kid. Leave your sanity at the entrance and your patience in the bin." They both ignored him. Serala plucked another flower off Tala's ear.

"Did it-they-say anything else? If we're right, and it was the Beast God, then they want to die. Some of us are already trying to find a way to kill them anyway. But that can't be it. Not for Vail to have gone through all of this! The Jungle is huge! There was no guarantee at all that you would actually meet, no matter how smelly he made you! To say nothing of how likely you were to die before! He sent you alone into the Jungle, taking care of me, mostly dead and entirely helpless! What could possibly be worth the risk? Did *whatever* you met say anything else? Anything at all?"

"I don't think so. Nothing really important, at least, I'm pretty sure. It's all fuzzy, but I'm pretty sure I remembered everything important. The only other thing it said was something about the city of Tora, but there is no city with that name."

"Tora? I've never heard of that. Could it be a city that died out, or changed its name or something?"

"I don't think so. I've studied maps that are thousands of years old. Also, flower." Tala spotted a bud poking out of Serala's hair. They spent a minute combing through each other's hair to make sure there were no more buds hiding there, to Osson's audible annoyance.

"Could it be something from before maps? If that was the God, they've been around since the literal beginning. And you said they've been forgetting things. Maybe they forgot the city changed its name or something?"

"Fiahren was the first city ever founded, and I've seen the maps from that time. They're shitty, but you can still make out the cities."

"So, nothing, then? You've never heard of Tora before?" Tala hesitated, not missed by Serala. "What? What is it? You're thinking of something."

"I don't know. I don't. I just... I could swear I've heard that name before somewhere. 'Tora.' It's like a tickle in the back of my mind." He rubbed a hand over the back of his head, making sure the 'tickle' wasn't another parasitic plant trying to grow on him. "That's the only reason I even remember it being said. But I've been thinking about it all week, and I have no idea when or where I might have heard it. I think it's just because of the Somic. It messed me up really bad."

Serala seemed unconvinced. "Maybe." They continued walking in silence for a bit, only interrupted by the occasional flower bud that had started sprouting. They must have walked through a cloud of spores or something at one point without realizing it. "We can figure it out later. When we ask Vail about everything. For now, we should keep moving. I really want to get to Morungil and find out what in the Godsdamned Hells Vail was thinking!"

Tala wholeheartedly agreed with that sentiment.

"Uhh... Tala?" Serala sounded worried, making Tala and even Osson spin to look at her. She just gestured to Tala's waist, where a few flower petals were starting to show out from under his tunic.

"Godsdamnit!" Tala growled, quickly pulling down his pants. The damned flowers had some sort of pain-killing substance that they injected into their victims as they took root, allowing them to grow unnoticed. With his pants off, Tala could see the way the roots were bulging beneath the skin of his leg.

"Carefully, please," he asked Serala as she gripped onto the stem. She began gently pulling at the flower, and Tala watched nauseously as the roots slowly slid up and out of his leg, where the stem had been right below his hip. Osson sighed noisily.

"Why don't these things ever grow on you?" Tala asked him, irritated as Serala wrapped some cloth strips around his hip to help staunch the (thankfully slow) bleeding.

Osson just deadpanned at him before walking up and plucking another bud off Tala's arm. With a smirk, Osson placed it on his own exposed arm. The roots eagerly dug into his skin. A few moments later, the bud started twisting and writhing, as though in agony. Quickly, it shriveled up and turned brown, before falling off Osson, obviously dead, roots trailing behind it, landing on the ground with a pathetic *fwump*.

"I hate you," Tala said.

"Feeling's mutual." Osson rolled his eyes as he turned back to continue their trek. Serala patted Tala's shoulder in solidarity.

CHAPTER 37

*T*ora. *Tora.* The name was taunting him. It had been ever since he first heard... that creature say it. Tala couldn't shake the feeling that Serala was correct, that it was the Beast God, but he still found that a difficult concept to accept. A *God*! One of the nineteen creators who built the world! Made humanity! Until they reached Morungil, and he got the chance to question Vail, Tala did his best to just not think about it. If only he could get the name of that damned non-existent city out of his head!

Osson had even told them, one night when he and Serala were discussing possible locations, that there was no place by that name—or anything similar—on the other side of the Dustwall. How exactly he knew that he refused to share.

"But how do you know?" Serala had challenged, refusing to let it go. "Nobody knows what's on the other side of the Wall!"

"I just do. Drop it," Osson growled at her.

Tala was getting annoyed. This argument had been going on too long in his opinion. So far, he had been silent, letting

Serala take the lead as he thought back on the many little things he had heard Osson say since they met; odd sayings and references littered here and there.

"It's because he's been there. Or is from there. The Bodylands," Tala interrupted whatever Serala had been saying.

"What?" Serala scoffed. "That's impossible."

"So is my life," Tala pointed out, turning to Osson, who was glowering at him. Again. "I'm right, aren't I? You're from the Bodylands. Somehow." Osson didn't speak, just continued to glare at Tala. "Oh, come off it! You don't exactly hide it well. You swear by 'The Three' for Fire's sake! Who the Hells else could you be talking about? And how the Hells else would you know of any cities there? Even the Institute doesn't know what's beyond the Dustwall. So just stop pretending!"

"Sometimes I really hate you," Osson growled.

"Yeah. Feeling's mutual," Tala replied, rolling his eyes. Serala snorted. "Now would you just tell us what you know? Even if Tora isn't—or wasn't—over there, you're still probably the only person alive on this side of the Wall to have seen the place. What's it like?"

"Gods, kid," Osson swore. "Fine. Yes, I'm from there. No, I won't tell you about it. No!" He forestalled Tala's attempt to argue. "Trust me on this. You *do not* want to know. I've heard every story you people have about what the Bodylands 'might' be like, the good and the bad. So, take it from me when I tell you, it's so much worse than any of you people can even imagine. There's a reason nobody has ever gone there and returned, even in the early days before the Dustwall. And the hordes? Half of them aren't trying to invade, they're trying to escape. They don't care if they die trying; a quick death at the Wall is better than living in that place. You think your Churches are bad? Nobles who can make slaves of anyone on the street who catches their eye? That's nothing compared to the fear of joining the flesh farms. And there are no cities. Not ones like you're thinking. Whatever Tora is, it's not over there. If it ever was, it was destroyed a long, long time ago. Just like everything else."

Tala shared a wide-eyed look with Serala, who silently mouthed 'flesh farms?' back to him. Tala turned back to Osson to see him glaring at nothing in the canopy. Maybe he didn't want to learn more about the Bodylands.

"Okay. But how did you... cross the Dustwall, then? I've learned about it, seen paintings of it, that doesn't seem possible for a single man. There's a reason even hordes rarely break through," Tala asked.

"I didn't. I went around it."

"Around it? Like, you took a boat? I thought the Bodylands didn't have boats? Nobody has ever seen one." The Bodylands finding a way around the Dustwall was one of the world's greatest fears, but there had never been any sign of them doing so.

"They don't. They can make boats, big ones. Out of bone and flesh. But they always sink, no matter what. It's like the ocean itself refuses to let them leave. In the Bodylands, to enter the ocean is to die. The only swimming or fishing over there is in the lakes or the blood ponds. Most people—and I use that term loosely—over there believe that the Water God and his Blessed are responsible. I thought that too until I got here and found out he and his people vanished millennia ago. Now I have no idea."

Tala... was just not going to touch on the Water theory. Given his recent discoveries, it may be truer than Osson realized.

"Okay," Serala responded instead. "That's... disturbing." Was she talking about the bone/flesh boats or the blood ponds? 'Cause to him it was both. "Then how did you 'go around' the Dustwall if not by water?"

"I dug." Osson shrugged.

"You dug?" Serala asked dryly. "Under the Dustwall? Under all twelve walls that extend miles into the ground thanks to Earth wielders to stop people like you from doing exactly that?"

"It's thirteen now, actually." Tala corrected without thinking.

"What?"

"What? Oh. Sorry. But they added another wall a few years ago. With another five major fortresses on it, and however many minor ones. It was actually an Institute project. A horde attacked about a decade ago and was beaten, but only after they broke through the first seven walls. They had some sort of flying abominations apparently, big gas bag things that floated over the walls, filled with other, smaller abominations, that dropped out when they were killed. So, a bunch of Researchers in Mil Tec developed these giant crossbow things to launch a volley of hundreds of spiked balls really high into the air to bring down the gas bags before they could cross.

And they decided to add another wall to put them on instead of rearranging the existing ones."

Serala and Osson both gave him blank stares.

"You dug under all of that?" Serala asked, ignoring Tala.

"No. I dug around. Under the ocean. No Earth barriers to stop me there, or water to drown me."

"I'm sorry," Tala said. "You dug under the ocean? Are you joking? That would take years! Decades, even!"

"I can dig fast." Osson shrugged. "I think it only took me about ten years. I'm not certain—I didn't really have a sense of time down there. And I didn't know anything about what was on this side of the Wall, so I've never been able to figure it out. But it took a very long time, yes."

"Right. Okay. Well, I think I've had enough of this conversation." Serala stood up, patting herself down for anything that might have hitched a ride. "We've rested. I'm going to climb a tree and see if I can tell how close we are. The God Tree should be in sight by now, I think. If I'm not down in five minutes, I've been eaten again, so come get me."

Tala winced; that was not a pleasant memory. Rescuing Serala from the mouth of a tree that had almost fully swallowed her had given him more than one nightmare. And he knew it had given her quite a few more. Ever since, she had made a point of being the one to climb whenever it was needed. Some sort of psychotic, stubborn-spite response to her ordeal.

A couple minutes later and a scuffling sound up above brought Tala's attention to the thick branches, just in time to see Serala nimbly scamper her way down, dropping the last few feet and landing with a dull thud. She seemed perfectly fine, but he was still going to give her a check-over to make sure she hadn't picked up anything.

"We're almost there. Should make it in a couple more days." That was wonderful news! Morungil, finally! Tala couldn't wait to escape the pressing darkness of the deep Jungle!

Well, most of him couldn't. In truth, despite the nightmarish plant life that constantly harassed them (and the animal life that harassed Osson or Serala whenever they ventured too far from him), he had actually rather enjoyed the last couple weeks. Serala had taken Tala's entirely unnatural protection from the beasts of the Jungle as further proof he had met the Beast God, and it had done what it could to help protect him from the many, many dangers of the place.

Osson had refused to talk about it much (unsurprisingly), even beyond his usual reticence to engage in conversation with them. Although he had been speaking more and more as the days wore on, to the point he would actually engage in proper conversations with them now! He still resolutely refused to be involved with anything to do with the Gods, though, saying he wasn't being paid enough for that level of shit.

But despite the annoying, ever-present threat of the Jungle flora, and the welcome semi-absence of danger from the fauna, the journey had mostly been a less-than-relaxing couple of weeks spent essentially alone with Serala. Tala had enjoyed *that* immensely.

Without the burden of leading a whole group of terrorists, while protecting the most wanted criminal in the world, Serala had been able to relax. After Tala had forced her to deal with her issues with Osson, at least. As such, with no other real company besides each other, he and Serala had grown much closer together, to his (internal) joy.

After a few more hours of battling their way through the Jungle, which ended only when it got too dark to safely travel, Serala started the fire. Sitting on the ground, she leaned back against the tree Tala had relaxed on (he was fairly confident it was an inert tree) and laid her head tiredly on his shoulder. The act sent warm fuzzy feelings buzzing all through his chest.

"What's the plan once we do get there, exactly?" Tala questioned, trying not to move and thus dislodge Serala. While his two companions (mostly Serala) had told Tala quite a bit about the Jungle city, she hadn't been very forthcoming about how they were going to find Vail and the others once they were inside. (Thankfully, entering would be quite easy, as most of the city had no walls or even guards to stop infiltrators, the Jungle itself being more than sufficient for defense while Plant and Beast Blessed kept its nastier aspects away from the city.)

"Meet up with the others. Interrogate Vail on what in the Godsdamned ever-loving Hells he was thinking." Serala's ire towards Vail's whole throw-Tala-off-the-bridge thing hadn't lessened even slightly in the last two weeks. Whether it was out of personal concern for Tala himself or simply irritation at risking such a valuable asset to their cause, Tala wasn't certain. (He liked to think it was the former, given how comfortable she had become with such casual acts of intimacy, like using him as a pillow.)

"Yes, but how are we going to meet up with them? Is there, like, an established meeting spot? Or a safe house we're going to go to that will let them know we're there?"

"No. No meeting spots. And definitely no safe houses. I already told you we can't do *anything* suspicious in the city. Rare as Beast Blessed themselves are, Descendants are plentiful, and even we can't hide our tracks from them if they start looking for us. Beast trackers can follow a scent from one end of the world to the other once they've caught it. As far as you're concerned, in Morungil, you're not a Dissident. You've barely even heard of them outside of scary stories."

"Okay. Right. But then, how are we actually going to *find* the others?"

"We'll look around a bit."

Tala gave her the best deadpan glare he could, given she was practically lying down with her head still on his shoulder. He figured she got the point, even if she couldn't see his look.

"I know a few places they're likely to be. The arena, for one. Hopefully only as spectators, but it's been weeks, so I'm not going to hold my breath," she grumbled, and Tala could well understand her concern. As stoic as they could be, a few of their friends didn't handle idleness well. While it didn't sound to be quite as grand as the Grand Arena in Fiahren, anybody could enter the Morungil Arena as a gladiator for their daily fights with few questions asked. Dunlop, at least, would have been sorely tempted to enter. The risk of getting the wrong sort of attention was really the only thing that might stop the man. The others he could easily see as enjoying being spectators, if nothing else.

"Yeah. That seems likely. But where else? We can't just spend every day at the arena waiting for one of them to show up next to us."

"I know a few others. There are a couple of tea shops that Vail's fond of. The drink's not too popular there, not like it is in Fiahren, so there aren't many, and fewer that live up to his standards," she said with an eye roll that Tala could *feel*. Vail had a weird obsession with that drink.

"So, fights and tea? That's the plan?"

"It's Vail," she said with a shrug. "They'll all be avoiding anything Dissident-related, same as us, so there's not much else there that'll interest him. Believe me, we'll find him and Ilan at one or the other."

"Yeah, that tracks," Tala said with a sigh. Vail had to be the strangest person that he had ever met.

"It's better than him burning the city down for shits and giggles," Osson said as he came back into sight, having briefly left to relieve himself. If there was one subject that Osson was *always* willing to talk about, it was Vail. Mostly complaining about or insulting Vail, but still.

"He wouldn't do that," Tala protested, but even to his ears it sounded weak and half-hearted. Even just barely knowing Vail personally, Tala couldn't have confidently claimed that, but after hearing everything Serala and Osson had to say about the man over the last couple of weeks? Well... at this point, he wouldn't be surprised. Even Serala rarely said anything that Tala considered positive about her adoptive father. The way she shifted and coughed uncomfortably at Tala's protest made it all too clear what she thought about Osson's accusation, much to Tala's dismay.

"I swear. The way you two talk about him sometimes, it's like you think he's the Demon reborn or something." Tala chuckled, closing his eyes. It was late, he was tired, and having Serala leaning on him had left him feeling all sorts of happy, contented, and comfortable. He only barely heard Serala's awkward half-laugh about how Vail was "nobody reborn" before he drifted off to sleep.

CHAPTER 38

"That is a big tree," Tala breathed out, eyes wide as he stared up at the God Tree as it towered above the Jungle, absolutely dwarfing the city beneath it. He had heard the famous giant tree was, in fact, giant, but if ever he had been faced with the contrast between knowing something was big versus seeing and understanding it was big, it was now. Even the mountains of the Split were less impressive, even if the larger of them were still quite a bit taller.

"Are the leaves giant too? Or does it just have that many of them?" Tala missed the way Serala blinked in surprise at the question, too entranced with the tree, trying to discern any distinct shapes in the giant branches stretching out across the sky. The green of the tree's expansive crown was a roof covering the whole world.

"I don't know." Serala frowned at the tree.

"They're larger than most normal leaves, but not huge. There's just a lot of them," Osson said blandly, arms crossed as he waited for Tala to stop ogling the giant growth.

"How do you know that?" Serala asked.

"I've spent more time in this city than you. Leaves fall sometimes. More in the autumnal months. They're about the size of the average human. Mostly."

"Really? Do they all fall?" Tala couldn't imagine how the city could survive if the tree lost every leaf at once. The combined weight of that many giant leaves would probably crush the whole place. Anyone who did survive the fall would likely end up suffocating, or worse, in the blanket.

"No. Only a few. Maybe a few dozen throughout the year. The Church collects them as soon as they hit the ground. No idea why."

"Do you think it's true, then? That's really the Plant God?"

Osson merely grunted, which didn't surprise Tala in the least. The man still refused to talk about anything directly related to the Gods.

"I don't know. I was skeptical before, but with the whole 'wild Beast God' thing, I'm reconsidering," Serala responded, always happy to discuss theories about the Gods, unlike Osson.

"You don't suppose it being a tree would make it any easier to kill, do you?"

Serala snorted a laugh. "Please. Even if it was a normal tree, it would take forever to cut down just from its sheer size. As a tree in the Jungle? It would take a Fire Blessed just to burn a small chunk out. If it is the Plant God, even Anderas Anto probably couldn't scratch the bark."

"Pity. Imagine what you could build with wood that strong. And that much of it. We could build a fleet of unsinkable ships and invade the Wind Islands." That got a full laugh out of Serala, with even Osson chuckling a bit.

"Invade the Wind Islands in the mutilated corpse of a dead God! That'd be one for the bards to sing about."

Serala and Tala both turned wide eyes on Osson, who resolutely refused to look at them, although he couldn't quite hide the slight smirk on his lips. They shared a look before laughing again.

"That's the dream." Tala chuckled, shaking his head before bringing his eyes downwards. "So, this is Morungil, eh?" The moment they stepped out of the tree line, his eyes were drawn to the massive tree, so he hadn't yet examined the city that lived far beneath its massive branches.

"Aye. Welcome to the capital of the Jungle, the one and only city in the damned place." Serala dramatically flourished her hand toward a sight Tala would readily admit was absolutely beautiful. Morungil had no walls of any kind on the edges, so nothing blocked his view aside from the buildings of the city itself. Buildings unlike any from the other cities he had been to. Morungil was almost entirely made of stone and wood. The central structure of each building was stone, giant pillars of stone, with small windows and large doorways carved all around them at seemingly random heights and intervals.

Built up around the stone towers, spiraling out from the gaping doorways in a chaotic mishmash of architecture that deeply pleased Tala's Fiahren-born senses, were wall-less wooden platforms. They were built on top of, or extending out from, each other, turning one single stone tower into the central column of a living hive of activity and people. Almost all the signs of a domicile appeared in the higher platforms: tables and chairs, fire pits and cooking stoves (both of which seemed rather dangerous to him), couches and rugs, and even beds. Other platforms, most of the lower and ground level ones, looked to be various businesses, clearly selling food and/or drink, a variety of clothing and other accessories, weapons and armor, and many more.

All the many towers and their wooden platforms were connected to each other by an absolutely dizzying amount of hanging bridges that crisscrossed through the open air of the city: wooden walkways held together by intricately woven—or more likely *grown*—vines. Wooden ramps spiraled around the towers, passing each platform and allowing an easy, unbroken pathway all the way from the ground to the very tops of the buildings. As much as the chaotic mess of it all reminded Tala nostalgically of Fiahren, the sheer differences of the very foundations made it feel very alien to him. Even Kilatara hadn't left Tala feeling quite so far from home as he did now. And stretching above it all, so expansive and high up it seemed more like an alien sky than anything, spread the leaves and branches of the God Tree. A tree that very well might be one of the Gods themselves.

"It's quite something, isn't it?" Serala said lightly from beside him, smiling as she watched him soak in the sight of Morungil. One of the brightest parts of his unwilling journey was that Tala loved seeing the strange places in the world he'd never imagined he would get to, a part of him Serala had long recognized.

"It really is," he responded without taking his eyes off the city before him. "Are they all like this? The capitals, I mean. Fiahren, Kilatara, Morungil, they're all cities, but they're all so... *different* to each other and to everywhere else I've been. Unique."

"Aye. The lesser cities usually share similarities to their nation's capital, or multiple like some of the border cities, but the capitals themselves are all unique. Fiahren is the biggest and busiest in a lot of ways. Kilatara is the shiniest and has those storms. Morungil is sometimes called the Sky City because as much of its business is done in the floating Fal'marae as on the ground. Yerenta is—"

Tala interjected. "Fal'marae?" he questioned, vaguely recognizing the word.

"The platforms. They're called Fal'marae, or Falms for short. Or sometimes Marae. The ones above the ground are floating Fal'marae, or floaters, since they look like they're floating in the air around the towers, which are called Hale Kia'i themselves."

"Oh. Cool. What were you saying about Yerenta?"

"Oh, right. Yerenta is made entirely out of rock and stone. Almost the entire city is made of stone towers, kind of like these Hale Kia'i, but they're a lot bigger and... squarer. They also don't have Falms. Instead, everything is done inside the towers. Some of them are so big they take up an entire block by themselves and are almost like a small town of their own on the inside. It's called the Stone City for that reason."

"I've heard that, yeah. It's supposed to be kind of ugly, though."

"Eh, depends on the person. It's not nearly as colorful as Fiahren, but a whole city of giant stone buildings has its own appeal. And the place is full of nature, unlike Fiahren.

You could eat for a lifetime just by picking the fruits and vegetables that grow around the city. If you can get to them before someone else does, that is."

"Fiahren doesn't have a lot of that, does it?"

"Nope. Anyway, we should get moving. We aren't going to find the others standing here."

"Oh, right, yeah."

They cheerily ignored Osson's grumbled "Finally!" as they started walking again, crossing into Morungil unchallenged and unnoticed.

CHAPTER 39

"That's the arena I'm guessing?" Tala asked, gesturing out to the massive, circular structure in the distance. One of the few buildings easily as tall as the Hale Kia'i that made up most of the city, but significantly larger and without any Fal'marae circling it.

"Yep. There are a few more places to check on the way, but we should get there pretty soon." Serala had already analyzed all the other patrons of the teashop Fal'marae they were in. For all that she had said that the Jungle wasn't as generally fond of tea as Fire was, the "Tea-Top" (a name that Tala both loved and despised) was quite busy. The location probably helped, as the Tea-Top was, as the name implied, located at the very top of one of the taller Hale Kia'i in its area. It provided its patrons with an absolutely stellar view across Morungil and the nearby jungle.

Had they not been searching for their erstwhile companions, Tala would have loved to stop and spend some time in the Tea-Top, relaxing and enjoying the view. Neither of his companions seemed particularly inclined to do so, though, as they were already making their way across the shop to a walk-way on the other side, gently sloping downwards to connect with the Fal'marae of the next spire over. The Tea-Top had been the third teashop in their search for Vail and Ilan, and certainly the highest. Tala was still getting used to traversing the city by way of the hanging bridges. Walking on nothing but vines and planks of wood suspended hundreds of feet in the air had been rather terrifying at first, but his nerves were steadily calming with each one that he crossed with no issues.

"I'm surprised you're still with us, honestly," Tala said to Osson as they passed through a Falm grilling some sort of delicious smelling meat. "I half expected you to abandon us the moment we reached the city."

"With your luck, if I left, you'd never make it to Vail and the bastard would blame me. No. I'm taking you right to him so he can't claim I didn't complete my job in its entirety. Then I'll piss off and, with any luck, never see any of you morons again."

"Truly, your words warm the cockles of my heart."

"I will throw you off this damn bridge."

"Eh, been there, done that. And we aren't actually on a bridge right now."

"I will throw you off the next one."

"Throw him off and I throw you off," Serala chimed in, sounding far too chipper.

"Deal. I'll live."

"Vail will also hunt you down."

Osson literally growled at Serala.

"Down, boy. Or I'll tell Vail you admitted to us how much

you actually enjoy his company," Tala threatened, doing his best to maintain a straight face as they stepped onto another bridge. A feat made harder by Serala bursting into laughter.

Osson just scoffed. "Please. Even he isn't dumb enough to believe that."

"Wanna bet?"

Osson's glowering silence was like music to Tala's ears. Although that might have just been Serala's continued laughter.

They continued making their way towards the arena, going up and down, crossing bridges, and going down ramps as they checked every teashop, armory, and weapons store that was even remotely in their way. There were good odds that they could find Dunlop at least in such a place if he wasn't at the arena. They even checked a few of the forges in their path just in case, all of which were located on the ground and away from any Fal'Marae or Hale Kia'i to prevent any accidents from the intense heat of the flames.

Despite their diligence, the trio found no sign of their companions anywhere, and eventually found themselves staring up at the massive walls of the Morungil arena.

"So do we just go right on in?" Tala asked as he watched a pair of bored guards standing at the far end of the bridge. Just like the rest of Morungil, the arena had a multitude of bridges leading to it from various Fal'marae coming from every height and direction. Tala and his two companions were in a Falm selling (and renting) seat pads, with a bridge leading straight into the arena at roughly halfway up its height.

"Yep," Serala replied as she passed him and began crossing the bridge. "Is the Fire arena different?"

"No. Well-not really. Almost all the entrances are at ground level. The only ones higher up are in the Church's section, for their use only."

The trio passed by the two guards who barely even glanced at them, to Tala's mixed relief and amusement. The world's most wanted man, most dangerous man, and one of its worst (if unknown) criminals walking within feet of trained guards completely unrecognized. He wasn't complaining though; he really didn't need another Southtown. Or Lynmyr.

As they stepped through the entryway into the arena, Tala felt a wave of nostalgia course through him. It was incredibly similar to the Great Fire Arena. Staggered seating that could easily fit tens of thousands of bloodthirsty spectators all circled around a massive pit set into the ground. As his eyes roamed over everything, Tala could make out plenty of differences. The pit, which in Fire was a layer of sand over hard packed dirt, was more akin to a small field. Short green grass spread pleasantly from wall to wall, although the grass was clearly in better shape near the walls than in the center, struggling to survive amidst the mud and churned ground. If it wasn't for the ambient power of the Plant God supercharging its vitality and growth, Tala doubted even a single blade would have survived in there. Additionally, while most of the arena did appear to be made of stone, the seating itself was not. Instead of the long rows of hard stone that the Fire arena had, here there were long wooden benches to sit on, a far more comfortable experience for those who didn't bring or buy any padding.

"Have you never been to the Fire arena before?" Tala asked.

"No. I've barely spent any time in Fiahren at all. Hagan doesn't like us being in his city," Serala answered absently as she scanned the arena. It wasn't even half full, but there were still thousands of people scattered around the stands.

"Why?"

"Says we're too chaotic. Cause too much trouble." She shrugged. "He's not wrong, really. He hated having to call us in for the Ignis situation, but he didn't have much of a choice. Hey, bastard," she said, turning to Osson. "Can you find Vail? Do your little sensing trick?"

"No," he replied bluntly.

"Why not?" Serala challenged.

"There's not enough people." Serala stared skeptically at the many thousands of people scattered around the arena. Tala did too, though he had no idea what sensing trick she was talking about. Osson sighed as she turned back to him with a brow raised. "They're too spread out. I can't find one empty space when there's empty spaces everywhere. Not when none of them are moving. Doesn't work like that." Tala frowned, trying to puzzle out just what in the Hells that nonsense meant. Serala clearly understood it, to Tala's irritation.

"Fine. Do some eye trick and start looking around then." She huffed, dropping onto a bench and leaning back against the low wall of the next tier. Tala hesitantly sat next to her.

"Why don't you just look for him yourself?" Osson asked, frowning down at her.

"Because it would take all day for us to walk around checking every person. You can do it from here. So do it."

Osson grumbled but sat down a few spaces away from

them, crossing his arms and looking thoroughly put out. They sat silently for a minute before Tala broke.

"What are we-he-doing, exactly?"

Serala blinked owlishly at him for a moment before chuckling softly. "Right. Sorry. You know that thing Gazin can do with eyes? To let himself see things that are far away? He's doing that, looking for Vail or one of the others. If he doesn't find them, we'll go sit on the other side so he can look at the people around here."

"Oh, okay. Cool." They fell quiet for a minute, watching the pair of fighters currently in the pit brawl. They were both lightly armored, one wielding a club, and the other a shield and one-handed (and presumably blunted) ax. While Tala knew he was no expert on fighting, not with only a few months of training and almost no true experience, he couldn't help but feel that the two fighters were, well... utter crap. He couldn't think of a nicer way to put it. He was pretty sure that he could beat them both quite easily himself. Were they amateurs trying to make a career as gladiators or simply desperate for money—desperate enough to risk injury or death in the arena?

"Wait a second," Tala suddenly piped up, drawing a lazy eye from Serala, who looked like she was well on the way to falling asleep. "Osson's a Boney. How's he doing Gazin's eye trick?"

Serala stared tiredly at him. "Just... don't question it. Trust me. Just don't."

"But that doesn't make any-"

"I know." She cut him off, sighing. "Believe me, I know."

"There are no bones in the eye. Gazin said the eyes are tricky to mess with even for Fleshies and Bloodies, and they both are actually supposed to have control over them because the eye is all flesh and fluid. There are no-"

"It's 'cause I'm magic. Now shut up and stop distracting me," Osson interrupted. Tala had forgotten just how exquisite the man's hearing was.

"You're all magic. That doesn't explain-"

"I said. Shut. Up." Tala's mouth closed before he could even consider it. There was something dangerous in Osson's tone, something Tala hadn't heard before despite everything they had gone through. Serala glared at Osson, who resolutely ignored her.

Tala turned back to the pit, where the club-wielding man was slowly walking back to the tunnel, apparently victorious. The next pair of fighters' names were called out, the announcer's voice carrying through the arena with a strange rumbling undertone, more like an animal roar than a human voice. Tala peered over at the Church's section but couldn't spot the announcer in the private boxes from his angle. He figured it was probably some sort of Beast trick, allowing his voice to carry. It was louder and clearer even than Cacawari's voice in the Fire arena, despite their designs being so similar. The acoustics should have been nearly the same.

Tala watched in silence as the next pair of fighters entered the pit from their respective tunnels. They didn't seem much better than the first pair, wearing similar simple, dirty armor. One was wielding an ax and shield again, while the other had a sword and shield. As they began fighting, Tala decided he could still beat them both. They were better than the first pair, sure, but their movements appeared slow and obvious to him. Maybe all that training under the likes of Dunlop and the others had already had some effect.

Tala lost track of time as he lazily watched more fighters enter and leave the arena. Some of the fighters were truly horrible, and their fights were just pathetic. Although a few times, it seemed like they were just poorly matched against somebody far better, making them appear worse than they actually were. Most of the fighters were decent enough, he supposed, and gave an adequate enough showing to entertain the spectators. And while there weren't many, a few fights were absolutely spectacular, and Tala got caught up in the excitement of the crowd as they watched true warriors battle it out. Did the Dissidents ever use the pit fights as a way to find possible recruits? Some of the better fighters really were quite amazing. Not that even the best of them could compare to the monsters that Dunlop and Ilan were, but they might be able to hold their own against Lito.

Gods! Tala had never realized before that Lito was actually a fantastic fighter! His friend's eagerness to always join in on his training sessions, and Lito's lack of confidence in his own martial abilities, had made Tala believe that Lito wasn't all that skilled. Better than Tala himself by far, but not particularly impressive by any means.

Tala sighed, feeling sorry for his friend. Being around

such talented warriors as their other companions, they both had developed very skewed ideas of what a "good fighter" actually was. He'd have to find a way to boost Lito's confidence in the future, or at least get the boy to stop comparing himself to the monsters in their party.

As the names of the next two fighters in the arena were announced, something in the back of his mind perked up. Why? Tala considered the names that had just been announced, Poldun and—wait. Tala turned to Serala, also sitting up now, looking intently down at the pit as the two fighters emerged. One wielding a great sword and the other... two short sticks tied together by a short length of thin vine? Tala had never seen such a weapon before, if that even *was* a weapon.

"Is that...?" He trailed off, not sure he wanted to finish the thought out loud.

Serala responded with an aggrieved sigh. "Yep."

"Poldun? Really?"

"It is a fake name," she defended half-heartedly.

"Barely!"

They both stared in disappointment at the fighter with the two sticks as the fight began. Almost lazily dodging a quick swing from the great sword, he began to spin one of the sticks on the vine in a circle, the other held in his hand. His opponent clearly didn't see the spinning stick as much of a threat. He charged straight ahead, already bringing the great sword into another cross body cut that—blunted or not—would likely be a killing blow. The so-named "Poldun" once again leaned just out of range of the strike. Bringing the spinning stick around as he did so, he smashed it into the side of the larger man's face. The man spun halfway around and crashed to the ground. To his credit, he didn't stay down, and quickly—if unsteadily—pushed himself back to his feet. He brought his sword around into a defensive stance, clearly far more wary of the spinning stick.

As the fighters engaged again, Tala shared an exasperated look with Serala. It was painfully obvious to them both that "Poldun" was toying with his opponent, dragging the fight out and making it seem like a proper bout between two roughly equal fighters, to the exuberance of the crowd. Even using the strange maybe-weapon, he could have ended the bout with the very first attack had he so wanted, and still could end it at any moment he chose. As he whacked the other fighter one more time, the man fell to the ground once again, this time without making a single effort to get up. The crowd cheered excitedly for the unexpected victory by the much smaller fighter wielding such a weird weapon.

"Well then. Should we go congratulate 'Poldun' on his victory?" Tala asked, physically cringing as he spoke the very much half-assed alias.

Serala sighed. "I suppose so. Hey, bastard! We're leaving."

"Finally!" Osson muttered, not-so-quietly, as he rose to join them.

"You didn't see Vail, Ilan, or anybody else? Even with Dunlop fighting?" Serala asked skeptically.

"No. I did. They're across the pit."

"What!? Why didn't you say so?"

"I just saw them as the fight started. I wanted to watch Poldun fight." He shrugged. "The man's impressive, and it looks like they're leaving too."

Grumbling, Serala led them to the stairs and started descending, heading to the ground level where they could find Dunlop and, presumably, Vail and Ilan. As Serala continued to grumble, Tala glanced at Osson, who gave him a mean smirk and wink. Tala just shook his head and looked down, hiding a grin of his own.

CHAPTER 40

"They should be around here somewhere," Serala said as she scanned the open, wide grassy ring that circled the arena. It was filled with people, all standing around loosely by themselves or in small clusters, some waiting while others were talking to fighters, either congratulating or consoling them on their fights, cheering over money won or lamenting over money lost.

It didn't take long for them to spot Ilan. The man towered over almost everybody else there. He and Vail stood by themselves, a ring of empty space around them, as if everybody present were naturally avoiding the pair without even realizing it. Whether that was due to Ilan's imposing figure, Vail's conspicuous and ever-present hood, or both, Tala couldn't say. As the three of them began making their way over, Dunlop approached the pair, a few words passing between them before they turned to leave.

Serala whistled a series of notes, sounding much like birdsong, and Vail and Ilan's heads whipped in their direction. Dunlop's followed a second behind; he fell into a subtle battle stance with his hand on the hilt of his sword. The strange stick weapon he had used in the arena was nowhere to be seen. As Serala smoothly slid through the crowd into the empty space, followed by Tala and Osson, Dunlop stood straight, eyes wide. A relieved smile blossoming on his face as he took in the three of them. Even Ilan gave a small grin, the visible emotion a clear sign of how worried he must have been. Vail... Tala couldn't tell. With much of his face hidden in his hood as usual, only his mouth could be seen, and the shadowed lips didn't seem to have moved. But as Serala approached, he returned her hug without protest, if a little awkward and wooden to Tala's eyes.

Tala waited quietly as Serala turned and hugged Ilan. The large man bent down and wrapped her in a much more natural, warmer hug than Vail's. Tala thought he saw a glimpse of water in the man's eyes before he closed them, squeezing Serala tight. Leaving Those Three to their reunion, Dunlop approached Tala and slapped a hand on his shoulder as he stared him dead in the eye.

"It's good to see you. Both of you. We were beginning to fear the worst," Dunlop said, giving Tala's shoulder a squeeze. Tala's eyes flicked to Osson, standing bored beside him, but Dunlop completely ignored him.

"It's good to see you too," Tala replied, feeling both warm and awkward at Dunlop's visible emotion. The man was normally so awkward and stilted outside of training that seeing him so clearly care was strange. Not unwelcome, per se, but certainly unexpected.

"How did you survive? You and her both? When Denhei struck her, we were all certain she was dead."

"That's a bit of a long story. A long and confusing story. I'll tell you when we meet up with the others." Dunlop frowned but nodded, accepting and squeezing Tala's shoulder again before letting him go.

"And you've still got your sword, I see. That's good. It would be a terrible thing for that to have been lost in the Jungle."

Tala smiled, chuckling internally at Dunlop's words. Of course he had been worried about the sword. Maybe as much or more than he had been worried about Tala. Tala would have been offended if it wasn't so Dunlop.

"Dunlop. It's wonderful to see you too," Serala said, having moved beside them. Dunlop smiled back and squeezed her shoulder the same as he had Tala's. "Could you go and gather the others? At wherever you all have been staying? The four-five of us," she corrected herself, shooting a glare at the uncaring Osson, "need to have a talk before we join you."

Dunlop frowned, his eyes narrowing, but he nodded all the same. "Aye. These two know where to find us when you're done. It might take some time to get them all anyway."

Serala smiled and Dunlop turned and left. As he vanished into the crowd, Serala turned to Vail and Ilan with a frown.

"We need to talk. Somewhere private." Ilan regarded her blankly. But Vail, surprisingly, simply nodded in response without delay, like he had been expecting it.

"We can get a room. Follow me," Vail said in his usual monotone, turning and leaving without waiting for a response, Ilan right behind him.

Osson gave an aggrieved sigh. "Do I really have to-"

"Yes," Serala practically snarled at the man. Osson sighed again with an exaggerated roll of his eyes, moving his entire head in the process. Tala smirked and ignored him. For somebody with such a fearsome reputation who always acted so angry and aloof, he could be a real drama queen at times. Still, he fell into line behind Tala as they followed the retreating back of Ilan.

The four of them followed Vail—or, rather, the three of them followed Vail and Ilan—as they made their way through the grassy ground of the city. As strange as he found the place, the presence of the Falms and sky bridges meant there was light foot traffic on the ground, and they were able to quickly traverse the city to wherever they were going. A mysterious location that quickly formed into an exasperated sense of amusement as Vail finally led them up two levels of spiral ramps and into another tea Falm. *Of course* that would be where he was leading them.

Vail completely ignored his followers, unsurprisingly, as he walked up to the counter and spoke quietly to the woman manning it. When he dropped a few coins into her open hand, the woman nodded and dropped something small into his hand in turn. He didn't move as she turned away, and Tala waited awkwardly as he stood a few feet behind. The woman came with a serving tray carrying five cups and a large pot of tea, trying to pass it to Vail before Ilan stepped forward and took hold of the tray. The woman blinked at the giant man before smiling nervously and with a last glance at Vail, turned away from them.

With no more preamble, Vail turned and walked toward

the Hale Kia'i, not bothering to check if the rest were even there. Tala frowned, but followed alongside the others, trailing Vail as the man entered the opening in the giant stone tower. The inside of the tower was not what Tala had been expecting, but in retrospect he wasn't sure why he was surprised. The very center of the tower was an open hole, with a massive staircase spiraling around it, a landing wrapped around the staircase, between it and the walls, where Tala and the others were standing.

Tala stepped over and poked his head into the empty space in the center of the stairs, looking up and down. The stairs ran from the very bottom of the tower all the way to the top. Just seeing all the stone stairs made Tala's legs hurt. Thankfully, Vail didn't mount the stairs in either direction, and instead, turned to a door set in another wall of the tower, opening it and walking through. Tala and the others followed into a small sitting room with a few other doors leading off from it. Vail went to one and unlocked it with the small key in his hands, presumably what the tea matron had given him.

Following him inside revealed an even smaller room, filled only with a wooden table in the center surrounded by wooden chairs, one of which Vail unceremoniously dropped himself into. Tala followed suit as the rest sat in chairs themselves. Osson closed the door behind them all as he dropped, rather petulantly, into one of the remaining chairs, leaning back with his arms crossed and an angry scowl on his face. They all ignored him.

Vail poured himself a cup of tea. Tala felt awkward and uncomfortable as they all sat in silence, waiting for Vail to finish. The man filled up all five cups in the silence, passing them out to each of them. Tala thought Osson was going to knock his off the table, much like a naughty child might, but after a sudden glare from Vail, he simply took a disgruntled sip from the cup instead. At a complete loss for what to do, Tala lifted his own cup to his lips, blowing softly on the steaming beverage before taking a small sip. His brows shot up in surprise as he took another sip. He didn't recognize the flavor at all, but it was quite pleasant.

"Great. Now, Vail? What the fu-" Serala was cut off.

"Did you learn about Tora?" Vail rudely interrupted, staring intensely at Tala and acting completely oblivious to Serala's question. Tala blinked in surprise before feeling anger build. He hadn't even begun to think of how he might respond before Serala beat him to it.

"Really? Godsdamnit, Vail! What... Just-what the fuck, Vail!?"

Vail glanced at her, looking entirely unbothered. "Is that a yes?"

"No! I-it's a what the fuck, Vail! You really did plan that! Why? You threw Tala off the Godsdamned bridge!"

Ilan coughed on his tea, thumping himself in the chest with a heavy smack. Tala thought it had enough force to crush his entire rib cage had he been struck by it. "Vail. Really?" Ilan sighed once his coughing had subsided, looking and sounding as disappointed as Tala had ever seen him, putting his face into the palm of his hand.

"At least you didn't know," Serala muttered angrily, still glaring at Vail. Osson poured himself another cup of tea, having apparently already finished his first. Tala sipped more of his, anger still simmering but tempered by Serala's outburst. Vail ignored it all, aside from a quick glance at Serala, and continued staring intently at Tala.

"Tora. Did you learn-"

"Vail!" Serala screamed, gripping her own untouched cup of tea like she was going to throw it at him. "No! Explain! You! First!" A wave of fear smothered Tala's anger as he stared at Serala. This was the same girl who had laughed as she slaughtered her way through an army of trained soldiers. The same girl who had once offered to slit his throat like it was nothing.

"Does it-" Vail began, only to be cut off by Serala, who had apparently predicted what he was going to say.

"Yes, it matters! You threw Tala off a bridge! Into the Gods' Canyon! What were you thinking? He could have died! The fall could have killed him! The Jungle could have killed him! It should have! It almost did! What's so important about this 'Tora' that you would risk his life!? I've never even heard about it!" She was panting in her rage.

As much as Tala was trying to not stare at her, to look at the others and watch their reactions (Osson, the bastard, looking thoroughly amused now), his eyes kept being drawn to her against his will. A part of his mind wailed in despair, since fear wasn't the only emotion he felt at the sight of her all flustered with her face flushed. He mercilessly stamped down those thoughts.

Vail sighed, finally tearing Tala's eyes away to land firmly on the man. He didn't think he had ever heard Vail sigh like that. Like an actual person who could get annoyed. He took a breath like he was going to speak, but instead drank his tea, refilled the cup, and took another large sip. "I'll explain. After. But first I need to know: *did you learn about Tora?*" His tone of voice left Tala completely unable to do anything but comply.

"Ye-no-kind of?" Tala stammered. Vail's stern glare fell into a deadpan stare. Tala waited for him to say something, for any of them to, but they were all quiet, aside from Serala's still heavy breathing. Unsurprisingly, Tala broke first, and he tried to explain as best he could.

"I met a *thing* that mentioned Tora. Said it was a city. And some other stuff. It wanted me to find it, I think? It's all still really fuzzy. I had a bunch of Somic—Somiocanic venom—in my system at the time, so I don't remember it very clearly. I thought I hallucinated the whole thing, to be honest."

Vail closed his eyes and slumped back in his chair, looking disappointed in an uncomfortably normal manner. "That's it?" Vail asked, voice soft. "You don't remember any more? You don't know what, or where, Tora is?"

"No," Tala said, feeling oddly guilty. "I mean... I think it's a city. I'm pretty sure I remember *it* saying that. But I don't know where it is. Or was. I've never-I don't *think* I've ever heard of it before, though."

Vail's eyes snapped open, a slight frown on his brow. "You don't *think?*"

"What?"

"You don't *think*. You said you don't *think* you've ever heard of it before. Not that you've *never* heard of it. You stuttered. You aren't certain. You may have heard of it before." Vail was once again giving him that intense, almost fanatical stare.

"I don't know. Okay? But ever since I heard the name, it's been bugging me. I *feel* like I've heard of it before, but I have no idea where. Or when. Or why or how or anything. I know the names of every major city on the continent this side of the Dustwall. Even ones that have fallen. Even old names that aren't used anymore. From the very beginning. But none of them are, or have ever *been*, called Tora. If it is a real place, a real city, it's either in Wind or the Bodylands. Or the Water lands, wherever they exist. If they exist," he hastily added, remembering his promise to Wade. Although, from what Wade had said, Tala was fairly certain the Water people wouldn't be living in a city as old as Tora should be. Allegedly. If it was even real.

"It's not in the Wind Islands." Vail shook his head. Tala's brow furrowed: how in the Hells did Vail know what was—or wasn't—in the Wind lands? Even the Dissidents had said they didn't know anything about that place. "Os?"

Osson tsked, irritated. "I told you before that it isn't in the Bodylands."

"Could you be wrong?"

"No." Osson glared at Vail, who sighed and sat back again, tilting his head to sulk at the ceiling.

"Why do you think you *might* have heard of it before?" Vail asked, not looking away from the ceiling.

"I don't know. It's just been bugging me. The name. Like it rings a bell, but I don't know why. It's like... the memory of a memory. Like the memory of a dream. It's there, but *not*. I don't know. Maybe it's just because I was tweaked out on

Somic at the time. It *really* messed with my head. I'm pretty sure that's all it is."

"Fine." Vail sighed, sounding exhausted. Defeated, almost. "And you can't remember anything else that it said? Anything at all?"

"Not much. I think it wanted me to kill it and was disappointed that I couldn't. All the rest is really fuzzy, though. I haven't been able to sort it out, and I've been trying for weeks. I've just got some random words and nonsense in my head I can barely even grasp half the time. Kind of like a dream."

Vail didn't answer, but inside his hood, with his head tilted up, his eyes closed once more, he sighed sadly.

They sat there in silence once again, Vail not even drinking his tea anymore, just sitting still. Tala sipped at his.

Eventually Serala spoke up, her tone soft, still sounding angry, but it was only an undertone beneath concern and confusion. "Why did you... do all of this? Why didn't you tell me? Why haven't I ever heard about Tora before?" Tala peeked at Serala, clearly hearing a note of pain, of hurt, in her voice as she asked the last two questions.

"I don't know. Not really. Not much more than you. I was hoping that the kid could figure it out. He's smart. Clever. Learned in a way I never was or could be. He's pulled off a few miracles already, so I was hoping he could manage this one."

"And it was worth all of this? Throwing him off the bridge? Risking his life in the Jungle of all places?"

"Yes."

"Why? How?"

"That was the Beast God he met. The 'thing' that told him about Tora."

Tala's heart jumped, and Serala jolted in surprise at Vail's words too. They had assumed that it was the Beast God already, true, but to have Vail confirm it? And so casually at that?

"It was? You're certain?" she asked, voice little more than a breath.

"Yes." Silence again. Even when he wasn't intentionally being an ass, Vail was a difficult man to talk to. A sentiment Serala seemed to share, given her quiet, aggrieved groan.

"Okay. Vail. You need to talk now," she said, faux-calmly. "You need to tell us everything. The bridge. The Jungle. The Beast God. Tora. Everything!"

Vail sighed quietly, bringing his head back down and downing his full cup of tea.

"Alright. Where should I start?" he asked quietly, and Tala wasn't sure if he was asking himself or the rest of them. Even now, Vail was impossible to read like that. Either way, he seemed to figure out the answer for himself, for he started talking before anybody else had answered.

"I met the Beast God myself, in the Jungle, many years ago. Before I met you. Any of you." He made a small gesture towards Osson who, despite his belligerence and very vocal desire to not be there, seemed as caught up in it all as the rest of them. "He-it-they, whatever, told me the same things it probably told the kid, only I wasn't out of my mind at the time." Osson, Serala, *and* Ilan all snorted. Not that Vail paid them any mind. "I was lost in the Jungle and just happened to cross its path. Or it mine. Either way, we spoke. It realized what I could do, recognized it." *That* got a reaction out of both Serala and Osson, much to Tala's confusion. What could Vail *do*? "It wanted me to kill it. I tried and failed. I could hurt it, barely, but didn't have the power to do more."

Now Tala was really confused. What could Vail do that could hurt a God?

"Once we finally gave up, we talked. It wanted to know how I had my power. Said it hadn't seen it since the beginning. I told it about my past, and that's when it mentioned Tora. Called it the greatest of all cities. That it was the only place in the world my power could have come from. My former captors must have had artifacts or technology from there, to give me these powers. Old things, saved in the beginning, probably. The Beast God told me if I could find Tora, if it still existed, I would find the power to kill it—to kill all the Gods. I've been looking ever since, but I've never found anything. Not so much as a whisper. At this point, my best guess is that Tora is a city in the heavens. That's why the kid was my last hope. If Tora did ever exist in our world, he would know of it."

The room was silent again. All of them digested what they had just heard. Tala didn't know where to even begin. He was missing so much information about Vail and his "power" and origins that the rest clearly knew. Most of what Vail said was similar to what he could remember the God saying during his encounter, though.

"So, what? The power to kill the Gods is hidden in the heavens? The afterlife? 'Cause that's not very helpful to us," Serala said.

Vail shrugged. "I guess. Which is unfortunate, but it could be worse."

"How could it be worse?" she asked skeptically.

"The Gods aren't as invincible as they're portrayed. Water vanished. Beast is all but feral at this point. It barely remembers that it is a God and not just a weird animal. Plant is a tree." Serala and Tala made indiscernible noises in their throats at that. "Hm? Oh, yes, the big tree up there is the Plant God. It got tired of immortality and put itself into an eternal sleep, or near enough. It treed itself before Beast pissed off to lose itself as an animal. The Gods may not be able to die, but that doesn't mean they'll be around forever. Three are gone, more or less. Eventually, the rest will go the same way, probably. Lose their memories, go crazy, something."

"Six," Osson muttered. When they all looked at him, he sighed in irritation. "Six are gone. The three Body Gods did something similar to Plant. Except even more messed up, naturally. There's a reason you people think there haven't been Blessed in the hordes in millennia."

"Wait, what do you mean we 'think' there hasn't been a Blessed?"

"You've heard of the 'Abominations,' right? The really nasty ones? The nightmare monstrosities that are almost impossible to kill?" Tala nodded. "Those are Body Blessed. The ones who survived. What's left of them. Their minds and bodies broken, shattered beyond all reason under the Blessing of the Three."

The room stared at Osson in horror. Even Vail looked sick. The Abominations of the Bodylands hordes were little more than whispered legends. Horror stories rarely talked about. Few people even believed they actually existed, since each tale told was more terrible than the last. Nightmares made up by the veterans of the Dustwall whose minds had broken under the horror of the hordes, tormenting their dreams with twisted visions even worse than the reality they had witnessed. This was a topic even Tala didn't want to explore any further. Only the most demented of Researchers would ever want to learn more.

"Okay. Six Gods are... non-issues. Let's leave it at that." It was the first time Ilan had spoken since they sat down. Tala was impressed at how close-to-normal he managed to sound after what they had just heard.

"Agreed," Serala said, voice a bit shakier. She cleared her throat before continuing. "So that's, uh, everything about Tora. And the Beast God." She cleared her throat again, pointedly *not* looking at Osson. "But why do it like this, Vail? Risk Tala all by himself? Not tell anyone about it?"

"He wasn't actually by himself—you were with him," Vail pointed out.

"I don't count! I was in a coma! He had to care for me for weeks before he found the Carnival!"

"What?" Vail asked, sounding surprised. "Oh. How are you still alive?"

"Tala took care of me. It nearly killed him. A bunch of times."

"Oh." He turned to Tala. "People can't drink in a coma." Tala swallowed and nodded, feeling very uncomfortable.

"People die in around three days if they don't drink anything." Tala nodded again. "How is she alive?"

Tala swallowed again, noting that Ilan, Serala, and even Osson were looking at him questioningly. "I... would rather not say. Please. It's something I learned about back at the Institute and it only worked because of some... *very* specific circumstances. That I'm not going to talk about."

"Okay. We are going to talk about that later," Serala said slowly. Tala cringed. "Anyway. Again, why didn't you tell anybody about this? Even Ilan didn't know!"

"About Tala and the bridge. I knew about Tora," Ilan confessed.

"What? Why did he know and I didn't?" Serala demanded.

"You were still a kid when I told him." Vail shrugged. "We gave up trying to find it years ago. The kid here made me think there was a chance again."

"That's why? But why throw him off the bridge by himself?"

"Beasty wouldn't approach a group of people. The kid had a better chance by himself. Especially with my smell on him. And none of you would have let him go off alone in the Jungle like that. Not even Ilan." Ilan nodded in affirmation, despite glaring at Vail. "So, I didn't give you all a choice. And I was right. It worked. Even if it didn't matter in the end."

"This. This is why people hate you, Vail," Serala grit out through clenched teeth and closed eyes.

"Really? I thought it was because of all the people I've killed." Osson barked out a laugh, and Serala snorted. Tala didn't really see the humor in it.

"Gods. Fine. Well, it's done now. We're back. We're alive. I'm alive, and I wouldn't be without Tala. Just promise me, Vail, not to do anything like this again in the future? Please? And talk to me, us," she motioned to Ilan, "about shit like this first? Okay?" Vail sighed and nodded, although Tala had a feeling it wasn't a genuine promise. Serala seemed to think the same, given the way she sagged. "Whatever. I'm done. Is there anything else we need to talk about before meeting up with the others? Vail? Any other giant secrets you've never told me about that you'd like to share?"

"Eh. I'm good." He shrugged.

Serala's eye twitched. "Fine. Excellent. We're done then."

"Wait, hold on a second," Tala piped up. "I'm still lost here. What power does Vail-"

"Tala," Serala interrupted, pinching the bridge of her nose. "Just... later, okay? I know you're missing a lot but, please, can we not do this right now?"

"Uh, sure." Tala nodded. As much as he desperately wanted to know, he could tell how thoroughly *done* Serala was. He didn't like it, but he could wait. For her sake, at least. And to be honest, he wasn't too upset himself. He had a lot to think about, even just from what he had understood in that conversation—and some things to very specifically *not* think about. He just knew he was going to have nightmares from Osson's little reveal.

As they all rose and prepared to leave, Tala remembered something. "Oh, one last thing, actually!" he called, making the others stop and look at him with exhausted expressions. He turned on his heel.

Following the lessons Dunlop had drilled into him, he swung his arm and punched Vail in the face. "Ow! Oh, wow, that hurt!" Tala cursed, shaking his hand. He had hit Vail right on the cheekbone under his left eye.

"Ha!" Osson shouted, beginning a laugh that quickly turned into a cackle. Vail raised his head and stared Tala in the eye, a second away from murdering him. Tala gulped and stared back at him, terrified, but refusing to regret his action.

"You deserved that one, Vail. Let it go," Ilan said softly.

Vail's hackles raised. For a moment, Tala thought the man was going to attack him like a wild dog. Thankfully, he just grunted and walked towards the door, passing by Tala, whose whole body relaxed when it was clear Vail wasn't going to retaliate.

"Nice punch," Serala said, giving him a small grin, which he returned.

CHAPTER 41

"Gods! I feared I'd never see you again!" Gazin choked out as he tightly hugged Serala. He hadn't allowed himself to truly hope she had survived Denhei's blow, and had spent the last month privately mourning her, even as he did his best to keep the others' morale up. More specifically, Lito and Alina. The two of them had been devastated at the loss of their friends. Tala especially had haunted them during their time in Morungil, the lad having grown quite close to them both. At the moment, the two were wrapped tightly around him, hugging the lad for all they were worth, much like Gazin and Serala.

Reluctantly, he let the girl go, stepping back as Caida swept her up. He turned towards Tala, who looked at him over the shoulders of Lito and Alina. Gazin would have hugged the lad as well, but those two weren't looking like they'd release him any time soon. He merely gave the lad a watery smile, which was sheepishly returned.

Gazin allowed himself to fall back into an armchair. His whole body relaxed now that the stress and worry of the last month was over. Mostly over, at least. There were still questions to be answered. Despite his best efforts, Gazin had utterly failed to get the truth about the events on the bridge from Vail. He was certain Tala hadn't just accidentally fallen off and could tell that Vail knew more about it. The stubborn bastard had resolutely refused to share anything, though. What happened on the bridge, why they had come to the Jungle in the first place, or why they weren't sending every available person to search for Tala.

Gazin's unease had been growing steadily for the last month as Vail continued to behave like a normal, law-abiding person. Coupled with his fear over the fates of Tala and Serala, it had been a very stressful month for him. Now that half of the problem had—unbelievably—resolved for the better, he was determined to find out what was going on. And if Vail still wasn't willing to talk, well then, Gazin wasn't going to give him a choice! And the timing couldn't be better as the others took their own seats around the sitting room. Serala promised to tell them about everything the two had experienced after the bridge.

"Tala should start. I was unconscious for a while after the bridge—I only know what happened myself because of him," Serala began, gesturing to an uncharacteristically nervous Tala.

Tala told them about what happened inside the Jungle. The animal attacks, the plant attacks, the Somic that had left him completely delirious. Gazin wasn't the only one who was struggling to listen to Tala's experience in a literal living hell. Even Serala had a hand on the lad's shoulder in an uncharacteristic show of support. Gazin raised a brow at that, noticing something he had missed earlier: Serala was sitting right next to Tala. Not merely next to him, but right beside him. As close as she could be while still sitting on her own wooden stool instead of sharing his chair. That was an interesting development. Surprising, if only because it was Serala. Tala hadn't exactly been subtle about his infatuation with the girl, although he had at least tried to hide it. But for Serala to be showing such familiarity, such comfort in return? It only took weeks together lost in the Jungle for the girl to start opening up.

A chill went down Gazin's spine. He would have to have a talk with Serala to make sure she knew certain things about the world. He didn't trust that Vail would have explained things properly—if at all—to her. He wasn't entirely certain that Vail even understood what sex was or how it worked. He was not looking forward to that conversation.

As Tala continued his story and began talking about how he "managed to find a camp of people who helped" them, Osson, of all people, interrupted. "They all know about the Carnival. You don't have to keep that secret here. Courtesy of Vail there." Vail shrugged uncaringly when Tala looked at him, before sighing and continuing his story, albeit talking about finding the Carnival of Blood instead of a random "camp of helpful strangers."

"Hold on. How did you find the Carnival? We thought it was a myth until Vail sent the- uh, him there," Lito piped up, awkwardly pointing at Osson as he stumbled over what to call the most feared man alive while in his presence.

Now that was interesting. Not just Tala, but Serala, Ilan,

and even Osson were suddenly acting shifty. Tala started talking about hallucinating again before being interrupted by a loud sigh from Vail. A sound Gazin knew couldn't lead to anything good.

"No point hiding it," Vail said nonchalantly. Or sounded nonchalant, rather. Gazin could detect in Vail the signs of frustration, dark amusement, and... despair? What in the Hells was happening? "The kid ran into the Beast God. It told him how to find the Carnival."

The room was utterly silent, Gazin himself was easily as shocked as the day those two came back to the safe house in Fiahren with Tala in tow, telling a tale of how the lad had killed a Blessed.

"Yeahhh." Tala sighed, rubbing the back of his neck awkwardly. He explained meeting the creature he thought was a hallucination and it summoning a monkey-thing that led him to the Carnival.

Gazin closed his eyes and slumped back in his chair. First Vail, now Tala. Some days Gazin regretted ever leaving Earth country. Well, not really. Killing his former masters and escaping was still the best day of his life, but Gods did those two make said life complicated.

"You just happened to randomly meet a God? In the middle of the Jungle? Just by chance?" Gazin sighed out. From everything he knew about his companions, from everything he was reading in them since Tala started talking, Gazin was building a picture of the real truth behind events that he was very much *not* liking.

"No. I've met it before. I gave Tala something to draw

Beasty to him. Nothing came of it, though," Vail drawled out, and Gazin was sure he would have busted a blood vessel if he didn't have reinforced flesh. Suddenly, everything—almost everything—made sense. He *knew* Vail had been planning something in the Jungle, but this? Sometimes he forgot just how much of a psychotic madman Vail was, only to be brutally reminded at the worst times.

"Why?" Gazin breathed out, fighting the urge to strangle Vail. What could the bastard have possibly thought was worth risking Tala over?

Tora. Gazin had never heard of Tora. Apparently, that was the whole point: no one had, besides Vail, from the mouth of the Beast God itself (and Gazin was still struggling with the revelation that Vail of all people had personally met a God!). After Vail and Tala (mostly Tala) finished explaining everything they "knew" about Tora, Gazin had to begrudgingly admit he understood Vail's reasoning. And oh, how that hurt to admit, even if only to himself!

Once the group recovered from the revelation of the Beast God (for now, at least. Gazin knew they would all be struggling with that later), Serala took over the story, from her waking at the Carnival to their time spent trekking through the Jungle with Osson and a healed Tala. Gazin detected some hints of a bit more to that story too that was glossed over; he could well guess what must have occurred between Serala and Osson for her to not be glaring bloody murder at the man anymore. As she finished the tale, Gazin watched Tala curiously. The lad had been frowning to himself ever since the whole Tora thing. Was he feeling guilty over not knowing it, dashing Vail's greatest hope and reasoning for his entire ordeal? Gazin resolved to also have a talk with Tala later to make sure that the lad understood nobody blamed him, or even could, for not knowing the maybe-place.

"So that's it? Vail almost killed Tala, made him go through all of that, just to *maybe* learn about a place that *maybe* exists?" Lito exclaimed, sounding both infuriated and horrified. Gazin could well understand how the lad was feeling; it wasn't the first time he had experienced such emotions when dealing with Vail.

At Gazin, Serala, and even Ilan's tired nods, Lito all but exploded. "No! That-that's not okay! How could you do that?" He rounded on Vail, who stared back with a bored expression. "That's horrible! That's insane! He's our friend! Hells, keeping him alive has been our entire purpose for months! And you just throw him into-into all of that on a whim!? By yourself!?"

"Lad-" Gazin began but was cut off by Vail.

"Yep. It was our best chance at finding a solution, a *real* solution to having Them in the world. That's worth anything."

Lito made a strangled, choking noise. He stood there shaking, glaring at Vail, and Gazin had a bad feeling that if the boy wasn't stopped, he was going to attack. Luckily, before Gazin or one of the others had to step in, Alina grasped Lito's hand, not standing herself, but rubbing her thumb along the back of his fingers. She was also glaring at Vail, though she knew better than to let Lito try anything. Her touch helped calm the lad and he softened, losing some of the rigidity in his posture.

"I just... Even if Tora's real, how would we get to it? If it's so important, it probably would have been destroyed millennia ago. And that's if it even-"

"Say that again," Tala interjected.

"What?" Lito asked, blinking at Tala along with the rest of them. While Tala may have been looking—glaring—at Lito, it didn't seem like he was actually seeing him, but more like his eyes were just pointed that direction. A quick glance around showed Gazin that none of them seemed to know what had gotten into Tala.

"Say that again."

"...It would have been destroyed?"

"No. Before that."

Lito looked around, confusion and a plea for help clear in his gaze. They could do nothing but shrug at him in return. Even Gazin had no idea what Tala was getting at.

"Even if Tora's real?" Lito trailed off, only to continue as Tala absently nodded. "Even if Tora's real, how would we get to it? If it's so important, it probably would have been destroyed millennia ago."

Tala didn't speak; he just continued staring at Lito, brow furrowed and eyes absent. They sat in silence. Lito slowly lowered himself back into his seat, making as little noise as possible as they all waited for Tala to... finish whatever he was thinking. As a full minute passed, they started shifting uncomfortably.

"Tala, what are-"

"Shut up," Tala demanded, shocking them all. They never heard Tala talk like that before, much less to Serala of all people! She sat back, looking confusedly at Tala. Gazin doubted anyone had ever spoken to her like that before, aside from Vail, and possibly Ilan, and lived.

The atmosphere of the room had long since passed awkward, with even Osson and Vail feeling it, when Tala's eyes suddenly sparked to life, and the lad shouted out, startling them all. "That's it!" he yelled, ecstatic. "Tora! I know where I've heard of Tora before." He jumped to his feet, energy practically thrumming through him as he shuffled.

"Where?" Vail asked, sounding more serious and excited than Gazin had ever heard him.

"My parents!" Tala exclaimed, beaming at Vail.

"What?"

CHAPTER 42

Alina kept quiet, walking down the road beside Lito as Gazin and Tala repeated the same argument they'd been having for the last few days, ever since Tala's realization about his parents. The only one who seemed to fully believe Tala without issue was Vail. Within moments of Tala's announcement about his parents, Vail had jumped into action, sending Serala out with orders to all the local Dissident masters. The masters would use their own secret networks to find Tala's parents and have them sent to the city of Kurazil in Dust to meet up with their little group. Or, if that wouldn't work, to have a message sent in their place with a better location to meet. Serala hadn't seemed eager, but Vail had completely blown her off when she tried to argue.

That had been three days ago, and they had left Morungil the very next morning following the Jungle Road south to Kurazil. And Gazin hadn't stopped arguing with Tala since.

"I'm not saying I don't believe you, lad-"

"Really? 'Cause that's what it sounds like."

"But are you sure you weren't just dreaming and mixing

it up with reality? It'd be understandable with everything you've been through."

"Gazin, I told you already. I'm positive. It wasn't a dream, or hallucination, or mistake, or anything. I've heard my parents talk about finding Tora before! They said a lot of what Lito did: if it's real, if it still exists, how to get to it. I've heard them have conversations just like that!"

Alina couldn't find it in herself to defend him against Gazin. As much as she wanted to trust Tala, she had a hard time believing that he was right, that somehow his parents of all people knew about some legendary city related to the Gods that literally nobody else had heard of.

She wasn't the only one who was skeptical, either. She had talked with both Lito and Caida about it, and they both were like her. It was too random, too convenient. She had a feeling that the others were struggling with it too, based on their uncomfortable behavior whenever Gazin and Tala started arguing about it, although she hadn't spoken to them.

"I'm familiar with Somic, lad. I'm just saying it could have messed with your head more than you thought."

"The Carnival cleared it out of my system completely."

"Aye, but you were deep in its grip when you met the-the Beast God and first heard about Tora," Gazin stumbled, still struggling with the idea that Tala had met a God. They were all still struggling with his, and Vail's, revelations about the Beast God. "It could have mixed that idea with some inner desire to see your parents. The Carnival couldn't heal a thought already in your head, even if you didn't realize it was there!"

"Of course, I want to see them! They're my parents! I miss them! But that's not what's happening!"

Alina sighed, slowing her pace alongside Lito to put some more distance between themselves and the arguing pair. Tala and Gazin could both be incredibly stubborn when they set their minds to something, and now that they were set against each other, everyone else was suffering for it.

"I have half a mind to stick around and meet these parents of his. See just what kind of people are responsible for creating such an annoying little ass."

Alina twitched, hard, heart jumping as the Bone Merc spoke. the Bone Merc had left Morungil with them, much to their collective dismay, saying that he was heading south anyway and didn't care to stay in the Jungle any longer than he had to. He had kept pace with them, despite claiming to be traveling alone, but had mercifully stayed behind the group, rarely interacting with them. She desperately wished he had continued doing that; the man terrified her. She hadn't even realized that in trying to distance themselves from Tala and Gazin, Lito and her had fallen back near him.

"Why stop there? Why not go try to find Vail's parents, see who made him?" Lito asked casually despite his tenseness. Alina silently thanked him in her mind. If Lito was talking to the Bone Merc, then she didn't have to.

"Ha! Yeah, no. Even I don't want to meet whatever twisted monsters hate-fucked him into existence."

Alina cringed at the crudeness but couldn't help but silently agree. Before Southtown, Vail had been a strange and mysterious figure, one she—like everyone else in the

Dissidents—had wanted to know more about. Despite traveling with him for weeks, she hadn't learned any more. Until Southtown. After that, Vail had changed. He had grown more active, more involved, and the more she learned and saw of him, the less she wanted to do with him. She still didn't know how he had killed Lord Denhei on the Bridge, and she wasn't sure she wanted to anymore. the Bone Merc terrified her, for good reason, but there was something *wrong* with Vail. And the more she saw of him, the more she wanted to run away and hide.

"What a rude thing to say about your friend." She could have slapped Lito. Mouthing off to the Bone Merc! What was he thinking?

"He's not my friend," the Bone Merc growled.

"He says you're friends."

"He doesn't know what friends are."

"And you do?"

"Hmph." the Bone Merc grunted and fell silent, dropping his pace and falling behind them once again.

Alina turned to Lito with wide eyes. "Are you insane? You can't talk to him like that! He could kill you in an instant!"

"Tala does." He shrugged.

"Tala kills Blessed! And he's not exactly the picture of sanity!" She loved Tala dearly; he was her closest friend after Lito, but there was no denying there was something wrong with his head. Nobody else could have done, or would have even tried to do, the things he had. To say nothing of the fact he was clearly infatuated with Serala, had been since day one, and no sane person could ever have fallen for somebody who offered—offered!—to slit their throat as though it was a favor! Alina had had nightmares about that moment in the cave, and she was merely a witness! The fact that Serala was starting to show her own signs of interest in Tala didn't help the case of his sanity either.

"Point," Lito conceded. She knew he was thinking about the same things she was. Lito found Serala as physically attractive as anyone did, herself included, but a sharpened knife would probably be a safer bedtime companion than Serala. And would likely involve fewer knives too.

Lito shifted awkwardly, and Alina glanced at him. He had been acting strangely ever since they had arrived in Morungil. At first, she had thought it was because of Tala and Serala, that had thrown them all off, but even after they had both miraculously arrived alive and well, he hadn't gone back to normal. It was starting to worry her.

She knew Lito was having some issues, concerns about his place in the group and what he brought to it. He hadn't said much about it, but he was her closest friend—for years he had been her only friend. She knew him as well as she knew herself. He couldn't help but compare himself to the others and was finding himself lacking. He was an incredible fighter, but he didn't have the experience or overwhelming skill of Dunlop, Vail, or Serala. He didn't have magic like her, Gazin, or Ilan. And Tala wasn't even worth comparing himself to, though she knew that hadn't stopped him. It had never been an issue before, but spending so long in a group of such exceptional people, he was struggling with feelings of inadequacy.

She thought back to some advice that Caida had given to

her and Serala one time. "Sometimes," Caida had told them, "you have to be direct. Blunt. And say something affirming. Sometimes that will work better than all the subtle hints in the world."

"Lito?" He looked at her. "I'm glad you're here with me." She smiled at him and enjoyed the way his eyes widened as he was enveloped in a large blush.

"I-what-I-what?" Lito spluttered, and Alina had to suppress a giggle. "Where did that come from?"

"I was just thinking about it." She shrugged, trying to act nonchalant. "After everything that's happened. And whatever is going on between those two," she gestured to Tala and Serala, "I'm glad that you're here with me."

"Oh. I-I am too." Lito grinned goofily at her, and Alina did allow herself to giggle this time. They kept walking through the dense, dark jungle, staying adamantly on the road, and Alina was pleased to note that Lito was standing just a little bit taller. Prouder.

"Do you think those two will ever actually get together?" he asked after a few moments.

"I don't know." She shook her head. "I want them to be happy, but..."

"But she's completely insane?"

"Yeah."

"He's not exactly the picture of sanity either," he said, parroting her earlier words.

"Yeah." She sighed, hearing Tala and Gazin still arguing with each other. "Yeah," she repeated.

"Do you ever think we'll get together?" Lito asked.

"Yeah, probably," she said, not really paying attention. She was watching Serala fall back beside Tala and sling her arm over his shoulders as she finally told him and Gazin to shut up. "Wait, what!?" Alina cried, as she swung her head toward Lito so fast her neck cracked. He just beamed at her with that dazzling smile of his. She stared at him, shocked, entirely unable to think. She didn't even realize that she was beaming right back.

CHAPTER 43

"You just... *asked* if you two were ever going to get together?" Tala asked dumbly, looking at Lito in disbelief.

"Yeah. I mean, it felt like the right time, you know?"

"No. No, I do not. When did you do this, again?"

"Like... a week ago, I think? A couple days after we left Morungil." They had just snuck across the border of Dust and the Jungle the day before, sneaking through a hidden pass in the mountains the Dissidents had been using for millennia. It was dangerous to get to, since it required leaving the Jungle Road well before the border, but the fringes of the Jungle were much safer than the depths. Besides, a secret pass that couldn't be accessed or even found without knowing exactly which large boulder out of hundreds to push aside in the mountains made for the safest border crossing there was.

"Then why am I only hearing about it now?"

"I don't know." Lito shrugged, shifting awkwardly. "We weren't really sure how to tell you all. I mean, things haven't really changed much, and we don't want to distract you from everything, and it's all just kinda new, and we don't really-"

"Okay, okay. Calm down, I get it," Tala reassured him, amused. It was funny how flustered Lito could get about Alina, despite having officially begun to court her. It explained the weird looks the two kept sharing, at least. "So, what next? I don't really know how relationships go in the Dissidents. Or for nobles."

"There aren't really any set traditions or anything." Lito shrugged. "Nobles have their whole own way of doing things in each country, but we don't really care about that. She's not really a noble anymore anyway. But in the Dissidents, it's just kind of whatever and however you want to do things. But, to be honest, things aren't really going to change for us much. It just... *feels* different, I guess."

"Well, it's been a week and I haven't seen you two sneak off together or anything yet." They were now walking through the plains of Dust country. Tala would swear he could see it growing drier by the minute. Where there had been lush green grass, copses of trees, and bushes and other flora aplenty near the border, even just a little over a day's walk had led them into expansive fields of yellowish grass with thin trees and sick looking bushes. A few cacti could be seen here and there, one of the few plants that thrived in the desolate conditions of Dust. Tala had been assured that if they ended up traveling even further west, he would see little else but dry dirt and cacti.

Lito blushed hard and laughed awkwardly. "We haven't. We won't-I mean, we *will*, just... there hasn't really been anywhere to sneak off to. And she-we-don't really want an audience, you know?"

Tala just nodded, keeping his lips firmly shut as he tried not to laugh until he got himself under control. "Are you going to get married?"

"Eventually. Maybe. I think so. We probably won't bother with a ceremony or anything. For Dissidents like us, who don't really have a 'public' face, it's better to avoid drawing attention. When we decide we're ready for that, we'll probably just say that we're married. It's not like we want to get the Churches involved, anyway."

"Yeah, that makes sense. I can't imagine the Churches would be happy to perform marriage rites for people like us. Guess I haven't really thought about it before."

"No?" Lito asked, side-eyeing Tala in a way that made him immediately suspicious. "There's nobody you've thought about courting? At all?"

It was Tala's turn to blush and look away. "No. Why? I'm on the run for my life. Romance isn't really something I have time for."

"Oh? So there's nobody at all? Nobody who you can't take your eyes off of? Maybe someone with a penchant for stabbing-"

"Why now?" Tala interrupted, unwilling to let Lito finish his question. "You two have been together forever." The question did the trick, bringing Lito's focus back onto the topic of his relationship.

"It wasn't really all that sudden, actually." Lito sighed.

"I know I've been avoiding it for years. First, it was because she was a noble, even if deposed, and I didn't think she'd accept someone like me. And with everything she had just been through, it didn't seem right anyway. And I guess that just never really changed. I was scared. I love her, and I love being around her, even if I wanted more than to just be her friend. Honestly, it might have taken me years still before I tried to push for anything more."

"So, what changed? Why now and not in a few years?"

"Honestly? You did."

"What?" Tala shot a bemused eye at Lito.

"Not *you*, you. Just like... you in general. Everything that's happened because of you. Okay, I'm not explaining this well. Let me start over."

Lito fell silent for a minute, eventually taking a deep breath before speaking again. "Okay. So first, I guess, is that there was never really any rush. For me, us. I know being in the Dissidents, especially as deep in it as we are, isn't exactly safe, but the two of us have never really been in any particular danger. With her powers and skill, she's only really ever been in danger from assassins or Blessed. The first are kind of a moot point since nobody outside of us even knows she's alive. And Blessed, well, it's kind of a hard rule for all of us to avoid Blessed at all costs. Even though she could be a threat to them, it's way too likely that they'd kill her instead. And since I'm more of a spy than anything, and I always work with her, we've never really been in danger. Get it?"

"I think so. And since the two of you are never really in danger, there was nothing pushing you to act, right?"

"Exactly. We're still young. Have all the time in the world. It was more of an excuse for me to not do anything, I'll admit that, but still. And since she's a Descendant, an Awakened at that, she has even more time. For us, people like you and me, it's regular to start fooling around and courting and stuff once we're in our teens. Married in our early twenties. Regular nobles usually have marriages, or at least marriage contracts or something even before then. Sometimes as kids. But for Descendants, it's the other way around. They live so much longer that they rarely start anything serious until they're well into their thirties, usually forties or fifties. Everything before that is merely having fun. And I didn't want Alina to see me as just some 'youthful fun,' you know?"

"I didn't know that, actually."

"Really? It seems like you know everything sometimes."

"That's 'cause I'm a-I *was* a Researcher. Apprentice, but still. Learning about things is kinda what we do-did-whatever. I never learned much about Descendants though, 'cause it was too close to Arcane Research to bother risking. And it's not like most of us really care about the courting habits of nobles to bother skirting the line like that anyway."

Which was true, although Tala was finding this all interesting to learn about. He'd never given much thought to how different relationships might be for people who lived hundreds of years compared to the average folk who rarely ever even reached one hundred.

"Oh. That makes sense. Well, yeah. That's what romance

is like for nobles and Descendants. But the point is I was always too scared to push for more with her and thought I had plenty of time to wait."

"Okay. So how did I change that?"

"At first you didn't. Your circumstances were a bit different, what with killing Ignis Fatus and all, but we smuggle people all the time. The Dissidents and us two especially. With her powers and my skills, we're damned good at it. Slaves, recruits, criminals, other Dissidents. Getting you out was a higher risk than we're used to, but not exactly out of the ordinary for us. And whatever came next was for people like Vail and Serala to worry about, not the two of us."

Tala shook his head, sighing to himself. Despite everything that had happened, he still sometimes found himself caught off guard at how different his life had been compared to the others. Fleeing Fiahren had been the worst, most terrifying experience of his life. To Lito, who was about the same age as Tala, it was an ordinary event that he'd done dozens of times before. As much as Tala sometimes admired his friend, he was glad he hadn't had to live his life. Ignorant of Tala's internal musings, Lito continued unabated.

"But then Southtown happened, and everything went crazy. It's been drilled into my head since I was a kid: Run, don't fight. It's practically a mantra in the Dissidents. But in Southtown, we didn't have a choice. That was the first time either of us had been in a situation like that. Honestly, I thought I was going to die there. If it weren't for Alina covering us, we would have been overwhelmed. Well, Those Three might not have. They're freaking insane. I don't know how

Vail and Serala fight like that. And Ilan was a Stone Knight so... yeah. But the rest of us? We were screwed. And then the Blessed showed up." Lito broke off with a sigh, running a hand through his hair.

"I thought I had died and gone to the Hells. That wall of fire sweeping through, burning people to death in an instant. If he hadn't been so focused on you, we would've all been caught by it too and would've died right there. But then it all ends with you having killed two more Blessed? Two of the most famous? And surviving Anderas freaking Anto? Well, things changed. Suddenly, we were fleeing through Light, heading to Lightning, and the whole world was in chaos and we're trying to protect the most wanted man in the world with bugger-all of a plan. Suddenly, we weren't safe, either of us, and I didn't have all the time in the world to be a coward about it."

Tala pursed his lips but nodded along. He still struggled with the awkward feeling he got whenever his encounter with Anderas Anto was brought up. How could he possible explain that they had survived not because of their own actions but because Anderas had let them? Even if he tried, they'd never believe it. Not without telling them the truth about everything that had happened between him and Anderas. And Tala still didn't entirely understand that himself. Those were thoughts for him to struggle with on his own, though, late at night when he was trying to sleep.

"Southtown was months ago," Tala said, shifting the conversation back to Lito and Alina's new relationship and away from the confusing mess that was Anderas bloody Anto. "Why did it take you this long then?"

"Like I said, I had only started to think about it. Honestly, Southtown was so insane I thought it would be a one-time thing. We'd escaped Fire, escaped Elidor and Annelore and even Anderas freaking Anto. By the time we got out of Light, I thought we were safe again. Not like before, but that we'd be able to keep our heads down, stay hidden, and nothing like that would happen again." Lito made a sound in his throat, something halfway between a sigh and a laugh—a huff of pain and dark amusement. Tala could well understand the sentiment.

"So, while we were waiting around in Morungil, I decided it wasn't worth waiting anymore, and that I would talk to her about trying out being more than friends. I couldn't do it in Morungil. We were all grieving Serala and too worried about you. But then you both showed up, alive and unharmed, with the Bone Merc in tow. Again. Because screw you. And then there was all that about the Beast God and Tora. And then, we were on the road to find your parents who apparently know about this mystical city, and I was just feeling even further done with everything. I said fuck it and asked her if anything would ever happen between us, and she said yes. And then we talked and—yeah. We'll probably get married eventually. So, thanks, I guess, for pushing me into it even if you had no idea, you utterly insane bastard."

"Oh. Well, I'm glad things worked out for you," Tala said. At least that was true, even if he could have done without the multiple insults from Lito.

"Thanks, man." Lito smiled at him, an expression full of honest happiness. "So, what about you? Have you thought about pursuing a relationship with any of our illustrious and totally not-psychopathic companions?"

Tala groaned.

CHAPTER 44

Tala sighed contentedly as he finished up the last of his dinner. Their arrival in Kurazil had gone smoothly, entering the city with no problems. Seeing the many-tiered layers of the city that rose up from the lowest point on the shore of Lost Lake into the hills behind had been a wonderful sight. Seeing his parents, healthy and alive in a small Dissident safehouse tucked into one of the middle tiers of the city, had been even better. Even now, hours later, his eyes still felt sore from all the tears. He was incredibly grateful that the others—sans Vail—had decided to give him the rest of the day to catch up with his parents, just the three of them, before getting down to business. Ilan especially had abjectly barred Vail from interfering in their reunion, which Tala was especially thankful for. He wished he knew the man better so that he could do something for him to show his thanks.

The fish and vegetables had been cooked to perfection in the light broth and many different spices of the traditional Dustlands' dish, the fish being the Kurazil variation due to the abundance of them in Lost Lake. It had been so long since he had had a meal with his family. Even before his life had blown up, he and his parents were so invested in their work at the Institute that they hadn't been spending much time together as a family. Despite the circumstances, Tala was enjoying the opportunity to do so again. Beside him, his dad was also finishing up, while his mother was almost done.

Tala had seen and done so much since the last time he had talked to his parents that even after talking all day, dinner was still full of lively conversation: Tala told them about all of the ridiculous and wonderful and horrible things he had experienced over the last few months, and his parents shared in turn their much less chaotic adventures since becoming unwilling (and much less known) fugitives. Their time apart had also led to some small aesthetic differences. While his mom was largely the same as she been: dusky skin so pale it was almost white; fine, light brown hair that she kept in a loose, haphazard braid behind her head, Tala was still trying to get used to his dad's change in appearance. Tala had inherited his slightly darker skin tone from his dad along with the dark, curly hair that they both kept quite short—or both had. Moe-lo'Keahi had apparently decided that life on the run meant it was time to experiment with his looks. Instead of the tightly cut curls, Moelo had allowed his hair to grow out, making his head look like a small, dark bush was growing out of its top. Tala could already see where it was beginning to droop on the sides. He had also stopped shaving his face, and was sporting a dark, curly beard and mustache. Tala's mom didn't seem to mind the change, as far as Tala could tell, but he had caught her smirking more than once when his dad struggled to eat without getting food in his beard or mustache. Tala had never really considered growing facial hair before, and seeing his dad with both, he was feeling confident in his decision to continue shaving regularly.

The rest of the table had been fairly quiet as they ate, and Tala and his parents talked. Despite all of Tala's companions having reconvened to join them for the meal, they spent so much time with each other there just wasn't much conversation to be had. Additionally, quiet anxiety suffused the room as they all waited for the meal to finish. By order of Tala's mother, whatever business they had could wait until after they had eaten. As it was, Edana was the only person left who hadn't finished. Tala had a feeling his mom had intentionally been eating slowly just to make them wait on her.

Finally, she pushed the now-empty earthenware pot away from her as she sat back in her chair, eyeing the group calmly. They all stared back, anticipation clear on their faces, even Vail's. Osson (who was still around for some reason, despite his constant complaints) was feigning disinterest, but his eyes too were focused on Edana.

"Well, that was quite enjoyable. Anyone up for dessert?" she asked. Tala had to stifle a laugh as the whole table visibly flinched, hearing his father chuckle beside him.

"Perhaps later," Moelo'Keahi said, trying—and failing—to fully suppress his amusement. "I suppose it's time for you all to tell us why you wanted to meet? Not that we don't appreciate getting to see Tala, even if he damn near gave us heart attacks with everything that's happened to him the last few months." Moelo shook his head, but fear and pain hid beneath his father's silly dramatics. Tala had wanted to downplay the events but hadn't been able to bring himself to do so. Once he had begun, it had all poured out of him. Unloading everything to his parents—all the fear and anger and confusion he had felt since killing Ignis and through everything that came after—had been cathartic beyond belief.

"Yes. We want to-" Vail was promptly silenced. Ilan had grabbed his shoulder, squeezing hard enough to catch his attention. Vail shot him a glare as Gazin began speaking instead.

"Tact, Vail. Have some tact," He muttered before looking both of Tala's parents in the eyes. Tala did find it slightly annoying how his eyes swept from one to the other, passing over and ignoring him entirely. "We wanted to speak with you because we recently heard about a place that might have some importance to us. The only problem is that none of us have heard of it before, we don't know where it is, and we aren't sure it even exists."

Tala's parents both leaned forward, clearly intrigued.

"Tala, however, believes he has heard you two talk about this place before. So, we thought we would arrange this little meeting to confirm and, if nothing else, allow you three to reconnect."

"We appreciate that. But what's this place you all are so interested in? Don't keep us waiting," Edana ordered curiously.

"It's a city," Gazin said. "Apparently called Tora."

Tala's parents straightened in their seats before leaning back, having a silent conversation behind him. They had had many such conversations when he was a small child and would ask them questions about things they weren't sure if he was too young to know about or not. Being two people obsessed with learning and knowledge, they sometimes told him the truth even if they maybe shouldn't have. He had been terrified of going outside in the sun for almost a full year when he learned about skin cancer at the age of four. They had been a little bit more selective in what they told him after that.

"Where exactly did you hear about this "Tora" if you don't even know if it's real?" Moelo asked suspiciously.

"The Beast God told me about it. And Vail years ago when he met it," Tala quickly contributed.

His parents didn't even bother with a silent conversation this time, leaning towards each other and whispering ferociously right behind him. He couldn't make out what they were saying. Judging by the confused and annoyed looks on Gazin's and Osson's faces, neither could they. Tala couldn't help but roll his eyes. When discussing their research, his parents talked so fast that they didn't even finish their sentences before the other began. How they understood each other was a mystery even to him. All he could hear were starts like: "Do you?" "Could it?" "Beast?" "Before?" "Knew it!"

When they finally finished, his parents straightened again and gazed out at his companions, eyes narrowed. "And why do you-"

"Enough!" Vail snarled, finally losing his patience. "No more games! Have you heard of Tora?"

His parents shared a look before his dad sighed. "Yes. We have." Silence met his announcement, the group clearly waiting for him to continue. When his father failed to say any more, as did his mother, Tala had to bite back another laugh.

"Well?" Vail demanded.

"Well, what? You asked if we've heard of Tora. We have," Moelo said, so seriously Tala knew he was messing with them. Question asked, question answered. His parents could be dicks sometimes.

"Where is it?" Vail roared, making half the table jump.

"We don't know." Moelo sounded sincerely sorry.

Tala closed his eyes. They knew *exactly* where it was. Or, rather: strongly suspected, but didn't know for certain. He loved his parents.

Vail slumped back, looking as defeated as Tala had ever seen him. The rest of them weren't much better, sans Osson, glaring at Tala with a twitch in his eye.

"Now I see where you get it from," Osson growled, drawing everyone's attention. "Fine. Since the rest of you are idiots, I'll ask. Where do you *think*, Tora is?"

"Oh, that's easy!" Moelo chirped, sounding chipper. A table full of wide eyes swung his way. "We're pretty sure it's in the desert!"

"If it's still there, of course. If we're right, then it's a city that died over seven thousand years ago. There might be nothing left of it," Edana casually added, making all eyes swing to her.

Tala grinned. He loved his parents.

CHAPTER 45

"It's in the desert?" Gazin asked, skeptically. Moelo nodded. "Which desert, exactly?"

"The desert. You know? Dead center of the continent—pun intended—full of nothing but sand and heat and oblivion? That desert." Even Tala thought his dad sounded far too happy.

"Right. Okay. Just..." Gazin trailed off with a sigh.

"How do you know?" Lito asked, looking confused. "I mean, it's called the Dead Desert because nothing's in it. How could there be a city there? Or was there?"

"Because it wasn't always a desert. At least, we don't think it was!" Moelo said, leaning forward. Tala recognized the tone in his voice, meaning his dad was about to start monologuing.

"Think about it! The Dead Desert? That name is way too on the nose! And nothing about it makes sense! It's in the very center of the continent, almost perfectly round, but surrounded by lush plains and farmland! And it's not a long shift either! At least in Fire, there's a short stretch of ground between the plains and the desert, about a couple miles where the grass rapidly starts browning before vanishing, and the ground starts becoming hard and dry before turning to sand! That can't be natural! And the climate doesn't make sense! Cloud patterns, wind patterns, soil, water, the Dead Desert should only be the outskirts of the desert that makes up most of the Dustlands, not its own separate, worse place! Grass and trees and rivers that slowly taper off into cacti and bushes, not a bunch of sand! And certainly not that *much* sand! The Dead Desert is huge and full of sand dunes! And besides-"

"Stop! Stop," Gazin called, holding up a hand. "None of that means anything to us! Cloud and soil patterns? Maybe your son understands what you're talking about," Tala nodded absently, thinking about what his dad had said, "but I know almost nothing about any of that!"

"Well, you see-"

"No! No. The Dead Desert may be unnatural, or it may not. It doesn't matter to us. Why do you think that's where Tora is? Or was? Let's start with how you even know about Tora in the first place. Vail has been searching for decades and has never heard the name aside from the Beast God."

Tala's parents shifted uncomfortably, sharing another look. "There's a lot we can't say. Not because we don't want to!" Edana was quick to clarify. "But there are rules!"

"You're fugitives! You don't have to listen to the Churches anymore!" Serala pointed out.

"Not Church rules." Edana hesitated.

"Oh," Gazin said slowly. "Institute rules."

"Yes. Whatever happens to us, we took oaths that we won't betray. Not even here."

"What?" Tala asked, looking back and forth between his parents. "I never took any oaths! I didn't know there were oaths!"

"You're still just an apprentice, son. The oaths aren't for you," Moelo said, sounding actually serious to Tala's surprise. "There is far more to the Institute than you know about." Tala frowned. He hadn't had access to all of the Institute because of his status as an apprentice, but apparently there was a lot more than he had thought.

"We'll tell you all that we can," Moelo continued, addressing the room once more. "But there are many details you'll just have to trust us on. At the Institute, certain knowledge is accessible only to certain people. Even beyond the normal Researcher. Very few people have access to it all, but there were certain things we," he gestured to Edana, "were allowed to know. Some of those things were ancient documents, held safe in the Institute since before the Gods came. We learned about Tora from those."

"Wait, wait!" Lito cried. "I thought there was nothing before the Gods came! I mean, not *nothing*, nothing, but no cities or writing or anything? People back then were barely better than animals."

"That's the accepted teachings, yes." Moelo nodded. "Doesn't mean it's true. The truth is there was a lot. Fiahren isn't the 'first' city founded after the Gods. It already existed before the Gods came, as did the Institute. The Churches tried to destroy all knowledge of the times before the Gods, but some things remain. From what little we know, Tora was a great city, perhaps the greatest in the world at the time. The author certainly seemed to think so, as far as we could tell from the little that survives. It was the capital of its civilization, a shining beacon for the world."

"Then why has no one ever heard of it?"

"It was destroyed. All knowledge of it was, at least. Or all that the Churches could find. That's why we think it is—or was—in the desert. The desert that shouldn't exist, that doesn't make sense. Not to those of us who know about things like how different environments form. Our hypothesis is that when the Gods descended from the heavens, they destroyed Tora. Why? We don't know. Maybe the Torans resisted, refused to worship them. Or maybe Tora was such a majestic city the Gods felt it took away from their own majesty. Regardless, they destroyed it so completely that they killed the very land it was built on, and the lands surrounding it, to the point that there was nothing to grow back, leaving nothing but a desert of death. The Dead Desert."

There was silence as everyone digested what Moelo had just told them.

"But they didn't," Tala muttered, frowning to himself as his mind worked.

"Eh?" his dad asked.

"They didn't. Destroy Tora. Or not entirely, that is. The Beast God told me to find it. If they did destroy it, something must have survived, or it would know not to bother."

"It may have forgotten," Gazin pointed out. "From what you both have said, it may have forgotten that it was destroyed."

"No. It was certain. It said something about the city

being destroyed, but it was certain something still existed. Something important that could kill it. Or help kill it. It just didn't remember where it was, or something."

"So, what, lad? Do you want us to blindly venture into the most inhospitable place in the world in search of the remnants of a city destroyed by the Gods themselves?" Gazin asked.

"Not blindly," Edana chimed in. "The desert's almost a perfect circle. If it was formed by the destruction of Tora, then Tora, or what remains of it, should be in the very center."

"Oh, even better! You just want us to go to the heart of a place that even Great Hordes have vanished inside of!"

"The Hordes were unprepared," Edana pointed out.

"Yeah. We won't be," Moelo concurred.

"We'll bring water and snacks," Tala added.

CHAPTER 46

"You know, this feels kind of... anticlimactic," Tala said, staring out over the dunes of endless sand stretched out before him.

"Oh? How's that?" Lito asked.

"Well, I didn't think getting into the desert would be hard, per se, but we literally just walked from Kurazil right on up to it. It took a few days, but that's it. No running or fighting. No guards or Blessed to sneak past. And tonight, we're going to go into it. Just walk right on in."

"Yeah. We snuck into Kurazil, did our business, and snuck out. That's what's supposed to happen."

"I know. It just feels weird."

"That's because you're a magnet for chaos."

"Fair." Tala sighed, unable to argue with Lito's assessment. "Doesn't mean I'm not going to be worried about a Dust army on our heels or some new Great Horde falling on us."

"We're on the wrong side of the desert to hit a horde. And Dust's armies are all busy at the Wall and the borders.

With everything happening, they'd have to have seen your face themselves to bother with us right now."

'Everything happening' meaning the giant war that had well and truly kicked off while they had all been in the Jungle. A war that was largely Tala's fault, although he couldn't really find it in himself to feel guilty about it.

Neither did any of it affect them now. The desert was useless territory, offering neither food nor resources nor even strategic value to anyone, and as such was being ignored as ever by the warring countries. And why wouldn't they ignore it? The only thing it offered was death to anybody stupid enough to enter it.

Tala looked around at his companions as they made camp. Calling it camp was probably too generous, to be honest. They were just arranging a bit of shelter so they could rest away from the sun as they waited the day out, having reached the outskirts of the desert in late afternoon. They would wait for the sun to lower and the air to cool off a bit before venturing into the merciless dunes, where the heat would be their biggest enemy. It would also be easier to navigate at night, as the stars and two evening and night moons would make it easier to discern which direction they were going without having to calculate around the day moon's chaotic orbit.

They were all wearing light layers of clothing that fully covered their skin, similar to the common garb of the people who lived in the surrounding lands and had grown accustomed to the drastic temperatures of hot days and cold nights. It would help protect them from the heat and scorching rays of the sun during the day. They had many Fireland goods to help keep them warm at night: self-cooking foods, sticks and logs of firewood that would burn hot but slowly, bones and treated skins and furs of Fire creatures they could hold or tuck into their clothing for extra warmth. And they had water; boiled water, as much of it as they could carry. Most of it was being carried on the backs of three Dust camels they had purchased at a small village they had passed. One of the few animals—even among Dust—that might be able to survive in the desert long enough to reach the center. They were as prepared as they could be.

Once they had finally entered the desert, and traveled a couple days in, Tala reconsidered that thought. "I'm starting to see why nobody comes here!" He shouted over the wind, doing his best to hold down his edge of the large cloth that they were all hunkered under.

"Oh, are you?" Serala shouted back, holding on next to him. "And here I was thinking of building a vacation home out here!"

"Gruhhoommuuu," one camel grunted. Fitting the three camels under the cloth made for a very tight squeeze, but none of them were sure if the animals could survive in the sandstorm raging outside. They hadn't been willing to risk losing them and all their supplies. At least the camels had been cooperative so far, lying down in the sand without complaint and not moving. Tala could have done without the smell, though.

It made him wish Osson had stayed with them. He had departed from Kurazil with them but had left the group shortly after, to no one's real surprise. He had made it clear from the start he had no intentions of staying with them, only remaining as far as Kurazil due to going the same way, and his own curiosity about the Tora mystery. His curiosity had run dry at the idea of venturing into the Dead Desert. Most of the group had been relieved at his departure, but none of them would've been against the man creating a large bone structure for them to wait out the storm in. From what Tala had seen and, more so, the stories he had heard about the Bone Merc, such a thing would have been a simple feat for him.

Instead, they were stuck holding down the largest cloth they had to protect them from the rampaging winds and flesh-flaying sands. Which was getting easier, mercifully, if only because they were slowly getting buried in said sand. Thus, the cloth was being weighed down more and more, with less exposure for the wind to rip it away. Digging out of the sand later was a trade he was perfectly happy to make. Even with all of them working together, their strength would have failed eventually. They had barely managed to keep the cloth covering them at the beginning. Every second becoming harder until they had started getting buried.

"How much further till we reach the center?" Tala yelled to his parents, holding the cloth down on his other side.

"Another week, maybe two!" his mom yelled back. "It's hard to tell when there's nothing but sand around!"

"Grea-blarspsps," Tala spat out a mouthful of sand that had flung up in his face. He returned his focus to holding the cloth down.

"Just hold on till this passes!" his mom yelled, laughing at him. He didn't bother responding.

When the storm finally ended, the cloth had been buried

under so much sand that they couldn't stand up. Not even Gazin, the shortest of them. Every attempt they made to dig themselves out just ended up with sand cascading under the cloth, burying them even worse. Eventually, they gave up trying, leaving the whole process to Ilan. He stuck a hand deep into the sand surrounding them, slowly building it into long beams before they collapsed away from the hole. It took a few hours to move enough sand for them to finally work their way free, his limited powers having immense difficulty getting the sand to cooperate.

"Godsdamnit!" Tala growled, shifting uncomfortably. "I have sand everywhere!"

"Better get used to it, lad," Gazin grumbled, skin undulating in a distinctly disturbing way as sand trickled out of his clothes. "There's naught but sand in our near future."

"At least we're all alright. A storm like that could have easily killed the lot of us," Lito said, words contrasting with the heavy grimace he wore as he attempted to shake his pants out while still wearing them.

"Let's keep moving. It looks like the sun will be up soon," Serala called, frowning and clearly as uncomfortable as the rest of them. "We need to get as far as we can."

Looking disgruntled, Tala's parents once again took the lead, climbing up the nearest dune that had formed during the storm. They consulted with each other quietly for a minute before pointing at nothing. "That way."

"Wonderful, let's go," Serala practically growled.

Tala glanced up at the sky, trusting his parents were correct, but feeling the need to confirm for himself. When the sun came out, he could help his parents figure out any adjustments to their course. He picked up his pack and fell into line with the others, following his parents through the sands as the sky lightened and the cold air grew warm, until eventually it became burning hot.

"We should be getting close," his mom announced a few days later as they were setting up camp for the day. "We should be near the center. If Tora was here, we should reach it soon. Depending how big it was, we may even get there tomorrow." Finally, some good news! Spirits rose, and they finished setting up camp a bit faster than usual, eager to be done with their miserable desert trek.

"Getting close, eh?" Dunlop asked three days later, his expression deadpan. Despite his parents' assurances, nothing had changed. There had been nothing but sand, sand, and more sand over the last few days, and nothing but sand spread out in front of them as far as the eye could see. Dunlop, of all people, asking was a sign of how thoroughly exhausted they all were, and just what sort of moods they were in.

"It's been almost eight thousand years. We're probably standing in the middle of where the city once was," Moelo answered tiredly.

"The middle? Then isn't this it? Where we're going?" Lito asked.

"Figure of speech. But yeah." He sighed, looking around at all the nothing. "Probably not a good sign."

"What do we do then?" Serala asked.

"Keep going." Moelo shrugged. "We don't have the tools to pinpoint the exact center. But we're in the general area. Just keep your eyes peeled, I guess. Hey, Ilan!" he called. "Can you feel around with your magic or something? See if there's anything buried underneath the sand?"

Ilan shook his head slowly. "I don't have those types of powers. I don't even know if they would work in sand."

"Ah. That's too bad."

"After eight thousand years, even if anything does still exist, it might all be buried at this point with those sandstorms," Lito said.

"We'll deal with that if it comes to it. For now, let's keep going." Moelo sighed. Tala stayed quiet. They kept walking.

"Something's wrong!" Gazin suddenly said, voice cutting through the silence. They all stopped, turning to the very concerned man, who repeated himself. "Something's wrong."

"What? What is it?" Serala asked, anxious but not moving. None of them were, not until they were sure it was safe to do so.

"I don't know. I just... I can feel it. Something's wrong," Gazin answered, sounding confused. "My body. I can't feel my body!"

"What? Are you hurt?" Serala cried.

"Nay. Not like that! I can feel my body, but I can't *feel* it. Not like normal! My magic! It's not working!" Gazin cried, horrified.

"What do you mean?"

"I mean it's not working!" Gazin yelled, face white. "It's like touching Vail! My magic isn't working!"

"Mine neither." Alina called, voice shaking. Lito wrapped an arm around her, comforting her as best he could.

"Nor mine," Ilan said, seeming calm but for his furrowed brow. "It is like touching Vail." Tala frowned, wondering what that meant.

"How is that possible?" his dad asked, sounding more excited than since they entered the desert. "Something is blocking your magic? And Vail can do that? How?" He turned towards Vail. "Are you doing something? How?"

"It's not me," Vail replied, with an odd note in his voice. "But I think we're close to whatever we're searching for."

"Then let's move!" Moelo cried. Eyes gleaming with excitement, he raced over the sand, leaving the rest to follow.

CHAPTER 47

"Well, we found something," Tala muttered, staring at the sand before him. No one responded, not that he blamed them. What was there to say? They were all still, staring in shock at the massive wall of sand that stretched up towards the sky in front of them. Even looking straight up, he wasn't sure he could see the top.

They had first caught sight of the wall of sand hours ago, seeing it on the horizon as they crested a dune. They had thought it was another sandstorm and had prepared to bunker down if it came their way. But after hours of watching, the thing hadn't moved, growing neither larger nor smaller, nor moving off to the side. Was it some sort of mountain? A hill or bluff or other natural formation in the depths of the desert? Upon determining that it wasn't moving, and thus, likely not a threat, they had begun to trek towards it. After countless days with nothing but sand to be seen in all directions, anything that was different could be what they were looking for.

As they got closer, and the mysterious thing grew larger

in their vision, they had grown even more confused. It still looked like a giant sandstorm, but there was something wrong with it. It was a... *wall* of sand. Not a sand dune, like the countless numbers scattered throughout the desert, but a wall. A solid wall of sand thousands of feet high. A perfectly flat line of sand from the very top (as much of it as he could see, anyway) to the very bottom, where it met the dunes and the valleys between them. And it was almost perfectly flat as it stretched out to the sides, where it curved the further his eyes followed it. A circular wall of sand, perhaps?

"How is this possible?" his dad whispered, voice carrying through the silence.

"I don't know," his mom responded, clearly in awe. "Mr. Ilan? Could you do something like this?"

"No," Ilan said slowly after a few moments. "Even if my marks were working, which they still aren't, I could never make something this large. Nor this stable. Not with sand. A Blessed could, maybe. But even then, I don't think they could hold it. Not this still. Not for this long."

"Maybe it's not held together with magic," Tala voiced, drawing confused looks. "I mean, it was probably *made* with magic, but maybe it's held up by something else? Some sort of adhesive? Somebody, like an Earth or Dust Blessed, made this and held it up long enough for somebody, probably a lot of somebodies, to pour something over it. Like tree sap or something. It dries and when the Blessed releases their magic, the whole thing stays up on its own."

"It would be tighter." His dad shook his head. "When

sand gets wet, it clumps together and stays clumped when it's dry. This isn't clumped."

"How can you tell?" Tala asked.

"Look closer," his mom answered instead, walking closer to the wall until her face was inches away from it. "The sand is densely packed, but it's not actually clumped. Nothing is binding it together. It's just... *there*."

His dad joined her at the wall of sand, practically touching it with how close he was. "It's not supporting itself," he muttered. "There's no weight bearing down." He dropped to his knees and examined where the wall sharply transitioned into the loose sand of the desert. "No weight at all."

"Could it be Dark magic?" Lito asked, staying back by Alina's side and making no move to get closer. "Their magic does weird things when they actually use it. They can instantly disappear and reappear somewhere else. Cause rocks and arrows, and even other magic, to miss them even when it should be a direct hit. They can even make things float."

"I don't know," Edana answered, giving Lito an approving smile. "We know even less about Dark magic than we do the others. It's a good question though. Do any of you lot have any idea? You've probably seen some Dark wielders before."

"Not many," Gazin said, not turning his gaze away from the sand wall. "It does seem like something they might be able to do if they had the control and power for it. But I'm not so sure. They can make things attracted to each other, stick to each other. Gravitational pull, I've heard it called, whatever that means. But those things aren't motionless like this. And it would be pulling all the sand around to it."

"Gravity? Really?" Moelo exclaimed, turning his back to the sand wall with his eyes shining. "That's remarkable! I knew calling them 'Dark' was a misnomer, but I had no idea! Does that mean they're actually gravity wielders? No, no, that wouldn't make sense. They can teleport."

His voice lowered as he began muttering to himself, frowning at the ground with his chin held in one hand. "That's their best-known ability. Also kills them the most. Leave part of their body behind. Messy business. Very messy. Couldn't be gravity. Unless they're forming two different gravity fields and failing to account for the difference, part of their body caught in one and the rest in the other? But that wouldn't be teleportation. That'd basically be flying. Or being pulled through the air. Couldn't be fast enough. That kind of speed would kill them regardless. So not gravity. Something else." His head snapped up, looking at Gazin with wild eyes. "What else can they do? Or Dark animals? If I had a few abilities, I could compare and extrapo-"

"Love!" Edana practically yelled in his ear, making Moelo flinch and breaking his ramblings. "You can do Arcane Research later." She ignored the way his eyes lit up and his excited "promise?" "Right now, we need to figure out what in the Hells is this wall."

"Right. Right. You're right." Moelo visibly calmed himself down, turning back to the wall and speaking again. "So. Giant impossible wall of sand. Huge. Curves inwards. Implies a circle. Massive one. A wall of sand encircling something. Why? What? Clearly unnatural. Meant to keep something in? Or keep something out? But then why sand? Why not something stronger?"

"Well, it's big. Maybe they just needed a lot. And there was plenty of sand around," Lito suggested, gesturing to the desert surrounding them.

"No. Something like this? Too big, too much. Resource heavy. Power heavy, whatever magic they were using. Implies important. Too important to rely on something as weak as sand. They would've used something stronger. Stone, at least. Could've been a last-ditch effort? Desperate attempt? Not to contain, plenty of time to strengthen. Keep out? Plausible, but no. Still exists. Unbroken. Breached elsewhere? Big enough. But how is it standing? Why leave it up? If broken, whole thing should have collapsed. Unless separate. Non-reliant on self. No weight being borne. Destroy part, doesn't affect the rest. Should be easy. It's sand. Can't be that strong. Should be safe." He finished with a shrug, back still to the rest of the group. They were alternating between looking at Moelo and each other in clear confusion, none able to follow his rapid words and seemingly disjointed thought process.

None except for Edana and Tala, who were used to the way his genius mind worked when he got invested in a project.

"Dad, no!" Tala shouted, at the same time as his mother. They were both too late. Moelo had already unsheathed the knife at his hip and tossed it at the wall of sand. Tala and the rest watched in horror as the knife tumbled through the air, spinning in ways that could give Dunlop an aneurysm, and slapped side-first into the wall of sand. It pushed some sand out of the way as the knife slipped into the wall, point up, and stayed there.

"Huh. That was unexpected," Moelo said, staring at the knife that was just sitting in the wall of sand, unmoving.

"Ow!" Moelo grunted as Edana's hand impacted the back of his head. "What in the Hells were you thinking?" she screamed at him. "You could have brought the whole damned thing down on our heads!"

"No! I worked it out! Wouldn't make sense for it to fall from something like that. And it didn't! See?" He pointed proudly at the knife.

"Oh? So, you knew that the knife was just going to... *become* part of the wall, then?" Edana asked him in *that* tone. The tone, which Tala had learned from a young age, meant to shut up, apologize, and let it go. His dad had never seemed to learn that lesson somehow.

"No. No, I did not. And isn't that fascinating? The sand wasn't even supporting itself—it got displaced far too easily— so what's holding the knife up? Can't be the sand."

"Yes, love, I know." Edana sighed. "But could you not endanger us all like that again? You didn't actually know it was safe. You wouldn't be surprised at the knife otherwise."

"Eheh." Moelo laughed sheepishly, scratching the back of his neck. "Sorry. Sorry, everyone," he called out to the group. "I was right, though," he pointed out to Edana.

"Yes, and we're all very proud of you for being right and not killing us all." Moelo flinched. "Just be more careful."

"Right." He nodded.

"Now then. It isn't a wall, is it?" Edana asked.

"No. I mean-technically, yes. But it's not a wall wall."

"So, what is it?"

"That's the question now, isn't it?"

"I'm sorry!" Serala called to the pair, sounding annoyed and confused, but very much not sorry. "But what exactly are you two talking about? How is it not a wall wall? What does that even mean? And how, *exactly*, did you know that wasn't going to kill us all?" She gestured at the knife still resting point up.

"I already explained-" Moelo started but was cut off by Edana.

"Tala, honey? Would you explain while we work on this?"

"Sure." Tala shrugged, having expected that. He was used to how his parents worked. "Basically, Dad's a genius. Kind of an idiot, but a genius. Honestly, you should probably leave it at that." It wasn't the first time Tala had experienced a group of people glaring at him after dealing with his dad.

"We are *not* leaving it at that," Serala said shortly.

Tala sighed. "Fine. Basically, the wall is clearly unnatural, right? Well, that, and its size and shape, means it was probably built as a defense measure to protect the people inside it from something on the outside. But since it's a wall of sand, it wouldn't make for a particularly strong barrier, so whatever it was supposed to protect against probably broke through it somewhere else. We just can't see it from here. Since the whole thing didn't collapse when it was broken through, it probably won't collapse on us either, regardless of what we do to it."

"Okay," Serala said slowly. "I guess that makes sense. Although, that's a lot to risk our lives over."

"There's a lot more to it. That's just kind of the important basics. It doesn't really matter because, aside from the part where it won't collapse, none of its true anyway."

"Wait, what?" Lito interjected. "You mean you lied to us?"

"No. I mean the premise is wrong." He sighed at their blank looks. "The wall wall thing? He means it isn't a wall. It looks like a wall, but being a wall isn't its purpose."

"Then what is its purpose? Why was it built?" Serala asked.

"That's what we're trying to figure out. If it wasn't meant to keep something out, or in, then why go to the trouble in the first place? Usually, a wall is a barrier. Otherwise, they keep things up, like roofs or floors or something. But that doesn't really fit either because who, or what, would need a roof or floor this big? And if whoever did this can suspend sand, why bother with a wall at all instead of just suspending whatever you need where you need it?"

"Hang on!" Lito interjected again, looking more than a little confused. "How do you know it's *not* a wall wall? Meant to keep people out? Or in, or whatever?"

Tala shrugged. "The knife didn't go through the wall. Or hit and get stuck in it. It didn't even hit it with its point. It hit it side on and became part of the wall. If it was meant to be a defensive barrier, the flat side of a badly thrown knife would have just bounced off. And if it was meant to be an obscuring or intimidation thing, they could have done a lot better than just a bunch of suspended sand broken so easily. So, it's not a wall."

"Right. Sure," Lito said.

"What is it?" Tala asked again. "Suspended sand, easily

thousands of feet high, presumably forming a massive circle. Seems like a wall but isn't a wall. Won't collapse and doesn't keep things out. It's just a hells of a lot of sand. Clearly unnatural, but also kind of useless. I wonder..." He trailed off, slipping away from the others and approaching his parents where they were furiously inspecting the wall.

"I think I'm starting to understand how he managed to kill Ignis," Lito murmured as he stared at Tala's retreating back. The others muttered in agreement.

"Hey, Mom, Dad?" Tala said as he approached the two, who barely glanced at him. He could tell from how still they were, they were listening to him. "What if it's an accident?" His parents stared at each other for a few moments, then at him.

"As in-" his dad started.

"Side effect," his mom finished.

"Accident?"

"But how?"

"Gods?"

"Could be."

"Then what's holding it up?" Tala added.

"Magic," his dad said.

"Unintentional," his mom continued.

"Then what?"

"Why?"

"Why?" his dad parroted, frowning at the sand.

"Accident," Tala reiterated.

"Then-"

"Inside-"

"Maybe," Tala said.

"Could we?"

"How thick?"

"Does it matter?" Tala asked.

"Can't be much."

"Cloth?"

"Should work." Tala nodded.

"Half a minute?"

"Probably will tunnel."

"Knife hasn't moved," Tala pointed out.

"Should be safe."

"Should be."

"I'll do it," Tala volunteered.

"No!"

"No!"

"It should be safe!" he argued.

"The knife was a surprise!" his dad exclaimed.

"Now he cares." his mom rolled her eyes.

"Then who?" he asked.

"It's my knife," his dad said.

"No!" his mom scolded.

"What in all of the Godsdamned Hells are you talking about?" Serala yelled, faltering when three pairs of disturbingly intense eyes fell on her.

"I'm going in there." Tala flicked a thumb over his shoulder, pointing at the wall of sand.

"No, he's not!" his parents yelled in sync.

"It's perfectly safe!" he challenged.

"Allegedly!" his mom hissed.

"Then who?"

"Oh, for Mud's sake." The muttered curse cut through their argument as all eyes turned to Dunlop, who was tying a strip of cloth over his mouth and nose. "Straight in?" he asked the three of them, pointing to the wall of sand with a thoroughly annoyed look.

"Straight through." Moelo nodded.

"Good," Dunlop growled, and before anything else could be said, he turned and strode straight into the wall of sand.

CHAPTER 48

"Dun?" Serala called to the man who was standing completely still just inside the sand wall. "Dunlop? Everything okay?" There was no response. Tala shared a concerned look with his parents. Dunlop wasn't moving. At all. He walked right into the sand wall without hesitation, but froze before he got two steps in, one foot still raised just above the ground.

"Dunlop!" Serala rushed forward alongside the rest, all congregating around the unmoving Dunlop. "What's wrong with him?"

"I don't know," Moelo replied with his head tilted, frowning curiously at Dunlop. "But it isn't natural. Look at him, not even the slightest twitch. This is fascinating!"

"Mm." Edana hummed, staring just as hard at Dunlop. "He pushed the sand out of the way no problem. No, don't touch him! We don't know what's happening yet!" she ordered a startled Serala, who had been moving to do just that.

"We can't just leave him! He could be in danger!" she retorted.

"We all could be. But we shouldn't be reckless. Hon." She turned to Moelo. "Perhaps you should retrieve your knife first." She pointed to the knife that still lay unmoving in the wall.

"Right. Yeah." He nodded, and with extreme care, moved to grab the handle of the knife. The sand around it moved back with no resistance. He gripped the hilt and pulled the knife out of the wall. "Strange," he muttered. "There was no resistance at all. It might as well have been floating in the air." He looked back to where the knife had been in the wall. There was a knife-shaped indent in the sand. The hole where the hilt had been was deeper and misshapen due to his fingers digging in.

"I've never seen anything like this," Edana murmured, more to herself than them. "Condition?"

"Seems perfectly fine," Moelo said, flipping the knife in the air and then fumbling the catch, causing it to land with a soft thump in the sand by his feet. He quickly picked it up with a growing blush, laughing sheepishly.

Edana sighed.

"You didn't feel anything when you grabbed it? No force, prickles on your skin, anything?" she asked.

"No. I felt the sand around it, but it didn't have any resistance either. I barely felt it before it just kind of... floated away."

"None of you have ever heard of magic like this before?" She turned to address the rest of the group, who were still hovering anxiously around the frozen Dunlop.

"Nay," Gazin said, voice low. "Dark wielders can make it hard for a person to move, like the air is as thick as water.

I've never heard of them freezing a person entirely. He's not even breathing."

"Shit," Edana cursed. "I didn't think about that. Okay. Pull him out." She nodded to Serala, who didn't waste a moment before grabbing Dunlop's shoulders and pulling him back with force. He came tumbling backwards with far more ease than Serala had clearly been expecting. She stumbled back herself, falling to the ground and pulling him on top of her.

Dunlop spun to his feet in an acrobatic twist so fast Tala barely even saw him move, drawing his sword half out of its sheath before pausing, eyes locked on Serala on the ground. "The Hells'd you do that for?" he demanded.

"What do you mean?" she exclaimed as she pushed herself to her feet. "You weren't moving! Gazin said you weren't even breathing!"

"What are you talking about? I just stepped into the damned thing!"

"It's true, lad! It's been a good minute since you entered. You just stood there frozen 'til Rala pulled you out."

"That's absurd!" Dunlop looked around to the others, frowning as he realized just how close they all were compared to where they had been when he entered. "What in the Hells?" he growled softly.

Tala studied the sand wall, where Dunlop had been frozen. There was a perfectly man-shaped hole exactly Dunlop's size in the wall. He could even make out the rough shape of his nose and mouth under the cloth in the sand at the back of the hole. "Well, it's at least one person thick."

"I didn't stop! She pulled me out the second I stepped

in!" Dunlop argued, sounding uncharacteristically unsure of himself. "This doesn't make any sense," he whispered.

Tala sidled over to the Dunlop-hole while all attention was on Dunlop. He drew his sword and slowly pushed the blade into the hole, moving it around in the empty space. Nothing happened. It felt like he was just wiggling his sword around in the air.

"Tala!" His mom's voice was sharp. "What in the Hells do you think you're doing?" she demanded. Tala glanced back at her and the others and shrugged.

"Just checking. It seems fine. Just a hole that shouldn't exist." An idea struck him, and Tala unsheathed the dagger at his side, casually tossing it into the hole. The moment it passed the edge of the wall it froze, hovering in midair, not moving in the slightest. "Well. That's a thing." He looked back at the others, who were staring wide-eyed at the floating dagger. Pursing his lips, Tala cautiously reached out and grabbed the dagger, pulling it back to him with no difficulty whatsoever. He flipped it once in his hand, resisting the urge to look at his father as he successfully caught it. With another shrug, he tossed it back into the hole, where it once again stopped suddenly, floating in midair.

"I don't understand," he heard Lito mumble.

With another shrug, Tala reached out and lightly poked the tip of the dagger. It spun slowly, floating back a little bit into the hole until it stopped spinning and froze in place again. He reached in and grabbed it, feeling nothing different. He glanced back at the others, all of whom were just watching him wide-eyed. He bent down and grabbed a handful of sand off the ground, tossing it into the hole. It all froze the moment it passed the edge, hovering in place like the world's strangest patch job. He turned to his parents.

"I think it's some sort of stasis field," he said. They both nodded back to him.

"Yes. But how? That's barely even a theory!" his dad replied, eyes gleaming. Tala shrugged.

"Is it a barrier? Or is the entire place in stasis? If it is, how do we get inside? It'd be impossible." His mom frowned.

"We need to find out how deep the wall is first," Tala said. His mom nodded.

"Wait! Again, for the love of the Gods, wait!" Lito cried, sounding annoyed. "For those of us who don't know everything in the whole damned world, what in the Hells is a stasis field?"

"It's a field where everything is in stasis." Tala shrugged. He decided to elaborate, given all the glares he received.

"Stasis is a theory we had back at the Institute. Basically, it's when something is frozen in time. It doesn't move, doesn't age, doesn't grow, or decay, nothing. It just... sits there. Forever. Unchanging. It isn't a real thing, though. Or we thought it wasn't. This is kind of exactly what it was thought it would be like." He gestured to the wall and the floating sand in Dunlop's hole.

"And a field is, well, an area. In this case, an area where everything inside of it, or that enters it, apparently, goes into stasis. Only moving when influenced by an external force. If I'm right, we could've left Dunlop in it, and if somebody came by in a thousand years and pulled him out, he'd be in the exact same condition he's in now." The glares had turned into blank faces.

Tala sighed and turned back to the hole. He considered his sword, still held in his hand, and shrugged. He stabbed the sword forward. Pushing it into the back of the hole as far as he could without entering the hole himself, he moved it around, feeling almost no resistance as the sand shifted, making the hole deeper. He withdrew his sword and turned to his parents. "Well, it's deeper than I can reach. What now?"

"Let me try," his dad said, patting Tala on the shoulder as he took his place in front of the hole. He stepped forward until half of him was in the wall and half out. He turned around, being careful with his steps to make sure he didn't go all the way in. "I don't feel anything different. My fingers move. Blood seems to be pumping fine. It must only take effect if we're entirely inside the field." He moved deeper in, keeping only one foot outside of the wall. "Yeah, I'm still fine. Wait a bit, then pull me out." Before they could respond, he pulled his foot into the hole, freezing the moment his foot crossed the threshold. Tala couldn't help but gulp; seeing his dad frozen so completely was unsettling.

"We should leave him in there, the reckless fool," his mom growled.

"I see where Tala gets it from," he heard Serala mutter. He felt slightly offended as the others made noises of agreement. Rude!

"It shouldn't matter how long he's in there," Tala said, reaching forward and gently pulling on his dad's shoulders, pulling a bit harder when his dad barely budged. His dad came tumbling out of the hole. Tala managed to stay standing and steadied them both.

"I said wait a bit! I wasn't in any danger!" his dad exclaimed.

"Dad! We did wait. It's been nearly a minute."

"Really?" Moelo exclaimed, looking back at the hole. "Fascinating! It didn't feel like any time passed at all! Not a second! I was frozen like Dunlop was?"

"Exactly like him. You didn't move or even breathe as far as I could tell."

"Amazing!"

"Let me try," Tala said. His dad shuffled to the side, gesturing to the hole with a wide grin on his face.

"Now wait a minute!" Tala heard his mom object as he crossed into the hole, only to get jerked back at the same moment. He stumbled in the sand but kept his feet.

"Oh, come on! I just wanted to see what it's like!" he cried, freezing as he stared his mom in the face. "Uh... what?" She hadn't been there a moment ago.

"Boys!" She shook her head. "Well? Was it everything you hoped?" she asked, unimpressed.

Tala's neck twisted between the hole and his mother, glaring at him disapprovingly. "That-but-I... how long was I in there?"

"Only about ten seconds," his mom said flatly.

"Amazing," Tala whispered, sharing an excited grin with his dad.

"This is what I get!" his mom muttered, throwing her hands up and storming off to the side. "Marry an idiot husband!

Get an idiot son! 'He's a genius!' I said. 'Misunderstood!' I said. That's what I get for thinking with my twat!"

"Mom!" Tala cried, mortified. "What the hells?"

"What? You think he impressed me with flowery words? Orgasms! That's what did it! I was blinded by a man who actually cared about my pleasure!"

"It's the clit, son." His dad laid a hand on his shoulder and gave him a wink. "Never forget the clit."

"Dad! Eww! No! What the fuck? I don't want to know that!"

"Why not? You'll thank me for it one day. As will your girl there." He nodded towards the others, making Tala blush as he resolutely did *not* look their way.

"No! Gods! Just-rope, give me some rope!"

"Rope, eh? Nice. We've used roped before-"

"Dad!" Tala yelled. "No! What? No! Just... Up! Shut! Shut up! Rope! Now! Tie rope around my waist! Maybe that'll bypass the stasis field! Gods!"

"Oh. Right. Clever!" his dad said cheerily, taking a rope out of his own pack and tying it around Tala's waist.

"If this doesn't work, for the Gods' sakes, just leave me in there," Tala begged.

"No." His dad denied him with a smile.

"Dick." Tala turned and leapt into the hole, throwing himself as deep into the sand as he could.

CHAPTER 49

"What the-! Oh." Tala slumped in his dad's arms, realizing what had happened. It was incredibly disorienting to one moment be throwing yourself through the air, and the next to be on your feet, held up by another person. "How far did I get?" he asked dejectedly.

"Nowhere," his dad answered sullenly. "Froze in the air the moment your foot passed through."

"Damn. So, the rope didn't do anything?"

"No. It wasn't affected itself, but didn't stop you from being either."

"Well. Shit." Tala sighed. He turned to the others. "I'm out of ideas. Any of you have anything that might get us through?"

"We still can't use our magics," Gazin said, looking distraught. "Even with them, I don't know what we could do." Tala looked to the rest, none of whom seemed to have anything to add.

"Damn." He stared up at the sky, seeing the sand wall

stretching to the heavens despite being behind him, trying to think of something. "It can't be a coincidence. Some sort of anti-magic field leading up to this. How does that even work? Wouldn't it disrupt the stasis field?"

"Not necessarily." His mom answered his rhetorical question. "The anti-magic field could have been placed around this wall on purpose. An extra layer of protection to keep people away, if the desert isn't enough. Or it might just not affect it all. Nineteen types of magic from the nineteen Gods, and none of them can create a stasis field like this. It might not be magic at all."

"What could it be if not magic?" Lito asked.

"I don't know. Technology of some kind? There are theories about such a thing at the Institute. But to actually create something like this? I can't even imagine."

"And there's no magic at all that could do this?" Serala asked.

"Not that we know of. Research into magic is expressly forbidden, however, so we could be wrong. But that doesn't stop us from learning about it when we can. The closest would probably be Dark, I think. From what you all have said, it sounds like what we call Dark magic is actually some sort of spatial magic. But I don't see how it could make something this stable." Edana mused.

"An unknown type of magic, then?" Serala asked, with an odd note in her voice.

"Couldn't be. Magic comes from the Gods. It *is* the power of the Gods. Nineteen Gods, nineteen magics. How could there be other magics?" She received no answer.

"So, what then?" Tala asked. "How do we get through?" He received no answer either.

"What would happen if the stasis field was destroyed?" Ilan asked, contributing to the conversation for the first time and receiving puzzled looks.

"All the sand would come crashing down, most likely," Moelo answered. "Can't say what'll happen on the inside, since we don't know what's in there."

"How do you know that?" Lito asked.

"This sand isn't here on purpose," he replied, gesturing towards the wall. "It was built by sandstorms. Flying sand crosses the threshold and freezes, then gets pushed a tiny bit deeper by more sand. Assuming this has been here for thousands of years, that's more than enough time for sandstorms to have built it up. So, if the stasis field breaks, all that sand will fall straight down."

"How far away would we need to be to be safe from the falling sand?" The question rang out, and all eyes turned to Vail, surprised.

"With this height? I wouldn't feel comfortable being any closer than a mile. Maybe more. This isn't exactly a situation I have experience in." Moelo shrugged.

"Is it more than a mile deep? On the inside?" Vail continued to ask. Tala's eyes narrowed at the man, suspicious.

"Oh, easily," his dad answered. "Assuming the edge of the stasis field is a uniform circle, at this size and curvature, the radius would be miles long. But that would only matter if we had a way to get inside without getting caught by the field."

"I can," Vail said simply, matter-of-factly. It didn't even

sound like confidence, delivered as it was in his deadpan, almost bored way. It simply sounded like... truth. "I'll bring it down once I'm far enough in."

"Really? And how would you do that?" Moelo asked, skepticism on his face, but eagerness and excitement in his voice.

"The stasis field is magic. It won't affect me. And I can end it."

"Again, how? And how do you know it's magic?"

"I can feel it. Their magic may not be working, but mine is fine."

"Magic? What magic?" Moelo asked eagerly. Tala was just as curious, a feeling he could see reflected in the faces of many of his companions. Serala, Gazin, and Ilan the notable exceptions.

"Enough talking. You all leave, get a mile or more out. You'll be able to see the sand collapse. I'll do the same on the inside. Once I've broken the stasis field, you can all come find me."

"Wait! Wait! What magic do you wield? Why is it working when the others aren't? How do you know you can bring down the field? Why do you think it won't affect you?" Moelo cried, eyes wide and manic, in full Researcher mode, as Tala called it.

Vail didn't answer. Instead, he just walked up to the hole in the wall and entered it seamlessly. Fully inside the hole, well past the point where the stasis should have held him, he turned around, giving Moelo an empty stare that could be felt more than seen under his hood.

"Amazing!" Moelo whispered, staring starry-eyed at Vail.

"Go. Now. I'll only wait so long before I bring it down,"

Vail said, his voice still fully flat and somehow sounding more threatening for it.

"But-" Moelo started to object, before stopping as Ilan gripped his shoulder with his massive hand.

"Come. We will tell you what we can," he said, turning Moelo away as he spoke. Tala followed, mind buzzing as he added these new revelations to what he had already known—and suspected—about Vail.

They had been walking for more than ten minutes in total silence when Tala lost his patience. Ilan had promised answers, and Tala wanted them. "So," he started, speaking loud enough that he was sure everyone could hear him. "Vail can destroy a stasis field made with some sort of mystery magic that none of us have ever heard of before."

"Aye," Ilan grunted, the only response that Tala's not-quite-a-question received.

"Cool. Cool, cool, cool. Care to elaborate? Tell us what magic he has, maybe? Just to start with?"

"I don't think this is really the time for this, lad," Gazin warned.

"Oh? Well, I disagree. We're literally doing nothing but walking." He hadn't meant to sound quite so rude, especially not to Gazin, who had always been kind to him, but months of fear, confusion, and exhaustion were getting to him.

Gazin sighed. "Don't you think you owe it to Vail to at least let him explain first? He saved your life, and it's a poor way to repay him by digging into his secrets behind his back."

"That is why I waited! But I kind of feel like any debt I owe him was settled *when he threw me off that Godsdamned bridge!*" Tala yelled, unable to stop himself. "You all have saved my life. Many times over. And I appreciate everything that you've all done for me. But you were pretty open from the start: You were doing it for your own reasons, not for me. Which is fine, I get it. I'm still grateful for it. But I don't feel like I owe him shit anymore, and I want answers. Every time I learn something new about him, it just leads to more questions. So, who in the Hells is he, and what type of magic does he have? I know you know the answers, Gazin! I've been able to tell from the start that you know more about him than the rest of us combined. Except for Ilan and Serala. And you two can feel free to answer if you'd like."

Tala took a harsh, deep breath. He had been holding all of that in for so long. He hadn't meant to snap, but he wasn't going to let the chance pass. He'd have preferred to let it all out at Vail, and not the others, but Vail wouldn't have cared anyway.

"He's right, Gazin," Serala said, voice somber. "We should have told them long before now."

"We can't," Gazin argued, sounding desperate. "You know what will happen if that secret gets out. I'm not saying we don't trust all of you." His eyes darted to every person with them, including Tala's parents, before focusing back on Serala. "But you don't know what it was like. You were too young to remember. It was bad. As bad for us as it was for the Churches. It's better that the world forgets. Nobody else needs to know. It just adds more risk."

"The world isn't going to forget, Gazin! He's already breaking—you should be able to see that! He killed Denhei

Mishima! How many people-how many *soldiers* saw him do that?"

"Nobody will believe it! He's with Tala! They'll just think that the 'Blessed Killer' shared his tricks!"

"He murdered a Blessed with his bare hands!" Serala shouted. "I didn't even know he could do that! That's not just some clever trick! And he did it in *Lightning*! How long do you think it will take them to start putting the pieces together? He's been different ever since Southtown! I just thought he was feeling hopeful about the future now that we have Tala! I forgot *who he is*!"

"He isn't that anymore!" Gazin shouted back. "He put all of that aside when he took you in! He raised you like his own! I doubted him as much as anybody, but he proved me wrong! He did the best he could for you! If he was the same person, he would have left you for dead without a second thought!"

"Dude, what in the Hells did you start?" Lito whispered to Tala, who was watching the two fight with wide eyes.

"I have no idea," he mumbled back. He had never seen Gazin or Serala act like this. Especially to each other! Gazin usually treated Serala more like a beloved granddaughter than anything and vice versa!

Tala quickly scanned their other companions, trying to gauge their reactions. Ilan, who had technically started everything, was looking somberly off in the distance, eyes avoiding the arguing pair. Dunlop was looking almost as stoic as ever, though he had a deep frown as his eyes flicked between the two. Caida was watching them with wide eyes, horror and exhilaration in equal parts clear on her face. The mistress of secrets had clearly figured out what they were arguing about and was both terrified and thrilled. Such a reaction in *her* of all people worried Tala immensely. Lito and Alina seemed to be just as lost as Tala was, which was comforting in a way. And as for his parents, well, they were just quietly watching the fight, brows furrowed and rather resembling Dunlop at the moment.

"You weren't wrong!" Serala yelled, sounding as if it hurt to say the words. "I asked him, you know, about why he took care of me! I asked him for years! He did it because he felt guilty! My parents were his friends, or the closest thing he ever had to friends, and he felt guilty about getting them killed! That's why he took me in! It wasn't because he had a change of heart or had suddenly become a better person! He just felt bad that he had turned his only friend's daughter into an orphan!"

It was Tala's turn to frown. Why would Vail feel remorseful about their deaths? Had he been trying to save them and failed?

"So what? The fact that he even *could* feel guilty shows he had changed! He's been living as a different person for almost twenty years! He *can't* be the same!"

"He is," Serala said sadly. "He's only been hiding it. This entire time. For my sake. But I'm an adult now. He doesn't need to take care of me anymore. Whether people find out about him or not doesn't matter anymore. Whatever we find here, whatever is hidden behind that wall, doesn't matter. The hope of finding it already was enough. His facade has been cracking more and more since Southtown. Whatever comes next, he's going to reveal himself to the world again. It's just a matter of time."

"You're wrong," Gazin said desperately. "We can stop him. You and me. Ilan too."

"We can't." Serala shook her head. "You know we can't. Once he's decided he's fulfilled his debt to my parents, there will be nothing any of us can do. The best thing we will be able to do is try to aim him in the right direction, and hope it stops him from causing too much damage. He's raised me for nearly twenty years. I should be able to do that much."

Gazin was going to continue arguing when his back suddenly straightened, shoulders tense and eyes wide. "My magic's back," he whispered, bringing one hand up before his eyes and watching as the skin rippled and twisted across it. His head shot back towards the sand wall, and the rest of them followed his eyes on instinct. Off in the distance, the giant wall of sand was falling, like a curtain suddenly cut from its bearings all at once. Even at their distance, the ground and air rumbled as though there were an earthquake, setting off the camels, who began braying in distress.

"He did it," Gazin said, not sounding surprised.

"Aye," Serala replied tiredly. "We should get moving then. Tala. Everybody," she called. "I-we-know you want answers. When we get back to Vail, we'll tell you everything. Everything we can. But there's a lot even the three of us don't know." She indicated herself, Ilan, and Gazin.

"Serala-" Gazin started, before she cut him off.

"No, Gazin. They deserve to know. And it's my choice. He's never cared if people knew. He only ever hid it for my sake anyway."

Despondently, Gazin nodded. He clearly wasn't happy

with her decision but knew it was a fight he couldn't win. Tala, as confused—and now nervous—as he was, almost sighed in relief. *Finally,* everything would be answered.

"That is interesting. Quite interesting," his dad muttered, to which his mom mumbled in agreement.

"What is?" Tala asked absently. "That Vail has some huge secret they've been keeping from us?"

"No. Well, yes, but that's hardly a surprise. No, what's interesting is that the anti-magic field fell at the same time as the stasis field did. Either Vail found some way to turn them both off, or they were connected to each other. That can't be an accident."

"Oh." Tala blinked. In all the drama, he had barely even registered that. "But that implies-"

"Oh yes." His dad nodded.

"Which means-"

"Mhmm," his mom hummed in affirmation.

Tala turned to the rest of the group, who were already moving back toward the former sand wall, pulling the unhappy camels with them. "We should get going."

"Oh, yes!" his dad replied, the manic smile of promised secrets soon to be revealed on his face. Drama and Vail notwithstanding, Tala felt a similar excitement bubble up inside him.

CHAPTER 50

"Well, that's different," Tala couldn't help but point out, not that he really needed to. They could all see the way that the land changed from the endless sands of the desert to... well, still a desert, but with no sand, just dry, barren earth stretching out into the distance. There was no sign the sand wall ever existed other than the large sand dune that was left behind in an unnatural ring where the wall had once been.

"That's interesting," his dad corrected. "The land is completely dead. The stasis field must have been put in place after it died, but before it turned to sand like the rest."

"So, the desert wasn't always here then. Something created it."

"Indeed."

"But there's nothing here. It's all just empty. What about Tora? Where is it?"

"Destroyed," his mom answered, looking around at the vast emptiness around them. "This is the center of a desert that stretches for hundreds of miles. The kind of power it would take to destroy everything in that big of an area so thoroughly would have erased all traces of anything, even a city. Nothing would be left of Tora but dust. It may even be some of the sand that we've been in for the last week. It had to have been the Gods. Not even a hundred Blessed could do all this." They fell silent, gazing out at the devastation of the Gods.

"It's gone, then?" Lito asked. "Tora? Then what was the point of coming here? Why would the Beast God send you here if they destroyed it all?"

Tala shared a look with his parents. "They missed something. Or left it on purpose."

"What? How do you know?"

"Because if there was truly nothing left, then who put up the stasis field, how, and why?" Tala asked.

"He's right. There must be something in here worth saving. That stasis field and the null field around it? That's a lot of effort for nothing," Serala added, making Tala frown. She had called the anti-magic field a "null" field. He had never heard her, or any of them, call it that before. Why did the word sound so familiar? "We should find Vail. Then we can look for whatever was left here."

"After you explain everything to us, right?" Tala reminded her.

"Yeah." She nodded tiredly. "After that."

They continued on, walking as straight as they could with only the sun and moons to guide them. With no landmarks or distinguishable features, only the flat, dead land around them, it was hard to tell if they were going in a straight line.

In the sands, they had at least been able to use the remnants of their footsteps and the dunes as rough path markers.

Tala had just been starting to worry that they had indeed gotten turned around and were going the wrong direction when Caida called out. She could see Vail off in the distance, far to their right. When he peered over, Tala could just barely make out a blurry blot of darkness marring the horizon.

"Are you sure that's him?" Lito asked what Tala, and probably a few of the others, had been thinking.

"Who else could it be?" she all but snapped back. Caida had not been enjoying their trek through the desert, though she refused to be left behind. Her temper was short, and she had mostly just kept quiet and to herself since they had entered the oppressive dryness and heat of the sands. Not that Tala could blame her.

"It's definitely a person. And none but Vail would just stand in the middle of all this alone and not even try to make himself more visible. We're lucky he didn't lay down to take a nap."

"He's not that bad," Serala defended, before sighing. "But he could have done something to be easier to find. Come on, then." She turned and started leading the way.

It took them a few minutes to reach the figure, who was indeed Vail, standing perfectly still in the vast emptiness of the dead land with his hood still pulled over his head. Even during the hottest days in the desert, he hadn't removed that hood. The only time Tala had ever fully seen his face was right after they had rescued him from the guards when he killed Ignis.

"Vail! We almost passed you!" Serala chastised, glaring

at him. He ignored her, instead looking toward Tala and his parents.

"There's nothing here," he said flatly.

"That we've seen," Moelo pointed out. "There's something worth putting that stasis field up for. But before that, you owe us all some answers."

"No, I don't."

"You owe *me* answers. And I think everyone deserves to hear it all anyway at this point," Tala told him.

"He's right, Vail. After everything that's happened, they deserve to know the truth. Tala especially," Serala said gently. Ilan nodded in agreement beside her.

Vail sighed. "Fine. What truth?"

"All of it," Serala said sternly.

Vail sighed again. "Fine. Where should I start?"

"How did you bring down the stasis field?" Moelo jumped in eagerly.

"Null magic. Anti-magic you've been calling it. I can use it."

Tala's eyes grew wide, as did most of the others, except Gazin who was hanging his head sadly.

"Vail! Just... tell them everything. You're wasting time," Serala ordered, irritated.

Vail sighed again. "Fine. I could feel the stasis field was some sort of magic, so I used my magic to be immune to it. I walked in to here, could feel that I was still in the stasis field, and used my Null magic to collapse it. Happy?"

"How exactly did you collapse it? That field was massive! How much power do you have?" Moelo questioned eagerly.

Vail shook his head. "A bit of Null into it broke the whole thing. That's just how Null magic works. I can break or redirect magic easily. Usually."

"Fascinating!" Moelo exclaimed. "You said usually? When can't you-"

"Dad!" Tala spoke up, hating himself a little bit for it because he also wanted to hear the same answers. But they had priorities, and the minutiae of Vail's magic could be studied in the future. "We can ask him later. Right now, focus." He turned to Vail. "I've never heard of Null magic before. There is no Null God. Where did you get it?"

"What happened to staying focused?" He heard Lito whisper to Alina.

"We just spent days inside of an anti—a *Null* field, and now we're learning Vail has the same type of magic. I'd say it's pretty damned relevant," Tala retorted. Lito blushed.

"You just want my whole life story, don't you?" Vail asked drily.

"At this point? Yeah, sure," Tala replied.

Vail gave an aggrieved sigh. "Fine. Whatever. As a kid I was captured by Wind raiders. They experimented on me and hundreds of others. Thousands before me, probably. With things I've never seen elsewhere. Most of the people they were experimenting on died. I didn't. Don't know why. But I was a 'success' and got Null powers, stronger than any other 'successes.' Once I figured out how to use them, I broke out, killed a bunch of people, destroyed everything I could, punched the Wind God in the face, stole a ship, burned down the Wind fleet, and worked my way west until I reached these lands. I landed in Light, got a rude welcome, killed a bunch of people, and escaped again. Spent some time like that until I met the Beast God in the Jungle. It told me about Tora, that I could 'learn the truth' there, and I spent a couple of years trying to learn anything I could about it, and failing, until Os found me. We fought until I realized that a couple that had saved my life before had died in our fight. I owed them my life, so I adopted their daughter so she wouldn't become a slave or soldier in Lightning. I let Os go, had the Dissidents spread the word that he had killed me, and joined them officially. Anything else?"

Tala stared at Vail, eyes wide, as if seeing him for the very first time. That was *a lot*. And Tala was very much definitely going to go back through it all later. But at the moment, all of Tala's attention was caught up on one little detail. "That-that means-you are…?" Tala stumbled over his words, mouth not cooperating with the chaos that was his brain.

"The Demon? Yep. That's me. Live and in the flesh." Vail smiled sarcastically. "Surprise!"

CHAPTER 51

After Vail dropped his revelation on them, in his far-too-casual way, like it was barely worth mentioning, and not worth the time it took to tell, they all got over their shock—more or less—and decided to spread out in a line. Once they were within shouting distance of the two closest, they walked into the desolate wastes in the hopes that one of them would stumble upon whatever Tala and his parents were so certain was hidden out there. Well, it had been decided after Tala and his parents had finished practically drowning Vail in questions, most of which the man had—unsurprisingly—ignored.

"Why did you kill so many people?" Tala had asked. "You always left so much death and destruction in your wake. Why?"

"It was fun." Vail had shrugged. Shrugged! He had slaughtered people, innocent people, in the hundreds, thousands, all because it was *fun*!

Alina understood then why Gazin was so desperate to keep Vail's identity a secret. Why he had been so insistent Vail never be allowed to regress to 'who he had once been.' The

Dissidents may be terrorists—they had all long accepted that fact—but even they had limits on how far they were willing to go. Vail—the Demon—had none. Worse: he saw those limits, limits naturally embraced by all people who held even a fraction of sanity or a hint of morality or compassion, and thought it was fun to break those limits! Now she understood why even Osson, the infamous Bone Merc, had been cowed in the face of Vail's anger. Despite what history said, even he wasn't stronger than the Demon!

"Could Wind make more people like you?" Edana had asked, securing everyone's absolute attention.

"Not likely," Vail dismissed. "When I said I destroyed everything I could, I meant everything. The laboratory was in a few basement floors of the Wind God's palace, built into a cliff. By the time I was leaving, part of the cliff was collapsing into the sea. Including all the basement labs and some of the palace proper. The God's personal rooms among them. It all took a long drop into deep water. There's nothing left."

Alina had been able to feel how much his words pained Tala and his parents, even as they shared in the group's immense relief. Where the three of them would lament the lost knowledge, horrible as it was, even they couldn't be sad there would never be another Demon.

"What about the Wind Raids? Those stopped shortly before your arrival. Did you have a hand in that too?" Moelo had asked.

"I think so." Vail shrugged. "Wasn't really my intent. I stole a boat to escape the island and burned down the fleet that had been assembling there so they couldn't chase me. Burned down every boat, dock, and shipyard I could while I came west too. I don't know how to sail, so I basically just kept crashing into each island I could find so I could get supplies, then I'd steal another boat and do it again. Pretty sure I destroyed a good few thousand ships or so. And a few dozen towns."

"And you punched the Wind God in the face?" Tala had asked quietly.

"Oh, yeah." Vail had grinned at that, a thoroughly disturbing expression that Alina never wanted to see again. "When I was escaping the labs. Didn't exactly know my way around, and I ended up in his chambers trying to find a way out. Didn't realize who—or what—he was until later, after I became 'The Demon,' but it was definitely the God."

"That's why you were so certain that the Gods could be hurt! And feel fear!" Tala exclaimed. At Vail's—and all of theirs—confused looks, he elaborated, "In the cave, after we escaped Fiahren! You said that. It kinda stuck in my mind." He shrugged.

"Right. Well, yeah. I ran into the Wind God in his rooms, and I punched him in the face. He surprised me. At the time, I didn't know that wasn't supposed to be possible. I thought he was just some pampered princeling until I learned about the Gods. He was terrified, though."

"But if you can hit them, shouldn't you be able to kill them?" Tala had asked hesitantly.

"You'd think," was Vail's glib response. "But I tried it when I met Beast, with his cooperation even, and it didn't work. I could hurt him, but not enough. That's why Tora is so important. If the secret behind Null is there, we might be able to figure it out."

"Hey! Alina!" Lito called out from far to her left, breaking her from her recollections. "Caida found something!" Nodding back in response, despite being too far for him to see it, Alina prepared her magic. She had been placed in the very center of the long line they had made for this very purpose. Condensing her magic into small, shimmering balls hovering over her palm, Alina sent them shooting upwards into the sky, where they exploded into giant arrows pointing down the line towards Caida. With her job done, Alina turned and quickly caught up to Lito, who had been waiting for her.

"Do you know what she found?" she asked, entwining her fingers with his in a move that still caused a pleasant fluttering in her stomach.

"Nah, Tala passed it on to me. But he's excited. Took off running the moment he was sure I got the message."

"She could've found a strangely colored rabbit and he'd be excited," she couldn't help but point out.

"Yeah." Lito chuckled, one of her favorite sounds. "If it had purple fur, he'd spend the next two days obsessing with his parents over it before they all realized it was just covered in weird dirt."

"And then two more days obsessing over purple dirt." She laughed. Tala was her closest friend—after Lito, of course— but the boy was ridiculous at times. He had become even worse after reuniting with his parents, people who could not just follow, but properly engage with him about all the weird sciency-things he could get so excited about. It was endearing, if a little off-putting.

"Hey, Lina? Do you see that?" Lito asked, pointing to a blurry shape off in the distance. A few even smaller black dots approached.

"Yeah. One sec," she said, letting go of Lito's hand as she held both of hers in front of her face, fingertips pointing at each, letting her magic flow between her hands. Slowly, the dark blurs began to gain focus and take shape as she adjusted her magic until she could clearly see an image. Their companions were rapidly approaching some sort of ramshackle building, breaking up the monotony of the wastes. "It looks like a shack or a shed or something. It's small though. Couldn't fit more than a couple people inside."

"Huh. Well, it's something. We should hurry before the three of them lose patience and go inside," Lito said, referring to Tala and his parents. They were already poring over the outside of the shack, kept away from the doors by Dunlop standing sentinel in front of them.

"Dunlop's got them. Besides, they'll have to wait for the others regardless. Serala will kill them if they do anything risky before she gets there." Alina flinched at her own words. Although meant as a joke, they sounded far less humorous. Serala had been raised by the Demon. No wonder she was so twisted.

"Ah. She wouldn't. I think. Would she?" Lito asked hesitantly. "I mean, her and Tala definitely have a thing going on between them. She wouldn't hurt him, would she?"

"She was raised by the... Vail. She might think hurting him is a show of affection."

"No." He shook his head. "She knows better than that. She would've hurt him already otherwise. Besides, she was raised by Ilan too, more or less. The guy's quiet, and terrifying, but he's not exactly violent, is he?"

"No, he isn't," she agreed. "But he *has* been with Vail for over a decade, and he clearly knew Vail's past already. That's not exactly a stellar endorsement of his personality. And he's a former Stone Knight. How in the Hells did a Stone Knight end up with... Vail, and his adopted daughter in the first place?"

"I don't know." Lito sighed. "Maybe we should ask them? Now that they're finally telling us everything?"

"...Maybe let's suggest it to Tala and let him ask?"

"Yeah. That's a good plan. I like that plan. Let's go with that plan."

Alina smiled and re-entwined her fingers with Lito's, enjoying their quiet walk together until they reached the shack. Dunlop and Caida nodded to them in greeting, but Tala and his parents hadn't even noticed their arrival. Alina and Lito silently decided not to bother getting their attention, and just stood back, waiting for the rest to get there.

Once Ilan—the last of them—arrived, Serala finally strode forward, clearing her throat to get the Researchers' attention. When that failed, she walked up to Tala and slapped the back of his head, prompting a startled yelp from him, and a raised eyebrow from Alina towards Lito, who chuckled sheepishly back at her.

"Hello," Serala started. "Now that you three are back with us."

Alina idly wondered if Serala was aware of the irony of those words. "Mind sharing what has you so excited over a shack?"

"Well, it's here, for one thing!" Moelo exclaimed, practically vibrating with excitement.

"Yes. It is. Right here," Serala replied drily.

"What he means," Edana clarified, ever the interpreter for the other two, "is that it was built after the destruction—presumed—of Tora. It's clearly been put together with pieces of scrap metal. Some sort of steel, by the looks of the rust, and different pieces, maybe even different metals, based on the rough way it's all welded together. It definitely wasn't made by someone who knows a lot about welding and metalwork, but they did have a decent understanding of structural integrity. It's completely sealed, should be water—and sand—proof, not that either of those were an issue with the stasis field in place. But we can't tell you more without getting a look inside."

"What?" Moelo exclaimed. Again. *The man exclaims a lot,* Alina thought. "There's plenty more we can tell! Like it must have been built by someone without using magic! A Metal wielder wouldn't need to weld it, and a Lava user wouldn't have left such a rough, and focused, pattern. And a Fire Wielder likely wouldn't-"

"Dear!" Edana interrupted. "I meant anything more that these people would care about."

"Oh. Yes. Right," Moelo mumbled, nodding as he relented in his tirade.

Alina felt slightly offended at Edana's casual dismissal of their interest, as though they weren't even capable of understanding why the welding patterns were interesting. Granted, she wasn't entirely wrong, but she still didn't appreciate being dismissed like that!

"Dun, is it safe to open the doors?" Serala asked.

"As far as I can tell," Dunlop answered. "But I would suggest Ilan and I do so, just in case."

"Do it." Serala nodded, and Ilan passed her to stand in front of the rusted metal door of the shack. Tala and his parents scurried eagerly behind the two, trying to peek over their shoulders before getting pulled back further by Serala.

"We're clear. Open it," Serala ordered, one hand still holding onto Tala's collar as she practically held the boy to her, far closer than was strictly needed. Not that Tala was complaining.

"Opening," Dunlop called, grabbing onto the door's long handle as Ilan positioned himself next to it, giant sword in hand while Dunlop held his shield in his empty one. With a nod, Dunlop pulled the door open in a single motion, the door only slightly screeching as he did so. Immediately, Dunlop ducked behind his shield as Ilan brought his sword to cover him. The actions were unnecessary, as nothing happened. After a few moments of silence, and Tala and his parents standing on tiptoes trying to peer past the two, Dunlop peeked up over his shield, lowering it slowly as Ilan relaxed.

"What's in there?" Serala asked. "It's all dark. We can't see."

"Stairs," Dunlop said, voice bemused. "There's another door at the bottom. Nothing else."

"Bunker! It's a bunker! An underground bunker!" Tala whispered excitedly, his father sharing in his delight.

"We'll see," Serala said, not loosening her grip on him. "Same process, open the door," she ordered the two.

"It's dark down there. We'll need light." Dunlop told her.

"Alina, you're up." Serala gestured. Nodding, Alina joined Dunlop and Ilan, staying behind the two as she trailed the sunlight in behind her as she slowly descended the hidden underground stairway.

CHAPTER 52

"Opening!" Dunlop called, his voice echoing up the metallic tunnel the stairs were in. Tala was practically shivering in anticipation, completely ignoring the firm grip Serala had on him.

"Clear!" Dunlop's voice rang out. Light thumps sounded out from the hole as Ilan ascended the stairs.

"Well? What's down there?" Moelo excitedly asked before anyone else had a chance to say anything.

"It looks like a hallway," Ilan answered slowly. "There is a door at the far end and more in the walls in between."

"Any signs of life?" Serala asked.

"Possibly. It doesn't look abandoned, but if it was in that stasis field, then it wouldn't." He shrugged.

"Could there be people inside?" Serala asked, this time directing her question to Tala and his parents.

"It's possible," Tala said, turning his head as much as he could to talk to her.

"If it was in the stasis field," Edana agreed.

"If it was there since the beginning," Tala continued.

"There could be some of the first humans still alive down there!" Moelo finished. Tala heard Gazin let out a sigh.

"Right. We'll take it slow, check one door at a time. We don't know what's waiting for us," Serala ordered. "I don't suppose you three would wait out here while we make sure it's safe?" she asked Tala and his parents.

"Not on your life!" Moelo answered immediately, Tala nodding earnestly in agreement.

"Fine. But stay behind us, and don't open any doors. If there is anyone down there, you're the last we want to find them." She let go of Tala and made her way to the staircase, Tala right on her heels, his parents on his, and the rest following them. As they descended the stairway, Tala closely examined the walls and stairs, as did his parents, the entire place aglow in the eerie, unsourced luminescence of Alina's magic.

"Some sort of stone. No seams or anything. Probably Earth magic," Tala said. It was all beautifully crafted, if aesthetically bland.

"Yes." Moelo nodded. "I wonder if those are some type of torch," he said, examining strange bulbous shapes set high up on the walls, partly obscured by some sort of metal netting fastened over them.

"Could be. Looks like it might be glass. Think it might be like the gas lamps back home?" Tala said, also studying them.

"Something similar, at least," Edana added. "They're too high to reach easily, and if that is glass, then fire magic wouldn't be able to ignite them without breaking it first."

Nothing else broke up the dreary nature of the stairway though, no knobs, or levers, or anything else to indicate a way to turn the lamps on like in Fiahren. Tala kept an eager eye out for anything interesting as they descended, leaving security to the others. The descent didn't take very long, as the stairs were only about twenty steps or so. Upon reaching the bottom, Tala stood next to Alina. He peeked over Dunlop's and Serala's shoulders into the hallway ahead, already alight with Alina's magic.

"Strange," Tala mumbled to himself, taking in the hallway.

"What is?" Serala asked over her shoulder, not willing to turn away from the unknown ahead of her.

"All of it," Tala replied. "I've never seen designs like this."

"Like what? It just looks like a simple hallway," Gazin said from behind Tala.

"But-just look at it! The walls are painted. That type of beige isn't natural, nor how smooth it is! And those doors are weird! I think they're wood, but I've never seen wood like that before! And those two have windows in them! With glass! Glass windows in the doors! Inside! And what are those things in the ceiling? I'm pretty sure that's not glass, but whatever it is, I don't recognize it!"

"Neither do we," Edana said from where she and Moelo had pushed Alina aside and joined Tala in peeking past Dunlop and Serala. "He's right. The basic structure is normal enough, but the details are all strange. Everything is so... clean. And smooth. Even this door is weird."

She grabbed onto the door that Dunlop was keeping open. "It's metal, a strong door, but not the type of thing you would use to secure a bunker or anywhere else. There's not even a handle on the inside-look. It's just a metal bar stretching across at waist height. Actually, I think it opens the latch." She pointed to the latch sticking out from the side of the door, which would keep it from swinging open when shut, and then pushed the metal bar. It slid inwards with a small *clink*, and the latch retracted into the door. "It's a clever design. A door that can be opened without hands, at least from the inside, but is entirely insecure. There's no way to lock it or anything, as far as I can tell."

"Okay," Serala said slowly. "What does that mean?"

"It means this isn't some sort of bunker," Moelo answered for his wife. "Or isn't meant to be. I'd say this isn't even meant to be an entrance. An emergency exit, perhaps? We have such things around the Institute. In fact, I'd wager that this probably didn't even lead outside, originally. This staircase was probably inside of a building, once upon a time, destroyed with the rest of Tora. Somebody must have cleared it out after the destruction and built that shack on top to protect it. Or draw attention to it. Both, perhaps."

"Okay," Serala repeated. "What is this place then?"

"Oh, no idea!" Tala grinned. "We'll have to start poking around inside to figure that out! So, let's carry on with that, shall we? No point lingering in the doorway!"

"You're the-right. Fine. Let's go," Serala huffed and entered the hallway, dagger in hand. Dunlop followed her cautiously, while Tala and his parents followed less so with Alina and the rest behind them. Serala and Dunlop took up positions in front of one of the doors and nodded to each other once before Dunlop grasped the handle and pushed the door open, raising his shield in the doorway. He peered around before lowering his shield.

"Clear. But I don't know what it is."

Serala nodded and poked her head, looking around.

"You three can go inside. Gazin, stay with them, just in case. We'll keep clearing through."

Tala and his parents practically sprinted towards the room, stumbling over each other. They entered, entirely ignoring Gazin as he followed much more calmly. It was a tiny room with little more than a bulky desk-like table in it, one which Tala couldn't see past as it ran down to the floor, with two chairs in front of it and one behind. On the table were a few small items Tala didn't recognize, and an open container with a collection of strange implements, some of which reminded him of the pencils that had been growing in popularity at the Institute, but much thinner and neater looking. The largest thing on the desk was some strange sort of large, misshapen block. Tala walked around the desk without care, examining the object.

"I have no idea what this is," he said, prompting his parents to join him in a huddle. "I think that's glass on it. Like a glass pane was stuck in it."

Tala reached toward the handles set in the desk, assuming they had drawers behind them. "Wait!" Gazin ordered, making Tala blink up at him in surprise. "There could be something dangerous in those. I should check them first!"

"Oh, relax, Gazin!" Tala smiled. "This is clearly some sort of office. There won't be anything bad!" Gazin could be far too paranoid sometimes. If there was anything dangerous, whoever had used this room wouldn't have left it so unsecured! Probably.

It took only a couple of minutes for Tala to rifle through all the drawers. "Honestly, I don't know what half that stuff is. But it's definitely not whatever we're looking for. We can come back later if we need to anyway." As eager as Tala was to examine every little strange object, they did have a more important purpose.

He led the way into the next room, strikingly similar to the first, down to the same weird blocky thing on the desk. Every room, it turned out, was like that. The only difference was in the little objects on the desks, and the one room with the window in the door, which was larger but had nothing but a long table surrounded by chairs.

By the time they had gotten there, the others had cleared the entire hallway and were now congregated at the door at the far end.

"Hey! Every room is the same," Serala told them. "Let's keep going further."

Tala and his parents didn't object as they passed by the other empty rooms; they could always peruse them later. Once they were ready, Serala opened the door, and Dunlop pushed through, shield and short sword at the ready. Seconds went by in silence before he called "clear." Glancing at each other, the group filtered through the doorway. When he got through, Tala understood why Dunlop had taken longer than usual. The room they entered was huge and full of stuff Tala couldn't even begin to recognize.

There was metal, a lot of metal, but for the life of him,

Tala couldn't say what any of it was *for*. There were also many tables and more of those big desks. Most striking of all, was a single table clearly out of place, sitting innocuously a short way into the room, directly in front of the door. The only thing on the table was a small object Tala still didn't recognize. Beneath it was a sheet of paper, only it was impossibly white and smooth and cut exactly to be a perfect rectangle.

Tala shuffled forward with the others, eyes roaming the room. As he got closer to the conspicuously placed table, he could make out writing on the paper, but even though the words looked normal, he couldn't read them. There were only two of them, with a large number above and a small symbol beneath.

The group came to a stop in a small semi-circle around the table with Tala and his parents in the middle. He frowned at the device and the paper beneath it. Slowly, Moelo lightly gripped the paper and slid it out, careful not to touch the device.

"Can you read it?" Serala asked.

"Yes," Moelo said slowly. Tala glanced at his dad, surprised. All he recognized was the big number 1 taking up a full quarter of the page. "Barely. This style of writing is old. *Old*, old. Thousands of years, at least. I've only ever seen it in some of the oldest documents back at the Institute."

"What does it say?"

"Play me."

"Play me? What does that mean?" Tala asked.

Moelo scrutinized the strange device on the table, glancing between it and the paper before shrugging. "It has this symbol here." He gestured to the symbol on the paper. "Maybe we touch it?"

"Maybe we should wait-" Gazin started to say, but he was too late. Moelo had already pushed something on the object, eliciting a quiet click. Suddenly, the object lit up, and soft beams of light shot out of the top. They came together, forming the image of a small, sad man hovering in the air over the object.

"If you're watching this," a voice sounded from the device at the same time as the light-man's mouth moved, "it means our plan succeeded."

CHAPTER 53

"I've spent a lot of time thinking about how best to present this to you, whoever you are," the man said, his voice heavy with an accent unlike any Tala had ever heard. "But in the end, I truly have no idea. I don't even know if you'll be able to understand my words. How long will this recording have been waiting here? Decades? Centuries? Millennia? The fact that last is even a possibility is astounding. A testament to our arrogance, maybe, one way or another. Will you still speak the same language that we do? Or will my tongue be so foreign to your own that you may never manage to translate my words, and this will all have been in vain? I hope that isn't the case. And I will act as though it isn't, for to do otherwise is to give up completely, and I can't."

Tala was enraptured by the strange man, this "recording" of a man presumably long dead. What sort of magic, or technology, was this?

"So, with the assumption that you can understand me, or will be able to with time, I will tell you the story of what happened here. The mistakes we made that in our hubris have all but destroyed the world, in the hopes that in knowing what happened, in knowing what we did and how, you might be able to fix them."

"Maybe we will if you could get to the damned point," Gazin growled, and Tala couldn't help but agree. Whoever this man was—had been—he certainly liked to hear himself talk.

"With that in mind, I've decided the best way to tell you what happened is to let you hear about it for yourself, as it all was happening. Since the very beginning of the project, I have kept a video journal. Every day, after I would turn in for the night, I would record what had happened, big or small. It was a way for me to organize my thoughts, to speak my mind about everything. And it was helpful whenever I got stuck to go back and listen to my thoughts from earlier. It wasn't technically allowed to have private records of the project, no matter how informal, given the secrecy and importance, but after what's happened, I'm glad that I did. It's not like there's anyone left to punish me for it anyway. They are the only records we have—Hell, maybe the only records period—from that time. And hopefully, those records will help you to fix the world we have made."

The man reminded Tala of some of the more annoying Researchers he had known back at the Institute: men and women who thought so highly of themselves they considered their every word a gift of genius that all the rest of them should be thankful to receive. Those people could (and would) talk for hours at a time while saying absolutely nothing at all. Tala hoped this "recording" man would hurry up; his friends were looking about as irritated with his diatribe as Tala was.

"For now, though, I have compiled what I believe to be the most relevant parts of my journals over the course of the project and assembled them for you. Hopefully, they will provide you with everything you need to find a way to fix our mistakes. And though we will be long, long dead by the time you are seeing this, I ask that you do not judge us too harshly for what we have done. It was never supposed to turn out like this."

The lights on the device winked out, the small man disappearing with them. They stood in Alina's light for a few moments, silent as they waited for something else to happen. "Is that it?" Lito asked. No one answered.

Tala took a few moments to observe the room, seeing if anything stood out to him. Nothing did. He didn't have the faintest idea what anything in the room was.

"That doesn't make sense." Moelo frowned, closely examining the paper. "This was clearly an introduction of sorts. But of what? What does he mean by 'they destroyed the world?'" His voice had grown quiet, talking to himself more than them.

"There must be more recordings." Edana blithely ignored her husband muttering to himself. "That giant number 1 must mean this is the first recording. Perhaps we should spread out, look for more?"

"Like a scavenger hunt?" Tala asked. That was a game used to teach children at the Institute critical thinking skills, forcing them to solve puzzles and riddles to find hidden objects.

"Exactly. But I doubt it'll be as complicated as that," his mom answered. "There wouldn't be much point, not if he intended these to be heard."

"I don't know." Serala frowned, looking around. "We don't know what's down here. It could be dangerous."

"I don't think so," Tala disagreed. "This was some sort of research facility. Like the Institute, and they were working on some sort of huge project here. And that guy clearly wanted whoever found this place to know what happened. I think if we're careful we should be fine. Still, don't touch anything, not without one of us checking it over first." He gestured to himself and his parents, resolutely ignoring his dad sucking on a corner of the paper.

"Alright," Serala agreed hesitantly. "Go slow and stay in sight of each other," she ordered to the group. "And don't touch anything. If you find something, call out."

The group split up, everybody going around looking at different things. Even Vail was participating. Tala stayed still, thinking. Why scatter the recordings around?

"If you're watching this," a voice sounded, making them all jump and whip around, back to where Tala, Serala, and Moelo were still standing.

"Sorry! Sorry!" Moelo waved a hand at them. "Just wanted to see what would happen if I pressed it again."

Tala nodded as the others turned away. It was smart to check that there wasn't more in the recording. He tuned out the man's voice.

"What are you thinking?" Serala asked him, standing close to be heard over the recording.

"Context," Tala replied, elaborating at Serala's confused look. "It's the most likely reason he would have spread out recordings, instead of having them all right here. Or nearby, at least. He clearly wasn't trying to protect them, so they must be in places that will help us understand what he's talking about."

"That... makes sense, I guess. So, where do you think the next one would be?"

"No idea." He shrugged.

"Ah. Any idea what he's talking about? With the project and destroying the world and all that?"

"Not really. Unless he means Tora. Maybe the people here destroyed it? Thought they had destroyed the whole world? I mean, if this used to be inside a city, the entire place is a barren wasteland now. Maybe they thought the destruction had spread further than it did?"

"Oy! You two!" Lito yelled. "We found the next one!"

Tala peered over. Lito and the others had congregated on the far side of the room, off to their right. They hurried over, seeing another small table set against the wall next to a closed door. Another recording device sat on the table, as well as another sheet of weirdly white paper, blank except for a large number 2 on it.

"Guess it's next." Tala hummed, pressing the same button on the device. The same weird lights lit up, just like before, and an image of the same man appeared in the air again, sitting in a chair this time, and looking years younger.

"I can't believe it's started!" The man sounded exuberant. "Finally, after years of research, of pushing and defending our theories, the Avatar Project has finally been approved! When Professor Parker asked me to join his research team back during my undergrad days at university, I had no idea what I was getting myself into! His theories blew my mind! I wasn't sure at first, you know, when he first told me about his avatar idea. I mean, it sounded absurd! It went so far beyond normal mages! I mean, a master of magic is one thing, but to imbue a living person with the very essence of elemental magic? A fire avatar would make even William Harkness, old fiery Dick himself, the world's greatest fire mage, look like a rank amateur in comparison! Keeping my mouth shut about my doubts and playing along with Parker paid off, though. It got me both my master's and my doctorate in Elemental Arcanistry and an apprenticeship with Roger Mishima, one of the best electrical mages on the continent! His whole family has been electrical mages since the days it was still called lightning magic! I'm a certified doctor and master of electrical magic, all thanks to Parker!

"But now, thanks in no small part to my own contributions to his theory, the Avatar Project is going to become a military special project with the best toys money can buy! Parker told me they've already started construction on a secret laboratory on the outskirts of Tora! I guess the bigwigs in the government want to keep this whole thing right under their noses. Can't say I blame them, really, with what this will mean if the project is a success. But imagine, me! Living in Tora! The shining city! The jewel of civilization! Anyway, I'm heading out for some drinks. It's celebration time!"

The floating figure of the man winked out for a second, before being replaced by another version, sitting in the same chair.

"Got to tour the facility today. It was fantastic! First, it's like some spy movie. The building just looks like an ordinary office building with some basic security on the outside—gated access, simple guard booth, all that. Like somewhere a bank does its record-keeping. Even inside, it looks like a regular little office building. But take the stairs or elevator down? And blam! You step into a world of high-tech glory! Seriously, I don't even know where to begin! It's got everything! You know that five-hundred-million-dollar DNA splicer we said we'd need? We have three! They spent five hundred million dollars on a single machine, and then got two more for redundancy! It's insane!

"Oh! And I finally figured out why they set us all up in hotels for the last few months! They're expecting us to *live* there! Yeah! They have hundreds of rooms for us all to live in! And enough non-perishable food stored to feed an army for a year! It seems a little excessive to me, to be honest—I mean, living at work? It's a bit much. But they're taking the whole operational security thing seriously. I get it, I do. This project could be world changing and would be devastating if the wrong people got their hands on it, but still. At least we're allowed to leave the facility whenever we want. We're not prisoners. We just have to check in and out and follow other security protocols. No picking up women and taking them back to my place, unfortunately. But hey, I'm working on a super-secret government project! Totally worth it!"

The man blinked out, and this time didn't return. The lights on the device going dark once again.

"Did that make sense to any of you?" Lito asked, once again the first to speak. "I got the whole 'moving to Tora' thing, which means we're in the right place, I think, so yay? But I'm not sure I understood the rest of it."

Tala shared a troubled look with his parents. Oh, they hadn't understood everything, but they had gotten enough.

"What's DNA?" Dunlop asked.

"A theory," Edana answered absently. Like Tala, she was busy thinking over what they had just heard. "It's like... a recipe for what makes up living things. An old theory at the Institute. No one knows who created it or when."

"I've never heard of it," Gazin protested. As a Fleshy, he was an expert on all things body related.

"You wouldn't have. It would be... too small for you. DNA, according to the theory, would be so small it would be like taking a single strand of hair and shrinking it in half fifteen times."

"Oh." Gazin pursed his lips.

"What about the rest of it?" Serala asked. Tala shared another look with his parents. "What? What is it?"

"Well..." Tala hesitated.

"This avatar project he spoke of..." Moelo continued.

"Doesn't matter," Edana interrupted. "Not yet, anyway. Not until we learn more."

"But it could be-" Moelo was cut off by his wife.

"No, it can't." She shook her head. "That-it's not possible."

"What isn't?" Serala asked impatiently.

"No, she's right," Tala said, shaking his head. "It's not possible. Don't worry about it. We just need to find more recordings." Serala glared at him, and he stared back resolutely. Eventually, she caved.

"Fine. Let's keep looking." She waved a hand dismissively.

"Through here, probably." Tala gestured at the door beside the table. "I think it's leading us to the next recording."

"Alright. Dunlop?"

Dunlop stood next to the door, Ilan taking the other side while the rest of them split off. With a nod, Dunlop swung the door open, waiting for something to happen. When nothing did, he peeked around the corner. "Clear." He led the way into another hallway with a few doors, this one with the same hard flooring as the big room and white walls instead of beige.

"Well, I think we found the next one." Dunlop nodded to one of the doors, with a paper holding the number 3. After ushering the rest of the group out of the hallway, Dunlop and Ilan went through and cleared the other doors first. After securing the door with the number, they called for the rest to join them.

As Tala entered the room, he glanced at Vail, who had stepped aside, refusing to enter. He was staring blankly at the wall of the hallway. Weird, but Tala couldn't be bothered to try and understand Vail at the moment.

He examined the room with a critical eye. It was clearly some sort of small laboratory. Or something. Most of the room was filled with a large metal machine. In front was a lectern-like stand covered in switches and buttons and little glass bulbs. Next to the lectern-thing was a desk with multiple shelves, scattered with objects, some of which Tala actually recognized! Those were glass vials and a beaker. Clearly, it was some sort of chemistry room. On the desk sat another one of the recording devices. With little hesitation, Moelo pressed the same button as before, and the device started up.

"Well, the project has officially begun. We've begun working on isolating whatever it is in the human genome that allows us to wield magic. We have blood, bile, tissue, bone marrow, and more from hundreds of different people to work through, all with different levels of magical ability and elemental nature. If we can determine what makes one person better with fire magic and another with water, we can begin trying to amplify those abilities. Then artificially inducing an elemental compatibility and so on. It'll take a while, probably, but I'm confident. I've gone through all of our research and theories myself. I thought Parker was crazy, way back. Now I'm practically leading the charge to see it done. And you should see Parker! Every day the man looks like he's in heaven. Can't blame him, really. If this works out, his name will go down in history. All of ours will."

A blink out and in. The man was a little older now, a little more worn.

"Well, we've done all we can do. All that's left is to start human trials. I can barely believe it. A few years ago, this was Parker's pipe dream, and now we're set to begin trials on turning humans into Avatars—living embodiments of elemental magic. It's surreal. Oh, and I've forgotten the best part! Guess who we'll be conducting the trials on? Prisoners! Death-row inmates, to be exact! The first people in history to be given these powers will be murderers, rapists, and terrorists! They don't deserve to even know this project exists! Of course, that's why they were chosen. We don't expect the initial trials to go particularly well. Honestly, these people should feel honored: instead of being executed like the vermin that they are, they get to give their lives in the pursuit of scientific advancement! In bringing humanity into an entirely new era of magic! Their deaths will mean more than their lives ever did, and far more than their deaths ever should!"

The man blinked out, the device falling dormant again. The group stood still, nothing but the sound of breathing to be heard. Eventually, Caida broke the silence. "He isn't saying what I think he's saying, is he?" she asked with a tremor in her voice.

"We don't know that," Edana answered sternly. "They could have been trying to create their own Blessed. Or Descendants. Or something. Maybe that's why the Gods destroyed Tora. For their heresy. Or maybe the experiments destroyed Tora, and that's why the Gods banned Arcane Research, so nothing like that ever happens again."

Tala remained silent. His mom's words made sense, as they usually did, but he had a feeling in his gut that she was wrong. By the way she was wringing her hands, she felt it too.

"Let's keep going," Tala ordered, surprising himself. "We're not done yet." Silently, the group filtered out, Vail joining them without issue. "Dun, Ilan, anything important behind those doors?" Tala asked, feeling lightheaded.

"No. Not that we can tell," Dunlop answered stoically. Tala nodded, then gestured to the door at the end of the hall. Dunlop and Ilan went to clear it as the group shuffled back into the '3' room, sans Vail.

In his head, Tala put together the pieces. Everything that

the ancient man had told them in his recordings was painting a picture he still wasn't sure he could believe. Shuffling silently with the others after Dunlop had given the all clear, they left the hallway and continued on, moving through more rooms and hallways. They silently searched, each of them lost in their own thoughts.

Eventually, they ended up in a strange room. One wall was covered in glass windows, many of which had been shattered and sat empty. Around the room were more weird podium-like stands, covered in the same switches, buttons, levers, and little glass bulbs. Peeking through the windows, Tala saw down into another room, one that looked like a natural disaster—or many—had occurred in it. The others had clustered around another table with another device sitting on it, and a paper with the number 4. With a sigh, he nodded for his dad to start the recording.

"Initial human testing was, as predicted, disastrous. None of the elements worked, and all the subjects died. Well, I say none of the elements worked, but really, they did. They just... worked too well, I guess. The guy we imbued with the essence of fire exploded. He burned so hot there's nothing left to clean up except some scorch marks. Nice for the cleaners, bad for us, since we couldn't study his remains to figure out what went wrong. The rest went similarly: water swelled up and exploded, and what's left is too waterlogged to get any data from. Air... disintegrated, I guess? Regardless, there's nothing left. Earth turned to stone, unsurprisingly. A full-on stone statue, like something out of those old myths about gorgons. We had an earth mage try to turn him back, but it didn't work. The worst of them all was flesh. I'm not going to describe what happened—I'm trying not to think of it, honestly, even though I know I'm going to have nightmares anyway. Blood was disturbing, even if it was basically what happened to water, just red. But flesh was… that was just wrong. Space was nice: just… there one moment and gone the next. To be safe, the government will have agents on high alert out looking for her, same as air, just in case they happened to survive and appear elsewhere, but we're all doubting that. Anyway, back to the drawing board!"

A blink out and in.

"Null continues to evade us. We haven't even managed to make a failed avatar out of null magic. It's not a complete surprise, since the very existence of an anti-magic magical element screws with every magical law we know, but we were hoping to learn more about it. And so far, we've failed miserably. We have a couple dozen null mages working security over the prisoners in case they do survive, or something goes weird-wrong, but we haven't discovered anything consistent in their genetic makeup. I'd feel better if we could get a null avatar to work by the time we have the rest working. These will be people with unprecedented powers, and they're all the worst of the worst of criminal scum. We have plenty of security volunteers if we do get null working. We just need to figure out what we're missing."

A blink out and in.

"Trials are… progressing. Subjects aren't instantly expiring. And they're sometimes leaving remains behind for us to study, which has been incredibly helpful. The deaths are getting worse, in a way. Steam, as far as we could tell from the autopsy, boiled himself alive in his own skin. It was fast, mercifully, but even a few seconds must have been unimaginable agony. I'm actually feeling sorry for these people, for what they have gone through, and what the others will go through. Still, we were prepared for this. We knew what we were getting into."

A blink out and in.

"Null progress is still a bust. Everything else is onto human trials, whereas null is still stuck on mice. 'Course, it would help if *anything actually happened* when we imbued mice with null. We imbue a mouse with fire, and it either burns to death or exhibits fire magic of its own. Great either way! With null, just *nothing* happens. None have died, but none have exhibited any anti-magic either. Magic still works on them the same, be it fire magic to burn them or body magic to give them extra limbs or injuries or anything. We have no idea what the problem is! Stupid bloody null magic!

"Oh, and it gets even better! Some of the bigwigs have called in a couple of 'consultants' from the goddamned Research Institute of Fairhaven! This is supposed to be a *top-secret* project! Why are there consultants from the RIF that even know about the Avatar Project? Just because they work in that stupidly huge fortress of theirs doesn't mean they know anything more about null magic than we do! That fortress was built over two thousand years ago by King Eretrius when he joined the inquisition in their crusade to exterminate magic users! *He* had it built with null magic imbued into the very foundations! I've been there, you know? I visited the RIF, and it's goddamn weird to walk through those gates and just have your magic stop working! Maybe, if the RIF does have records of its construction, they might know how to imbue null into something. You know what? Maybe I was being too critical. The bosses might have an idea there, asking the RIF consultants to come help us."

A blink out and in.

"Well, the Researchers at the RIF don't approve of the Avatar Project. Can't say any of us were surprised. Those people are so used to working somewhere magic doesn't work, they probably aren't comfortable around magic at all. I've always said it should have been torn down after the war instead of being turned into a monument, and later a Research Institute. And the consultants couldn't even help us with our null problem. They say we're messing with things we don't fully understand. I say we have some of the foremost minds on all things magical and mundane working on this project. The sheer amount of knowledge present here is astounding. They can go back to hiding behind their magicless walls. I've got some ideas for null anyway, and the rest of the project is going smoothly. Mostly. Some of the subjects have had weird reactions we weren't expecting before they expired, but I doubt it's anything major."

A blink out and in.

"I've been saying for a few weeks now that we may have been a bit too dismissive of the RIF people. Now I'm almost certain, even if no one else will agree with me. Something is... wrong with the project. We ran another batch of tests today, and I'm worried about what happened. When we imbued the electric subject, parts of his body turned into electricity and formed back into... his body. Human body. I know what I saw. I'm a master of electrical magic, trained by Roger Mishima himself. Before he died, the subject successfully turned part of himself into electricity and then turned back. It was fast, and I admit it's hard to see even in the slowed-down recordings, but it *happened!* And that *shouldn't be possible!* Not even the wildest theories about the avatars included that, because *the math doesn't check out.* Nothing that we're doing should give a living person the ability to do something like that! I've never even heard of somebody doing something like that. Not even the greatest mages in all of history could do that. Turn part of their body into an element? Sure, easy. Turn it back? Into a living, working, functional body part? Never! I don't know. Maybe the others are right—I didn't see what I thought. I mean, I've been going over all the math, all our formulas, and nothing explains it. That has to be it. I must have been mistaken."

A blink out and in.

"I think we're making progress on null imbuing. We were going about it all wrong. The mice were showing nothing, but I've been thinking about how null works. Or, what little we know about it, and how different it is to the other magics. I think it isn't working on the mice because they aren't sapient beings. Null magic isn't just anti-magic—it's the interfering with other magics. Rerouting them, redirecting them. How would a mouse know how to do that just because we gave it the ability? Unfortunately, if I'm right, the only way to test null imbuement is to try it on a human subject. And since we wouldn't dare risk making a prisoner a null avatar, one of the volunteers would be needed. And given how... gruesome the results have been on the prisoner trials, I'm not sure if that's really even an option. I'll keep working on it, though. I'm growing increasingly worried that we're missing something in the avatar project. A null avatar on our side would make me feel a lot better."

A blink out, and the device went dormant.

"For fuck's sake!" Moelo shouted, making them all jump. "This-this-I don't know what to say! Why? Why spread these out? Why not just tell us everything? He's jerking us around like toys here!"

"He's giving us time," Edana answered, and Tala could see how she was faking her calm. "Time to understand what he's saying. And to see. This-down there," she gestured to the windows, "must have been where they were experimenting on people. Where they were trying to create the-these avatar things."

"The Gods, you mean?" Moelo growled. A shiver went through the room. They had all realized it, but to hear it spoken aloud was something else.

Tala didn't know what to do. He didn't know what to think. What these... recordings were saying contradicted everything he knew about the world. Even everything the Dissidents had taught him. He wanted to laugh. Or cry. Or both. He wanted to run. Run away, to the Far Shore, to Water, run until he fell off the edges of the world that probably didn't exist.

"But-how?" Lito asked. Pleaded. He sounded as broken as Tala felt. "That would mean... They were created! They were human! Are human! How!?"

Alina put an arm around him, drawing him close to her, even though she was clearly struggling as much as he was—as much as they all were.

"Keep going." The cold, angry voice cut through them all. Vail looked murderous. As much as Tala wanted to stop, just stop, he wasn't going to argue with the Demon.

Like a funeral procession, the group continued through the room, through the facility. Ilan and Dunlop only performed cursory checks as they went. More hallways, more doors, until they came to one with the number 5 stuck to it. They trudged into the room, forced on by the sheer presence emanating from Vail.

The 5 room was a small bedroom. Through another door, Tala could see a sink like the ones they had in Fiahren. Only Fiahren and some of the Fire cities had pipeworks. Maybe Lord Ishaan hadn't been the first person to ever think of using pipes in such a way. The thought gave Tala a headache.

The device sat innocuously on a desk near the bed. Moelo started it with an almost angry jab. This time the man looked completely different: his hair was cut short, he seemed tired, exhausted, and was staring out with a half-dead glaze in his eyes.

"It's working? It's working! I can't believe I got this to work! I... I should explain. Journal. Journal everything. Journal. It's been weeks since my last entry. Things are... things have... I don't know where to start. Everything just... went wrong. That day. We were doing trials. New batch. We thought they might work. Years of work, months of failures, altering and refining the formula. Spirits were high. We thought it might be the day we did it. The day we succeeded. The day it all ended.

"Well, it ended. We did something. I don't know what but something. The trials. I should talk about the trials. The trials started like normal. All the subjects were secured, vitals and everything else monitored. Injections went fine, imbuement went fine. No instant deaths, none of the subjects started going out of control. Everything was looking perfect. A few minutes later, still no problems. The subjects were alive, conscious—they were fine. We thought we had done it. But minutes passed, then more minutes passed, and then things started going... wrong.

"The first thing we noticed was the lights. Slowly, steadily, they were growing dimmer by the minute. That shouldn't have been possible. The enchantments in this place should have lasted for years. Then the equipment started to fail: every machine, everything that ran off electricity, just sputtered and stopped. That happened to everything. We tried to use magic, and it didn't work! And then the screams began.

"The subjects. The prisoners. We could see them in the test chambers, strapped down on their tables, writhing as they shrieked. As they erupted. I'll never forget that sight: the fire subject burst into a pillar of flame. Ice froze into a giant block. Water flooded, mist disintegrated, animal shifted into a thousand different creatures all at once—all the subjects started dying just like their predecessors had. We thought they were all dead or dying. Just like before. We were wrong.

"Earth, the statue of a man, once flesh turned to stone, broke his bindings and rolled off his table, landing on his feet with a thud I will never forget. Space glitched—that's the only word I have for it—and started appearing all around the room, sometimes in two or three places at once. Metal melted around his bindings, pooling onto the floor, and rose again in the shape of a man. All of them, alive, somehow. Almost all. Some didn't survive, somehow. Most of those imbued with higher magics didn't, space being the only exception. Sound shattered in a scream that will haunt me for the rest of my days. Time stopped, frozen in a moment, and then, before my very eyes, grew younger. I watched as her hair grew and shortened, as her skin grew taut and her breasts firm before she began shrinking, and in a matter of moments had shrunk from an adult woman to a teen girl, to a child, to a baby, before vanishing entirely.

"Twenty had survived. We couldn't do anything but watch. These were the avatars we had spent years working on, decades for some, only they were so much more than that—so much more than we had ever dreamed. We shouldn't have waited even a moment before exterminating them all. But we did. We were transfixed by these people, these creatures we had created. We waited and watched as they reformed themselves in their human shapes. That was our final mistake. We didn't send in the security forces to put them down—we didn't activate the kill switches to terminate them, if they would have even worked at that point. We watched as they grew into something *more*. And then they attacked.

"Those testing rooms were so secure we had once joked that gods would have been unable to escape them. The avatars we had created broke out like they were made of paper. And then they started killing people: janitors, doctors, security. They slaughtered everyone they could. It was chaos. Madness. I saw friends and coworkers mowed down by magics greater than any I had ever imagined. And when security tried to fight back, nothing happened. Their guns simply didn't work. Of course, they didn't: guns work on magic, the same as the rest of the facility. The rest of the whole damned world. Magic that is now the sole providence of the avatars. Some of the guards tried other means, knives and batons, even a chair, anything that could be used as a weapon.

"That's when I first realized I hadn't made a mistake all those months ago. That electric subject *had* turned into electricity briefly and turned back, for the avatars were now doing the same. Every hit that the guards struck simply went through, like trying to stab fire with a knife.

"I only survived because of the null guards. The ones that were on duty had already been killed, but it didn't take long for the rest to come swarming in. We thought we had more than twice the number needed to contain all the avatars. Once again, we were sorely wrong. Dozens of masters of anti-magic fought against the twenty avatars, and they were all slaughtered. They bought the rest of us time to flee the observation rooms, however, which I will be forever grateful for. I had no plan other than to get as far away from the monsters we had created as possible, but Anders had another idea. While he wasn't a master by any means, he did know a few null magics. It's why I had enlisted him to help me with my problems in creating a null avatar, after all.

"Well, he decided if there was ever a time for us to try

out the null serum on a human, it was then. He dragged me to our lab, where we had been working on the null formula, and made me help him start the null imbuement on himself, the crazy bastard. It worked, though. I can't say why exactly—I only have theories—but it worked. Mostly, at least. He didn't go through the same... transformation. Regardless, Anders said he felt fine, powerful. Like a god, he said. A god of magic. He could feel the magic all the way in the observation room, like the avatars were shining beacons, each one blazing like the sun. He rushed off to fight them. He didn't even wait for me to tell him how bad of an idea that was.

"I followed him, like an idiot. I don't know why. Curiosity, perhaps? I wanted to see what a null avatar could do. Or because he was my friend, my colleague, and I didn't know what else to do. Either way, I watched through the doorway as he attacked the avatars. And he won, at first. As powerful as the avatars had become, they were new to their magics and weren't prepared to face a null wielder as powerful as them, or close to it. He managed to kill the mind avatar with nothing more than his fists and a broken piece of metal rod. Her body didn't shift from the blows, not with his null magic suppressing her. It was a sweet moment of victory. However powerful these avatars were, they weren't invincible.

"It didn't last long. Even with the overwhelming power of the null avatar, he couldn't resist the remaining nineteen all at once. They tore him apart. Metaphorically. What they actually did was far worse. But even with him dead, they had just witnessed one of their own die, despite the incredible power she wielded. That seemed to bring them out of their rage, and instead of seeking only to kill, they escaped the facility instead. Like a horde of demons loosed from the deepest pits of hell, they stormed their way out, destroying everything in their path. Once again, I survived, this time only because they cared more about fleeing this place than anything else. Not that there were many of us still alive by then. And even fewer after they had left.

"The next few weeks—the last few weeks—those of us who survived have been trying to... well, do what we can. There are a few dozen of us left, out of hundreds. At the moment, we're trapped down here. All the exits were destroyed in the avatars' escape. There's still air, thankfully, and enough food and water for us all to survive for lifetimes, but that's it. Nothing else works: computers, lights, heating. Everything that used the magic of the nineteen surviving avatars has stopped working. I haven't felt so much as a spark from my electrical magic, no matter how hard I try. Far too many people who survived with injuries have died in the last few weeks because none of our healing methods work: flesh, blood, and bone magic are as dead as my electrical magic. Fire, water, steam. Even space, the only of the higher magics whose avatar survived, isn't working.

"Over the last few weeks, when I haven't been trying to dig out survivors, caring for the wounded, or digging our way out of this place, I have been trying to get this video diary of mine working. The magic that powers it is as dead as my own, but magic isn't the only way to generate electricity. Those eggheads at the RIF use it, after all, and no magic works there. It's taken a bit of time, but I managed to put together a small crank generator and some simple wiring to power this thing. I'm not totally sure why I've bothered, really, but since I managed it, I thought I would record everything I could about what happened. I'm sure that, eventually, the government will get people down here to save us or find out what happened here.

"If nothing else, if we're all dead from suffocation or we collapse an exit on ourselves trying to dig our way out, at least this journal will remain to tell them what happened. If the avatars haven't killed them all, that is. I doubt that, though. Powerful as they are, there's only nineteen of them. They may be able to escape Tora, maybe, but they'll be put down eventually. They aren't gods, after all."

CHAPTER 54

The recording continued, unaware and uncaring about the effect it had on its audience. It blinked out and in. The man looked defeated, spent, and when he spoke, his voice had a hollowed, dead quality.

"It's gone. It's all gone. I don't… I don't understand. We dug out the emergency stairwell past the accounting offices, since it wasn't nearly as damaged as the others. The door should have led us inside the surface building. But when we got out, we were outside. There was nothing. Anywhere. Everywhere. Just, nothing. No buildings, no people, no Tora. Just, nothing. Empty, dead land as far as the eye could see. I thought I was going crazy. We all did. Mass hallucination. Some trick left behind by the light avatar. But it was true. We found remains. Small, shattered pieces. Of metal, of glass, of steel, and stone. Remnants of buildings, streets, cars, people. They destroyed it. Tora. The greatest city that ever was. Erased it from existence.

"I don't understand. The power required to do that is… it's incomprehensible. What happened to the army? The arcane university? The archives? Some of the strongest mages on the planet live in Tora. What happened to them? What-what did we create? A few of the others went out to explore. See what they could find. Any answers, any survivors, anything. We stocked them up with food and water and sent them off. We'll see what they return with."

A blink out and in. The man appeared better, healthier, but was obviously in shock.

"It's worse than I thought. Worse than I could have imagined. I already told you how far the devastation spread. My coworkers walked as far as they could before running out of food and found nothing. Well, that's only the start. See, I managed to get a radio working off a larger generator I was able to scrape together. We got hold of the Research Institute of Fairhaven. They keep an old-fashioned radio maintained, because of course they do! Well, we spoke to them, and they told us what they knew. I think we may have destroyed the world.

"In the months since we created the avatars, everywhere has gone to shit. Magic has stopped working. Not just here, in the facility, or in the general area of Tora. Everywhere. Magic has stopped worldwide. Specifically, the nineteen types of magic we made successful avatars of. The implications of this are staggering, to say the least. I knew there was something wrong with the avatar formula, but it was far worse than I ever imagined. Heh, I feel like I've been saying that a lot lately. Is my imagination just that small? Maybe I'll try to figure out just where we screwed up later.

"The world, though. Everything, literally *everything* in the world worked on magic. With it suddenly just stopping one day, the world broke. Planes fell out of the sky, ships were lost adrift at sea, volcanoes controlled and suppressed for centuries erupted all at once. Everything the modern world was built on, everything forming civilization as we know it, all just stopped. I can't even begin to imagine what the death toll must be. And what about astronauts? The people stuck up in the orbital space stations? Reliant on magic simply to have air to breathe? Or the colony on Antura? The first lunar colony in the history of mankind? Are they gone too? I can hardly bear to think about it.

"Oh! And it gets even worse! The collapse of *everything* with the disappearance of magic isn't it! No, the RIF knows about the avatars! Well, they don't know about them exactly, and definitely don't know we're responsible for them, but they've been hearing increasing rumors of men and women with incredible powers, with functioning magic, causing devastation all over the continent! Tora isn't the only city that's been destroyed, even if it is the only to be destroyed so... thoroughly. None of us knows what to do. We tried to create another null avatar. From the rumors the RIF has told us, the avatars haven't all stayed together. We thought if we could make another null avatar we could hunt them down, fix this... apocalypse we created. It didn't work. Jenson, our volunteer, died. The life just... disappeared in him. Like his very essence was sucked out of his body. Or something. I don't know—I'm no poet. At least it didn't seem painful. Or was quick, at least. I don't know why it worked for Anders. Maybe because he could wield null already? Maybe it was luck? I don't know, but we'll keep trying. What else are we going to do?"

A blink out and in.

"Another failure. Five more dead from null imbuement. I don't know where we're going wrong! The others want to stop the experiments, and I can't find it in myself to argue with them. These aren't prisoners: rapists and murdering scum already sentenced to death. These are my friends, colleagues, people I like and respect who are dying because of my failures. I'll keep working on the formula, but there will be no more tests.

"On another note, we've kept talking to the RIF, and things are getting worse. The avatars are continuing their campaign of destruction. We had to tell the RIF what we know about them. They had already realized we were at fault, unsurprising since some of them had worked on the project, and two even came in person that one time. They still weren't happy with us, not that I blame them. Unfortunately, they don't have any better ideas than we do. They aren't even sure if the RIF will be safe from the avatars, despite its null protections. They've never been tested against such raw power, and they don't have the equipment to work on their own null avatar. The secrecy of the project is now biting us in the ass, I guess. Some of the others are losing hope. I don't know what to do."

A blink out and in.

"We have an idea. It is, quite frankly, a horrible idea, but it's something. We're trapped in the middle of the wasteland that once held Tora. More of us have left, trying to get out, most returned in failure. Some haven't. So, Allison gave us an option, an option that is becoming more appealing by the minute. She's a time mage, and a decent one, according to her. She thinks she can suspend us, the whole facility—what's left of it—in time, for a few years. It's not really a solution, but it's something. Come back in a decade, see what the RIF can tell us about the world. Maybe they'll have figured something out. About magic or the avatars. Something to fix the problem, or something that will help us fix it. It was our mistake, after all. It is our responsibility."

A blink out and in.

"I've been trying to figure out what went wrong with the avatar project. I've been poring through every note and theory and data point in the project since its conception, all those years ago. And honestly? I don't think it was a mistake in the project. I know how that sounds, but I can't find even the slightest error in our work, much less one big enough to have caused all this. But if the error isn't with the project, then what's left? An error with magic? It's absurd to even think—our understanding of magic has worked flawlessly for millennia—but it's all I have left. And I noticed a point I made myself before, when going back through these journal entries of mine: null doesn't make sense within the boundaries of our understanding of magic. Could that be the key to all of this? Why the project went wrong, why null imbuement isn't working now? Because there's a mistake somewhere in our understanding of magic itself? I don't see how that's possible. Everything we know about magic has been built on what our ancestors taught us, our knowledge increasing generation by generation, stretching back to before the beginnings of recorded history. Our understanding of magic has worked for untold millennia. How could it be wrong?"

A blink out and in.

"We're going into stasis tonight. Allison thinks she can get us at least five years, maybe a few more. I'm conflicted about it, if I'm being honest. It feels like running away from our problems, hoping somebody else will solve them while we're gone. I know it's our best chance at this point, but still. I'm at a loss on null imbuement. What does it matter if our understanding of magic is wrong anymore? Most magic is dead to us anyway, under the sole control of the avatars, somehow. Knowing where our mistake was won't fix it, and fixing it is more important at this point. So, we're going into stasis tonight. I can resume my work in a few years when we wake up anyway."

A blink out and in.

"Seven years, apparently, that we were in stasis. Not bad on Allison's part. Nothing has changed in our area, which isn't surprising. It's weird to think that seven years have passed, though. Seven years gone in the blink of an eye. Even outside you can barely tell: the land is as dead as it was before. Maybe a little more barren, a few less signs of Tora remain, for all that's worth. We managed to contact the RIF again. They were relieved the stasis worked but had no good news for us. The world has barely even begun to recover from the collapse of magic, and on the continent, things are even worse with the avatars running around. We've been talking about what we should do next. The lead idea is to do another round of stasis, once Allison recovers. Seven years took a lot out of her;

it'll probably take a few days, maybe more, for her to recover enough to do it again. In the meantime, I'll keep working on null and my theories about magic."

A blink out and in.

"Fifty years. I can hardly believe we've been going in and out of stasis for fifty years. It's been a little over a month for us, yet fifty years have passed in the world. Most of my friends and family outside of the project are probably dead now. Of course, most of my friends who were on the project are dead too, but who's counting? The RIF are still up and running, and we've been in touch with them again. Remember how before the last stasis there were some disturbing rumors, about how people were calling the avatars living Gods and all that rot? Well, apparently, these cults around the avatars have grown. The 'living Gods' or 'earthly Gods' or 'old Gods' or whatever people choose to call them is a fast-growing religion. I guess it's not surprising: fifty years in a world devoid of most lower magics and the avatars would seem like Gods. Especially since they don't appear to be aging. It's almost funny, in a way. Just how badly did we screw the world up with our little project? I swear, I'd clock Parker a good one if he had survived."

A blink out and in.

"Well, it's not much, but for what it's worth, I think I figured out where the project went wrong. Surprise! It's exactly what I thought! Our understanding of magic, stretching back to the earliest days of human civilization, is wrong—was wrong—whatever! See, we always thought magic came in elements: fire magic, water magic, metal, flesh, etcetera. And we thought even the higher magics were the same, just 'higher' elements like space, time, mind, and the like. Magics that existed but were less physical in nature. Well, I'm pretty sure now that's all wrong, and that's why null magic never made much sense.

"See, I've come to realize that there is no such thing as 'elemental' magics *at all*. It's all just magic, and the way magic interacts with different aspects of the world. So, a fire mage isn't wielding fire magic, he's wielding magic and using it to interact with fire. An easy mistake to make, especially for our earliest ancestors. They summon a ball of magic, it's a ball of fire, of course. It's fire magic! Simple! And since they can't summon any other type of magic ball, they must be a fire mage who wields fire magic! That's what we always thought! That's how magic worked! But we were wrong! That first fire mage simply summoned magic, and his magic meshed well with fire! Looking back, it's obvious, really! People can learn to wield other magics regardless of how talented they are with their natural element!

"Anyway, how does this relate to the avatars, you ask? Simple! We thought we were imbuing the subjects with *fire magic*. Instead, we were imbuing them with *pure magic*, and pure magic's *ability* to interact with fire! That's why they had so much more power than they should! We made them *living beings of magic*! And that's why all fire magic stopped elsewhere in the world! The ability to control fire with magic was imbued into the fire avatar! Magic still exists—it just can't control fire anymore! We took control of fire away from magic and gave it to a living person! A person who—and I checked his record—killed over a hundred people in a bombing!

"Granted, I do kind of sympathize with him: his daughter died in a drunk driving accident and the perpetrator was released on a technicality." The man shrugged. "He was rich and had connections. But seriously! He bombed a charity gala! He killed the guy who killed his daughter, yeah, but also a hundred other innocent people with him! And now that man might be immortal, with power greater than almost anything else in this world, and is being worshiped as a living God! And I've checked the other avatars' records too. Fire is one of the *better* ones! We ruined the world and handed its remains off to a bunch of immortal monsters all because nobody bothered to ask however many thousands of years ago *why* their magic did what it did!? It's all a fucking joke!

"Oh! I figured out why null wasn't working too! It's because null isn't an element! What we call null is just magic *interacting with magic. Itself. Magic controlling itself!* The greatest minds in history were stymied by what is basically magic stroking its own dick! Well, I'm the man who solved what none of them ever could, so I say that *I'm* the greatest mind to have ever lived! Also, that's why it keeps killing people when imbued with it: we were pumping them full of pure, unrefined magic until their bodies literally couldn't take it anymore! Anders only survived because he already could use it and was familiar with it! Had his formula been any stronger, he probably would have died too! So, there we have it, folks!

"We didn't just make avatars: we might as well have gone and made actual magical Gods! Who cares if it's all a misconception if we can't *do* anything about it? What's left of my null work is stuck here with us. How would we even find somebody capable of using it anyway? Anybody who isn't a null mage won't have the power to challenge even a single avatar, and if we try to give them more, they'll die! We're screwed!"

A blink out and in.

"One hundred years. One hundred years it's been since we created the avatars/living Gods/overpowered wankers! And oh boy, has the world *really* gone to shit! The religion that's been forming around the avatars for the last century? I don't know about the rest of the world, because not even the RIF has been able to contact anybody anywhere else. But the entire continent of Caminen now worships the criminal shits we gave godlike power and immorality too! Fairhaven, apparently, was the last city—according to the RIF—to fall under the sway of the new religion, as none of the Gods have even come close to it. Dominant theory amongst the RIF—and us, admittedly—is that they were scared the RIF might be a threat to them due to the null factor of that damned fortress.

"Their independence couldn't last forever, though, as about a year after we last entered stasis, followers of the avatars wormed their way in and infected the city! And last year the fire avatar himself, who is now being known as '*The God of Fire*' if you can believe it, settled himself in Fairhaven and called it the capital of his nation! Yes, that's right, the fire avatar is no longer just a religious figure but is now the god-king of his own nation! Only took a hundred years for one of them to pull that shit! Probably all the fighting with each other delayed them.

"Oh, yeah! Apparently, the 'religion' around the avatars splintered and turned into factions, each one worshiping a different avatar as the 'true king' of the 'Gods' while the other Gods are still worshiped, only as 'lesser' and their followers are 'enemies' because whichever 'God' 'wins' the 'war' will be named the king of the 'Gods' in 'heaven,' where the 'Gods' 'descended from' because they couldn't decide on a 'king' for themselves! So, they 'came to the world of humans' to have people fight each other over who gets to be ruler instead! I guess they spent the last century coming up with that bullshit story!

"Anyway, Fairhaven has apparently been renamed 'Fiahren'—which is nonsense, but I guess it's similar and sounds kind of like fire? With a really bad accent? Exotic fire?—and is now the official capital of the 'Fire God,' who is a 'God and doesn't need a mortal name.' Bitch, his name is Jeremy. Jeremy Mariah Antloos. I mean, I don't blame him for not wanting to be a God with that name, but nameless? Really? For reasons nobody seems to understand, on our end or theirs, *Jeremy* has declared that the RIF—newly renamed the Research Institute of Fiahren—is an independent institute working under the banner of the Fire God and is not to be harassed or interfered with in any way, and its members are to be protected and treated with respect. The RIF has agreed to those terms, naturally, and in return they've agreed to contribute all their findings and creations to the benefit of 'Fire,' but they don't know why he made them the offer in the first place! He didn't even try to take the RIF by force, and when one of his 'Blessed' tried to storm the Institute—failed, of course—he personally executed them.

"Oh, yeah, the Blessed. Apparently, the avatars are capable of bestowing absurd amounts of elemental magic on people of their choosing. Not sure which of them figured it out first, or how, but they can give people powers similar—if much lesser—to their own. These people who have been 'Blessed by their God' are by nature stronger and more versatile than even the best of mages from the old world. They even have the avatars' ability to physically turn into their element! I don't want to go into stasis again. Every time we wake up, the world is even more absurd and shitty than it was before!"

A blink out and in.

"Things have gotten worse. Again. It's not a surprise, really, but we had hoped. First, I guess, is that we've had our last contact with the RIF. The 'Church of Fire,' which is the organization devoted to Jeremy Motherfuckin' Antloos as the best God, has officially taken over Fairhaven—Fiahren—and the surrounding areas. *Jeremy* is still ultimately in charge, but the new 'High Priest of Fire' and his subordinates run the day-to-day operations of the 'Fire Nation.' They've also begun a purge of the city, including the RIF, removing every detractor to their 'holy cause.' Even friends and neighbors are turning on each other, reporting each other to the 'Church of Fire' for any hint of dissent. Anybody who has been accused and found guilty of being a heretic, a dissident, is being given a choice: execution or slavery. That's right: slavery has been brought back! As a punishment only, so far, but history has shown us how *that* will turn out.

"Anyway, despite Jeremy's edict about the RIF a few decades ago, the Church of Fire has been quietly purging them along with the rest of the city. Doctors, researchers, even cooks and janitors have been disappearing. A lot of them are living in the RIF now, afraid that if they leave, they'll disappear too. But the Church has appointed 'overseers' of the RIF, loyal minions who routinely visit to inspect the place for any signs of heresy. They've had most of their equipment destroyed with the reason being that they were 'relics of the old world' and thus 'existed against the will of the Gods,' whatever that shit means. The RIF has hidden what they can, but the Church is actively trying to remove all traces of history from before the avatars came. They kept the radio in a secret room until we came out of stasis so they could tell us before hiding the radio away for good. We're now entirely cut off from the outside world once again.

"There was some other news about the state of the world, although most of it's bad. The other avatars have been setting themselves up in cities and declaring themselves rulers of sovereign nations too, conquering the surrounding lands. At the rate they're going, the entire continent will be ruled over by the avatars, each with their nation and warring against all the others to keep the myth of this 'heavenly throne war' going. With the Blessed leading their armies, no one can stand against them. And when two Blessed clash, the devastation they can cause is extraordinary. While the avatars themselves are apparently sterile, thankfully, their Blessed are not, and their children and grandchildren are born with natural powers equal to all but the most legendary of mages of the old world. These 'Descendants' are rapidly becoming the backbone of the new Churches' forces. And much like the Blessed seem to share in the avatars' longevity, the 'Descendants' also inherit increased lifespans. So far, no Blessed or Descendant has died of natural causes. The RIF theorizes that the Descendants, at least, aren't immortal, and will die of old age eventually, but without being able to properly study them, they don't know how long that might take. Hundreds of years at least, it's looking like.

"There is some small amount of positive news, at least. During this last decade of stasis, the RIF got into radio contact with the Skipps Institute on the island of Essetir in the Ungolian sea to the east. Took them a hell of a long time to figure out non-magic electricity, but they have been stuck on an island in the middle of the ocean for generations now without magic. Essetir is part of an archipelago with plenty of food and resources, so it's not a surprise they survived. Our radio isn't strong enough to reach them, unfortunately, but the RIF have given them everything they know about the avatar project. At least there'll be somebody out there trying to solve this shit, free from the avatars and their churches. For now.

"As for what we who remain here will do, we haven't decided yet. I'm not sure if we'll bother going into stasis again: without the RIF to contact, it feels more pointless than ever, and we're all getting tired of it, especially Allison. Her life for the last couple of years—our time—has been cast big magic, rest, cast, rest, repeat. I don't know how much longer she can do it."

A blink out and in.

"Well, this is it. My last entry. I don't have a whole lot to say here, really. I'm ready to be done. Everybody else has left, except for me and Allison. We loaded them up with food and water and set them out in all directions. With any luck, at least some of them will survive and make it to Fair—Fiahren, and manage to get to the RIF. If that doesn't work, they'll bypass that place entirely and make for the coast, steal a boat or something to get to Essetir. If they can get my work on null imbuement to Skipps, then maybe, one day, they'll be able to make a null avatar of their own and do what we couldn't: fix our mistake and rid this world of the avatars. Even with all my work, I don't know how long it will take them, though. They don't have the equipment, the resources, any of it. All they will have is hope. I can give them that much, at least. The avatars have, so far, kept to the continent.

"Even the water avatar, who would have the easiest time leaving, has stayed, so we're hoping Skipps remains free of the avatars' influence for long enough to replicate my null imbuement. If any of the avatars and their people take to the oceans and find those islands, that will be the end. That's why Allison and I have stayed here, are going through with this moronic last resort plan. With the RIF taken over by the Fire Church, if Skipps falls, we will truly be the last hope for the world. A false hope, probably. Who alive today even knows of the name 'Tora' aside from the avatars, the RIF, and Skipps? Who would ever even think to come here? In the middle of a long dead wasteland? A desert, apparently, as the avatars destroyed this land so completely that the entire place has started turning to sand! The RIF told us that the center of the continent, where we are, is forbidden by the 'Gods,' claiming there is nothing here but a desert of death!

"So as a final, last resort, a just-in-case the Skipps plan fails, Allison and I will make this place, this secret lab, a memorial that stands untouched through time. We have all the surviving work on the project here, all my work since, on both null and the nature of magic, and we have more null imbuements prepped and ready to go. We will give our lives to preserve this place, this last, desperate hope for the future. I have adjusted the imbuement formulas, and tonight Allison and myself will turn ourselves into avatars, albeit far weaker ones. I will imbue myself with null and Allison with time. Together, we will die. She will erect a temporal stasis field around this facility, a large one, so that it will remain untouched by the passing of the years, no matter how many may go by. I will craft an anti-magic field so that neither the avatars nor their followers will ever be able, or at least willing, to make it this far. Only a null wielder will have the ability to bring down the stasis field, and the null field with it, and none of the avatars will ever suffer one of those to live, so we know they won't be working for them. This is our last, final effort to fix our mistakes."

A blink out and in.

"Well, listener, whoever, whenever, you are. There you have it: the true history of this world. We made the avatars, the beings you probably know of as 'Gods,' right here in this very facility. Right here, we destroyed the world as we knew it, killing billions in the process, and unleashing evils the likes of which the world has never known. I hope that you are here as scientists, archaeologists, academics simply seeking nothing more than to unearth secrets lost to the past, and that these new Gods themselves have long been lost to history. If that is not the case, as I fear may be, and you are here, somehow, as part of a desperate struggle against the Gods, well, then, you've come to the right place. If you made it here, you have null magic yourself. You should be an enemy of the avatars, the Gods, as your very existence is a threat to their dominion over this world. And you have, hopefully, followed the path of these recordings and seen what you need to make more null avatars. We have left instructions for the entire process and prepped everything we can to make it as easy for you as possible. I have spent years making sure the process is as safe for anyone as it was for Anders. I have full confidence that, if you do accept this request, you will be capable of finally ridding the world of the avatars, once and for all. I beg you, now, to take up this duty, and to fix our mistakes. For the last time, I am Dr. Martin Griffith, signing off."

Tala stood still, frozen, mouth agape. He had known, suspected, where the recordings were heading, but this? Never in his wildest dreams could he have imagined this!

A sound rang through the silence of the bedroom. Then it rang again. Frowning, Tala turned to Vail. The man was shaking. "Ha. HA. HAHAHAHAHA!" Vail was laughing. Hood thrown back, face alive, he laughed, a laugh that would haunt him for the rest of his days, for there was nothing sane, nothing good about it. "Don't you understand!?" Vail cried out, looking at them all with manic eyes and a worse smile. "They're human! They can be killed! AHAHAHAHAHAH!" He laughed. Tala stared in horror, feeling the chilling fingers of death creep their way down his spine. He could do nothing but watch as the Demon laughed.

CHAPTER 55

"Wahahaha!" Lord Endellion's boisterous laughter rang out across the hall, washing over the revelers, feasting and drinking. "Oh, you all should have seen how the rest of those dirty mud suckers ran away after that! So brave they were with a Blessed backing them up! But there ain't no thing such as bravery when faced against Anderas Fuckin' Anto, I say! So cheers, I say! Cheers to Anderas Anto, who sent those Godsdamned mudders running right back to the shit from whence they came!" Endellion roared, swaying so hard that he almost knocked himself down when he turned to Anderas, mug thrust out in the air.

A resounding cheer echoed as the rest of the hall roared their own acclamations towards Anderas, who gracefully rose from his seat and gave a sweeping bow to the room with one hand tucked under his chest as the other swept out to the side. The cheering erupted even louder. Not a noise could be heard aside from the thundering yells and pounding of boots on the floor and mugs on the tables. Anderas lifted his own mug, filled with the mulled wine he preferred, towards the crowd before taking a deep (much shallower than he made it look) drink, to the crowd's joy.

Once the cheering and applause settled down, and the revelers turned their attention back to each other instead of him, Anderas let himself fall gracefully back into his seat. Endellion's accounting of the day's battle had been surprisingly accurate, given how inebriated the Lord of Huobak was, and Anderas couldn't deny the thrills of pride he felt at being celebrated so. Even if the Mud Blessed (one Lord Faulton, as Endellion really should have known) hadn't put up much of a fight. Or a fight at all, really, aside from his tidal wave of mud move, which had been all too easy for Anderas to deal with. Truly, Blessed who were unaccustomed to fighting others at their level were really disappointing. It almost—*almost*—made Anderas sad that Annelore and Elidor were dead. Those two had made for quite the challenge, even if he would have preferred to fight them one-on-one, or at least elsewhere where he wouldn't have needed to hold back quite so much. Although, that wholly unexpected outcome, courtesy of Tala'Keahi, had let Anderas move his (admittedly rather nebulous) plans forward by a good century at least.

Finishing his wine, Anderas rose smoothly to his feet, signaling to his personal servants he was leaving. The celebratory feast after their victory that day had been quite enjoyable, and planning for it had begun well before the actual battle had. Endellion had been that certain about their inevitable victory. But Anderas was growing tired of it. He had been in Huobak for a couple of months now, and there were no ears left for him to bend, at least none he could do anything with at such a rowdy celebration. So, having drank and eaten his fill, and allowed the masses and local lords to celebrate and honor him, as was their wont, Anderas happily took the opportunity presented to him once Lord Endellion became quite distracted with a rather forward serving girl. He left the feast and returned to his rooms, slinking down into a plush chair in front of the hearth to enjoy the pleasant silence broken only by the crackling of the fire.

He cracked one eye open to survey his servants, who had taken chairs for themselves to relax and indulge in the many spoils they had secreted away from the feast.

"Where's Surya?" he asked after the unexpected absence of one of his most trusted friends and servants.

"In the city, milord. There have been some... rumors, that she wanted to verify, that have preceded official channels."

"Oh? And what rumors are those?" he asked languidly, already closing his eyes again as he relaxed further into the plump chair. The nervous energy he felt sparking through the room caused his eyes to both open as he focused on Ulian. It was unlike his guard, any of his trusted servants, really, to hesitate when they were in private.

"She's been gone all day, sir. She should be back soon. It would be best to wait for her to confirm anything," Ulian told him.

Anderas nodded slowly, a frown marring his brow as he turned back to the fireplace. She could be investigating many possible rumors, especially now that the war had ramped up into full swing. Still, the clear discomfort that his servants were showing (clear to him, at least, who had personally helped train them all in subterfuge) had him worried. He relaxed as best he could while he waited for Surya to return but couldn't find that same place of tranquility.

He had lost track of time, staring into the dancing flames of the hearth as he worried, when she finally slipped through the door. Whatever rumor she had gone out to confirm was indeed true, and very bad.

"What is it?" he asked, forgoing pleasantries as he stood to face her.

She eyed him worriedly, then glanced between Ulian and the others, none of whom were relaxed anymore. "What have you told him?" she asked.

"Nothing," Ulian told her simply.

"Fantastic." She exhaled harshly.

"It's true then?" Ulian asked, an uncharacteristic quiver in his voice.

Anderas grew even more concerned; there wasn't much that could shake his guardsman.

"Yes," she replied shortly. "All of it."

"All of what?" Anderas asked with forced calm. It wasn't like his servants to circle an issue like this, much less one that he knew nothing about.

"Rumors, sir. News from Lightning that I have confirmed to be true. Or as much as I can here, at any rate."

"And this news is...?" Anderas asked.

"Tala'Keahi may be dead, sir. And Denhei Mishima as well."

Anderas blinked. That was most certainly *not* what he

had been expecting to hear. "I see. That is unfortunate. May be dead?"

"His status is unconfirmed, sir. But by all accounts, he did fall off the Gods' Canyon Bridge and into the river. No body has been found, but it is unlikely, if still possible, that he survived."

"I see. So they went into Lightning, and then tried to make for the Jungle. Interesting decision, that. And Denhei Mishima? Is his death related, or did his 'ancient family techniques' finally fail him on the battlefield?"

"Related, sir."

"So, Tala took out another one of us with him, did he? Well, even if he is dead, at least his legend is secure."

Surya hesitated, drawing another frown to Anderas' face. "Not exactly, sir. It seems, actually, that Tala wasn't responsible for Denhei's death. Not directly, at least."

"So, he taught his companions his Blessed-killing tricks?"

"I don't believe so, sir."

"Tell me everything," Anderas commanded.

As Surya spoke, Anderas felt himself grow increasingly... anxious. Tala and his group had vanished without trace for months, only to suddenly show up in Lynmyr with the Bone Merc? Who helped them reach the bridge, then promptly abandoned them? (Which wasn't exactly out of character for him, if they hadn't actually hired him, but then why would he help them in the first place instead of capturing Tala himself for the bounty?) "So, Tala is likely dead, as well as the girl." Anderas nodded along. "How did Denhei die, then?"

Surya shared a dark look with Ulian and the others.

"That's the thing, sir. After Tala fell, that man, the one in the cloak, he... fought... Lord Denhei."

"Fought as in...?" Anderas asked, growing annoyed with his servants' continuous stalling. Was that man a Blessed? A Descendant prodigy? Surya had already denied any use of Tala's tricks.

"As in beat him. To death. With his fists. Sir."

Anderas felt himself grow pale and would have sworn that a chill wind had suddenly swept through the room. "Elaborate."

"Accounts are confused, but also unanimous, milord. The cloaked man attacked Lord Denhei with nothing but his bare fists and beat him to death. Apparently, Lord Denhei recognized the man after they started fighting and was terrified of him. The man showed no signs of wielding magic himself, however."

Anderas stood frozen, picturing the events Surya had recounted in his mind's eye. All too easily could he picture that cloaked man from Southtown fighting a Blessed. All too easily could he see the look on Denhei Mishima's face as his magics were suppressed, entirely outside his control. All too easily could he imagine the fear Denhei must have felt in that moment.

"That is impossible," Anderas heard himself say in a half-choked whisper.

"Aye, milord. But it seems certain that is what happened."

Anderas took a deep, shuddering breath, then another, as the previous had been far too shallow. "We are leave-" He stopped, taking in the tired, alcohol-flushed faces of his ser-vants. "We leave first thing in the morning."

"Yes, milord." Surya nodded a bow. "To Fiahren?"

"Yes. No. the Bone Merc, where is he?"

"He was last seen in Genigul, to my knowledge. I think it is likely he is headed to either Narville or Bulabar."

"Then we make for Bulabar. Osson and I need to have a little chat."

"Yes, milord." Surya nodded. "What about Huobak and Lord Endellion? And how will you explain this to Soleil?"

"Mud just lost a Blessed to *me*. They won't dare come near this city for a while. Even if they do, Endellion is, for all his faults, a decent ruler and a strong fighter. Huobak will be fine. I'll explain things to him in the morning. And Soleil will understand. Even he wouldn't challenge me on this, not beyond what is required of him."

"Understood, sir. We'll be ready to depart by dawn."

"Good. See to it." Anderas nodded, making his way over to the desk he had been using since arriving in Huobak. He had plans to make and would work through the night. He wouldn't bother trying to sleep, not when any rest he might manage to steal would be interrupted by blood and screams—and laughter.